THE ART
OF SCANDAL

THE ART OF SCANDAL

SUSAN LOUGHNANE

POOLBEG

Published 2015
by Poolbeg Press Ltd
123 Grange Hill, Baldoyle
Dublin 13, Ireland
E-mail: poolbeg@poolbeg.com
www.poolbeg.com

1

A catalogue record for this book is available from the British Library.

ISBN 978-1-78199-942-4

Typeset by Poolbeg Press Ltd in Sabon.
Printed and bound by CPI Group (UK) Ltd, Croydon, CR0 4YY

www.poolbeg.com

About the author

Susan Loughnane lives mostly on planes between London, Ireland and New York. She house-shares in Notting Hill but still calls Dublin home. She also occasionally crashes on a couch in Brooklyn, New York. Finally, this extravagant property portfolio includes the ownership of a drawer in a house in County Clare, where she dreams of living some day with lots of cats. She also dreams of running a yoga studio one day.

Susan is best known in Ireland for playing Debbie in the hugely popular RTÉ series *Love/Hate*, for which she won the IFTA for Best Supporting Actress in 2013. In the UK, Susan is known for playing the series regular role of Chloe in *Hollyoaks*.

Susan is a portrait artist but, as she has attachment issues with her paintings, it will probably never be a profession.

The Art of Scandal is her first novel.

Acknowledgements

For my parents, who have always shown such blind faith in nudging me towards my dreams, no matter how off the wall and unstable they were. Mam and Dad are also to thank for making sure I was a well-read child. From *Can't You Sleep, Little Bear?* to *Little Women*, we always had our bedtime favourites!

I hang out with my boyfriend, David, in the vain hope his funny, strong and confident personality will rub off on me. A lot of my humour comes from a decade of spending time with this lad, so imagine how great his book would be!

Making my brothers, Eoin and Brian, laugh was my ultimate goal as a child – they were my first idols and I still want to impress them. In addition to them, I now have the new goal of impressing my niece Sophie.

The character of Sophie is in no way associated with my niece (my character existed first), but she is in fact an amalgamation of my five girlfriends. Thanks, ladies, yiz are only gas!

The feline friend in the book, Sasha, is strongly based on my cat Tiddles and she would be furious if she didn't receive an acknowledgement. Well, actually, in true Sasha style, she wouldn't give a s**t.

Thank you to all my agents at Lisa Richards – particularly to Faith and Lisa. Your encouragement right from the start gave me such confidence.

Also thanks to the wonderful editor Gaye, and to Paula and everyone at Poolbeg. Your enthusiasm for this book has made it such an exciting process for me.

A massive thanks to my friend and unofficial career coach Caroline Grace-Cassidy.

To my walking buddy and art friend, Jim Fitzpatrick, thank you for all the chats and laughs – I could write a million books out of our conversations!

Thanks to the Fennellys and the Loughnanes, there is certainly no shortage of interesting characters in my life! Thanks to Granny, the Queen of the Family – you're a hoot.

Thanks to my London family, in our crazy little flat-share, and to everyone at the Portobello Gold, for all the cups of tea/glasses of wine whenever I needed fuel or inspiration.

A little nod must also go to my Granddad Kieran, who was the funniest man I've ever known. He would be absolutely loving this whole book lark.

For my family and David

Prologue

I answered the door of Winnipeg Cottage and Mo Brady was standing on the doorstep, wearing wellies and a raincoat, her hands on her hips. On leads extending from her chunky wrists were two skinny Doberman dogs, glaring at me threateningly. There was a chubby Rottweiler, also on a lead, sitting slightly behind the others. He was licking his crotch.

I wrapped my cardigan across my chest as a cool breeze swept up the path, carrying half a dozen orange leaves into the hall. The threat of a typically brisk Irish autumn was in the air.

'What do you want, Mo?' I asked, taking my eyes off the Rottweiler and fixing her with a firm look. My head was pounding, and my heart was in my throat, but I kept my face expressionless.

'I'm delivering a message to you from everyone in this village. And we both know this isn't the first. We want you gone. Do you hear me? You and your repulsive, wildly inappropriate activities. Get out. Go. Pack up all your shit and leave.'

I made a deliberate effort not to roll my eyes in exasperation.

'I'm not leaving, Mo. This is my home.'

'I'm warning you. We know what you're up to. If your grandfather knew you were using his cottage as some sort of erotic, hippy, arty-farty, orgy-whorehouse,' she spat the words out like they were pieces of her dog's excrement, 'he would be turning in his grave.'

At this point I suddenly felt the blood racing around in my veins, red-hot and angry. She had no fucking clue how my granddad would feel about any of this. I knew him better than anyone. I swallowed a lump the size of a giant gobstopper down my throat with fierce determination. Words were spinning around my head, waiting eagerly and impatiently to be launched at this woman, but I fought to hold them back. I knew better than to poke the dragon. She took a deep breath and a quick glance over her shoulder, and then turned back to me, fixing me with an intense glare.

'Don't test us, you little slut. *Get – the – fuck – out – of – this – village*,' she said slowly and quietly.

I looked her square in the eye, and took a minute to strengthen and compose myself.

'You and your dogs don't scare me, Mo. Now get off my property or I'll call the police.'

'You'll regret it.' She turned and stomped away, nearly choking the poor Rottweiler as she dragged him behind and his legs scrambled to keep up.

As soon as I had the door closed, my knees buckled and I sank to the floor.

Sasha strolled up to me, meowed knowingly and rubbed herself off my shins. 'How did I get myself into this mess, Sash?' I asked her as her little head brushed off my slipper.

Chapter 1

Two months earlier, all was lovely and calm in Winnipeg Cottage. I closed the door and took a deep breath as I stood in amongst the suitcases and boxes in the hall. I watched the dust particles floating around in the early summer sunlight that streamed in through the blinds. I surveyed my new home. I wandered in and out of the still, quiet rooms. Each seemed to be steeped in character and wisdom, the very walls told stories without saying a word; every bump and bend in the wonky but sturdy foundations contained a memory.

I inhaled the familiar smell and atmosphere into my lungs and it somehow seemed to filter down through every extremity of my body, folding around me like the softest cotton blanket.

I grabbed a box in the hall labelled '*bedroom*' and carried it up the narrow wooden staircase. I hadn't any intention of unpacking at this moment but felt I might as well get a small start made. I surprised myself by bypassing the room I used to stay in as a child, and dropping the box in my granddad's room. It was the main bedroom and as I was now the lady of the house I took my place on the throne. Not the loo obviously! A part of me felt attached to the other sweet little room with its beautiful dormer window that protruded from the roof and the ornate iron-frame single bed. But the main room was beautiful in its own way. The ceiling was sloped, as there was no attic. There was a sink in this room – a beautiful old basin with two Victorian brass taps. There was also a birdhouse on the windowsill so you could watch them come and go from the bed. I would have to put some seeds in it. I opened the window to let some air in.

I drifted back down the stairs and into the entrance hall, having wandered through the entire cottage, like a fish swimming dreamily around a bowl. I dropped to my knees in front of the dusty old sixties-style telephone table by the door – a position I'd occupied countless times as a child. I pulled out the drawer and flicked open the faded-yellow metal phone/address book inside. I did it all without thinking, without blinking, possibly even without breathing. But as soon as I heard the click of the latch and the metal cover swung back with the same enthusiasm as it always had, revealing the notes, numbers and addresses delicately written inside, in the elegant handwriting of my grandmother, I sighed. My eyes welled up. I sank back, resting my backside on my heels. As tears slid down my cheeks, I pressed the metal cover closed and then released it over and over again. An old habit.

I had studied this address book a million times. My granddad had left it just so after my grandmother died, which was before I was born. And I must have been a pretty simple, easily entertained child as it gave me endless amusement – clicking it open, closing it, and clicking it open again.

Since my very earliest memories, the cottage had always been a little haven of stability. I remembered studying the Yeats poem 'Lake Isle of Innisfree' in school and I always thought of Winnipeg as my version of Innisfree. No matter where I'd ever been in my life, I could always hear Winnipeg in my '*deep heart's core*'.

At this point in my life, I needed the cottage more than ever.

It had been more than just a home to my grandfather too. It connected him to his brother, Joe. Joe helped him build the cottage and emigrated to Canada once it was completed. Granddad gave the cottage the same name as the city Joe moved to. That way he could always say he and his brother both lived in Winnipeg.

I wiped my eyes with the back of my hand and propped my right elbow up on the cushion part of the telephone table, the part you sit on to make calls. I snuggled my chin into my palm so that my neck was stretched out and my nose was pointing up in the air. With my other hand I stuck my index finger into the hole of the number eight on the old telephone sitting gracefully on the table. I drew it around as far as it would go, withdrew my finger, and watched it dutifully rotate back and click into place. I remembered feeling so grown up doing this as a child, using a phone just like the adults did. Even now a feeling of sophistication came over me as I created an imaginary phone number, sticking out my pinky finger dramatically as my index finger did the dialling, and held the cold heavy receiver against my ear waiting for it to ring. The phone line had been cut off but I played along just to amuse myself.

I eased my stiff, tired body up off the ground, stretched my legs and walked into the quiet living room. I felt like an oversized person standing there in the middle of the room.

I was contemplating the feeling you get when you stand in a place you frequented as a child, how the walls feel closer and your limbs feel enormous, when I was suddenly jolted back to reality by a soft voice behind me.

'Hello?'

'Jesus!' I put my hand on my heart.

She was by no means a threatening presence, but the unexpected nature of her visit made me jump out of my skin.

'No no no, my dear, I'm not Jesus. God love you, you must be hallucinating,' she stated with her characteristically straightfaced humour. The memory of this regular figure from my childhood came immediately flooding back to me. She put her hand on my shoulder. 'I'm Mrs Mac–'

'Mrs Macaroni! Oh my God!'

'It's Mrs MacInerney, darling. Not Jesus, or your God . . . but I did love how you used to call me Mrs Macaroni so I'll let that one slide. How nice it is to be back in this cottage.' She sighed and looked around. 'I've really missed wandering in here since your grandfather passed. Sorry, pet, I just noticed the back door open and I just couldn't resist a peek in for old times' sake. I wondered had poor old Dónal risen from the dead like our dear Lord who you seem so fond of mentioning . . .'

'Well, it's great to see you, Mrs Mac. You look . . . exactly the same.' My eyes started welling up again. She did look remarkably like time had had no effect on her whatsoever. It wasn't necessarily a good thing. For as long as I could remember she had always looked about ninety-two years old. Her white hair fell around her shoulders in wispy curls, and her large heavy eyes still protruded dramatically from her face, exuding a permanent twinkle of mischief. She had always been a good companion of my grandfather's. They had been as thick as thieves for as long as I could remember. He often referred to her as his 'ladyfriend'. He even proposed to her once, at his seventieth birthday. It was the only time I had ever seen my grandfather even slightly inebriated. I was in my late teens at the time and we organised a party for him at the parish hall. She didn't take the proposal seriously, which was a good thing because I was pretty certain he didn't remember it the next day.

'Oh Katie, it's a real delight to see you. You've become such a beautiful young lady. You here for long?'

Her soft hands were wrapped around mine in a manner I

found strangely gentle and comforting. They were warm without being too hot, and almost a century of regular hand-cream use had resulted in them feeling like wrinkled silk.

'Well, I've moved in actually . . . I still can't quite believe it. It just sort of happened.'

'Oh Katie, that's wonderful!' She smiled broadly, showing a set of too-perfectly aligned dentures.

'I didn't spot you at the –'

'I didn't go,' she interrupted. Her face fell, and she looked down at her hands, still holding mine. 'I'm so sorry, Katie. I couldn't face it. You'd think that at my age I'd be used to funerals. But this one I just couldn't . . . He was my last . . . real friend. Now all I have is my sister in Birmingham. And sure she doesn't know who I am. De-men-ti-a.' She spoke the last word in an exaggerated manner, pronouncing every syllable almost too clearly. It was as though the word had a power of its own that seemed to overwhelm her. Then she widened her eyes and shook her head. 'But it's really fantastic to have you here, Katie. It is.' Her broad grin was back.

'Let's have tea,' I decided.

I sank into the three-seater couch and tucked my toes into the folds of the cushions. Mac sat at the other end. Sasha purred as she basked in the sunlight that poured in through the large living-room window. I would hardly have known Sasha was in the room if it weren't for the loud hum of her purr. It was like a backing track to our chitchat. Her deep, rich, brown fur blended perfectly into Granddad's favourite antique Dralon armchair. She looked up occasionally, keeping an eye on proceedings as we sipped our tea and laughed at old memories.

'Are you still painting, Katie? I recall Dónal telling me you did a Fine Art degree over there in the States.' Her eyes sparkled as she seemed to study me intently.

'I did, yeah, but I . . . haven't painted in a while, no . . . I suppose I just haven't had the motivation – or the inspiration perhaps.'

'Well, maybe the beautiful west of Ireland will inspire you again. You did some wonderful paintings here when you were a youngster. You had an incredible ability for capturing the spirit of a person, not to mention a remarkable likeness.'

'I've been mostly doing landscapes actually . . . well, while I was in college I did. I haven't done portraiture in a really long time.'

'Well, you'll find some of the most beautiful landscapes round these parts.'

'Who would have thought I'd end up back here again? I couldn't believe it when they said this place was mine.' I shook my head, still bemused by it all.

'He always said he'd leave Winnipeg to you. He was very adamant that you would have it. I'm surprised that you wouldn't have expected it,' she mused, her long-fingered hands gently encasing her teacup.

It had been ten weeks since Granddad passed and I unwittingly became an overnight homeowner.

'I suppose I just hadn't really thought about it.' I shook my head, my mind still adapting to the whole thing.

'I have to say, though: I didn't expect you to move down here. You're full of surprises.' She smiled.

'Well, things just sort of fell apart in New York.' I twisted the cord of my hoodie around my finger. 'I'd been there almost eight years but when I came home for the funeral I realised that I had no reason to go back. And when I discovered I'd inherited a house here I just thought . . . why not stay? It felt like . . .'

'Fate?' she finished for me with a hint of a mischievous grin tickling the corners of her mouth. 'Well, frankly, I'm thrilled you're here. You, Katie McKenna, are just what Ballytiernan needs to liven it up. Stuck in the eighties we are around here!'

'Well, I'm planning to lay low, Mac. I won't be getting up

to any mischief if I can avoid it.'

She threw her head back and let out a loud short laugh. 'I know you. You're more like your mother than you would like to think. She was far too wild for this place. She couldn't wait to see the village grow smaller as she hit the well-worn road to Dublin. But, boy, was it fun having her around!'

And her eyes seemed to dance as she looked over at the old family photos still gathering dust on the mantelpiece.

Chapter 2

Without the photographic evidence, I would never have believed my mother had been brought up here in Winnipeg Cottage. If you'd only just met her you'd bet your bottom dollar she was born and bred in South County Dublin, with a silver spoon in her large, outspoken mouth. Like a perfectly camouflaged predator in the jungle, she had slotted herself right into my dad's outlandish millionaire lifestyle. You'd never have a clue she was a Ballytiernan bird underneath her scaly chameleon skin.

My parents had never really been the 'parenting' types. They regularly informed me (with little concern for how it might upset me) that they'd never intended to have a child. But along I came out of the blue and, quite frankly, I refuse to believe that it made any difference to their lives, as they didn't behave like any other parents I knew. To put it bluntly, my parents were swingers. I wasn't even entirely sure my dad was in fact my biological dad. Just like Prince Harry (who for this reason I believed for many years was my soul mate), my red hair seemed to have come from absolutely nowhere. There wasn't a single strand of red hair on any family member's head, on either side. Even a red beard or moustache would have helped, but no. In fact, not only was my dad's hair black, but his skin was actually quite sallow, but that might have been a result of all the time he spent on a yacht. My lack of resemblance never seemed to bother him though; likewise, I think Prince Charles and the royal family are firmly in denial.

Anyway, my supposed father, a very savvy and intelligent man (another reason why I could not believe we were related), made a considerable fortune in the eighties, investing in property. As the Celtic Tiger boomed in the nineties and into the noughties, my dad became wealthier and wealthier, and he and my mother enjoyed a wildly extravagant lifestyle. Then he retired from it all and sold almost everything just before the collapse of the economy, the jammy dodger. So, even after the downfall, they were still minted, unlike the rest of the country. However, they were somewhat aware of the grim reality, in their own unsympathetic way. My mum liked to regularly complain in a mock working-class accent that 'this bleeding recession is wrecking the buzz'.

Anyways, back to the eighties: little changed in the McKenna household when I came along. I think had they had triplets it still wouldn't have had much of an effect on their lifestyle. I'm sure losing the baby weight was the greatest of my mother's concerns. Despite all this they weren't completely terrible parents.

It was always exciting and glamorous in our family home. My parents regularly had sports stars, famous actors and musicians over for ostentatious dinner parties or wild poker nights. I never knew what celebrity I would bump into when I arrived home from my piano lesson.

My parents' ignorance of the world outside their bubble meant it became impossible as an adult to please them. My mother, who was particularly lost in a bizarre world of vanilla-martini-mocha-frappuccinos, just couldn't understand why I was nearly thirty and hadn't become a famously coveted artist yet. She would roll her eyes and come out with a classic line such as, 'Had *I* chosen to be an actress, I'm sure I would have become a Hollywood movie star'. And then she would proceed to tell my father how lucky he and Angelina were, for if she had, she would be married to Brad Pitt right now. 'And isn't that lucky too for their little refugee rainbow family,' she would conclude.

My parents didn't really know what to do with me as a young child. It was as though they had never been children themselves. The whole thing seemed to baffle them. If I didn't want to enjoy a glass of brandy with them and discuss jazz music, or Victoria Beckham's botched boob job, I was alien. And that was how Granddad and I became best buddies. I was left for long periods in Ballytiernan, while they went off on cruises or on 'adult only' holidays in Ibiza. Knowing how I was being brought up in Dublin, Granddad created a much more stable environment for me when I was in Ballytiernan: a proper balanced dinner every evening, a fixed bedtime every night, and he always read me a story before I went to sleep. I was his only grandkid, as my mother, like myself, was an only child.

So here I was back in his cottage. It wasn't easy. The little house was very blatantly lacking his large jovial presence. An almost constant flow of memories bombarded me from every crevice of every corner. But it was just what I needed. To escape New York. To get as far away from the city as possible. Far removed from the heartache, humiliation and downright messiness of it all.

I took Sasha with me. It took my parents a day and a half to notice she was gone. And that was only because the housekeeper pointed it out to them. I figured I was rescuing her from a life of solitary, albeit opulent, isolation. She quickly found all the sunniest places, as cats do, and seemed relatively content. However, I did wonder whether she found her new surroundings to be rather bleak and grim compared to the life she was used to. She had been a cat of ultimate luxury; her delicate paws had never graced anything other than marble floors and the softest of carpets before now. I wondered had she noticed the lack of under-floor heating and thought this a crude, slum-like environment. But I was glad to have Sasha. With her there I didn't feel quite so alone in the middle of the isolated countryside.

I patted Sasha's little head the following morning as she tucked into the tuna I'd put in her dish.

'Be good,' I told her and headed for the front door.

I waved over at John Joe as I strolled down the driveway. My dad had arranged to rent out the field at the side of the cottage ('good grazing land') to John Joe, a local farmer. He was a strange lad, John Joe. A happy-in-his-own-company sort of creature with a magnificent unibrow and a big toothy grin. But I quite liked having him there. He kept to himself and always seemed cheerful.

It was also good to have a bit of income from the field, even if it was a minimal amount. I knew I would probably have to continue to chip away at my inheritance over the next while or else sign on for social welfare. But of course I was keen to do a bit of work if I could get some. So I set off on a little mission to find myself a job in the village. If there was a coffee shop to be found in Ballytiernan I wasn't going to leave it without a job, I told myself firmly as I marched down the road. Okay, it wasn't my number-one career choice, but painting wasn't really an option. It was a bit of a solitary occupation, not to mention a penniless one. For now, I was determined to satisfy my artistic urges by doing elaborate cocoa swirls on the tops of cappuccinos.

The village was basically exactly as it had been when I was last there. In fact, it now appeared even smaller if that was possible – just tiny – almost like a model country village. The only changes were: two of the three pubs had shut down and Tuohy's Greengrocer's was now a Spar. Church – exact same. Graveyard – exact same. Post office – exact same.

One new addition: Mo's Teacup. That was it.

My future employer, I thought – I bet she's a warm friendly, homely woman who'll take me under her wing and treat me like the daughter she never had, and even set me up with one of her sons, and it won't be weird at all.

In I trotted to Mo's Teacup, full of this optimism.

A wide woman with an apron and short hair greeted me with a grunt that vaguely resembled 'Howya'. She was cleaning the glass on the front of a display cabinet containing impossibly delicious-looking tarts, cakes, muffins, scones . . . My mouth immediately started watering. Yes, I could absolutely work here, I thought. How perfectly things were all going to fall into place! I could just feel it. I could feel it in my tummy. It rumbled approvingly.

'Excuse me,' I began with a confident smile. 'Are you, perchance, Mo herself?'

'Perchance I am indeed,' she retorted with a hint of mockery that I chose to ignore.

I wasn't exactly sure why I had tried to impress her with fancy lingo in the first place. Obviously it fell on very unimpressed ears. But I was not discouraged. Still smiling, albeit a little less enthusiastically, I persevered.

'Right so, em . . . Are you looking for staff at the moment?'

Silence.

'Can I give you my CV?'

'I don't know. Can you?'

'Yes, I . . .' I waved my CV in its envelope at her.

More silence. God, this woman really was a tough nut to crack.

'Em . . . I'm looking for a job,' I finally attempted. At this stage my smile had seriously waned. 'I'm really . . . hard worker.' Oh dear, now my English was failing me. I now sounded like it wasn't my first language, except I had a Dublin accent so it resulted in me looking like an idiot. I might as well have said 'I am job.'

'Okaaaay,' she said slowly.

She took my envelope, her eyebrows raised as though this was all quite entertaining to her.

I left. Well, almost. I could hardly have been expected to leave without a cake. I chose a strawberry tartlet, paid the strange lady and went home to stuff it into my face for some much-needed comfort. My only hope of employment in the village had been a source of amusement to the prospective employer. Well, at least someone had got a kick out of my efforts. I had lost my determination but at least I had a cake. I trudged home to my granddad's little cottage.

Just as I got in the door I felt my mobile phone buzzing.

'Katie, is it?' a woman's voice barked down the phone rather aggressively.

I knew immediately who it was.

'Yes?'

'Do you know Farrelly's?' she pressed on.

The one and only pub left in Ballytiernan.

'I do.'

'Right so,' Mo continued. 'Jim is interested in giving you a go over there. Mary, who makes the sambos for them on Mondays, Tuesdays and Wednesdays, did her hip in at set dancing last night. Are you capable of shlapping together a few ham-and-cheese sambos?'

'Yes. Definitely,' I chirped.

'She also jumps in behind the bar occasionally when it's needed. Do you have experience with that sort of thing?'

'Absolutely,' I lied.

I had employment. Sort of. And luckily too, because Sasha was about to eat me out of house and home. I was hardly in the door and my little companion was marauding around, pestering me for more food. She had killed a sock, and was keen for me to see it and praise her, but obviously that was not satisfying her nutritional needs.

'I have a job, Sasha!'

The sassy little cat didn't even acknowledge my excitement.

'So long as you put food in my bowl we're good,' she mumbled as she strutted out into the hall swishing her hips, her tail high in the air. Well, she didn't actually say anything but that's what she would have said if she could.

Mac answered her phone just before it rang out, thankfully, as I was bursting to share my news with a more vocal audience.

'I got a job in Farrelly's!' I bellowed down the receiver before she had finished saying hello.

'You're not serious? That's fantastic, Katie.' Mac sounded genuinely pleased. 'Don't let Jim scare you though, pet – he doesn't mean to be the way he is!'

Jim was a short, googly-eyed man with a few wisps of hair combed across his head. Looked older than he probably was: anywhere between fifty-five and seventy. As well as an evident lack of social skills, he wasn't a man who understood the concept of personal space – or breath-freshener for that matter.

'Mo didn't mention you were such a fine-lookin' girl,' he announced, his nose inches from my chin and his tiny stature making every effort to broaden out. 'You could do with a bit more meat on your bones! I like my women to be chunky.' His eyes lingered on my belly bulge which was the only area containing any of the chunk he was hoping for. 'You're getting there though. I'll start you off on a tenner an hour, eighteen hours a week, with the potential for a raise if you pack on an extra pound or two. We'll say a euro for a pound, that's a good exchange rate – ha ha!'

I was momentarily concerned I had entered a brothel looking for employment, the way he was examining me. But no, it was definitely a pub. An old, slightly dilapidated, but somehow charming pub. Despite Jim, I felt immediately at home. There was a relentlessly friendly atmosphere that somehow prevailed. However, almost everything was in need of repair – anything that wasn't actually looked out of place. There were flecks of sawdust all over the ground, gathered in heaps in the corners. There was an ever so slight – but nevertheless present – smell of cat piddle. The upholstery on the seats was distinctly from the seventies. Not like it was seventies imitation, no. It just hadn't been reupholstered since then. If you looked carefully, you could just about make out a pattern of pineapples framed in little diamond shapes. However, this pattern was barely visible through what I imagined was beer, sweat, puke, and possibly piss embedded in the fabric. Some of which was more than likely older than I was.

I looked back at Jim who was still inspecting me. I self-consciously wrapped my loose cardigan across my chest, even though I didn't have much of a chest to hide.

'Yes. A few ham sandwiches and you'll be a fine woman indeed. And we can help you here with that. Sure you'll be making plenty of them and I won't mind if you sneak a few away for yourself.' He winked with a chuckle.

I would have recoiled at this persistence only it somehow seemed harmless and even endearingly clueless.

'And sure 'tis nice to have a fresh, pretty, young face all the same,' he went on happily. 'What do you think, Fred?'

A scruffy, fair-haired lad, about my age, maybe a bit younger, appeared behind a keg as he lowered it to the ground behind the bar with a groan. He straightened himself and looked over sympathetically with a knowing lopsided smirk. He had a slightly crooked nose, a small scar just in the middle of his two eyebrows and kind, piercing blue eyes. Something about him seemed familiar; it made me relax a bit, counteracting the efforts of Jim.

'I'll show you round,' Fred offered warmly.

I followed him behind the bar and into the small, very basic kitchen where he showed me the sandwich-making supplies.

'They do like them cut in triangles.' He stood there awkwardly, suddenly less comfortable in himself, and continued, 'I'm Fred by the way – I pull pints here in the evenings.' He shuffled from one foot to the other.

I smiled. 'I'm Katie – I make sambos here Mondays, Tuesdays and Wednesdays, apparently.'

'Well, depending on how long you can stick *him*,' he said, smiling warmly again.

My eyes locked with his and my stomach seemed to tighten. A grin spread across my face and I looked at the ground. I noted that it needed a good hoovering.

'Don't worry, you'll get used to the smell in this place . . . eventually.' He played with a little hole at the bottom of his jumper.

I tried not to look at him too much, but something was niggling at me and I couldn't figure it out. I couldn't shake the feeling that he was somehow very familiar. I didn't think it was just in my head, because he seemed to be looking at me with strange uncertain glances too. Although maybe I just had some of Mo's strawberry tartlet stuck to my face from earlier. I swiped at my mouth region with the back of my hand but there didn't seem to be anything there. He was still looking at me with a vaguely unsure expression, like he wanted to say something but was holding off.

'Have we met . . . before . . . ?' I broke the silence, but trailed off. It felt like a silly question the minute I'd said it.

'Actually, I think so.' He ruffled his hand through his hair, leaving it sticking up in places at the back. 'Is your name Katie McKenna?'

'Yes.'

'I grew up in the house right next to your grandad's cottage – well, just round the corner on Fleming's boreen. I still live there actually – well, in the little bungalow on the other side of the house.'

My mouth fell open. 'Freddie Flanagan? No way!'

I couldn't believe it. I hadn't stopped smiling since I met this guy and now I just couldn't help laughing. He started laughing too.

'This is ridiculous!' I said.

My face went red and I silently warned myself not to giggle for too long or I'd look like an airhead.

'I know!' he nodded.

I had to hug him. I couldn't not hug him. Maybe it was a little strange but I leaned towards him and squeezed him in a big hug. He hugged me back. He smelt lovely too. Like lemon and cut grass.

Chapter 3

The Sunday before I was due to begin my new bar-service/pub-grub career, boxes arrived at Winnipeg Cottage. The last of my New York belongings. My stomach sank as I realised there was nothing left of me in that city. My existence there had diminished to memories. So Seb had lumped everything I owned into a few boxes with not so much as a note or card or goodbye message . . . I dug around . . . nope. Nothing. My eyes welled up, but I shook my head and swallowed the lump in my throat.

I had really prided myself on my ability to get back up off my arse pretty quickly and get on with things. I had started fresh, in a whole new part of the world and everything. Although, deep down I wasn't quite sure if I had really dealt with the break-up and everything that had happened. I had been upset – there was no denying that. But had I just been mourning my granddad or was it both? Anyway, it didn't last too long. I gave it a few days and that was it. Nasty little thoughts of Seb occasionally crept into my consciousness, though, like a virus, making me angry. Deep down I knew it wasn't resolved for me.

We'd lived together. He knew everything about me, every silly little thing. He knew that I folded my loo roll eight times before I used it – I would never crumple. He knew basically everything.

Then one day I told him my granddad was dying and I had to go to Ireland to say goodbye. What happened that day still stunned me when I thought back on it. Although he seemed distracted, he expressed some sympathy and wrapped me up in his arms as we sat together on the couch. I talked about my granddad. I lamented the fact that they would never get to meet each other. Seb would have liked my granddad. Everyone did. Seb said nothing, just listened. He stroked my hair and I continued sobbing softly into his chest. He got up to make me tea. He always knew what I needed without having to ask. Even in my grief I knew I was lucky to have Seb. I watched him squeeze the tea bag. He was what you would call an ethnic beauty. His mother was Puerto Rican, lending his skin a caramel tone. He was tall and thin, shaped like a clothes hanger with broad shoulders but not a lot of muscle. His style accentuated this. He always wore well-tailored suits, blazers, slacks – always with elegant loafers or smart dress shoes. He had incredible bone structure, full lips and a face that looked intelligent and effortlessly sophisticated. His image was completed with hair that was always well-coiffed.

He sat down beside me, handing me the cup with the handle towards me. Then he tucked my hair behind my ear and gently whispered, 'I think this might be for the best.'

I thought perhaps I had misheard him. I sniffled, 'Hmm?'

'I think maybe we need some time apart . . . so . . . every cloud . . . you know?'

I actually laughed. I thought it was an inappropriate joke. He was pretty good at those. I put the cup down and looked at him. I gradually stopped laughing when I realised he wasn't laughing with me. He was looking at me with this strange expression, like there was an insurmountable guilt or regret there, but he was trying with all his might to disguise it. I knew him too well. My eyes bored into his, but he didn't budge. My mouth suddenly tasted like salty sour apple.

'Kat, I'm serious. I think it's time for me to . . . try other things . . .'

It was like he was trying to make it seem simple and uncomplicated but there was something deeper there. And it felt like a big something. It felt massive. Like a giant elephant that had always been sitting there in the living room of our apartment, but that I had been oblivious to all along. Why had I always been so oblivious? I searched his eyes for an answer but he looked away from me.

'What do you mean "other things"?' I spluttered, feeling as though the elephant was now sitting on my chest. 'What sort of other things? Is it one thing in particular? Someone else? What is it?' My eyes were stinging and everything seemed to start to spin. I could hardly believe what came next and I still couldn't get my head around it three months on.

He took a deep breath and looked down into his lap. 'I think it's time for me to try something less . . . inverted.'

'*What?*'

'Cock.' He lifted his head ever so slightly and looked at me with a grimace. Then he covered his face in his hands and I heard a muffled 'Sorry, babe' through his fingers.

I wasn't sure whether to laugh or cry; the room was spinning faster and faster.

'If this is a joke, Seb, it's fucking hilarious!' I spat every word out drenched in a particularly viscous sort of sarcasm.

He said nothing. I stood up. Then I sat down again. I was too dizzy to stand but I didn't want him on the couch beside me so I started pushing him off the couch with my hands and then with my feet. I was forceful and soon he gave in and stood up. He looked extremely uncomfortable and awkward. I didn't care. I looked up at him, a steady stream of tear-blobs flowing from my eyes, and plopping off my chin into my lap.

I silently begged him to put me out of my misery and tell me it was all a really un-funny joke. He didn't. He was looking more and more uncomfortable as the minutes passed, each one slower than the next, and his face seemed heavy with a deep sadness.

It was real. Could this be real? Was he actually gay?

'Are you gay?'

He shrugged. So was that a yes? When? How? Why? I had so many questions. I was horrified. I was mortified. Was the whole relationship a big lie? Did everyone else but me know?

People had occasionally made suggestions but I had always just presumed they were joking. I had laughed about it. 'As if! Could you imagine?' I'd said.

After all, he was my soul mate. I reminded myself that this could not be possible, as I knew everything about him. Or I thought I did. So had other people seen or heard something and not told me? Was everyone laughing at me? 'God love her, she hasn't got a clue her boyfriend is a big flaming pink queen! The poor idiot. How does she not see it?' Did he even find me attractive? Had he ever loved me? Did he love men now? Had he been secretly horrified by my lady area? Did he think about men when we had sex? These thoughts rapidly flooded through my head like molten magma, covering my brain, frying it and destroying every notion I had ever had. I could almost feel my heart break, like a bone or anything else breaking. A snap. I could feel my cheeks getting violently hot. How could he have lied to me for so long? I was such an idiot! How had I not known?

Despite all my fury and aggressive urges, I couldn't bring myself to shout at him because he looked so miserable. And even though he was hurting me beyond belief, it couldn't be easy for him. I swallowed my rage and tried to think of something calm to say.

'Do you not love me?' I finally asked quietly. It was hard to know which one of us seemed more pathetic than the other.

'I don't know, Katie. I just need some time to figure it out.'

'Is there someone else? A . . . a man?'

'Well, I've been experimenting a bit, I guess.'

'With who?' My jaw hung open.

'No one you'd know.'

It felt like I was trying to swallow a gobstopper. Unsuccessfully. A big massive lie that felt like it was stuck in my throat. I felt majorly duped.

It was all a charade.

Three years.

I was officially a beard.

I suddenly felt abandoned, and utterly alone. I looked at him, searching his eyes. But he stood firmer now, colder. My Seb wasn't there, just a stranger standing in front of me, breaking my heart.

'Don't worry, Katie.' He put his hand on his hip and kept his feet rooted to the ground, rather awkwardly. 'You'll find someone else, you'll get over it.'

My Seb would never have said that. I stood up, gathered every last bit of strength I had, willing myself not to projectile-vomit all over the place, and I walked straight out the door.

'I am so fucking over it,' I said aloud to myself, briefly stirring Sasha from her snooze. She gave me a blank look and went back to sleep, curling her tail around herself. I was ready to bury those feelings in a deep dark part of me and ignore them. I was beginning a new life.

I opened the delph box to dig out Muggins – my favourite mug – for some much-needed tea and finally, lo and behold, I found a note: *'Muggins fell off a shelf and smashed so I threw him out. Sorry!'* was scrawled on a Post-it.

Okay. Stay calm, Katie. It's not the end of the world, just the end of a mug. I'll use the 'Gorgeous Granddad' mug I got Granddad for his 80th birthday. It's fine. Totally fine.

So I popped on the kettle and stood there, watching the little red light on the switch, trying to suppress the mounting rage building in my gut. All the humiliation and devastation was flooding back and I didn't seem to be able to control it. Man, I really needed this tea. Knowing this red light was triggering some sort of red rage within me and also knowing a watched pot never boils, I felt myself rotate away from it. But instead of just standing there with my back to the kettle, I continued to move on a sort of autopilot towards the back door. It felt like cinematic slow motion, and that I was an external, impartial observer of my actions.

I picked up pace as I descended the steps into the garden. I leaped over the low fence with surprising determination and ran. I ran through Old Mr Healy's empty field and continued past the sheep in Dennis Daly's field. I didn't notice their reaction to the intruder – my eyes were almost closed against the wind, and tears were streaming down my face. For God's sake, Katie, this is by far the stupidest thing you have ever cried about. A *mug*! I told myself Seb could shove Muggins where the sun don't shine for all I cared. Ugh . . . I wouldn't actually want to do that to poor Muggins. That would be considered mug cruelty. I wiped my hands over my eyes and cheeks, and gulped down my tears.

I could just keep running, I thought, like Forrest Gump after Jenny leaves him. Yes! I wasn't crying, I was liberating myself – these weren't tears of sadness, they were tears of freedom. I was breaking rules, setting new world records and stuff, like Forrest Gump did. I would run all across Ireland, news cameras would follow me, crowds of people would cheer me on! Like Adele winning awards for break-up songs, I was going to win awards for break-up athletics! I wasn't sure how but I had a feeling there was likely an Oscar in this for me.

I began sprinting, feeling wild and free and spontaneous . . . through a clump of trees into the next field and then *Wham!* –

right into the backside of a big brown cow. *Moooo!*

Blackout.

'Eck!'

Something slobbery was licking my face. I could feel grass on one side of my face and the other side was throbbing, and burning hot. And now, it was also becoming moist and sticky. I shifted around and discovered that my face-licker was a large dog, the owner of which I vaguely recognised.

A lopsided smile teamed with scruffy blond hair. The piercing blue eyes looked at me with bemusement. I realised who his eyes reminded me of: they were like Daniel Craig's. In fact, he looked a little like Daniel Craig. Although, I'd never really fancied Mr Craig – but there was an extra something about Fred. His clear eyes and shrewd gaze made my cheeks blush.

He had changed so much from my childhood memories of him. The scar above his nose hadn't been there when he was younger.

We had played together non-stop as children. I remembered how I used to cry when I had to go back to Dublin. I would wave out the back of the car window at him, bawling crying. As an only child I threw tantrums a lot when I wasn't getting my way. I was hoping he didn't share that memory. He had also been much skinnier as a boy. Since then his shoulders had broadened out a lot, and his eyes seemed lighter and yet deeper, if that were possible. They were the colour of the sea in those pictures of exotic beaches in travel magazines. A breathtakingly clear blue. I did remember getting lost in them when we were kids but mostly because his eyes always seemed to be dancing with excitement when he spoke. He had a mind that was constantly switched on, a mill of ideas for new games and inventions running through his head. He was the most entertaining boy I had ever met. We used to climb trees and race around the fields spotting different animals, and he always knew so much about all the animals and flowers. Even though he was slightly younger than me, I learned more from him than I did in school. And he was so gentle the animals never feared him. The sheep would let him touch their wool. He was often wary of ewes though and wouldn't go too near. But once their baby lambs were a little older they didn't mind him playing with them. The little lambs would follow us, climbing up rocks, and Freddie always helped them to find a safe way down. I was fairly enamoured of my little explorer friend. Was it any wonder I hated leaving? Was it any wonder I was drawn back here?

Just as I had always remembered, he still carried a big stick in his hand, which he was now tapping off the ground.

'Thank you, dog . . . you can stop that now,' I grumbled, petting the soft doggy ears as I sat up. I wiped the slobber off my cheek with my sleeve. I was too embarrassed to look up.

'Are you okay?' Fred asked.

'Yep. Just a little . . . damp.'

'Bessie here alerted me to a trespasser,' he announced, indicating the dog at his side, who remarkably resembled her owner in a comic sort of way. 'And I wasn't going to leave you lying here, was I? Bess was very concerned. Weren't ya, Bess?' He ruffled her ears playfully, which almost made it seem as though she was nodding dutifully along with what he was saying.

I trudged along beside Bessie and Fred towards his bungalow, feeling like a proper idiot. I was grateful that they weren't a pair who asked a lot of questions.

'Tea?'

'I could do with a cup all right.'

I felt like a total perv checking out his ass as he filled the kettle. It was a pretty perfect bottom, wrapped up nicely in a pair of faded jeans. Bessie seemed to catch me looking so I averted my gaze. My eyes wandered around Fred's cosy kitchen. It was neat and organised. Very straightforward. Everything was clean. Everything had its place: the football boots and wellies lined up neatly at the door, Bessie's food bowl on a mat near her doggie bed. No bells and whistles, with the exception of a few quirky additions that seemed almost accidental. A photo of Fred with two children, a boy and a girl, playing rock-the-boat, was stuck to the fridge with a Chelsea football-boot fridge magnet. A blue disco ball hung out of the ancient-looking lightshade above the table – it looked totally out of place but nevertheless it seemed to work somehow. I noticed the droopy eyes of a bodiless ceramic Basset Hound whose large head sat alone on the sideboard. It had an opening around the top, and its shiny collar read '*Biscuits*'.

Fred caught me looking at it.

'Do you want a Twix?'

'Oh no . . . I mean . . . I was just looking at the Basset Hound jar . . . it's interesting . . .'

'Yeah, my sister – do you remember Evie? She got me that last Christmas from a car-boot sale . . .'

Evie was a good five or six years older than us so as kids we had mostly stayed out of her way. She'd always seemed way too cool for us. I gathered she was still pretty cool if that cookie jar was anything to go by.

Fred placed a massive mug of tea in front of me and hovered the jug of milk over it. 'Say when.' He began to pour.

'When,' I smiled.

He returned my smile coyly and stopped pouring.

'You sure you don't want a Twix? I was about to ask you anyway . . . or I have some Jaffa Cakes if you'd prefer . . .'

'Oh. Well, a Jaffa Cake would be lovely. I don't know who in their right mind could refuse a Jaffa Cake.'

I began to nibble my Jaffa Cake.

And then I said: 'Can you please not judge me based on

what just happened in the field – you know, when we become colleagues in less than twenty-four hours' time? In fact, let's just pretend it never happened, okay?'

'Pretend what never happened?'

'Thanks.' I smiled, holding his gaze.

All of a magical sudden I had another friend in Ballytiernan. I now had a grand total of two real proper buddies there. Mac and Fred. Two greater people it would be hard to find, and I knew straight away how lucky I was to have fallen on my feet with a job and two friends already!

In a sense Fred and I – we had sort of grown up together. Except it was a fragmented friendship and, because of that, over the years we had drifted apart. He had gone away to a boarding school in Galway, and my visits became less frequent as I got older, as my parents felt they could leave me on my own in the Dublin house when they went away. Eventually we just drifted completely out of each other's lives. But now here he was. I hadn't even contemplated that he could possibly be there. But why wouldn't he be?

I sighed contentedly as I sank back into the folds of my couch and switched on the TV. I was starting to feel less and less alone in this small little remote village.

That night I had a fairly standard phone conversation with my mother, in which I told her the excellent news that I had progressed from coffee-making to sambo-making.

She sobbed into the phone, 'Who even *eats* ham-and-cheese sandwiches? Builders with their bums out and dirty fingers?' and then she wailed dramatically: 'Who are you?'

The sounds coming down the phone line were so loud and theatrical, at one stage I was sure I saw Sasha look up and roll her eyes.

Afterwards I lounged in the living room with a jam doughnut and a glass of wine, and flicked open my reliable little three-year-old white MacBook. I convinced myself it would be a totally normal thing to do to check out my new best friend on Facebook. As one does. There was so much I didn't know! Was his name Fredrick, Fredmond or Alfred? Or was it just Fred from the get-go? What were his religious and political views? Did he have any interests? A girlfriend? Favourite TV series? Any music preferences? These were questions one would not have asked as a child. The most I would have found out about him back then was if he had an innie or an outie belly button, and even that I couldn't remember.

We had chatted briefly over tea and Jaffa Cakes but he hadn't really revealed much. He wasn't one to waffle on about himself, and I wasn't able to stay long because I remembered I had left the back door of the cottage open . . .

He didn't seem like a complicated kind of guy, but I did sense he was private and there was more to him than met the eye. He was obviously a totally different kettle of fish to Seb, who was very much an open book (well, except when it came to his sexuality . . .). So this quiet, sort of mysterious and yet uncomplicated man was a refreshing change. All right, I suppose what I really wanted to know was did he have a girlfriend? Wasn't that what Facebook was invented for anyway? *Not* that I was interested in being his girlfriend or anything. I just wanted to keep up to date with my new friend's status. I typed '**Fred Flanagan**' into the search bar and a list of profiles came up but I knew which was his straight away. It said Ballytiernan for hometown and the profile picture was a photo of Bessie wearing a Mexican sombrero hat. This made me smile. But other than that there wasn't a lot of information on him. A few pictures his friends had put up of him on nights out and on a stag – none very flattering. He was obviously the type of person who blinked every time a photo was taken. There was no relationship information. I clicked '**Add Friend**' anyway.

I certainly was in need of a few new friends, now that all my friends in New York thought I was sad and pathetic. I was probably now a laughing stock for being Sebastian's beard for three years without realising it. Maybe they even thought I turned him gay and everything! They were probably musing over how manly I was anyway. I basically had the same amount of boob as most men and maybe I even had really broad shoulders without knowing it! That's why halternecks never looked good on me! Oh my God, it suddenly dawned on me – I was basically a man – that's why he was able to stay with me for three years. All I was missing was the twig and berries. And I was obviously attracted to gays and I attracted them right back. My first crush was Stephen Gately. And the time when my best friend Sophie and I went to our first ever concert with no adults, when we were thirteen, he definitely looked at me. Yes, it was a jam-packed concert at the Point but he looked down from the stage and right into my eyes. Sophie said she saw it too. But then he turned out to be gay. I should have known then that unrequited love for gay men would be a curse that would follow me for the rest of my life.

Chapter 4

I quickly fell into the rhythm of the little village, and soon felt like part of the grotty old furniture in Farrelly's. Although I got the distinct feeling I was jazzing things up a little bit. I was definitely one of very few young women of my age bracket in the village. In fact, there was a glaringly obvious lack of young people there. It was almost blatantly missing a whole generation. Just gone. Poof! Like I imagined it was in Ireland during the famine. Between the ages of twenty and thirty-two, there were really only a handful of us scattered around. They were generally the ones who had got married early, settled down and perhaps taken up the family business, or they were socially awkward and still lived with their parents. In fact, at times it almost seemed like Fred and I were on our own in our generation. I happily got the impression he was delighted at the new arrival – he started calling me his 'new-old pal'.

As my shifts coincided with Fred's we had so much fun that work didn't really feel like work. However, I'd hardly been there a wet week and I already felt like I'd made a lifetime of sandwiches. I was hoping to venture behind the bar soon to mix things up but, otherwise, there didn't seem to be much scope for climbing the career ladder at Farrelly's. There were only six of us working there in total. There was Jim, Fred, myself, and Jim's nephew Cormac who seemed to possess a lack of social skills similar to his uncle's. Cormac fell into the 'socially awkward living-with-his-parents' category. He was beyond creepy, he was fairly unaware of boundaries and his brain-to-mouth filter was non-existent. So he basically said exactly what he was thinking at all times. And his thoughts were frequently disturbing. I quickly learnt to zone him out pretty efficiently. There were also two lads, Igor and Albert, who worked in the kitchen Thursday to Sunday, relieving me of my sambo-making duties, and offering patrons of Farrelly's a higher standard of pub-grub during the weekend.

I usually finished my shift at ten. Mac then joined me for an after-work Guinness that neither of us ever paid for. Mac almost always asked me the same thing.

'When you going to start painting, Katie?'

Mac's passion and enthusiasm for art was coming out her ears, as it had always done. I recalled that her craft of choice was tile painting. She lived in a small old terrace house along the road into the village. I had visited it many times as a child; it was one of those handy locations to call into, as you would pass on your way. I remembered being totally fascinated by a wall in her little courtyard at the back. It was a massive mural. She was constantly adding to it with new tiles and I would bound through her house, hardly saying hello, and race to the back to discover the new tiles. Occasionally she would allow me to help her to paint a tile and I would sign it. My chest would expand with pride seeing my signature scrawled in the corner of those few tiles.

'How's your wall coming along, Mac?' I asked, after one particularly busy Wednesday evening, as I dragged myself onto the barstool beside her. I was too exhausted to fob off her questions about my own art so I decided to initiate a conversation about her work instead. As much as I appreciated her encouragement, I knew I would never paint if I felt pressurised.

'Full. They've even started leaking down onto the ground, but finally I'm bored with it now. Twenty years doing the same shite. I've moved on. I'm doing erotic sculptures now, Lord bless us and save us! Don't look at me like that, Katie. I have as much of a right to explore my sexuality as a young one like yourself does.' She whipped out her phone, a cheeky grin spreading across her face and showed me a photo of one of her sculptures, if that's what you'd have called it.

I gasped. 'Jesus, I'm sure there are ways to explore sexuality, other than crafting a massive you-know-what out of clay!'

'This is none of the Lord Jesus's business, Katie.'

'It's lovely though,' I added, seeing her disappointment at my lack of enthusiasm. In fairness it was quite well made. 'Sorry, Mac. It's very impressive. The pubic hairs are very . . . life-like.'

'Have you never done any naughty paintings or anything yourself?' she asked slyly.

'Well, yeah, when I was a teenager I probably did.'

'It's very liberating, you know.' She sipped her Guinness. A creamy moustache lingered on her top lip and she grinned at me with her eyes crossed as she had always done when I was a kid. It still made me laugh. Probably more so this time because she was rubbing her thighs like a pervert.

It wasn't long before I started jumping in behind the bar when it got busy, but I soon got restless just pouring pints. I watched Fred making cocktails. I then made messy sub-standard versions of those cocktails. He teased me playfully and I found it hard not to blush.

One Saturday night Fred's sister Evie and her friends commandeered the bar for a rare night away from their families. To say they were a rowdy bunch would have been an understatement. They loudly insisted that Fred made the best cocktails in Ireland. It was quite possibly true but for a nice guy he was remarkably militant about how he made them. It was his way or the highway.

'Hiya, Freddie! Can I've a Margarita please!' slurred a happy bottle-blonde member of Evie's pack. 'Oh, no salt, please,' she added as he was about to salt the rim of the glass.

'Well, I don't want to make you a Margarita so,' Fred stated firmly.

I couldn't help laughing from my perch at the side of the bar.

The bottle-blonde shrugged and said 'Go on so'. She knew he was right.

Although I wasn't working, I had popped into Farrelly's anyway because the quietness and solitude at Winnipeg was driving me up the walls. Sasha's company was lovely and I was very grateful to have her there – however, it was fairly limited. All the conversations were one-way, except the ones where I imagined her response. And I presumed it wasn't healthy to do too much of that. So I was propped up at the bar with Terry, my favourite customer, helping him with his crossword.

'Fred, what's the capital of Indonesia?' I shouted as he passed me carrying a handful of lemons and three Margarita glasses.

'Eh . . . Jakarta.'

'Thanks. So is that *J-a-q* . . . ?'

'*J-a-k-a-r-t-a*,' he replied hurriedly. 'Sorry, Katie, I'm a bit busy here.'

Fred had a massive order of cocktails and the regulars were getting restless for their drinks. God forbid they'd have to wait a few minutes for their precious pints.

'Oh goodness, sorry – here, I'll help!' I jumped up, perhaps a little too eagerly, and ran around behind the bar. 'Sorry, Terry, you're on your own. I wasn't much use anyway!'

'Ah, no, Katie – you shouldn't have to do this,' Fred said as he diced lemons briskly.

'I'm happy to!' I grinned, wrapping a little black apron around my waist.

'Thanks,' he smiled gratefully.

He was right though. There should have been two people scheduled to work. But Jim was trying to cut corners. The Ballytiernan nightlife wasn't a hugely lucrative market and, even though he had the monopoly, being the only pub in the village, the business was still struggling. So it was somewhat understandable. But having Fred working on his own on a Saturday night was just plain bonkers.

'Katie, put the kettle on, will ya?' shouted Terry.

'It wouldn't suit me, Terry!' I responded.

I took a couple of orders and busied myself pulling pints. They weren't even appreciative, some of the regulars.

'About time.' That was one lad's response when I handed him his Bulmers. He was lucky I didn't pour it over him.

Fred and I worked together at a harmonious yet focused pace for almost two hours and it eventually started to quieten down.

Fred added the finishing touches to what seemed like the hundredth round of cocktails of the night and passed them over the counter. He looked over at me as I topped off a Guinness for Paddy Longface.

'Thanks for that. I seriously owe you. How about a cocktail while I'm at it? Lady's choice. Anything you fancy . . .'

'Okay. What if I asked for a Manhattan but wanted it shaken not stirred?' I teased coyly.

'Well, that's not possible.' He firmly held my eye contact. 'It's just wrong.'

I giggled. 'Oh, I have an idea! I'll make my own. You can supervise and I promise I'll do it perfectly!'

'Am I a cocktail Nazi?' he asked, biting his lip.

'Yes. I think I fancy a Whiskey Sour. I might as well join all these ladies getting salmonella from the egg whites,' I joked.

As I shook up the ingredients in the mixer as vigorously as my scrawny little arms would allow me, I noticed Fred laughing at me.

'Is that your sex face?' he grinned.

'What?' My cheeks immediately went scarlet. 'No!'

'Well, you're not doing it right if you're not making a sex face.'

'You're *such* a cocktail Nazi!'

I had stopped noticing the smell of cat piddle in Farrelly's. That was around the time when I realised I was really enjoying working there. I particularly liked being behind the bar. On days when I wasn't working I found myself missing it, missing Fred and even Terry and Jim.

I even missed Paddy Longface, despite the fact that he frequently puked red wine at the end of the night and it was horrific to clean up. Paddy Longface was a failed magician. He had joined some sort of circus troupe in his late teens, he informed me, but it didn't work out. He spent the rest of his life trying to make it as a freelance magician, but there just wasn't the market for it, he insisted with a defeated shrug. For all his efforts he really did look like a magician. He had a long face (obviously) with a narrow beard hanging off the end of it and a full moustache that he kept impeccably twirled at the ends. His nose looked like a light bulb, veins meandering down towards the tip of it like little streams joining together and culminating in a large red bulb.

I was hearing his and all the local old men's life stories for the first time so I wasn't yet bored with them. I was informed this would not last long, but for now I found it fascinating. In fact I wanted to capture it all.

There was something undisturbed about the place and the people. Like they hadn't changed with the times. There was almost an Amish feel to the village, like it had just stood still over the years. I regularly took my phone out when Jim wasn't around and snapped pictures of the characters on the other side of the bar. Instead of listening to what they were saying I would be taking photographs on the sly. They rambled away, lost in their thoughts and memories, and I would nod along attentively while simultaneously taking pictures. I wasn't even particularly discreet – I would have the phone out in front of them – but I did avoid telling them I was taking pictures because I didn't want them to pose. But they never copped on. Or else they simply didn't care. In fact, they probably enjoyed the attention. I showed them the finished images of themselves after I'd double-filtered them on Instagram. 'Jaysus, don't I look well,' was the general sort of response I got.

But I loved catching them unawares. Terry with his head in his paper, diligently filling in his crossword; Paddy Longface rolling a cigarette, or shuffling a deck of cards, or playing battleships with Barney; Barney with his colourful dicky bows; Silas with his mouth full of braces, and a big grin showing them off. At seventy he had decided to spend some of his pension money on finally fixing his teeth. And why not? He looked great. His teeth weren't the whitest, but they were all there and now they were getting straighter and he was going to look fabulous. That's what I always told him. But, with or without braces, these men all made wonderful subjects for impromptu portraits. The lines on their faces told a million stories before they even spoke a word. Sometimes the story I created about them in my mind was better than the one they told me.

That was what I loved so much about images: you could decide for yourself what the story was. My hands were itching to pick up a paintbrush again. This came as a surprise. The urge hadn't hit me in such a long time. Maybe Mac's persistence was actually having an effect on me. Despite having studied to be an artist, I had spent the last few years completely uninspired. Yes, New York is undoubtedly an inspiring place, but unless you're loaded it's also a massive struggle to get by, and a struggle to resist the party scene. Any spare time or money I had was spent on partying. Partying very quickly replaced art as my hobby. I was still unsure as to why I had really stopped painting though. Maybe I had become disheartened with my abilities when people stopped buying my work. Or maybe I had just been stuck.

Who would have thought that little backwards Ballytiernan would lift the curse? I felt freer here. Unshackled. It really was a surprise. But then there were so many little stories to be captured or indeed unearthed. It gave me that excited feeling where my toes wiggled and my stomach seemed to dance.

Chapter 5

Getting out the paintbrushes basically seemed to be the answer to all my niggling thoughts and questions. 'Simples.' And on top of everything else it would give me a purpose. A quest. Something I had so desperately been yearning for in my life. A distraction from my thoughts.

So one evening I decided to take another look at the boxes that had been so lovingly sent from New York by my darling ex. I began unwrapping all my canvases and art supplies and the smell of oil paint, mediums and turpentine immediately filled the small cottage. They had been wrapped up and hidden away for almost three years and still the smell was potent once they were released. I inhaled deeply, tickled by the familiar giddy feeling of creativity and escapism. This smell was a unique one; it was toxic. Not only was it the sort of smell that made you feel dizzy and high with chemicals, but also with inspiration . . . or potential inspiration . . . the fear that inspiration would not come also lurked in that dark part of the mind. Like any smell it seemed to be a portal for memories. With every inhalation feelings and emotions from a bygone time wrapped themselves around me and my eyes glazed over as I unloaded my trusty tools. The bristles of my brushes were old and hard. I would need to get new ones. The lids on some of the paint tubes had been carelessly left partially screwed. They would need to be replaced. But almost everything else was ready to go. My white spirits, my pallets and mixing trays . . . and finally my big old pieces of art. The weight of some of them almost caused me to topple over, trying to pull them out of the boxes.

And then they were there, placed haphazardly around the room. My creations. A bit vulgar. Large imposing canvases with chaotic city scenes. I had never done small paintings. I wanted drama. I wanted to create pieces that would envelop the viewer, overwhelm them, dwarf them. To recreate the effect of standing in Times Square itself. Nowhere could make you feel like a teeny tiny ant quite like Times Square did. And I wanted my art to achieve the same result. On top of this, I liked to make things difficult for myself. It was almost as though deep down I hadn't really wanted to sell them. Seldom would you find a person in Manhattan who had an apartment or space big enough for them. Therefore they never sold. That was my excuse for giving up hope. But the truth was probably that a small part of me was self-destructive. I created these massive pieces that would be redundant. Perhaps I had wanted to convince myself that I was unappreciated in my time, like one of my all-time heroes Van Gogh. I wanted to be a broke, starving, tormented artist. Like when Don McLean said in his song about Van Gogh that the world was never meant for one as beautiful as him . . . That song had always given me goose bumps. In fact, it occasionally made me cry on days when I was feeling melodramatic. The idea that the mind of the artist is too astounding for the world to handle. What a concept. To be that brilliant. To suffer in that way for art, for your 'sanity' . . . I envisioned myself as this genius trapped in a world where I was misunderstood, slowly going crazy . . .

But then it turned out I didn't have the commitment to

stick to it and so I just got a regular job instead. I probably wasn't ready to go crazy and kill myself for my art. Sometimes a girl just wants to earn money doing a regular job and party while she's young. The tortured artist thing just seemed too exhausting.

'Oooooh, now there's a smell I like!' Mac's voice floated in from the kitchen, gently cutting through my thoughts.

She had let herself in through the back door again.

'I'm sorry, dear, do you mind if I come in?' she added as an afterthought.

'Not at all, Mac! I'm in the living room!' I shouted.

'Well, what have we got here?' Her head appeared around the door, with a warm curious smile on her weathered but bright face.

'Oh, just a few little oversized snapshots from another life,' I answered softly.

As I looked at the body of work spread around the room it struck me how truly intertwined it was with my old life. The large dramatic canvases were jarring in this new environment.

'Indeed,' Mac agreed. She fell silent and stood with me taking it all in. Drinking the atmosphere they imposed.

I wondered if she wanted to ask me questions or if she was forming her own opinions. I wondered if she found the high-rise buildings of the big city and the bustling streets overwhelming.

'I can almost hear the noise,' she finally said lightly, as though in a trance. 'And feel the warm smoky air and smell the pollution.'

I smiled at her. She was right. Each painting was like a window into this other world, and they seemed to succeed in having the desired effect of consuming the viewer.

'Do you miss it?' she prodded.

'No,' I answered, surprised by the strength of my own conviction. 'I'm relieved not to be there,' I revealed, to myself as much as to her.

'There is an undeniable passion though,' she added thoughtfully.

'You know Renoir said: "*When I paint flowers my mind has a rest.*"' I moved back and sat down on the couch and tucked my feet under my bottom. 'I've always felt that way about cityscapes. I can just let loose with the brush and the movement of the city just flows onto the canvas. It always gave my mind a rest from the hectic life over there.'

'I see,' Mac nodded, her heavy eyes studying me. 'I presume you don't feel the need for that particular release here, in Ballytiernan.'

'True that,' I agreed.

'I challenge you to start something new, Katie.' She sat down beside me. She had such a gentle energy, despite the fact that she was being somewhat forceful with her intentions.

'Figurative work. That's the next step on your artistic journey,' she cooed.

I laughed. 'My artistic journey?' I couldn't help sneering a little bit.

Mac ignored it. 'Yes. Your artistic *fart-tistic* journey.' She smiled and crossed her eyes. I chuckled. 'Not something boring though,' she added firmly. 'Go on, try something raunchy. Erotic art. You know you want to.'

I wondered was she getting high on the paint fumes.

Chapter 6

It was a divine Monday morning in July. You never knew what to expect in Ireland, but when a beautiful sunny morning came along I grabbed it. It could always have rained within the hour. So I threw the strap of my Nikon SLR over my head, and stuffed my feet into an old pair of running shoes. I spooned some tuna into Sasha's bowl out on the step, to encourage her to spend the day outside. Then I stroked her silky little brown head and bounded down the steps into the garden. I hopped the fence and set off across the fields. The grass was a rich, almost emerald colour after a winter of rain. It seemed to roll out ahead of me, rising and dipping, the shade of green lightening and deepening as it followed the unbridled pattern of the landscape.

This environment has got to be good for the soul, I thought as I skipped through the fields. The camera was making my bouncy joviality a bit tricky but I did my best to frolic when the terrain was even, and took more delicate steps over rocky areas. I found both gaits equally enjoyable, and the inconsistency liberating. However, as I passed Dennis Daly's sheep, I was a little bit more sheepish than they were. I hurried past them quickly, hoping they had forgotten my little 'moment'. I presumed they had, given that a sheep brain is probably fairly basic.

I reminded myself to focus. I was seeking inspiration for my new collection of paintings. As I ventured farther towards the next field I came across the cows, including the one I rear-ended not so long ago . . . The landscape was undeniably magnificent but my gut feeling was that there was nothing I could do to improve it. And, furthermore, there was the niggling fear that I wouldn't even do it justice, rendering the whole effort pointless. Perhaps I was being defeatist or perhaps Mac was right. It was possible that the thing that would tickle my creative fancy this time would be portraiture. These thoughts were hindering my mission to find inspiration so I decided to forgo the original game plan and simply enjoy my little excursion. I bounced over the hills just like Julie Andrews in *The Sound of Music*. I even did a little twirl, because I felt like it.

Bzzzzzzzzzzzzz . . .

My singing and frolicking was interrupted by a loud, intrusive buzzing noise. It was coming from the direction of Fred's field . . . I trotted over to give him a piece of my mind about noise pollution, but found myself coming to an abrupt halt. I was rooted to the spot, my jaw hanging open as though to catch flies. Fred was there all right, but I no longer wanted to give him a piece of my mind. However, I could think of several other things I wanted to give him. He was shirtless. The early July sunshine was reddening the tops of his shoulders. An enormous fluffy sheep was sitting calmly in his lap as he skilfully sheared away massive clumps of wool with composed concentration. I stood there silently, concealed by shrubbery, and watched with fascination as the sheep was gradually being transformed into an all-over skinhead. I definitely had not expected Fred to be so muscular. Frankly, he was ripped . . . Not quite like Henry Cavill in the latest *Superman*, but not a million miles away either. Henry Cavill didn't have the sexy Irish farmer tan marks though. But that probably explained why Fred was topless, trying to get rid of them. I felt a bit creepy standing there watching him. All I needed was a trench coat and I could have been arrested. Seeing as I was already your standard pervert, I thought I might as well take a few photos. So I snapped away merrily, telling myself I was more like a secret-agent spy than a pervert. It was a perfect composition, just what I was looking for to kick-start my inspiration. I couldn't have imagined something so ideal just falling into my lap. I was so struck by the moment that I nearly laughed out loud. I had to admit it wasn't quite the inspiration of Van Gogh, but I was excited about what I could create with it. I was in the mood for this. It would be cheeky and maybe a little tacky too. But so what? Nothing wrong with a bit of tackiness from time to time. I was brought back to earth with a thud when I felt a little buzz in my pocket. Oh shit! God, *no*! I tried not to panic as I desperately rummaged in my pockets for my phone before the ring tone kicked in.

Too late. 'Telephone' by Lady Gaga blared mercilessly out of my pocket. Fred stopped what he was doing and looked around. I bolted like Usain Bolt. I ran as fast as my legs would carry me while fumbling to stop the ringing.

It was Sophie. I really couldn't cancel the call; we hadn't spoken in way too long. But why now, Sophie? I huffed. Why this moment? She could have very easily interrupted one of my long meandering, mostly one-way conversations with Sasha. But no. She chose to ring at this of all moments. I silenced it until I was far enough away, and kept running. I really was becoming quite the runner, I thought as I gasped and puffed.

'Feck sake, you always choose the worst time to ring,' I finally whispered, panting.

'Well, hello to you too! I haven't heard from you in five weeks, Katie McKenna, and this is how you answer the phone to me?'

'Sorry,' I wheezed, bending over behind a tree, clutching my side.

Sophie, my best friend, really had a remarkable knack for finding the absolute worst moment to call.

'What's going on?'

'Just out for a little jog.' I tried to sound nonchalant.

'As if! You don't have the patience for jogging. You're up to something. I know it! Why else would you have accused me of calling you at the "worst time"?' She was using her nagging voice and my ears were not enjoying it.

I figured I might as well just come out with it, to shut her up. Anyway I had nothing to be ashamed of. Yes, it was a bit perverted, but isn't all art perverted in some way?

'I was spying on a half-naked man who was shearing a sheep.' Despite still feeling the need to whisper and the stitch in my side, I did my best to speak calmly and clearly. I didn't want to have to repeat it, if at all possible. 'Oh, and I was taking photos of him. Don't worry – the police are probably on their way by now to arrest me for gross creepy conduct.'

A beat.

'That's why you're panting into the phone like a pervert?'

'Yes, that would be why.'

'Okay. You just moved to the middle of the country a few weeks and you've become a lonely pervert already! Oh my God, and Sasha is there with you too, isn't she? You're a Crazy Cat Lady! My best friend has become a crazy cat pervert. Am I going to have to initiate some sort of an intervention?' She sounded deadly serious and genuinely concerned.

I rolled my eyes. 'Sophie! That's disgusting. I'm not a cat pervert. I'm a man pervert who lives with a cat. A pervert of men, not a man pervert . . . Anyway! I'm panting because I had to run. Because *you* rang and my cover was blown.' I squeezed my waist to try to ease the cramp.

'Right,' she said with authority. 'This all sounds disturbed.

I'm actually very concerned. When was the last time you've had any sexual activity, Katie? No, wait. Don't even tell me. It was Seb, right? A gay man. That is all sorts of wrong. I know you're heartbroken, Katie, but you really need to get back up on the horse, yunno? God, you're practically a nun. Or a virgin. Or both. And when are you getting back to New York? It's been outrageously boring here without you.'

She finally took a breath.

That was a total lie (New York had never been and never would be boring, and Sophie was the life and soul of every party in the East Village), but I appreciated the lie anyway. Sophie and I had been best friends practically since the first day of secondary school. We were both sent to a posh school in Dublin city centre, where neither one of us had any friends. But somehow, inevitably we found each other, and like two magnets we were drawn together in a sort of effortless way, and that was that. We'd been basically inseparable ever since. We even moved to New York together, almost straight out of school, and both signed up to go to college there.

I was really missing her now, and I felt bad about being so lousy at keeping in touch. I decided I would send her a parcel, with Tayto crisps, Barry's tea, Lily O'Brien's chocolates, a bottle of Mickey Finn's Apple Whiskey Liquor and a handwritten letter, retro style! All of our favourite treats.

But first, I was desperate to start painting. It simply couldn't wait. I had to start immediately. I'd never had much patience once I was inspired.

I was buzzing when I got back to the cottage. I was so giddy and hyped up that I forgot to be mortified over Fred. Or else I didn't care. Well, I decided that I wasn't going to be embarrassed anyway. I was an artist after all. Artists sometimes have to sacrifice being normal for art. I hurriedly threw on my painting jumper – a massive old comfy cotton sweater I had robbed from Sophie's dad years ago. It had maths equations printed all over it, and in the middle it read

'*Albert Says: E= MC²*'. It was a total nerd attack. It was so nerdy that real nerds, like Sophie's dad who was a mathematician, would never wear it. It was a step too far. Like an Irish person wearing a jumper with a shamrock on it. But I decided that I got away with it because I was just a wannabe nerd. Over the years, I had covered it in splashes and blobs of paint. I liked to think it was a pretty cool combination of left brain meets right brain. I threw my rebellious ginger curls up in a messy bun on the top of my head and got myself into painting mode. I popped my iPod into the dock and stuck it on shuffle. Bob Marley's 'Buffalo Soldier' came on. Sasha watched me, totally unamused, from her Queen Bee armchair as I sang along with a terrible Jamaican accent.

As I danced around I scanned the room, surveying all the paintings: propped on the couch, leaning against the TV and on the windowsills. I was really itching to start new work – however, I had no fresh canvas, as I hadn't yet been to an art shop.

And then it clicked. I knew what I was going to do.

'*Helloooooo!*' Mac's voice echoed from the kitchen. I had invited her around for tea and completely forgotten about it. 'I brought some cakes from Mo's. Good Lord in heaven above that woman has a broom up her arse. Excuse my French.'

'I think maybe I don't need sex,' I said out loud.

'Right,' said Mac, letting herself into the living room. 'No, I have to say I disagree. It's not a normal way to live, Katie. Think of all those priests, God love them. They're not right.'

'But I have art.'

'You certainly do, but painting these buildings is hardly going to get you off, my dear.'

'But they are, Mac! Well, no, not the buildings – but the men! I've realised what my next project will be! Are you excited? You should be – it's going to be amazing. It's just hit me. These paintings are merely backgrounds. They're waiting for a story to complete them. I'm going to paint my next project onto them.' Words were bursting with gusto out of my mouth and my arms were gesturing wildly. 'Men, Mac. Naked men. Irish farmers, naked.'

'Naked men? Ballytiernan men?' Mac's eyes glimmered.

'Yep.' I nodded. 'I already have one – see.' I thrust the photo of Fred into her hand and continued, 'Sort of. Don't worry, it's nothing strange. I just happened to be out walking and I spotted him in his field and took a quick snap. That's all. A lucky opportunity really.'

'It's a lovely shot of Fred – you've captured him very well,' she said softly, but I wasn't listening.

I ploughed on. 'Irish characters, taken from their rural environment – suddenly transported to another place entirely. But nothing about them has changed. They're on the streets of Manhattan, but completely unaware of the bustling metropolis surrounding them.' I took a breath. Mac was looking at me with an unreadable expression. 'Oh God, I've gone mad, haven't I? Sophie's right. I am becoming a totally desperate, perverted saddo . . .' I trailed off. Then another thought hit me. 'Or, maybe in actual fact I'm becoming the artistic genius I've always dreamt of being and the modern world will misunderstand me as a sad pervert. Maybe a hundred years from now people will realise, "Oh my God, she wasn't a sad pervert – she was an artistic genius!" Alternatively, there is a grim possibility that I'm both, Mac. The miserable truth is that a lot of artistic geniuses were sad perverts. Well, maybe that's a bit extreme. But Gauguin for example, whilst capturing the beauty of the women of Tahiti, gave them all syphilis. But the men I want to paint are adults! And I have no intention of giving them syphilis or –'

'I think you need to get away from these paint fumes for a while,' Mac firmly interrupted. 'Let's go make tea.'

'Am I gone loopy, Mac?' I asked as I cupped my tea in my

hands. I knew, if anyone would, Mac would give me the reassurance I needed to hear.

And indeed she did just that.

'Absolutely not, Katie, I think this sounds like a brilliant idea. Male artists painted naked women all the time. Why shouldn't a woman paint a series of naked men?' Mac had voiced exactly what I had been thinking.

'Well, I suppose the naked male form isn't quite as beautiful as the naked female figure,' I mused. 'But perhaps it could be more of a satirical sort of beauty, rather than sexy and moody.'

'I don't see why it can't be both! Funny can be sexy.' Mac looked almost as excited as me about the idea.

Her enthusiasm gave me the confidence I needed. I was going to do this. I already had one to start off with. Well, he was almost naked and that was definitely enough considering there was a sheep involved. Let's not make things strange, Katie, I thought.

I knew straight away which painting I wanted to use for Fred and the sheep. I inspected it after Mac had left. It was perched in front of the fireplace, waiting for this new addition. Asking for it. It was a perfect fit. It was a busy, daytime, blurry painting of Times Square in summer. Approximately one square metre in size. Not the biggest painting, but I had a gut feeling that this would give it the impact it deserved. I chose the clearest photo I had managed to get of Fred and the sheep, and printed it as large as I could make it. I started sketching from the photo straight away. I used a pencil and drew directly on top of the paint. It was hard to see the markings but I knew they were there and knew where it was going. I outlined Fred and the sheep into the middle of the painting, cars whizzing past on either side. Little scraps of wool flying around. People in summer dresses, shorts and flip-flops strolling past – completely unaware, or unconcerned perhaps. My eyes started to hurt, trying to see the pencil markings, so I dug out a blue marker and boldly used big confident lines to mark where the new additions would be placed. I could see it more clearly this way. With the blue marker added, my painting, as it was, was destroyed. It was scary. A good sort of scary. Something better was happening. I could feel it in my bones, right down to my toe bones.

Chapter 7

As soon as I realised I was really attracted to Fred, I immediately became goofier than Screech from *Saved by the Bell*. Why couldn't I just remain cool? It was such a shame because we'd been having such good craic working together. Freddie and I had always got on like a house on fire – when we were kids we used to say that he was the house and I was the fire – but there was never any awkwardness until now. He hadn't been a gorgeous child. He was cute but not gorgeous. Freddie was friend material. His big brother Seán was another story. Seán was gorgeous, but of course I had always been too shy to talk to him. Fred on the other hand was my pal. But now he was a sexy man. A proper man, and all of a sudden it was like a light switch turning on in my head. He was hot. Freddie Flanagan was super hot. And for some dreadful reason I had lost the ability to function normally around him. It was like an automatic chemical reaction that happened without my consent.

I tried to convince myself that I wasn't really interested in him in that way. It was because I was painting him! Of course, it often happens that when you're painting someone they become fascinating to you because you are exploring their features so intently while working. That was what I told myself anyway. But I didn't really believe it. I was smitten. There was no point in denying it. For the sake of my sanity, I had decided to assume he didn't see me the day I was creeping up on him – wishful thinking. I changed the Lady Gaga ring tone straight away so he wouldn't recognise it if it rang in his company – clever thinking eh? I hoped he hadn't registered it in the past. That was actually about the only clever thing I did. I was definitely not clever when I noticed his nose was a little pink and I asked did he get burnt out in the field on Monday. Luckily, it was likely that he would have been out in the field – anyone could have guessed that. I was just thankful I wasn't stupid enough to ask if the farmer's tan had improved at all. However, my cheeks instantly went red and I fumbled my words and even dropped a glass when I was around him. It just slipped out of my hand when he came up behind me. And I felt myself get sweaty like a thirteen-year-old boy talking to a hot older girl at school.

I was painting him, semi-naked, into the middle of Times Square. Him and the sheep, of course. Unfortunately, as Fred was unaware that he was my new muse, this made me feel a little like a psycho. I felt like that character in a movie that ends up killing everyone. I really didn't want to continue being the strange one with the weird secret fetish. It wasn't even a fetish – it was art! I was going to tell him. Get it out in the air, so he could form his opinions and be done with it. Then I could stop acting so strange.

I bounced into Farrelly's for work, looking my most fabulous. If I was going to reveal how crazy I was I was at least going to do it in style. I had gone to Galway at the weekend to get new paintbrushes and I also bought myself some nice new summer work clothes with my fairly poxy wages. A floaty little Penny's summer dress. 'Twas cheap and cheerful but there was no denying I looked foxy in it. There was a pretty high possibility that I was the number one sexiest sambo-maker that ever existed. Fred was already there so I sashayed past him. I was so caught up in my efforts to look cool and uninterested I forgot to say hello.

I was prepping my sambo station for the evening's orders when Jim bustled in.

'Well, hi there, Katie!' he breezed. 'Jaysus, girl, you're not going to a wedding. Are you trying to get yourself some action tonight, is it? If only your sambo-making was as good as your style we'd be flying!' He lowered his eyebrows. 'Listen, Katie, I know our Fred is a fine man, but don't be letting that distract you. Ha! Remember now, you have to butter the bread all the way to the edges. We do things properly around here, okeydoke?' He spoke fast, bombarding me with what he probably thought was a joke, but what felt to me like an exposition. Behind Jim I could see Fred wiping the surface of the bar. He must have heard.

I felt my cheeks flush with embarrassment as I tried to think of something smart to say. I knew the perfect sassy response would come to me two hours from now, when I least needed it. For now I was totally stumped. He paused, almost like he was giving me a chance to retort but, tragically, nothing came out of my mouth.

'Anyway you look far too glamorous to be working here – people will think you wandered in by accident,' Jim continued loudly. 'Here, put this on.' He threw me over a black T-shirt with a Guinness logo on it, wrapped in a plastic packet. 'I think we should all be wearing these. Guinness kindly sent me more this week. At least now people will know who is actually working here and who isn't.'

'It's Ballytiernan, Jim,' Fred interjected. 'Everyone who comes in here is a regular. They know who works here. If they need a T-shirt to tell them then they probably shouldn't be having any more to drink.'

'Just wear them, okay?' Jim responded.

Fred shrugged. He was already wearing one anyway.

I took mine out of the bag and looked at it. It was basically a tent.

'This is extra-large men's size. Don't you have —"

'Anyway,' Jim interrupted, clicking his fingers, as though to focus our attention. 'I'm headin' out for the evening with a lady friend so you two are responsible for not burning the place down, right?'

Well, this was a nice development. We had the run of the place, on a quiet Wednesday evening. Even if I was now dressed in a tent, at least I could enjoy a relaxed fun evening with Fred. I needed a drink to relax me, and stop me behaving like an awkward praying mantis.

'I've left Drico and Hubes out the back.' Jim nodded towards the backdoor. Drico and Hubes were his black Alsations, named after his favourite Irish celebrity couple, of course. 'They tore a hole in the garden fence at home, the messers, so they can't stay there. If they escape all the sheep in Ballytiernan will be slaughtered before midnight.'

'Your choice of drink, darlin'?' Fred read my mind as the door closed behind Jim's dumb, probably hairy, ass.

'I'll just have a Guinness, thanks. And maybe a shot of tequila too . . .'

Fred laughed. 'Fair enough. Actually, no. I'm going to make you a cocktail. You deserve one the way Jim goes on at you.'

'Ah no, don't go to the effort,' I responded shyly. 'I'll be grand with the Guinness.' I appreciated his attempt to lift the embarrassing mood Jim had left behind, but I didn't want sympathy. Especially as he was about to find out what a creep I was. Well, just as soon as I was drunk enough.

'Come on.' He smiled in that cheeky sort of way that made my stomach lurch. 'Sure I've nothing better to be doing.'

'Umm . . . okay, you've twisted my arm. Cosmo with . . . vanilla vodka maybe?'

'Oh.' He looked impressed. 'Sounds good. I'll make two.'

By the time eight o'clock rolled around I was already fairly giddy, and I wasn't supposed to be finished my shift until ten. But there was no way I was making any more sambos. I was on sambo strike, I told Fred. Instead of making sandwiches I was doing tequilas. My excuse for not doing my job, if anyone asked, was that we were out of ham. I probably definitely did not throw the rest of it to Drico and Hubes out the back, if that's what you were wondering.

I was propped up by the bar for the rest of the evening getting steadily drunker. I was quickly joining the ladies of Ballytiernan in becoming a devoted fan of Fred's cocktails. And as the newest member of the fan club I felt it was my responsibility to try all of them.

'Mmm . . . this one tastes like . . . more.' I took a big slurp through my straw, and swallowed a burp. 'What's this sugary one called?' I inquired, almost slipping off the stool I was perched on. 'Whoops! Fred, have you ever noticed these stools are slidey?'

What was that? *Slidey* isn't a word! Get it together, Katie, you are a classy bird, I scolded myself.

'Yeah, absolutely! Everyone slips off those stools. They've caused some serious injuries over the years,' he replied, his face solemn.

'Really?'

'No, just you,' he laughed playfully. 'That's a Caipirinha . . . and . . . wow, you're certainly putting them away!'

He smiled at me, those incredible eyes lingering on mine. I gave him my squinty evil eyes as I slurped up the end of my sixth cocktail through the straw. I just about managed to stifle another burp and I decided I should slow down a smidgen.

'Freddie?' I blinked slowly at him. 'Where have you and your magical Caipirinhas been all my life?'

Was that too much? I couldn't believe I was flirting so

outrageously. With Freddie Flanagan! But we'd been new-old pals for weeks now and it was about time someone made a move. He was much too sober and dignified. Plus, frankly, I was feeling rather frisky, and had gained a substantial amount of Dutch courage. He put another strange-looking concoction in front of me, then came around the bar with another one for himself. He sat up on the stool beside me. Without thinking, I glanced at his cock. Shit! I couldn't believe I did that. But it was right there inside his jeans, practically asking to be looked at. I immediately studied my drink, desperately praying he hadn't noticed.

'This one is strong!' I winced, 'Are you trying to get me drr–'

Before I'd finished flirty sentence number two the door of the bar swung open and Fred began waving enthusiastically at whoever had walked in. I swivelled around to see Georgia Salpa strutting towards us. Nope. Not Georgia, but perhaps an exotic, bronzed goddess even more beautiful, if that was possible. And more tanned. And slightly bigger boobs that were only just about squished into her tiny white vest top, which served very successfully to accentuate her deep chocolaty tan. I wasn't a lesbian, but I could have licked her skin it looked so good. I looked down at the big black Guinness tent I was wearing and felt completely ridiculous. I looked like a little kid wearing her older brother's hand-me-downs. Or even her overweight father's hand-me-downs. I was a tragic sight. In comparison this Georgia Salpa doppelganger bird really was a fucking vision. All three remaining stragglers in the old-man corner of the pub stopped their grumbling and drinking and blatantly stared at her as she passed their table. One man's dentures fell out of his mouth and into his pint.

'Katie, this is Isabelle, my sister's au-pair.'

I nodded over-enthusiastically with a big smile plastered across my face. Of course she was. How could his sister bear to have that ride living in her house?

'Hi,' she chirped. 'Oh my goodnezz . . .' She paused, giving us all a moment to take in her beauty and then recompose ourselves, gathering our jaws off the floor and putting our eyeballs back into their sockets. 'It took me agez to get Conor and Emily to sleep – zey kept wanting anozzer story and anozzer and anozzer!' she laughed, flicking her shiny brown locks out of her eyes, which sparkled mesmerisingly.

'Well, in that case you definitely deserve a drink, Izz! Your usual?' Fred offered kindly.

They're probably having sex, I decided.

'You know me too well, Fred,' she purred, touching his forearm delicately.

They're definitely having sex, I concluded glumly.

Fred should have got a prize for not looking at her overwhelmingly perfect boobies. But then he probably sees them all the time when they have hot sex, I thought. They probably bounce up and down on his face like balloons. I tried to keep my own eyes away from them; I'd already let them wander inappropriately one time too many this evening. If she even donated a third of each breast to me I would probably get myself a nice little C-cup out of the deal.

I decided to be a good girl and not be jealous (they are actually two lovely people and they deserve each other, I decided – they'll probably make ridiculously beautiful, bilingual babies) and we actually ended up having fun, the three of us. A happy little trio. No bitterness.

Around midnight, after downing several more of Fred's toxic but addictively delicious cocktails, we mustered up every bit of sobriety we had left to close up the pub properly, telling the remaining stragglers to kindly fuck off home.

Then we called the only cabbie in Ballytiernan, George Best, to take us into Galway. Not the footballer obviously. George Best the taxi driver would find it difficult to see a football at his feet on account of his massive belly.

'Woo-wee, Freddie, what did you do in a past life to deserve a night out with these ladies?' was George's greeting.

He sped along the empty country roads at an alarming speed, but we had brought some vodka for the road so we were too busy drinking it to worry, and he managed to very irresponsibly knock about fifteen minutes off the usual hour-long journey into Galway.

Chapter 8

I woke up the following morning with a pounding headache. My eyelids felt like lead and my head felt like a bowling ball glued to the pillow. There was no lifting it without immense pain. I had forgotten all about the agony of a hangover after months of being basically dry, and this was a cruel reminder of the evil side of alcohol. On top of this agony, my memory of the rest of the night was unfortunately coming back to me, when all I wanted to do was forget everything. I prayed to God to make it all go away, but no, he was probably off dealing with actual real problems, and people who deserved his help.

Well, as I recalled it, we eventually wandered into a place called Karma. I headed straight for the bar with tunnel-visioned determination. As such, I found myself separated from Fred and Isabelle. It seemed to be impossible to get served. A guy who looked like a younger version of my boss Jim sidled up beside me.

'You must be a Louth girl.' His breath smelt like Tayto Cheese and Onion crisps and cigarettes.

I blinked. Huh? Then it dawned on me that this was some sort of chat-up line.

'I'm not, no.' I leaned my head back away from him.

'Where ya from so?'

I blinked. It felt like a long time since anyone had chatted me up. I was unsure of how to shake him off.

'Newfoundland,' I lied very unconvincingly and without even trying to change my accent. I was hoping he wouldn't pursue it as I wasn't even one-hundred-per-cent sure where Newfoundland was.

'Oh.' That stumped him momentarily. 'What do you do?'

Ugh. I always hated that question. 'I'm an . . . engineer?'

'What kind?' he pressed.

I restrained myself from rolling my eyes.

'Civil?' I responded. I couldn't think of any other kind of engineer. I started looking around furtively, silently begging Fred to somehow find me.

'No way! Me too! Who do you work for?'

Ah crap. What were the odds?

'McNamee's.' The minute I said it, I remembered that McNamee's was a brand of brown bread . . . but whatever, it sounded plausible . . .

However, the confused look on his face indicated that he wasn't buying it.

'I need to wee. Bye.'

Well, getting drinks had been a big fat fail. I hadn't even made eye contact with a barman. I stumbled around looking for my sort-of-buddies, dreading the likely outcome that I would find them wearing the faces off of each other in a corner.

'Katie!' I was halfway up a crowded staircase when I turned around to find Fred walking up behind me. 'I've been looking everywhere for you. Izzy's on the dance floor, come on!' He took my hand and gently pulled me back down the stairs. My tummy did a little flip-flop. Oh man, he had a lovely hand. Not sweaty, but not cold either. Not too soft. Not too hard. Just perfect. A nice man-hand. Fitted around mine like a glove. I thought about lacing my fingers through his and giggled to myself, imagining how weird and awkward that would be. Or if I tickled his bottom, or licked his neck, or smelt his hair. The kind of things a stalker/serial killer would do. It always entertained me to think of how doing one creepy thing like that could completely and irreparably change someone's opinion of you in an instant.

As I followed him through the crowd I wished Isabelle would just feck off so I could take him somewhere private and ravage him. Naturally, when we got to the dance floor, our beach-babe buddy was surrounded by admirers. I think they possibly thought she actually was Georgia Salpa. Spotting us, she mouthed '*Help!*' So we pushed our way through and rescued her.

My memory went fuzzy at that point but I was fairly sure I did actually need to wee for real at some point because I abandoned them once again and the next memory I had was finding my way back to them. Typical, wasn't Whitney singing '*Ooooo, I wanna dance with somebody . . .*' And it was like a scene out of *Dirty Dancing*. Isabelle was grinding up on him, all sexy. If I tried that I'd look like a pasty-white, ginger, flailing idiot, but she looked like some Latino babe out of an R&B music video. I stopped in my tracks, looking at them. It was mesmerising and heartbreaking all at once. It was almost as though people around them had cleared a space on the dance floor and everything had slowed down. Nothing else existed, just the two of them. I felt like Sandy in *Grease* watching Danny Zuko dancing with Cha-Cha, the best dancer at St Bernadette's. But, unlike Sandy, I didn't stand a chance against Isabelle. Let's face it, Katie, a third wheel is all you are, I decided.

I was brought back to cold reality by the skin-crawling motions of someone's crotch gyrating against my ass. I whirled around to find the civil engineer in painfully close proximity to me. His sweat seemed to be evaporating off him and surrounding me, creating a two-person steam room.

'Hey, Louth Girl,' he breathed into my face. More sweat was pouring out of his head and down his neck and gathering in a pool on his T-shirt. His eyes were bulging and his head was thrusting back and forth rather aggressively towards my face.

'No. No. Newfoundland, remember? Not Louth!' I shouted, inching away and shaking my head.

'I always knew I'd end up with a Louth girl. My mother is from Louth. You look just like her. My dad's actually Austrian, which is why my arms are so hairy!'

His hands were now holding my hips tightly and it was all starting to feel like a strange nightmare. For some reason, as my mind raced, I wondered if he was any relation to Joseph Fritzel.

'Oh my God, is that your mother?' I pointed emphatically towards the other side of the club, and in the brief moment he was distracted I bolted. I couldn't believe he'd fallen for that. I was half laughing/half crying as I fled the nightclub as fast as my high heels would allow me. I stumbled into a cab waiting outside and was gone.

Chapter 9

Winnipeg Cottage stank. Sasha had done an almighty poo in her tray, and I really couldn't be bothered taking it outside and clearing it out. To make the situation even less appealing, the rain was bucketing down out there. Sash couldn't have given a solitary shit about the smell, even though it was her solitary shit that caused it. She was happily snoozing away in her Queen Bee armchair. She had even turned over on her back with her paws up in the air to emphasise how little she cared. Needless to say, the smell was not helping my hangover. I trudged over, still wrapped up in my big soft leopard-print snuggie. Using my index finger and my thumb I dragged the litter tray over to the door and from there I hooshed it outside with my foot.

'Sasha, you better not need to poo again today.'

I washed my hands, plodded back to the couch and sank back into it, wrapping my snuggie around me and tucking my toes under a big squishy velvet cushion. I flicked the channels on the telly mindlessly. I really didn't feel like facing the world. I had been planning to spend the next few days locked away finishing my *Sheep-Shearing in Times Square* painting, but even that wasn't appealing to me right now. I looked over at it as I sipped hot chocolate from the Gorgeous Granddad mug, and for whatever reason my stomach sank looking at it. I had been telling myself it was about the art all right. But deep down I had developed feelings for Fred. Somehow in my sad little mind I had convinced myself there was something there between us, and this could be a fairytale ending. Now looking at it made me feel a bit pathetic. Like a teenager doing a doodle of her pop-star crush, and lusting over it.

I knew deep down that I wasn't ready to give up on this project, even though it was all I felt like doing at that moment. The concept still really excited me like nothing had before. So I concluded that maybe the way forward was to start on another one. Take the focus off Fred for a while. Put him on the back burner.

So I was going to need more men. And I didn't have a clue how I was going to go about finding them. I'll sleep on it, I said to myself.

I reluctantly dragged myself out of Winnipeg Cottage the next morning and marched down towards the village in search of my second man-muse. There was the remainder of yesterday's hangover still going on but I ploughed onwards bravely, determined to ignore it. I had made a small effort to disguise the grogginess. A lick of mascara, pink lip gloss and a pretty, floral Anthropologie dress.

Overnight I'd had a light-bulb-over-my-head moment. I had miraculously come up with a brilliant idea of where I might start my search. It was clearly the obvious answer. Billy Hanlon was a regular in Farrelly's. King of the chat-up lines. He was an arrogant dick, but I figured he was just cocky enough that, if I chose my words wisely, this project would appeal to him. Plus it might get the ball rolling on the project. There was a certain energy about Billy that made me feel as though his involvement would spice things up. I didn't know if it would be in a good or bad way, but I was willing to take the risk. An added bonus was his gang of loyal cronies who just might want in on the game too. Because if Billy jumped off a cliff – well, they would consider it the best idea since putting spoilers on cars.

I patted down my fluffy windswept curls as I approached Billy's garage. Billy was the proud owner of 'Billy's Garage', an establishment that put vile spoilers and other cheap-looking go-fast-thingies on Honda Civics and other knacker cars. This served to encourage the already inflated egos of the delinquent youth of Ballytiernan and surrounding towns.

Michael Jackson's 'Billie Jean' was blasting out of a surprisingly loud, dusty stereo in the corner as I entered. I noticed two CAT boots sticking out from under a relatively unembellished Golf GTI. He obviously had a lot more work to do on it to make it adequately ridiculous-looking. The rest of the creations in the garage were much higher up on the scale of absurdity.

'Excuse me?' I called.

No answer. Hmm . . . should I go over and turn down the stereo or just give him a little kick? I figured I would enjoy the kick more so I chose that option.

Sadly it only took the one kick to get Billy's attention and he slid out, swiftly coming to an abrupt stop almost directly under my dress. I jumped back.

'Hi.'

'How can I help you?' His cheeky grin was framed by his ridiculous handlebar moustache, but he looked less idiotic without his usual Colin Farrell wannabe beanie hat. In fact I hadn't ever seen him without it before. I was glad to know it wasn't permanently surgically attached to his head.

'Em . . . I was hoping we could have a chat . . .' I began.

As I had predicted, Billy didn't take much convincing. A few innuendos and some polite fake laughter later, and I had my second man-muse lined up. I decided it would be best if I took photos of him and I would paint from the photos: the least possible time spent in his naked company, the better. Outside would work best for natural light, but I offered to call round on Sunday at lunchtime and we could close the garage and take the pictures inside, to protect his modesty.

'No, no, I'm all for doing it outside, babes – nothing to hide!'

'Okay . . . great.'

I broke eye contact and took a few steps back towards the door, as his intense stare was making me feel uncomfortable.

'Don't go gathering a crowd or anything,' I added apprehensively. 'I want to keep it on the down-low for now.'

'Of course! Sure who would I be telling?'

'Cheers, Billy. See ya Sunday.' I smiled confidently and turned to leave.

'Em . . .' he muttered loud enough to make me pause, and turn back to him. 'So how naked are we talkin' now?' he asked, pushing his hair out of his face awkwardly . . . he seemed a little less confident all of a sudden, which surprised me.

'Well, only what you're comfortable with, of course.'

'All right . . . grand, grand. See ya tomorrow, sweet cheeks – Oh! And I'm obviously going to wear my beanie hat, yeah?'

I hadn't really been thinking about Fred since Wednesday night. Well, that was a lie. I had been telling myself not to be thinking about Fred. But certain thoughts did cross my mind occasionally. I only checked his Facebook page once or twice, and that was only because the mouse accidentally clicked on it. In fact, I was quite proud of my restraint. I hadn't gone near his painting. Which I knew was a shame because it was beginning to look really good. My passion for it had temporarily faded a little bit, which often happened during the process of creating something. Especially when emotions got involved, which was sometimes inevitable. I told myself

I'd get back to it, and get started on Billy's one in the meantime. I was more than a little anxious about how that one would unfold. I had an uncomfortable feeling Billy would somehow find a way to throw some sort of spanner in the works, pun/double entendre intended . . .

The main entrance to Billy's Garage was closed when I arrived on Sunday afternoon, with my trusty SLR hanging round my neck. I rapped on the shutter. No response. I walked round the side of the garage. The tractor we had decided he would be sitting on for the painting was out in the field ready and waiting. That was a good sign. I knocked on the back door.

'*Just a second!*' Billy grunted.

I didn't like the noises that were coming from inside.

Less than a minute later the door swung open and my jaw fell. Billy stood there, completely naked except for his beanie hat and wellies . . . and with a semi-erection.

'Looks impressive, doesn't it?!' he beamed.

I didn't know where to look. It took a vast amount of self-restraint not to fall to the floor in a fit of hysterical laughter. If Sophie had been there I would have been a lost cause but, being on my own, I somehow managed to control myself and swallow the laughter. He grabbed his coat off the hook on the door, threw it over himself and marched past me out into the field. I gathered my jaw up off the ground and followed him, more than a little apprehensively. He hopped happily up onto the tractor, threw his coat onto the grass flamboyantly and started arranging himself.

'Maybe we should . . . cover up your . . . you know . . . penis?' I offered.

'Absolutely not! This bad boy is the main attraction.'

I was starting to feel like it was looking at me. Or aiming at me! *Ew!* We would just have to get this done quickly.

Unbelievably, the photos somehow turned out quite . . .

charming. I certainly hadn't expected that to happen. Well, I hadn't known what to expect, but as soon as I saw the semi-erection I thought it was all over. I lost all hope of getting a good shot. But shockingly I found myself able to zone it out. In my mind's eye I covered it with an imaginary modesty rectangle. And then I was able to focus on finding some charm. And it just happened. I was probably going to have to do something to conceal the 'main attraction' when it came to doing the painting (I would figure out how to do that in preliminary sketches), but Billy actually photographed quite well. He was remarkably comfortable in front of the lens.

I decided I would put him in my long painting of Broadway. It was a dreamy painting of the famous Manhattan road in the early hours of the morning, in the rain. I figured the rainy mistiness would help with blurring out certain unsavoury bits.

The canvas measured about seventy-five by one hundred and fifty centimetres. I remembered being so proud of that painting when I completed it. I just loved how the lights from the cars and the billboards were reflected on the glistening wet pavement. I had somehow achieved an effect that made the watery surfaces sparkle. I wasn't even sure I would be able to recreate it – it just sort of happened. And I loved the people darting about huddled under umbrellas. A small part of me was dreading touching this one. I really had a soft spot for it. And what if this time I couldn't get the sparkly surfaces just so? But ultimately I was confident that I wouldn't regret it. The new addition would see Billy and his tractor driving down through the traffic in the rain. I was going to have to paint over the main yellow cab in the foreground in order to pop Billy in. So I was slightly concerned about losing this lovely big dash of colour. It felt to me like the painting needed the colour in that place. It occurred to me that maybe I could put a big blue umbrella in Billy's hand, as a nod to one of my all-time favourite artists Renoir and his famous *Les*

Parapluies painting. There was something about *Les Parapluies* that made my body gently sway while observing it. It was a painting with so much movement that it felt wrong to stand still looking at it. So I found myself gently rocking back and forth. Like you would with a good song. Without intending to. It would be marvellous if people wanted to sway looking at one of my paintings. How could I create that with this? I would just have to go for it with that intention in mind and hope it turned out that way.

Maybe it was to do with being Irish, but I always loved painting a rainy scene. I liked rain, in life as well as art. It could be so calm and almost still, like a mirror, and yet, on the other hand, it could be full of emotion and chaotic movement.

I threw on my *'Albert Says'* jumper and got to work on *Billy Does Broadway* straight away that night. I sketched away with pencil on paper long into the night, before even touching the canvas. I did have an undeniable attachment to this painting and I was reluctant to completely change it without lots of preparation. My rough sketches helped me to gain a familiarity with the shapes, and figure out where all the other elements of the original painting were situated. Then I could understand how to make the new composition work. I had to take out the yellow cab and slot in Billy and the tractor, all the time maintaining the symmetry and not overcrowding any one area. Once I was totally convinced it would look good, I boldly attacked my previously completed canvas with assured certainty.

It suddenly struck me how free I felt painting in my little isolated cottage in Ballytiernan, compared to the pressures of being in New York, where I had studied, and where I had so many friends who were great artists but struggled to get noticed. I had felt so intimidated and swallowed up by an environment steeped in such enormous talent, but with such a competitive undercurrent. Without all that, I was all of a sudden a much braver artist. I no longer cared how my work compared to that of other artists. I was no longer concerned with whether my ideas were actually my own ideas or if someone else had thought of them first. I could feel a change in my attitude. I was so confident and liberated I decided there was no reason for me to leave Fred's one untouched. I vowed to get back to work on it over the next few days.

Just to give it a little lift, I created a transparent solution with turpentine, linseed oil and yellow ochre. I spread it thinly over Fred's painting, covering the whole surface. It had the desired effect of lifting the mood even more, creating a daydream effect. I left it to dry and returned to Billy.

I enhanced the sheen on Billy's torso and legs, and made his moustache glisten, to make it look like drops of rain had whirled in under the umbrella, blitzing him lightly. If you didn't know him personally you might think he was handsome, I thought to myself with a grunt of laughter. Especially if handlebar moustaches were your thing. And semi-erections.

Chapter 10

I was dreading seeing Fred in Farrelly's on Monday. But I walked in with my head held high. I didn't feel I had anything to be ashamed of. I hadn't made a move on him on Wednesday night. I had not made a complete idiot of myself. Not that I was aware of anyway. I decided I would just keep to myself and make sambos, buttering the bread all the way to the edge like a good little sambo-maker.

But Fred, on the other hand, was full of the chats.

'Why did you leave on Wednesday night?' He was straight out with it.

'I sent you a text. I was tired. Also there was a guy who actually looked like the love child of Jim Farrelly and Joseph Fritzel trying to have unconsensual dry sex with me on the dance floor.'

'Seriously? When did this happen – where was I?'

Em, you were having dry sex of a consensual nature with Isabelle, remember? I didn't say this. Instead I just shrugged.

'It was grand. Luckily I made a cunning and stealthy getaway. I've realised I should basically be a spy, or an escape artist or something – I've missed my calling,' I stated matter of factly. I was pretty pleased with my composure. Maybe now that Fred was off the market and his painting was on the backburner I didn't need to be a goofy idiot any more. I could go back to being my normal smart-arse, not romantically deluded self.

'Oh. Okay . . . Well, it's a shame you left. It wasn't the same without you.'

Why was he coming out with this jibber-jabber? I didn't want to appear childish and jealous by saying 'Well, it looked like you and Isabelle were having a grand little party just for two . . . a *porno* party . . .' or something more intelligent and cutting. But anyway I just smiled and kept my mouth shut. I slid the buttery knife across a slice of bread carefully and placed a slice of cheese on top, followed by a slice of ham.

I was growing frustrated with him now. He was still standing there in front of my table. I didn't know what he wanted. It did seem like he felt a bit guilty about how it all ended, and it was almost like he wanted to say something else. But I kept my head down, to indicate that the conversation was over.

He ambled off back towards the bar and I pressed the top slice of bread down on the ham with the palm of my hand. Perhaps a bit too hard.

The time dragged on that evening without much conversation, but there were lots of sambo orders to mindlessly occupy me. After a while I trudged into the bar to pour myself some juice, and stretch the legs. Fred perked up when he saw me, seeming eager to start up a conversation again.

'Bessie has been asking about you a lot lately,' he smiled, as he pulled a pint of Smithwick's. 'She wants to know when you're going to come by for more tea and Jaffa Cakes.'

Was this an invitation? This was unbearably frustrating. I wanted to give him a scathing look and tell him to shove the Jaffa Cakes up his rear end. But he probably did not deserve that. He was only being friendly. I really needed to know how serious things were with him and Isabelle. Maybe it wasn't what I had presumed at all? My heart fluttered a little with hope. But I hated the whole 'is he/isn't he available' thing. I felt like a child pulling petals off a daisy. But I was too shy to just ask him outright. I cursed myself for not being more forward. I had lived in New York for most of my adult life – had I learnt nothing from the Yanks?

'Katie!' Jim shouted, interrupting our conversation. 'What are you doing floating around behind the bar? I have an order for four more sandwiches over here!'

I headed back to the confinement of the little kitchen and got cracking on the rest of the sandwiches with a heavy sigh. Farrelly's was always fairly busy on a Monday night, on account of the Ballytiernan Ladies Club having their weekly bingo session there. So I was making sandwiches constantly until after ten o'clock, when they finished up and went home to their beds, exhausted from laughing.

Mac arrived late, just before they finished up. She wasn't fond of bingo and was not quite as jolly and frivolous as the rest of the ladies. But she hated the thought of being a social outcast so she always made an appearance. There was one thing she had in common with the rest of the ladies though and that was a huge fondness for Fred. She also seemed to have some sort of intuition about my feelings towards him. Her face always changed when she saw the two of us together. Like she was watching a romantic movie or something.

'Does he know about the painting?' Mac nudged me as I delivered a sandwich to a lady near her.

'Not yet, no,' I whispered.

'Ah right.' She winked.

I didn't want to tell her that I had put it on hold while I was feeling sorry for myself because he hadn't returned my affection. So I left it at that. Any time he said anything to me, though, I could see her out of the corner of my eye watching us with raised eyebrows.

Jim asked me to stay and clean up as the ladies had created quite a bit of chaos so I was wiping down the tables with a damp soapy J-cloth when Hurricane Billy hit Farrelly's.

As usual, his loyal followers flanked him. I rubbed my eyes a bit too vigorously with my hands.

Billy headed straight for the loo with two others, probably to powder their noses so to speak, and the rest of the gang spread themselves out, moving the tables around as they pleased. I tried to remain calm and not let this ruffle me.

'We'll have nine ham-and-cheese sambos, woman!' a large-toothed, rather hairy member of the pack bellowed in my direction, as though I had a hearing problem. 'No, wait! Pete, did you say you want two sandwiches? *Pete!* One or two? Two? Okay, actually make that ten. Not nine, ten, yeah?'

'We stopped serving sandwiches at ten o'clock,' I said flatly.

'Ah yeah but . . . go on like.'

'We're out of bread,' I lied, without any effort to sound convincing.

I was continuing to wipe the crumbs and spillages off the tables where the ladies had been, when I suddenly felt an almighty smack on my arse. I whirled around instantly, my face flushing crimson.

'*Billy!*' I exclaimed with a warning edge in my voice.

'Hey, sexy! Well, have you got over the life-changing shock that is Billy's cock?' he sang loudly, a big stupid grin on his face.

I was stunned. We had agreed not to tell people about the painting, and technically he wasn't breaking that agreement, but he was making an outrageous implication which floored me. I wasn't quite sure how to react or if I would ever recover for that matter.

I shot him vicious daggers with my eyes. If looks could kill he would have been reduced to a bloody mess splattered all over the bar.

My eyes drifted to the bar behind him and, without a doubt, Fred had heard it. He was busy wiping out a pint glass with a dishtowel and was wearing a very intentional 'oblivious' face, but there were no two ways about it. He had to have heard it.

My eyes brimmed with tears, and my already red face grew even redder. My arse cheek throbbed. I was infuriated with myself that I couldn't think of anything to say to fix this mess and redeem my dignity. I ran for the loo, the J-cloth still in my hand, before I could make the situation even worse by crying in front of everyone.

Getting drenched walking home in the rain was the perfect end to an outrageously shitty day. Shortly after the arse smack came the sack. Jim had asked me to come into his office, which wasn't really an office, but a dark, damp shed that smelt of dog and stale beer.

'I've a bit of bad news now, Katie . . .' He looked at me like he genuinely regretted what he had to say. 'I'm afraid I have to let you go. Mary says her hip is all better and she wants to come back to work here. My obligation is to her, because as you know she's been working here on and off for no less than ten years and, well, I just can't afford to keep the both of you on.'

I had known all along this could happen, but I couldn't help being saddened by it nonetheless. In fact, I was a little surprised by just how gutted I felt to be leaving. I had got attached to the place. I would have no excuse to see Fred any more. Even though nothing more had happened between us, I had really liked having him as a friend. Also I had grown to like Farrelly's. Jim wasn't a terrible boss – he was a little tactless and inappropriate at times, and he generally operated on a 'do as I say not as I do' basis but, despite all this, he was a good guy deep down.

'I will pay you for the next two weeks, but Mary wants to

come in tomorrow so . . . that's it, I suppose. I'm very sorry to see you go, Katie. I hope you'll still pop in for a few drinks now and then?'

'Of course I will – sure where else is there to go?' I laughed. 'Thanks, Jim.' I couldn't think of anything else to say. I was exhausted.

I returned to the bar. Fred's head was buried in a cloud of steam as he was taking apart the coffee machine. I ignored Billy's gang who had lost interest in me anyway, but I stopped in front of Fred and put my elbows on the bar as though I was a customer ordering a drink. He looked up.

'Will you still be my friend?' I asked.

'What?'

'Mary is coming back tomorrow so I won't be working here any more.' I smiled sadly. 'Will you still be my friend anyway?' I repeated my question, my eyes wide open and watery.

'Of course.' Fred returned my sad smile.

'Do you promise?'

'I promise.'

And I left. I dragged my feet through the rain puddles, feeling very sorry for myself. I did believe Fred when he promised that he would continue to be my friend. But still I felt alone. I thought about how I had no one to talk to who really knew me. What I really needed now, I thought with my heart heavy in my chest, was Seb. I needed to tell him everything, hear his voice telling me that it would all be all right. Then I would fall asleep wrapped up in his arms, feeling warm and safe. I needed him because without him I felt alone. I couldn't help blaming myself for everything. Why had I run away? Why hadn't I stayed and done everything to convince him to try to love me again? Why was I all alone in the middle of nowhere?

As I walked along, I began loudly singing the '*Les Mis*' song. '*On my ooown . . .*' I hardly sounded like Samantha

Barks, mainly because I lacked her restraint, and generally her talent – but the passion was all there. And it felt good to get it off my chest. I felt epic and dramatic trudging along in the rain, belting it out. Who was going to hear me anyway? Who was I going to upset with my shrieks and wails? No one. That was who. I bellowed on, throwing my arms around and singing at the top of my lungs, serenading the full moon, which was high in the sky above me. It looked on approvingly. My clothes were drenched through and I really felt like I was Éponine. I was completely lost in her world as I reached the totally out-of-tune crescendo. I sang until my throat was hoarse, with my eyes closed and my head back, rain pouring on my face.

'*Bravo!*'

I whipped my head around and, driving slowly beside me, was Fred's truck.

'*Aaaaaagh!*' I screamed and practically leapt out of my skin. His window was down and his hands were not on the steering wheel because he was clapping them enthusiastically.

'Sorry to interrupt this magical moment,' he laughed, 'but I came to offer you a lift.' Even if he had tried, he couldn't have wiped the smile from his face.

I died. Well, not really, but I wished I had.

'I am supposed to be your friend, after all,' he continued. 'So I felt bad thinking of you walking home in the rain. I couldn't have imagined how magnificent a spectacle it would be.' He was really laughing now, a big belly laugh. 'I'm sorry!'

I shot him a warning look.

'I'm sorry, please get in. I feel terrible now for laughing at you.'

'You should feel honoured to have witnessed that,' I said defiantly and crossed my soaking wet arms across my chest.

'I do! Really. Come on, let me take you the rest of the way home.'

I slowed down my determined march and he stopped the car. I stomped around to the passenger side and climbed in.

We drove in silence.

'I can tell you're trying not to laugh.'

'I've forgotten all about it, I promise. What are you even talking about? I have no idea.'

I could see his shoulders shaking and even his voice shook with compressed laughter as he spoke.

'Fuck you.' I kept my eyes on the road resolutely but I could feel the corners of my mouth twitching into a smile. Damn it.

He looked across at me as he slowed the truck to a stop outside Winnipeg.

'It was actually kind of adorable.'

He was flirting! I was sure of it. I bit my lip. I was bursting to ask him if there was anything between him and Isabelle. Was she his girlfriend?

'Fred, can I ask you a question?'

'Of course. Anything.' He turned to face me, giving me his full attention.

My heart stopped. Why did I feel like a shy, nervous teenager around him?

'Why . . . does one shear sheep?' I chickened out. 'Is it for the wool?' I tried to make it sound like not such a stupid question.

Nevertheless he looked a bit confused by the question. 'Em . . . well, it can be for wool, but nowadays it's mostly for the benefit of the sheep really. Some farmers sell the wool but it's not really worth it, I don't think.'

'Thanks.' I clicked open the door handle to get out. 'It's important that you know something.' I looked back at him, my face solemn and serious. 'I didn't pee on your car seat. My clothes are just very wet.'

'You're entertaining, Katie, I'll give you that!' he shouted after me as I walked away from the truck.

I flicked on the lights in Winnipeg, turned on the heating and wrapped myself up in my snuggie on the couch with a cup of tea and a KitKat. I never liked turning on the heating in the summer time, but I needed all the comfort I could get, and the temperamental Irish weather could go screw itself. I was still feeling sorry for myself. I would be lost without Farrelly's. Maybe I would just still show up almost every day and become a drunk sad old local.

Sasha immediately sensed my sadness and uncharacteristically rushed over to me for a cuddle. Generally Sasha was a cat who kept to herself, but whenever I needed some love, like *really* needed it, her emotional intelligence absolutely astounded me – every time, she dutifully forgot all about her cool unattached demeanour and climbed right up onto my lap and rubbed her head lovingly off my chin. And then she'd curl herself up as close as she could physically get to my heart, almost as though she was trying to warm it. It was one of the most truly touching things I had ever experienced. And because it was so totally contrasting to how she usually behaved, it made it all the more poignant.

I snuggled Sasha, grateful for the rare opportunity, and nodded off to sleep.

I awoke a few hours later with a neck ache from the awkward position I'd fallen asleep in. Sasha had abandoned me and gone back to her armchair. I stretched my arms and looked around groggily. Despite the isolated location, Winnipeg was a soothing environment, and I was glad of it. My granddad's lasting presence in it was comforting and, without making dramatic changes, I was starting to make the little cottage mine. Just minor additions like my graphic patterned rug, and my fat, smiley, miniature Buddha statue, were adding an essence of 'me' to the place. The antique decor chosen by my elegant, classy grandmother in the fifties/sixties and the little gadgets and knickknacks my granddad had collected over the years, contrasted nicely with my few modern belongings. It made for a wonderful eclectic mix of old and new. I was really starting to love my little home.

Despite all this, however, and despite Sasha's rare bursts of amazing affection when I really needed it, I had to admit I was a bit lonely and isolated there with no other human being. Sasha was always a good listener, but our conversations were obviously a bit one-sided. And I was worried that Sophie was right – I was prematurely becoming a crazy old cat lady, way before my time. On top of this, now that I had no job I would be spending even more time on my own here.

I sighed heavily and flicked open my laptop to check my emails. As if she had read my mind, I had an email from Sophie.

Katie, I got your parcel. You are absolutely the most wonderful friend a girl could have. However! I'm worried about you all on your own out in some backwards village in the middle of nowhere.

And . . . I'm worried about me too . . . I broke up with Chris yesterday. It's serious this time, we're properly over. I need you, KitKat, and you need me!

SO . . . I'M COMING TO VISIT! Can't wait, we're going to get so wasted that we can't feel our faces, like the good old days! I arrive on Friday and I'll be staying with you for a fun-filled ten days! So stock up your wine cabinet – Bally-whatsitcalled won't know what hit it! YIPPEEEEEEEE, BABY!!

I clicked into my SuperValu online shopping account and added a few bottles of wine, tequila and Captain Morgan's spiced rum to my shopping cart . . . I also put some biscuits in. I couldn't have a guest coming and have no biscuits. And Tayto crisps. Having no Taytos would have been a crime against humanity.

Chapter 11

The next morning the rain was still pelting down outside. All I wanted to do was stay in bed, all cosy and snug. I'd had a nightmare about Fred catching me singing in the rain. Oh no, wait. That was real. I pulled the covers back up over my head, remembering the shame of it. But I knew I couldn't wallow in self-pity forever and I had to figure out what would be my next move. Would I find another job? Or would I commit myself completely to my art and slowly run out of money and then cut off my ear, staple it to one of my paintings (possibly using it to conceal Billy's cock) and then die of starvation and blood loss? And subsequently become world famous for my outstanding talent. Hmm . . . both options had their advantages and their disadvantages.

As I lay in my big cosy bed, looking out at the rain, I came to the conclusion that I wasn't ready for another real-world job just yet and, as for the second option, well, it was about time I finally fully committed to my inner demented artist. I was old enough and bold enough now, and I had nothing to lose. I was a lost cause anyway. So it was decided I would devote myself to art. I stroked my ear. Who knew? It could have been the last time I did . . .

So I had to start thinking about who would be the subject of my next painting. I dragged myself up and headed to the kitchen to make porridge. On miserable days like this I always needed my porridge to get started.

Despite the likely tragic outcome of my new chosen path in life, I was determined to keep going and not get sucked into depressive behaviours so early into the process. One thing I'd always been good at was picking myself up and ploughing on when times got crap. And this time would be no different. My paintings were looking good. Better than I could have imagined. I was almost getting itchy to show them to people. I always got super scared showing my art to people but then it was such a high hearing the oohs and aahs. I buzzed off it.

I had got back to work on Fred's painting and it was actually almost finished. Billy's one was progressing nicely, despite the fact that he was an asshole. I had no idea what my plan was for the paintings. I wanted to do a collection of five or six anyway.

By the time I'd finished my porridge the rain had eased off, sun was poking through the clouds optimistically, and Sasha was scratching at the back door to go out gallivanting. So we both decided to take ourselves outside for the day. I slipped into my red Mackintosh and black Hunter wellies. We bid each other a good day. Sasha darted into a bush, her tail high in the air, and I set off.

I had no real plan, but sometimes when you don't know what you're looking for an opportunity just slaps you in the face. And, believe it or not, that is exactly what happened. Although I would have preferred it not to happen quite so literally. I was almost at the village square when a big truck carrying bales of hay drove right through a puddle I was walking past. A tsunami of rainwater cascaded over me, soaking me from head to toe.

'*Dickhead!*' I shouted, wiping the wet mud off my face.

I felt cold water seeping down the back of my neck. I

shivered and squeezed my eyes shut. I thought I had dressed appropriately for the weather but I hadn't prepared myself for big obnoxious truck drivers.

The truck slowed to a stop up ahead and started to reverse back towards me. Shit. I immediately regretted the dickhead remark. I wasn't in the mood for an argument.

'Katie McKenna?' A burly man, somewhere in his forties, with a squashed nose and a big infectious smile, leaned over awkwardly, peering through the open passenger-door window at me.

I squinted up at him. It had all of a sudden turned into a brightish, glaring sort of day. I put my hand up to shield my eyes from the brightness.

'Yeah, why?'

I recognised him – he had been in and out of Farrelly's a few times. He was one of the shyer members of Billy's gang. He looked a little like Mel Gibson but broader and squidgier. More rough around the edges. He had dimples that were almost hidden with coarse, black beard-hair. But somehow they had a charming effect on his face.

'I'm really sorry about that – I can be a bit clumsy driving this thing sometimes.' He chuckled, shaking his head bashfully. 'I'm Gerry – I live round on Cassidy's Lane. Can I give you a lift somewhere? I feel bad about drenching you like that.'

I obliged. I wouldn't usually get into a truck with a stranger but I did know the guy, sort of. We had to drive around the village to get back to my cottage, as he couldn't turn on the narrow road. He was indeed quite hazardous in the truck. We went up on the kerb a few times and hit off a lamppost going around the corner outside the butcher's. It was hard not to find his goofy lack of coordination endearing though, especially as he was so well-intentioned.

There was a plastic black-and-white cow bobbing on the dashboard with big red lips in a wide grin. She was wearing red sunglasses, and shorts pulled down to reveal her bum at the back. It was crude, but in a forgivable, cheeky way. He had the Gorillaz' 'Clint Eastwood' song playing out of his old cassette player. He was nodding his head along to it rather comically in the same rhythm as the cow, as he drove slowly along the winding roads. I sensed he wasn't the sort of man who was going anywhere in a hurry.

'Gerry, would you like to come in for a cuppa?' I asked when we pulled up outside Winnipeg.

Go for it, Katie, be an opportunist. No time like the present.

I popped on the kettle and ushered Gerry back out into the hall towards the living room. I hurried him through immediately before I could stop myself. I was a bit apprehensive. I hadn't shown the paintings to anyone except Sasha. It was always a vulnerable feeling when people were seeing your work for the first time, regardless of who they were. I felt like I was the naked one not the subjects!

Needless to say, his eyes popped out of his head when they caught sight of Billy's painting.

'By the way, I didn't sleep with Billy, if that's what he's been implying,' I said immediately. 'I just wanted to tell someone, because, yunno, it was a bit upsetting the way he made it all sound in front of everyone in Farrelly's and I couldn't defend myself without telling everyone about the paintings and I'm just not ready to do that. It's a long-term project and I'm only starting. I don't want to cause trouble for myself so soon. I just want to quietly go about my work and see what happens when they are completed. I really want to keep it quiet for now, you know? But it's important for me to tell you, just so that someone knows, that Billy and I never . . . you know. This was as far as it went, and even this was fairly unpleasant if I'm honest.'

'Yeah . . . I did sort of think it was probably another one of Billy's tall tales. He's always been one to put a skin on a story. Also I thought something was going on with you and Fred. Ye do look like you have a laugh together, the pair of ye.'

'Nope. Not Fred and certainly not Billy.' I sighed and Gerry looked at me sympathetically.

'I don't really like Billy all that much.' He shrugged. 'But it's easier to just get on with him to be honest.'

'Yeah. I understand that.'

'Do you mind if I . . . take a closer look?' he asked kindly. 'Please do!'

He walked over to the paintings, shaking his head like he couldn't believe they were there, right in front of him, in all their glory. He was looking at Billy's one as though he really wanted to touch it to be sure it was real. But he restrained himself, holding his hands together behind his back respectfully. Then he looked at the other. He leant in, his nose just a few inches from the sheep.

'These are something else, Katie,' he finally whispered, standing back again away from them to take it all in. 'I've never seen anything this impressive right in front of me. You have some real talent there, young lady.'

'Thank you, Gerry – that's nice of you to say.'

'Fred's a good lad. You sure there's nothing going on there? I think he has an eye for you. Hung like a donkey he is too. I used to be on the GAA team with him and we'd always say he was the longest in the shower if you know what I mean. We would say it to piss Billy off but it was probably true.' He laughed hard and then coughed like a long-term smoker.

Fred? The longest in the shower! I felt like I shouldn't be hearing that and I found it very difficult to suppress a giggle. I figured it would have been inappropriate to ask how long.

'I think Fred might be seeing that Isabelle bird.' I hoped Gerry might deny it, put me out of my misery. There was always a chance he knew something I didn't.

'Oh, she's quite a lady that one,' was all I got back.

I sipped my tea and wondered how Gerry would react to my next question. It was worth a shot asking him anyway. I had to take risks and be fearless about approaching people if this project was ever going to work. So I took a deep breath and launched into it before I could chicken out.

'Well, anyway, while I have you here, there's something I want to ask you. I'll totally understand if you would rather not, but I just wanted to ask you anyway. I sort of need a few more volunteers for this project. I was wondering if you would like to be a part of it? Like, you know, to be one of my models?'

'Me?' He looked at me with his mouth slightly open, his cheeks flushed pinkish.

I could see he was a little bit chuffed but couldn't disguise his shock. He seemed a bit dubious, like he had a sneaking suspicion I was pulling his leg and would burst out laughing any second. I looked at him very seriously and when he realised I wasn't joking his face lit up and then it immediately dropped again. He shook his head.

'I couldn't do something like that . . . I don't know . . . Are ya sure you'd want me in it?'

'Of course! You'd be brilliant!'

'But I'm not, you know . . . I'm not like Billy. I'm a bit . . . well, rounder, I suppose.'

'Gerry!' I looked at him and could see his insecurities surfacing behind his eyes. 'Has no one ever told you that you look like an Irish Mel Gibson?'

He burst out laughing bashfully, and looked at me sceptically like he thought I'd been taking hallucinogenic pills. 'Yeah, maybe if Mel Gibson fell out of the ugly tree and hit every branch on the way down,' he scoffed.

'You do! Really, I'm not lying to you, Gerry, and I'm not coming on to you either. Firstly I think I'm a little bit too young for you and secondly I can see by the band on your finger that you're married anyway. But, honestly, you look just like him. Back when he was a hottie, in his *What Women Want* days. You could be his brother! Seriously. I'm surprised no one has ever said it to you.'

Gerry laughed again, still unsure, but I could see I was slowly convincing him. He took a gulp of his tea and grinned.

'Who in Ballytiernan in their right mind would tell me I look like Mel Gibson? You think Billy or one of the other lads is going to say it to me over a pint some night?'

Ten minutes later Gerry was lifting a bale of hay off the back of his truck and carrying it around the back of the cottage. I couldn't believe I'd managed to talk him round. I was quite proud of myself for being so forward. Maybe I had learnt something from the Yanks after all!

'Maybe you could be . . . you know, forking it?' I suggested. 'Just give me a second – I'll go grab a garden fork from the shed.' I hurried off to battle my way through the cobwebs in my granddad's shed.

When I got back he had taken off his jumper, T-shirt and jeans, and was standing beside his hay bale awkwardly in his socks and underpants. It was sweet though. The socks were striped red and yellow and one of his big toes was poking through a hole in the front. I knew immediately it was going to be a lovely feature of the painting.

'Maybe I'll leave my underpants on . . .' He shifted from one foot to the other.

'Of course! I can always edit them out in the painting anyway.' I smiled.

He exhaled apprehensively, loosened the bale and forked a big clump of hay up. He then composed himself with a determined air of decided confidence. He pulled in his belly and puffed out his chest and stuck the fork out in front of him enthusiastically with a big grin on his face. I laughed encouragingly as I took some pictures. His hands on the fork were positioned perfectly in front of his crown jewels so I knew, if I edited out the edges of his underpants to look like he wasn't wearing any, it would still leave something to the imagination, and I wouldn't have to go creating something using my imagination. He wasn't quite as comfortable and arrogant as Billy had been but his bravery and self-assertiveness won him extra brownie points.

'Gerry, this looks fantastic!' I beamed. 'You're putting Billy to shame!'

Gerry took a moment to blow gently on his tea as we sat in the kitchen chatting. It looked kind of funny: such a big guy daintily blowing his tea. Aside from the Gorgeous Granddad mug, the only cups I had were my grandmother's antique bone-china teacups, so I had given him his tea in one of those. The image of him holding the little teacup made me smile. I was suddenly struck with a thought.

'I'm sorry to ask you this, Gerry, but I just have to. Could I grab you quickly for another shot? Just one last one? Pretty please . . . ?' I smiled and clasped my hands together and my efforts at an endearing plea were met with raised eyebrows. I persevered. 'It's just, you look so great with that little teacup.' I laughed. 'You have no idea what a great image it makes!'

We scooted back outside and he left his jeans on this time – just whipped off his T-shirt and jumper, puffed out his chest once again. He perched himself on the edge of the hay bale, crossed his legs and posed very gracefully with his teacup. He had one of those faces where he hardly had to do anything to be funny, but when he posed like this he had me bent over in stitches laughing.

'You're a born performer, Gerry! Where has this little talent been hiding?'

'So this whole fandangle is on the down-low, is that right?'

'Yeah, I'd be really grateful if you didn't talk to anyone about what I'm doing for the time being. Thanks, Gerry.'

I was walking around the side of the cottage with him as he carried the hay bale back to the truck.

He glanced back at me with a mischievous twinkle in his eye.

'Do you know your mother used to baby-sit me? Vivienne Joyce, wasn't it? Before she was married, like. Me and my brothers really used to fancy her,' he confessed, with a cheeky grin that made me laugh. 'There was something sort of wild about Vivienne . . .' His eyes glazed over.

I looked at him with my eyebrows raised.

'Sorry. But she was my first proper crush! I was mad about her for years,' he went on enthusiastically. Then he added coyly, 'Only don't mention that to my wife Mo, she can be a bit –'

'Mo?' I interrupted. 'Of Mo's Teacup?'

'Yep, that's the missus!' he chirped.

'Em . . . you don't think . . . do you think . . . she'll be cool with you being in my paintings, Gerry?' I pressed.

'Oh.' He looked momentarily concerned, but quickly brushed it off. 'Don't worry, Katie, I'm sure she'll love it! She loves when I take my clothes off. Well, sometimes she does. I think.' He smiled confidently, but I could see a flicker of something troubling in his eyes.

'Gerry, if it's not too much to ask . . . maybe don't tell her about it just yet? I'm not asking you to lie to her – just don't say anything. Could you do that?'

'I'm not very good at lying.' He looked a little perplexed.

'You don't have to lie! That's what I'm saying! Just say nothing if she doesn't ask, Okay?'

'Yeah, I suppose I could do that.'

Chapter 12

I tried to put the niggling worry of Mo out of my head. Instead I focused on how excited I was to have the two new Gerry paintings to work on. I decided to do them as a diptych. They were a charming little duo and I knew Gerry was really going to stand out in the collection over all. He just had an undeniable charm. He was so amiable and yet surprisingly cheeky.

My thoughts wandered, unauthorised, back to the Mo dilemma. I had a sneaking suspicion she wasn't going to appreciate sharing this side of her husband with the world. What if she was possessive of him in that way? This thought troubled me. I couldn't help wondering if I was doing something wrong in this instance? Was I invading the private life of this couple, without intending to, and then potentially sharing it with the world? Was this going to seem like I had no respect for Mo's private relationship with her husband? But it was only supposed to be a bit of fun – surely she would realise that?

Anyway, I couldn't let these things inhibit me. I needed to be fearless for the sake of art. And it wasn't like I was sleeping with these men, after all. I was merely creating something.

And it was important to me that this collection be truthful and unrestrained.

It wasn't hard to know what canvases I would use for these two new paintings – it was practically meant to be. I had already done a diptych in my Manhattan series; it was the Statue of Liberty from two different angles. I knew right away that Gerry would look just divine painted in underneath her. I got into my '*Albert Says*' jumper, which was going to need a wash soon, took a deep breath and got to work.

I started on the one with the teacup first. It was one of those paintings that just flow onto the canvas. I didn't even need to do a lot of sketching to prepare, like I'd done with Billy. In fact, when I started to sketch, I just wanted to move on to the painting immediately. I didn't have so much patience with this one but I had confidence. Sometimes a painting just works with minimal effort. It creates itself, and it can surprise even the artist with what it becomes. Michelangelo once said '*Every block of stone has a statue inside it and it is the task of the sculptor to discover it.*' I always liked this idea that art creates itself and we, as artists, are merely facilitating it. It is a humbling thought, but also made me feel like I was serving a greater purpose.

Gerry had a pinky-white Irish skin colour, but his arms and face were darker and more weathered than everywhere else. I squished out a large amount of titanium white onto my palette. I put some cadmium red next to it, a dash of burnt sienna, the tiniest blob of yellow ochre and a small bit of cobalt blue. I gently mixed these together until I was happy with the skin colour. I gradually added more burnt sienna for the arms and face, and some raw sienna for the shading. It began to come to life. For this layer he would look quite smooth – I would have to let it dry and wait for the next layer to put in the expression lines and the chest hairs and work more on the shading. But already the painting was somehow reminding me of Rodin's *The Thinker*. The character was completely different, of course. And the fact that it was a painting, with such an unlikely setting for a naked man to be drinking tea, made it completely unique. But there was something about Gerry, the way he composed himself . . . When he was standing up, in the first set-up we did, he was confident, yet aloof. Then when he sat down he seemed content and wistful . . . there was more to him than met the eye. He seemed like a thinker! Or maybe I was getting carried away.

I almost didn't hear the doorbell on Thursday morning as I bounced around Winnipeg Cottage, happily working away on my new diptych and shaking whatever bit of booty I had to a vintage Destiny's Child CD. Except for Sasha, who was rambling around with blue paint on her tail (whoops!), I had been on my own, undisturbed, painting away since Tuesday evening. I was merrily shrieking away to 'Bootylicious' and I think the doorbell probably rang a second or third time before I snapped out of my zone and noticed it buzzing.

I skipped out into the hall and froze. Fred was peering in through the net curtain on the window at the side of the door. The minute I registered his face, without thinking I jumped back behind the doorframe of the living room and out of sight. Then I immediately felt like a tool. He had seen me, I had seen him, our eyes had met and I had jumped out of sight. Katie! What was that? You're a *moron*, I scolded myself. There was no way I could recover now and act cool and composed. What the hell was wrong with me? I gathered myself together, and tucked the loose stray curls behind my ears. I peered around the doorframe and did a pathetic little 'mock relief' gesture before I walked towards the door sheepishly. I unlocked all the bolts and chains, as gracefully as I could manage, and opened the door.

'Fred! Hi!' I blurted, perhaps a little too enthusiastically. 'So funny. I thought you were a burglar or something. *Ha-ha*.'

I sounded demented.

'Ha, oh right, yeah.' He was distracted, looking at something on my nose.

I swiped at it and rubbed blue paint off with the back of my hand. The same colour that was on Sasha's tail. Great. I'd probably sat in it too. God only knew how it had got everywhere. I swiped my hand across my arse, not that that was going to remove oil paint. Then I noticed there were big dirty blotches of paint all over the palms of my hands. Mostly dirty-looking brown and grey colours. Nice. I shoved them into my pockets. I never seemed to notice the disgraceful state I got myself into when I was on my own painting. Then the minute someone would see me, it became so glaringly obvious.

'That was some lovely singing you were doing in there.' He tried to keep a straight face but I could see a grin crack in the corner of his mouth.

My singing was definitely not lovely and he knew it. I always sounded like an excited seal when I sang. And this was the second time he had suffered this vile sound. He was still looking at the blue on my nose, but I didn't want to swipe at it again with my filthy hands and draw even more attention to how disgusting I was.

'Sorry.' I attempted a cheerful smile. 'Clearly you've not caught me in my finest hour.' I laughed and patted the mass of curls sitting haphazardly on the top of my head quickly before hiding my hand again.

He nodded, a smile still tickling the corners of his lips. I raised my eyebrows. His mouth spread itself into a big charming grin as always.

'No, you look great!' He seemed genuine. 'That jumper is brilliant. The equation, $E = MC^2$, it suits you . . . because it's about energy and you . . . well, you're so full of energy . . .' He paused and bent down to pet Sasha who sashayed past him out the door. 'Sandwich-making, singing, maths, and I'm presuming some sort of painting . . . or maybe you and Sasha are becoming members of the Blue Man group. Well, is there anything you don't do, Katie? I hadn't really pegged you as the maths-y type though.'

I scrunched up my nose, a bit embarrassed. I felt like a fraud.

'I don't really understand the jumper, if I'm honest. I just robbed it off my friend's dad . . . I suppose I'm a faux nerd.'

He laughed at me. He laughed at me a lot, I noticed. I wondered was there a chance he was laughing with me, instead of at me? Did he think I was funny in an intentional way? Probably not, given that it wasn't particularly intentional. No, my humour was definitely accidental.

'Maybe you're just a different type of nerd.' He shifted his weight from one foot to the other. 'Well, anyway, Jim asked me to drop this in to you. It's your wages, I suppose. A redundancy package maybe?'

'Yeah, right!' I rolled my eyes, accepting the little white envelope. 'I'm pretty sure Jim wouldn't understand the word *redundancy*. Would you like to come in for a cuppa?'

'Oh. Em . . . well, I have to go back and round up the sheep with Bessie. Then I gotta go to Galway and back with the van to pick up some kegs for Jim. Then I have to be back in Farrelly's by six.' He blew out his cheeks and widened his eyes, like he was exhausted already, just thinking about it all.

'A woman's work is never done, is it?' I raised my eyebrows.

He laughed again. 'Good one,' he smirked. 'We miss you in Farrelly's. It's not been the same since you left. Mary does make a fine sambo, top class in fact. But she's a bit grouchy . . . I miss our banter.'

'Hey!' I folded my arms. 'You sayin' my sambos weren't top class?'

Damn. He looked hot. Why did I have to look like shit when he looked so lovely? He should have warned me before calling over. Ah, what would be the point? Who was I fooling? I probably would only have looked very slightly less shit. I might have washed my hands at best.

He mimicked my pout and I got a sudden urge to lunge forward and plant a kiss on his perfect pouting lips. I didn't.

'I gotta hit the road,' he said, clasping his hands together.

I noticed he had avoided answering the sambo question. I furrowed my brow at him.

I paused. Standing in the doorway looking at him. I didn't want him to go. Would it be really uncool if I asked him again would he like to come in? He had already politely declined. But I wanted to invite him into my little world of Winnipeg Cottage. I now had four paintings, and they were shaping up pretty nicely, and I felt ready to show someone again. Well, I was ready to show Fred. Really I just wanted him to know in particular about his one. For my own peace of mind, so I didn't feel so oddly about it. Even if there was a considerable risk that he was going to think I was a sick perverted stalker forever. He was the only one who didn't actually know he was a subject and he would have to find out eventually. Now that there were four paintings I hoped it would seem less weird on a personal level.

'Can I . . . Do you mind if I show you something really quick, Fred?'

'Sure.' He raised his eyebrows.

'Okay. Actually. Sorry.' I held up my hand in front of him, stopping him as he stepped through the door. 'First, you have to promise not to jump to the conclusion that I'm a total creep. Because I'm not. I'm an artist." I gestured at my blue nose for evidence. I beckoned him through the door and we walked into the hall as I blabbered away. "Sometimes we artists have to capture moments – as they happen – and create something – with them.' I hesitated at the door of the living room. 'Do you promise?'

He looked baffled but, 'Yeah, I do,' he assured me.

I stepped aside as he walked in.

'Wow!' He stood looking around.

I followed behind him and stood a bit away from him so he wouldn't feel any more uncomfortable than necessary. I tried to see his reaction without staring. He seemed completely shell-shocked. I stood back by the wall. My cheeks were turning a brighter shade of red, and I was glad the curtains were closed so it wasn't so visible. However, the fact that the room was dark did possibly make me seem like a bit of a weird hermit serial killer. And now that I thought of it, the various printouts and rough preliminary sketches stuck up on the walls possibly looked like a sort of collage or shrine created by an obsessive demented lunatic. Shit. I really hadn't thought this through. It wouldn't have surprised me if he had taken out his mobile and called the police, there and then. I was feeling more and more like Robin Williams in *One Hour Photo* or something.

I longed for Fred to say something else, just to break the awkward silence in the room.

Finally Fred spoke. 'Wow!'

The same word he had used before. But at least it was a word. He had said something, he had made a noise, and that was a start.

I inhaled. I hadn't realised I'd stopped breathing.

He inspected the paintings individually: 'Billy . . . Gerry . . . and that's me.' His eyes narrowed. 'That day I was shearing . . . last month . . . in the field. That was you!' He pointed at me, laughing. He was really laughing now. 'You! That was you with the Lady Gaga ring tone . . . I don't believe it. I *knew* there was someone there. You actually took a picture of me . . . I'm not going to lie, this is a little weird.' He was laughing even harder now. I couldn't tell if he was laughing with disbelief or amazement, or both. 'You are unbelievable. These are fantastic.' He shook his head.

I started to blush. I loved being praised for my work, but I was never sure how to handle it, how to act demure and humble. And I was still unsure if this was in fact genuine praise. Or whether he was just keeping me sweet so that I wouldn't hack him to pieces with a meat cleaver, and dispose of his body in the little old stream that ran through Ballytiernan.

He looked back at me and smiled with what seemed to be a mixture of fascination and bemusement. Phew, I thought. It mustn't seem as crazy as it does in my head. Maybe he really does like them.

'Gerry's ones aren't so great yet,' I began. 'But I think they'll look good in the end. I can't get his nose right in that one . . .' I walked over to it. 'See there, it's a bit . . . long or something, I don't know. It's just not him yet. It's annoying because I really want to capture what's in his expression and . . .' I paused.

He was looking at me silently, his eyes wide.

'You don't really think I'm a creep for taking the photo of you on the sly, do you?'

'Em . . .' he backed slowly out the door, 'I eh, gotta go . . . No, I'm joking.' He laughed softly. 'I think you're fantastic. And I'm actually totally flattered that you wanted to paint me.'

'Thanks!'

We both laughed. Mine was definitely a laugh of relief, and my cheeks were slowly cooling down, hopefully returning to a normal colour.

'Well, anyway, I really do have to go. I don't think you're psycho, I promise! Bessie is waiting for me . . . Do come back into Farrelly's someday soon for a Cosmo or two?' I thought I noticed the slightest hint of a wink. 'Yes?'

We moved out towards the door.

'Well, my best friend Sophie is coming on Friday – oh, that's tomorrow! Goodness, it's nearly the weekend!' I squealed, clapping my hands. 'She's coming tomorrow! I might see you over the weekend so. I'm sure Sophie will want to check out the local talent!' I raised my eyebrows up and down with a playful grin, like Milhouse from *The Simpsons*. 'That's my Milhouse impression.' I realised I had to explain it.

'Right. Well, maybe stick to the painting and the singing for now!'

I pushed him off the step playfully. 'See ya at the weekend.'

'Okay, I look forward to it!' He turned to leave, then looked back. 'You really do look great by the way. Even with that brown blob on your chin.'

I rubbed my chin. What was the use? It had been there the whole time.

'See you soon, chin-blobless I hope!' I called after him. 'You'd better be in top Cosmo-making form!'

He turned back around and bowed, all gentlemanly.

'At your service, madam.'

As he walked away I gazed after him, feeling little flutterings in my tummy. I hadn't had those feelings about someone in a really long time. That excitement, and the giddy energy sparked by the possibilities of a potential connection with someone. It felt nice.

I was buzzing. I was feeling so damn good about life I challenged myself to do the one thing I almost never did. I went out for a run. Exercise would do me the world of good, I convinced myself. And maybe tighten up my jibbly belly bits.

There was a stream at the end of the field behind the cottage and a path ran alongside it. I used to play and swim there with Granddad when I was little. The stream went past the far side of Fred's bungalow. But I decided to look straight ahead as I passed. I didn't want to push it and seem like a total stalker. He was more than likely on his way to Galway by now anyhow.

I felt great when I got back from my run. Well, I say run – in reality I ran for about ten minutes puffing and panting and then gave in and walked the rest of the way, attempting a little jog every few minutes, clutching my sides if I went too hard on myself.

The Tesco truck arrived at five, just after I got in the door. I finally did a much-needed restocking of the kitchen cabinets and, most importantly, the wine cabinet. As I went around filling the cupboards and making the place all clean and homely, I kept replaying the conversation with Fred in my head, over and over. I analyzed it inside-out and upside-down. He had definitely been flirting, I decided.

But what about Isabelle? Had I completely imagined that incredible sexual chemistry between them? He hadn't mentioned her today. But then why would he? I hadn't asked about her. I should have asked him about her. Sasha was weaving around my legs, meowing and looking up at me with wide expectant eyes, which interrupted my incessant Fred-thoughts. I filled her bowl with tuna and got back to work.

Chapter 13

I walked down the village with a spring in my step the next morning. I was like one of those little chocolate men in the Crunchy ad from the nineties – I definitely had 'That Friday Feeling'!

First, I was meeting Mac in Mo's Teacup for a coffee and to say goodbye before she left for Birmingham to look after her sister for a while. Then I was going to collect Sophie off the bus from Shannon.

I strolled into an almost empty Mo's Teacup. There were two women at the window who didn't seem to notice my arrival. They were huddled together, but despite their close proximity they were shouting their gossip at one another – or, at least, the one with the blue rinse was. I sat down with my back to them and waited for Mac. A young teenager came over to take my order and I asked her for two lattes and a selection of buns.

'So anyway!' Blue Rinse Lady shouted. 'This young Dublin lassie who's moved into Winnipeg. Have you heard about her?'

I froze. Was she actually talking about me when I was right behind them?

'Ah yes, that sweet girl who works in Farrelly's? Katie Something-or-other.' The second lady was a chatty character named Sheila. She was a regular at Farrelly's, particularly during bingo nights. She had soft white hair and today, as usual, she wore a pink bow perched on the side of her head. Her back was to me but it was the bow that gave her away.

Mac bustled in and I gestured to her to keep quiet as she approached and took the seat opposite.

'So apparently she takes nuudie photos of men . . . you know, the willy part and everything. And then paints them!'

My mouth hung open and I looked across at Mac who appeared to be mirroring my gobsmacked expression.

Sheila giggled excitedly. 'Sounds fun! I'd love if my Liam got involved! He can be very sexy when he wants to be.'

Blue Rinse Lady scowled and continued, 'You would in your eye! Young Billy Hanlon was traumatised. She lured him into her cottage, spiked his drink or something and took photos of him in the nip. That's what Mo tells me anyway. Billy's mother Bernie is Mo's sister, you know. Mo seems to be very put out by the whole carry-on. She has forbidden Gerry to go anywhere near the girl, for fear he'll be lured in. Gerry is such a gentle, obliging man. He'd be a prime target.'

'Ah, but I don't know if I really believe all that,' Sheila said with a gentle laugh. 'She's a very pretty girl, Katie. I can't imagine she would need to drug men. I'd expect she has plenty of willing gentlemen callers. And sure don't you know that Billy lad is a divil for putting a skin on a story?'

'He's been to the doctor to be tested for that AIDs and the chlamydia and all those things,' Blue Rinse stated firmly. 'God love the lad, his mother is beside herself. Say a few decades of the rosary for him, will you?'

'I will indeed.'

The two ladies put on their summer coats and headed out the door.

As soon as they were gone Mac burst out laughing. 'Blind

as bats, those two! What are the odds that you'd be sitting right behind them?'

'Can you believe it?' I fumed. 'What in God's name is Billy doing fabricating such a story? And Mo! What business is it of hers?' I lowered my voice, remembering whose coffee shop I was sitting in. In fact it was more her business than she was even aware of. But still, I was furious.

Our lattes and buns arrived, but my appetite seemed to have walked out the door with the two ladies.

'Never mind them, Katie. How is it coming along?'

I leaned in close to her and whispered, 'I've just started two paintings of Gerry.'

'Gerry?' Mac's eyes looked like they were about to pop out of their sockets. 'Mo's Gerry?'

'Yep.'

Mac stopped at the nearer bus stop, as she was heading in the direction from which Sophie was coming. I spotted Sophie's bus pulling up down the road on the other side. I gave Mac a hug goodbye and ran down the road past the church. I let out a little squeal and dashed across the road and ran alongside the coach as it slowed and pulled into the stop, looking up through the dark windows, trying to spot my buddy – like an excited child who'd had too many Skittles. I couldn't make her out, it was too dark, but there was no mistaking her when she came down the steps at the front of the coach. Wiry blonde hair, similar texture to my own but managed far better, big emotional brown eyes and that large charming smile the Americans were always so fond of.

At school Sophie was the beautiful petite blonde girl all the guys adored. I was her lanky ginger sidekick. I had nicknamed Sophie's eyes the Avatar Eyes, because they were so large and emotive. They were surrounded by thick, long eyelashes. She got away with murder, batting those eyelashes. It was a talent. With the help of those eyelashes Sophie had bagged herself a dream career as a high-end realtor selling apartments to the rich and famous in Manhattan. She really suited New York. When we moved over she fitted in straight away. We hadn't been there a wet week and she was telling the taxi drivers how to get where we were going, haggling with traders on Canal Street, and she knew all the best bars and clubs. She seemed to have an inbuilt trendy-club sat-nav system. I had simply watched her in fascination. We were very different, Sophie and I. But she got my sense of humour like no one else. We had always sung from the same hymn sheet.

'C'mere!' I gave her a big bear hug. 'I can't believe you're here! In Ballytiernan! You and . . . your whole apartment . . .' I said, apprehensively eyeing her luggage.

We chattered excitedly the whole way to Winnipeg Cottage, despite the fact that we were hauling two impossibly large pink suitcases behind us along the uneven footpaths. I tried not to curse her and her ridiculous over-packing. She had only just arrived after all and I didn't want to start things off by scolding her. I should have expected it anyway; it was textbook Sophie. Whenever a group of us went on holiday, she would arrive at the airport with the biggest suitcase and proudly declare, 'I win!'

There was so much to talk about. Sophie was the sort of friend that no matter how long it had been since we'd seen each other we automatically picked up where we'd left off, as though we hadn't been apart for a second. I was dying to tell her all about my new life, but I wasn't sure if she wanted to talk about all the shit she had going on.

We nattered away like excited schoolgirls about all sorts of silly little things for most of the way and then finally, panting and exhausted but glad to be almost at Winnipeg, I asked, 'Do you want to talk about the split?' I looked at her. She hadn't even broken a sweat, the bitch. I was bloody dying. She probably had the lighter bag!

She brushed a perfect ringlet out of her eye and shook her

head. 'I need some wine before I can even begin, Katie!'

I turned the key in the lock and we bundled inside.

'I *love* this adorable little gaff,' Sophie enthused as she explored the cottage, 'It's *so* you, KitKat. Except like, a rural, bogger version of you.'

'Yeah, thanks! Who would have thought I'd become a country bumpkin? I think you're gonna like this little room.' I wandered into the room I had stayed in as a kid. 'The windows are really cute, look. There are more pillows and blankets in the press if you need them.' I walked back out into the corridor. 'Aaaaand here is my room – nice, isn't it?'

Before I'd finished talking, Sophie had opened her bag and was folding her pyjamas on the pillow beside mine. I looked at her with my eyebrows raised.

'What? I'd be scared and lonely over in the other room all by myself!' she protested.

I laughed.

I headed back down towards the kitchen. 'Tea, wine, or Prosecco?' I shouted up.

'Do you even have to ask?' she sang back at me.

'Prosecco it is, baby!'

I popped the bottle and poured two generous glasses, the bubbles dancing to the surface with exuberance. I then took two strawberries out of a bowl in the fridge and rinsed them. The liquid fizzed excitedly as I dropped one into each glass.

'To a week and a half of good times and good riddance to naaaasty New York boyfriends!' I announced, as she arrived down into the kitchen.

We clinked glasses and headed into the living room.

Sophie gasped. 'You're painting again!' she squealed the minute she laid eyes on the big canvases. 'Oh my God, Katie, these are hilarious! And brilliant! Where did you find the men? You can't have been spying on them all!'

'No!' I exclaimed.

I told her all about Fred first, seeing as she was involved in the accidental spying incident. Perhaps it might also have been because I was dying to talk about Fred. I'd been thinking about him non-stop since he dropped by and I was absolutely bursting to get it all off my chest.

'So, I really like him, Soph, but I just don't really know where I stand with him. I've no idea what's going on between him and Isabelle. But if there's anything at all there, I don't stand a chance against her. You should see her – she's honestly the biggest ride I've ever seen in real life. Her boobies are like big, bouncy, silk pillows from heaven.'

'You sure there isn't a thing between *you* and Isabelle?'

'No way! She'd never go for me.' I laughed.

'Don't be ridiculous, KitKat – you have your ginger charm – you're not totally hideous – despite being ginger obviously . . .' She ducked a swipe of my hand, and giggled. 'But, seriously, not all guys go for that sexy busty kinda girl – it can be a bit too obvious, yunno?' She looked like she actually believed that nonsense.

I crinkled my nose. 'As if! That's just bullshit us normal girls go on with to make ourselves feel better. She's a goddess. He would seriously need to get his head checked out if he picked me over her. And aside from all that, I'm pretty sure he thinks I'm riding Billy anyway.'

I then told her about the whole Billy fiasco. I should have explained it all to Fred while he was at the cottage, but I'd been too overwhelmed with showing him the paintings and everything.

'Listen, I'm so sorry. I've been waffling on about all my silly issues,' I said, interrupting myself. 'You have some proper shit going on. Are you ready to tell me about what happened with Chris? Or should I top up your glass some more? Or should we just start doing shots and get fecked off our tits?'

Sophie laughed but her breathing was heavy from the

110

minute I mentioned his name, and her eyes clouded over. The girl should have been an actress; those eyes could sell a billion movie stubs.

'Oh Katie, it's so complicated. He really messed me around this time, but . . . I got him back . . . *bad* . . . in the worst possible way . . . I really shouldn't have done it. I'm a terrible person.' Her Avatar Eyes widened and she bit her lip, guiltily. 'I honestly didn't even do it intentionally . . . it just . . . happened. I think.'

'What happened? Wait! Tell me what he did first. The dick-face.'

'Well, it was the usual really, but this time it just tipped me over the edge. Jules rang me on Saturday night.'

I couldn't help rolling my eyes; Jules was one of those people who always had to be the one to deliver bad news.

'I was staying in because I had a load of research to do for work, on the Kanye apartment. Anyway, she rang me from Fat Baby –'

'Classy joint,' I interjected sarcastically.

'I know. Ugh. And she took great pleasure in telling me, pretending to be a caring friend – you know, the way she does – that Chris was there. And of course he was completely plastered, and some girl was all over him. So that was what Jules said, and deep down I guess I knew she wasn't making it up. You know what Chris is like – it's nothing new. He thinks he can get away with this shit when he's drunk, yunno?' She took a deep breath and gulped down some wine. 'But we have been through this shit so many times and the last time it happened I told him it really had to be the last time. And he promised me! He promised it would never happen again. He was so serious, Katie. I really thought he'd meant it. He promised me he would change for me. Because he didn't want to lose me. So I didn't know whether to believe Jules or not. I guess I knew deep down he wasn't going to change . . . but I needed to know for myself. So I went down there – it was a shocker that I even got into the place. I was wearing a tracksuit.' She took another big breath.

It was probably a top-dollar Juicy Couture tracksuit, I thought to myself. Too classy by Fat Baby standards. Most of the chicks there looked like prostitutes.

Suddenly, those big brown eyes welled up with tears, as I had seen them do a million times before because of Chris.

'Aaaaand, lo and behold, there he was, wearing the face off some Jersey Shore slut, with her orange ass hanging out of some tacky glittery hot pants, and his disgusting hands all over it.' She wrinkled her nose. 'Ugh! I hope he has herpes all over his hands now – if that's possible.' She wiped the tears from her eyes. 'That was when it hit me, KitKat. I honestly never wanted to touch those hands again. I guess I needed to see it, for it to hit home with me what a disgusting pig he is.'

I was glad she'd seen it. Even if it hurt her, it was true she needed to witness it. I exhaled loudly and widened my eyes like I was ready to punch someone. Chris was lucky he was an ocean away from me right now. I had hit him before and I would do it again. It was a year ago – I saw him with a girl and I punched him in the face. But the bruises on my knuckles hadn't yet healed before Sophie took him back. It pissed me right off but I realised I couldn't help her. She needed to figure it out herself. And, thank God, she had finally seen the light. I unclenched my fists and shakily sipped my Prosecco. This deserved a toast. But I didn't want to be obnoxious and celebrate her heartache. So I silently toasted to myself.

'Wait. It gets worse,' she whispered. 'You won't believe what I did.'

I topped up our glasses and sank back into the couch beside her, throwing my pink sparkly fleece blanket on top of us.

'I didn't say anything to him. I left him with her.'

'Damn right,' I couldn't help interrupting. 'He doesn't deserve anything from you. He's got away with way too much already.'

'I know, I know. You don't need to convince me any more. Anyway. I couldn't be bothered getting upset, hitting him, shouting at him, running away, him running after me . . . I've done all that before. I'm finished with that. I really am, Katie. I'm finished with him. I know you've heard it before but this time I mean it.'

'You have no idea how glad I am to hear that. And I do really believe you this time.' I gently clinked my glass off hers. I couldn't help myself. It was so subtle I didn't think she'd even noticed.

'Hold on. There's more, remember?' She pulled her knees up to her chest and tucked her feet under my bum to warm them. 'So, as I said, I left. And for whatever reason, I'm pretty sure I wasn't really thinking straight, I went around the corner into La Caverna. I ordered two double Jägerbombs and a can of Red Bull. And I sat up on a vacated bar stool and drank it all. I just felt like getting really drunk and I guess I couldn't bear the thought of going home alone. Drinking alone is probably sadder though. But, anyway, guess who arrives at the bar beside me, completely out of the blue? Obi! Fucking Obi. Aside from Chris himself, he was the last person I wanted to see.'

Obi was Chris's best friend. I actually had a soft spot for Obi, but Sophie had never had much time for him – just because Chris behaved like an idiot around him. But, personally, I didn't see why that was Obi's fault. Chris was the one being the idiot, obviously because he wanted to impress his friend, and he was an idiot generally anyway. And although Obi didn't do anything to discourage his antics he was definitely the more sensible and reasonable of the two. That was what I thought anyway, but Sophie just blamed any of their mischief on Obi. I thought it was a bit unfair actually.

Sophie was biting her lip now.

'Oh God. Don't judge me. Please.' She put a cushion up in front of her face. But I could see her squirming behind it. 'I fucked him, Katie,' she blurted out.

I gasped. Loudly. This was crazy shit. I was speechless.

'My memory of it is very, very fuzzy but I definitely slept with him. We were both wasted. I told him what had just happened, and he told me that he never thought Chris deserved me, that I was too good for him. The next thing I remember, I'm waking up in his bed without a shred of clothing on me. I can't believe I did it. I don't do that sort of thing, Katie!'

'I know you don't,' I agreed softly. 'Is there any chance you just fell asleep in his bed naked?'

'Maybe,' she muttered sheepishly.

'You must know if you had sex with him, though. Surely you would remember that big black rod?' Obi was an African American beast of a man. Think Didier Drogba on steroids and you have the right idea.

'No. I do remember. Of course.' Her eyes widened suggestively and her cheeks went rosy. 'I'm not going to lie. It was outrageously good sex and I felt terrible but I felt great too. I'm an awful person, aren't I? Not only did I cheat on Chris, but I cheated on him with his best mate. His best mate with a massive black penis. It was the size of my arm.' She squealed and held up her forearm, her hand forming a fist. 'Tell me I'm an awful person, Katie. Go on! I deserve it.'

'I will not tell you that. It is untrue,' I said firmly. 'Does Chris know this happened?'

'Not exactly. I just rang him to tell him that it was over and to fuck off out of my life. That I never wanted to see him again. Then I booked flights to come here, organised leave from work and counted down the days. I didn't answer his calls or reply to his texts. I ran away from it all. And I ran to you. *Ta da!* Lucky you. You won the visitor jackpot.'

Wow. There was a moment of silence as I took it all in.

'Well, that is some serious payback.' I finally said. 'I completely approve. I know I shouldn't, but I just love it. His best friend! Sophie Elizabeth Powell! That is . . . Wow.' I shook my head in disbelief.

I went to the kitchen to put two Dr. Oetker pizzas in the oven, and then returned to the living room with a bottle of Merlot.

'Holy Mary Mother of God, who would have thought our lives would have turned out like this?' I laughed. 'You doing the nasty with your boyfriend's best friend, and me probably still in love with a gay man who pretended to love me for three years before coming out.'

Sophie shook her head. 'What are we like?' she sighed and flopped back into the couch, almost spilling the red wine onto my lovely cushions. But my head was too full of thoughts to care.

I looked at Sophie. I was so desperate to ask about Seb. I prayed that my voice would sound calm and somewhat detached. I didn't want her to hold back telling me anything for fear I'd break down.

'Sophie, how is Seb?' I remained still, now sitting awkwardly on the edge of the couch. I tried to look less awkward. I leaned back and spread my legs out wider. I wasn't sure why I thought that would look more detached and laid back, but the result must only have looked forced.

Sophie was silent for a minute, playing with one of the little tassels around the bottom of her top.

'I didn't know whether to bring it up. I'm not sure what to tell you.'

'Tell me everything obviously.' I tried to hide the desperation in my voice. All sorts of thoughts were flying through my head about what he might be getting up to, now that he was living life as he had always secretly wanted to, without me holding him back.

'Well, for a while he was in great form,' she began. 'I mean not in *great* form. Obviously he missed you. He asked me about you when I saw him. He was really keen to ask me how you were. Said he felt terrible and really wished you hadn't left so suddenly, and he said he just wished things had happened differently. He said he couldn't believe you weren't in his life any more and a massive part of him was completely devastated. He actually said: 'I've lost my best friend.' I told him he should have been more careful with your feelings and what he did wasn't right. I also said you were *my* best friend not his.' She smiled coyly.

I nodded, mustering up a smile to show appreciation for her loyalty. 'So . . . ?' I pressed eagerly.

She paused again, considering her words. This worried me.

'Well, soon after you left, he . . . partied. A lot. He was out every night. He lost his job.'

My mouth fell open. Sebastian had been a head curator at the Manhattan Museum of Art, a job he had worked practically his whole life for. He had worked for years in smaller galleries and museums, volunteering while he was in school and doing internships throughout collage, and he worked very hard after college and two years ago he was offered the job of his dreams at the MMA. The night he was offered the position we went out for dinner at one of New York's most expensive restaurants to celebrate, and I'd never seen him so happy. I just couldn't believe it now that he had lost the job. It seemed impossible. What had happened to my Seb? I suddenly felt a pang of guilt and overwhelming sorrow flooded over me. I should have been there for him. He must have been going through something terrible. Coming out can be very difficult for some guys and I had just deserted him when he needed me most, just because I was humiliated and heart-broken. Had I been too self-involved to recognise that he needed help? My eyes pricked with tears.

'So where is he now? How is he? What is he doing?'

'We don't know,' Sophie answered quietly.

'Huh?' was all I could manage to say. I was speechless. How could she have waited so long to tell me all this? What did she even mean?

116

'What do you mean you don't know? How do you not know?' I fought back tears of overwhelming guilt.

'None of the gang have heard anything from him, Katie. The apartment is empty, he's not answering his phone and he seems to have just . . . disappeared.'

All of a sudden I felt my stomach fall like lead. It plummeted down through my arse and through the Earth's surface into the core of the planet.

'I need to call him,' I said, immediately panicked.

'Katie, do you not remember what he did to you?' she said softly.

'But he might need me,' I protested.

'He was the one who cut you out of his life. He lied to you for three years, made a mockery of your relationship. Wasted three years of your life. Then he didn't even explain himself properly. He showed you no courtesy or respect. I know I can't talk about how you should be treated in a relationship. Clearly I have no clue. But I know that he doesn't deserve anything from you. If he needed you he wouldn't have treated you that way. Anyway – his phone isn't active any more. Try as much as you like, you won't get through.'

'What about his mother? Has anyone tried contacting her? Or his brother?' Did anyone even file a missing persons report? Was he actually missing?

'Calm down. Chris spent like five hours trying to find his mother's number in the Chicago Directory. He eventually found it after ringing like a hundred different people with the same surname. She answered and told him that she knew where Seb was but that she didn't want anything to do with it. Then she said that we should leave him be and hung up.'

'I need to go and find him,' I breathed. I stood up.

'What are you going to do?' Sophie tugged my hand gently, bringing me back down onto the couch. 'You gonna search the length and breadth of America to find him? There's literally nothing else we can do, Katie. Just have some more wine and relax. He's probably in some rehab in Utah, having the banter with Lilo. Seriously, Katie. Please don't let this upset you – he really doesn't deserve any more of your tears. Let's forget about Seb and Chris now and have a fun few days together.'

Chapter 14

I woke up the next morning spooning Sophie. Friday night had ended up being a girl's night in. I eventually put Seb out of my head. Sophie, God love her, used every distraction technique in the book, and eventually settled on getting me plastered with rum. We didn't even bother mixing it in the end, just passed it over and back between us, gulping it. That was the last thing I remembered. I sighed and stretched my arms up into the air. Sophie rolled over to face me and rubbed her eyes.

'Do you remember the voicemail you left for Fred?' she croaked.

'What?' I closed my eyes, trying to rummage through the baggage in my brain, but couldn't find any memory of it. 'No, you're joking, right?' I finally concluded.

'I'm afraid not.' Her laugh was raspy. 'Don't worry. You just said that he had a lovely bottom and that Bessie shouldn't judge you for looking at it.'

My head still glued to the pillow, I squinted at my phone and dialled Fred's number. 'You better not be messing with me. I'm calling him.'

She shook her head at me.

'Hello?' I murmured when he answered.

'Hi,' was his very ambiguous response.

'Can you please not listen to your voicemail – just delete it straight away, please – thank you,' I begged softly.

'Too late!' I could hear the crack of suppressed laughter in his voice.

'I see.' I squeezed my eyes shut. When I opened them Sophie was silently giggling into her pillow. I wouldn't have known only I could see her shoulders shaking. 'Right. See you tonight.'

I hung up and the two of us burst into a fit of laughter.

We hadn't fully recovered by the time the evening rolled around but we decided that hair of the dog was definitely our remedy of choice. We decided to start off the night in Farrelly's so Sophie could put faces to names and all that. We planned to spend about an hour – no more than two – in Farrelly's. And then we would ring George Best, the driver not the footballer, to take us into Galway in his death cab at about eleven.

So we put on some get-in-the-mood-for-a-night-out tunes, opened a bottle of Pinot Grigio and spent far more time than necessary getting all jazzed up in our best glad rags. Sophie put some oil treatment in my hair and spent almost an hour blow-drying it to look like hers. While I don't think it really went exactly to plan, it did look a hundred times better than usual. I looked in the mirror in the bathroom and I was pretty impressed with her work. She somehow made it look tame and even delicate.

'Can I keep you here forever, please?' I asked and gave her a kiss on the cheek.

I somehow ended up wearing a pair of black leather short shorts with a standard shirt. Sophie convinced me that my legs were my best feature. But it took more than that to get me to put on the teeny shorts. A tequila shot sealed the deal in the end. We teamed my outfit with heels I couldn't walk in.

Sophie looked me up and down. '*Swit swoo!* I don't know if Ballywhatsitcalled is ready for those legs in those shorts, girl!'

'Probably not!' I laughed. 'We need to get out of here before I chicken out and change into something else.'

Sophie had pulled all her curls to the side, held together with some clips and a flower from the front garden of Winnipeg.

'It's bogger chic. I'm a karma-chameleon, adapting to my environment, mon,' she announced proudly, in her best attempt at a Jamaican accent.

I smiled. Sophie and I were like two peas in a pod. Jamaican was generally our accent of choice when doing voices. I had missed that. I squeezed her in a hug.

We sang 'Karma, karma, karma, karma, karma, chameleon', clutching on to each other for dear life, as we teetered down to the village in our ridiculous heels. We sang the chorus twice and stopped because we didn't know the rest.

Sophie turned to me, one eyebrow raised, 'You do know that we absolutely have to get Billy back for what he did to you on your last night in Farrelly's, right?'

'Oh, I don't know, Soph.' I wasn't one for that sort of thing. I might have been a lot of things, but vengeful was just not one of them. Maybe I was just too lazy? But I knew Sophie would be in her element. She really got off on a bit of sweet revenge.

'He humiliated you, Katie!' she exclaimed passionately. 'He absolutely cannot get away with it! It is my job as your best friend to defend your honour and take him down. Take him down to Chinatown.'

'Ha. Sophie, we're not in some sort of hip-hop girl gang.'

'We'll see . . .' She winked with worrying determination.

We arrived into a jam-packed Farrelly's and Sophie made a bee-line for the bar as though she'd been in there a million times before. Her head was held high, her chest was out and she always adopted a supermodel strut when entering bars. I had always concluded it was an effort to make up for her small stature. When she arrived at the bar, Jim was closer to her and looked at her to take her order, but she was desperately trying to catch Fred's eye.

'Hiya, Jim!' I said, pushing in beside her. 'We'll have two pints of cider, please!'

'Ah, Katie! Great to see you! We miss you around here! It's nice to see you've taken my advice and eaten a few sambos. You look much better now. You have a bit more junk in the trunk, if my eyes don't deceive me. Still not quite as large as I like my ladies, but you're getting there.' He finished pouring the pints. 'There you go, love – these two are on the house.'

'Ah, thanks, Jim. You're very good.' I smiled, popped a straw into my cider and pulled Sophie away.

'Did he . . . ?' Sophie was dumbfounded. 'Did he just tell you that you had put on weight?'

'That would be correct, yes, Sophie.'

'Did he say . . . did I actually hear him say that you had junk in your trunk?' She was almost too outraged to react or merely clarify what had happened.

'That's what he said, yes.'

'What the –?'

'You'll notice men around here are completely lacking any ability to be tactful. But you do get used to it. And they don't really mean to cause any upset.'

We wandered through the pub with our pints. Sophie turned heads. Not quite as many as Isabelle, but not too far off either. We found two vacated bar stools at the far end of the bar, where Fred was working.

'Here to check out the talent, are we?' he teased. He was lining up four pints of Guinness and waiting for each of them to settle before topping off their heads. 'I'm Fred.' He freed up one of his hands and stuck it out to shake Sophie's.

'I know!' she replied smugly. 'I'm Sophie.'

'I knew that too, actually.' He grinned, winking over at me, causing my tummy to do an unauthorised flip-flop.

True to his word, Fred made us some top-quality Caipirinhas and vanilla vodka Martinis and it wasn't long before I could sense Sophie shifting restlessly beside me, her eyes darting around in search of some mischief.

'Hey, Freddie Flintstone! Can I request a tune, Mister DJ?' Sophie was definitely getting restless.

'What is it?' Fred responded.

'"Eye of the Tiger",' we both said in unison.

'No.' He shook his head.

'He never says yes to "Eye of the Tiger",' I told her, pouting.

'How about the *Baywatch* song?' She leaned forward eagerly.

'He definitely won't play the *Baywatch* song.'

'I could fall asleep to this music,' Sophie huffed. 'Fred, do you know it's a Saturday night?'

'He'll stick some Daft Punk on soon."

'What's the deal with that guy?' Sophie pointed over to the other side of the bar at a sixty-something American guy who always wore a bowler hat and spoke with a dodgy faux-Irish accent.

'That's Mr O'Reilly.'

Mr O'Reilly was a strange character all right. He always called me 'darlin'' and said things like 'Lord bless us and save us' in as thick an Irish accent as he could possibly attempt. But everyone knew he was from Detroit and only moved to Ireland last year to 'get in touch with his roots'. However, his behaviour suggested that his main motive was to find himself a young Irish bride. I managed to avoid his advances on several occasions by convincing him Fred was my boyfriend. It was convenient too as I sort of enjoyed playing pretend with Fred.

Sophie was still curiously looking over at Mr O'Reilly, tapping her fingers off the edge of the bar.

'Like what's the story with his –?'

'Oh yeah, the glove? I don't know actually, I've been meaning to ask someone.' I had noticed that he always wore a white leather glove on his left hand. I just presumed it was a tribute to Michael Jackson or something. He was just about weird enough that that was possible.

'Fred? Come here!' I smiled. 'Why does Mr O'Reilly always wear that glove?'

'Has no one ever told you?' he asked, leaning over the bar towards us, his eyes dancing like he was about to reveal a big scandal. 'Well, legend has it he wears the glove to conceal an operation he had before he came to Ireland. He apparently had a hand transplant because his hand got mangled in a machine at work.'

Sophie and I wrinkled our noses in unison.

'But get this,' he continued, as quietly as he could in the loud bar, leaning in as close to us as he could get. 'The new hand he got put on is the hand of a woman – he got it specifically in some sort of exclusive clinic in Alabama so that he can masturbate with a woman's hand. But obviously he doesn't want everyone to know so he wears the glove.'

Sophie and I both gasped and then immediately fell to pieces in fits of laughter.

'Well, you certainly know how to put a skin on a story, don't you!' I sighed, clutching my stomach, which had a stitch from all the laughing.

'Seriously.' Fred raised his eyebrows. 'Why else would he wear just one glove?'

'Fred, is there a big sign over our heads saying "Gullible Fools"?' Sophie asked, nearly choking on her laughs and gasps. 'Also, that's a vile thing to come up with – and there I was thinking you were a classy dude.'

'You don't believe me?' he asked with a wry grin as he

popped half a lemon into a hand-held press and squeezed it into a glass over ice and vodka. 'Hey, Terry!' he called, and poked Terry who was sitting on the other side of Sophie.

Terry, as always, somehow managed to be completely absorbed in the *Crosaire* crossword on the back of *The Times*, scribbling away at it in the middle of a packed pub. He looked up over the top of his glasses.

'Terry, what is concealed under Mr O'Reilly's glove?' Fred asked smugly.

'A woman's hand, Freddie,' Terry answered matter-of-factly and disappeared back into his newspaper.

Fred looked at us, his arms folded, a look of chuffed delight on his face.

I turned to Sophie, who looked like a light bulb had just gone off over her head.

'I need to see this,' she announced.

'None of us have ever seen that hand,' Fred replied, shaking his head.

'Until now,' Sophie finished, a look of pure determination in her eyes.

I sensed impending doom. Or hilarity. Or both.

'Drinking games,' she declared, her eyes wide. 'Let's get everyone involved. I'm thinking flip cup, beer pong, kings . . . Fred, have you got any plastic cups?' She batted her large eyelashes at him.

Fred looked at me and I shrugged and smirked back at him, happy to go along with Sophie's little game, but taking absolutely no responsibility.

Fred paused and then sighed and passed over a tube of plastic cups.

'Thanks!' Sophie beamed then turned around to face everyone in the pub. '*Drinking games!*' she loudly exclaimed and the whole pub looked at her.

It was remarkable. Within twenty minutes Sophie had the majority of the pub involved in her little games, and not only involved, but getting very competitive. This was the first time I'd ever seen anyone play drinking games in Farrelly's. It just hadn't seemed like that sort of place before now. But if anyone could make it happen, it was Sophie. They had even formed teams based on what areas of the village they lived in, east of the stream or west of the stream. I watched her in amazement. She had an incredible ability to get people together, joining in, having fun, and her games never failed to be entertaining.

If only it hadn't all been for another purpose. Sophie always had other motives for doing these things. She was full of plans and tricks.

There were still a few reluctant people sitting around not keen to join in and unfortunately Mr O'Reilly was one of them. But not for long. Sophie made her way over to him and flirtatiously begged him to come join us. He insisted he wasn't very good at games, but sure how could he say no to a 'beautiful young Irish lass'?

'Why don't you take that lovely white glove off? You can't play flip cup with a glove on, Mr O'Reilly!' she giggled, a ringlet falling adorably over her eye. She flicked it back behind her ear and blinked at him.

'Oh, there's no need for that.' He smiled firmly.

'I insist!' Sophie pressed. 'Sure it'll get filthy with all the drink flying around.'

Mr O'Reilly stiffened. 'Actually, I'm a bit old for games now, to be sure. I have to be getting home, darlin', it's very late altogether.' With that, he took his trench coat off the back of the stool he'd been sitting on and breezed off out the door of the pub.

I couldn't help laughing at her fallen face. 'Nice try, Soph! I guess we'll never know! That must be the first time you've ever scared a man out of a bar.' I found this very entertaining.

She looked like a kitten who'd just been trod on.

'But look at all the fun you've created!' I encouraged. 'Come on, your team are losing!'

We soon forgot about Mr O'Reilly and got our game on. Even though we were clearly the pros of the game we still managed to lose a lot and therefore drink a lot. I noticed Fred disappear out the back, most likely to bring in another keg or a box of crisps or something. Sophie was stuck into a ridiculously competitive round of flip cup and my team had been knocked out so I gave her a nudge and a wink, telling her I'd be back.

I knocked back the end of a particularly strong Bombay Sapphire with tonic, winced, and determinedly set off after Fred. I was feeling brave and confident. On nights out with Sophie I always felt like this. We buzzed off each other. Seb had always said I had a wild streak whenever I was with her, a certain mischievous glint in my eye. On the way through the kitchen I grabbed a few slices of Mary's ham to throw to the Alsatians. I wandered out to the shed where Fred had disappeared.

Drico and Hubes were delighted to see me.

'Shush!' I told them and gave them their ham. They wagged their tails and tucked in.

'Need a hand lifting anything?' I raised my voice and asked innocently.

Fred appeared from behind the big wooden door of the shed. He looked me up and down and smiled.

'Hmm . . . do I want help lifting a keg, from a skinny Dublin girl with six-inch heels on?'

'I may look skinny, but I have serious guns I'll have you know,' I protested. 'And abs of steel. Also Jim tells me he's glad to see I've been eating a few more sandwiches so I'm basically fat now.' I didn't care. I was never one to care about my weight – it was never really a big problem, thank God. I grabbed my ass. 'He thinks I have a voluptuous bottom.'

'You do have a great bottom.'

'On that topic, I've never had much of an opinion on your bottom to be honest,' I told him, smiling coyly.

He smirked. 'Are you sure that's true?'

His smirk softened and we both fell silent.

His eyes looked hungry in the dim light. Or maybe it was just my imagination, but I was nevertheless encouraged. I walked towards him, trying to look sexy, but of course I stumbled in my heels and fell forwards onto him. Shit!

'*Wahay!*' he teased, catching me.

'I'm grand. I'm not drunk or anything, just a little stumbley. Can I blame the heels?' I blinked at him, and then gathered myself reluctantly out of his arms.

He stepped back to examine the heels. 'They do look pretty menacing all right. Speaking of menacing, you and Sophie are quite a pair. Farrelly's would be a huge success if you guys were here every night. With all the games . . . and you . . . looking like that.' He paused, looking straight at me, his eyes deep and clear.

I kept my eyes glued to his, even though every instinct urged me to look away. But I desperately wanted to hold the connection.

'Well . . . there *is* something in here you might want to see,' he suggested.

'What is it?' I whispered as soon as we were both squished inside the shed.

It was dark, but I could feel him close to me, his breath on my neck. We were about the same height, with my heels in the equation. I had my back against the cold brick wall, which somehow calmed down my racing heart.

'I can't remember,' he whispered back and my heart skipped several beats.

I reached out my hand and found his fingers, tentatively lacing mine through them, scared he might pull away. But he took it as an invitation and leaned his body into mine. His perfect, delicious torso pressed against mine. He smelt amazing. My knees weakened but as it happened that wasn't a problem because his very alert body held me up against the wall. I could feel every bit of his anatomy pressing gently but firmly into me. My breathing got heavier as his lips drew nearer. Everything felt like it was in slow motion, but in a really good way. His mouth finally found mine. His lips brushed my lips softly – so softly I wasn't sure if it even happened. But then he kissed me, and again and again. A series of small kisses, getting more and more intense. Then he stopped, gently brushed my curls off my shoulder with the hand I was not clutching onto, and started gently kissing my neck, shoulder and collarbone, sending little shivers right down into my toes.

The words 'Just fuck me,' slipped gently out of my mouth before I could stop them. He paused. I wasn't sure if he had heard me. Then I wasn't sure if I'd actually even said it out loud or in my head.

The back door of the pub opened and the noise from inside spilled out. We froze.

'*Fred?*'

'Yeah – Jim – coming now! Just getting a keg out here.'

His hand fell away from mine, and he stepped back.

'What's takin' ya so long? Do ya need a hand?' Jim's voice was getting nearer.

I plastered myself against the wall, and stayed very still.

Fred hoisted a keg up into his arms. 'I'm here, it's grand. Jaysus, who licked the butter off your scone?'

Fred was gone.

Chapter 15

Tears stung my eyes as I stood there, on my own in the cold shed, wanting to scream. I slid down the wall and sat on my heels, with my head in my hands, and stayed there. I took a deep, shaky breath and let it go.

It was for the best, I told myself. You don't want to be the girl who has sex in a shed, with a guy who she's not actually even dating. Not officially. But now he probably thinks you're that girl. Fantastic, well-done, Katie, you wanton whore! Suddenly, Billy's proclamation of my contact with his cock came flooding back into my memory and I squeezed one eye shut, thinking about what Fred must be concluding.

I stood up, composed myself, and went back inside. Luckily the toilet was near the back door so I snuck in there to fix myself. I needed to calm down my burning cheeks with a lot of concealer and powder. I looked in the small broken mirror on the wall and gasped at the sight of myself. It was like Shinesville, Tennessee, on my forehead. I blotted my powder puff all over my face frantically.

Sophie came skipping in almost right away after me.

'Tell me!' she squealed. 'Tell me right now, you saucy minx!'

'Nothing happened, Soph, well actually, yeah, we had an – *amazing* kiss.' I sighed. 'But nothing else.'

'Well, that's something! God, Katie, what more do you want? Have you caught the slut bug off me?' she laughed. 'Oh, KitKat, he's lovely. He's so right for you. He's totally your type. Well, your original type, before you got sidetracked by gay pretty-boy Seb . . .'

I smiled at her forlornly as she rabitted on and on. I wasn't really listening any more. My head was still spinning from the kiss. I'd never, ever had such a powerful kiss in my life. Maybe it was because I'd been wanting it for so long, but it had exceeded all my fantasies. You know, like when you're really hungry, food always tastes amazing. Or maybe it was because it was with an actual straight man for the first time in I couldn't remember how long. It was like fireworks. But it had ended so suddenly. I wanted to remember every second and relive it again and again. Had he heard me telling him to fuck me? Oh God, why couldn't I have just kept my mouth shut?

'Katie!' Sophie's hand was waving in front of my face. 'Snap out of it, yeah?'

'Sorry, yeah, you're right, what were you saying?'

'We ready to go? We need to hit Galway soon or we won't get in anywhere.' She carefully topped up her lipstick. 'And your make-up is a mess, hun – sort it out!'

I laughed at her honesty as I got back to work on my face.

Farrelly's had quietened down when we went back in and Fred was over at the back of the bar, flashing the light switch and ringing the bell for last orders. I pulled out my phone and dialled George Best, asking him to come pick us up.

Sophie immediately started rallying troops. Isabelle was up for going, as was Fred's cousin Rory, who seemed eager to stay by Isabelle's side. A few other lads agreed to come along.

'Fred! You coming?' Sophie demanded when he got back to the bar.

'I can't.'

My heart sank. I didn't look at him, just busied myself rummaging in my bag even though I didn't need anything.

'I have to clean down here – then I have to help Jim bring in all the wood from the van outside,' he said through gritted teeth. '*Then* we're setting up a stage for the trad session tomorrow night. It's going to take at least two hours, probably more. I'm off tomorrow, so he wants to do it tonight, while he still has me. There's no way he could do it on his own.'

'What about Cormac? Can't he do it?' I piped up. I couldn't help myself. I knew Cormac would be working tomorrow, but he never lifted a finger. He just hovered around playing some World of Warcraft thing on his iPhone. It was my biggest pet peeve while I was still working there.

'Yeah, you and I both know he'll have some sort of back problem when it comes to lifting something. He always does. Jim knows it too, which is why he isn't letting me go until it's done tonight.' He smiled resolutely, his eyes lingering on mine.

I could feel my cheeks burning underneath all the powder. I hoped it was doing its job adequately.

As I put my coat on, I tried to keep up the appearance that I wasn't too bothered about him not coming but I caught his eye again and I was sure he could sense my disappointment.

'Come back in here tomorrow night, yeah?' he suggested. 'The trad group are playing and my brother Seán will be down from Dublin. We'll probably have a lock-in.'

'Sounds fun,' I said.

We poured ourselves into the back of George's taxi outside. The gentlemen decided to let the girls go ahead and George's brother Pat was going to follow with them behind us, in his minivan. So it was Sophie, Isabelle and myself.

'I haven't been in Galway since the Gaeltacht when we were – what, fifteen?' Sophie gulped down a swig of Bacardi from a Coke bottle and shivered.

'Looks like nothing's changed!' I laughed at her and she passed me the bottle with a twinkle in her eye.

'I love Galway,' Isabelle chirped. 'I have been zer five or six timez now wiz zee kids! It is so beautiful.'

Sophie immediately turned to Isabelle, like she had forgotten she was there until she piped up.

'Isabelle! Hi!' She smiled and nestled up to her like they were new girlfriends. 'So . . . are you having a nice time here in Ireland? It's a beautiful place all right! How long have you been here? What do you think of Irish men? Do you have those magnificent eyes on any one in particular?'

Sophie sounded like Cilla Black, the way she was chatting away, full of charm with the big fake smile. She had clearly missed her calling as a dating-game-show host.

'Oh yes, Irish men are wonderful, so friendly and kind,' Isabelle replied politely. 'I've been seeing Rory for a while now, but he has been in Dublin the past few weeks which has been sad for me. But he is back now! We are having fabulous sex.'

'You're having great sex with Rory? That's wonderful!' I chimed in, perhaps a little bit too enthusiastically.

Sophie nodded, her Avatar Eyes open wide as though this was the most interesting, important thing she had ever heard. And she certainly wasn't subtle about it. She kept looking back around at me and winking dramatically. I swallowed my giggles.

'So no interest in Fred then, no?'

'Oh no! Fred is like my bruzzer. Freddie is like family to me! And he is not my type at all, too scruffy for me. He is lovely though, very respectful. He doesn't hit on me like ze ozzer men. I think actually maybe he is gay.'

I felt myself stiffen and I knew Sophie sensed it off me. Given my history with men, this was probably the most sickening blow she could have delivered, right to my gut. I wanted to punch her annoyingly perfect face. Even more than I did when I thought they were fucking. And I was disgusted to think she would do that sexual grindy dancing she had done in Karma with someone she thought of as a brother!

Sophie had the good sense to diffuse the situation and distract me immediately. She turned back to me. 'Oh! I texted my cousin Sam and he's going to meet us at Halo, with a few of his friends. And he's bringing pills.'

'Soph. No pills.'

'I'm joking!' she smiled. 'Or am I?' She raised her eyebrows, and twisted her mouth into an evil grin. 'Maybe I'll slip you a little something . . . "*Do you really know your friends?*"' she said in a deep voice, mimicking a government 'party safely' TV ad.

I was suspicious Sunday afternoon when I woke up with a relatively un-hung-over head. I was praising and thanking the hangover gods for their mercy when I remembered that it was mostly due to my own sensible behaviour. I patted myself on the back as I headed down the stairs. I had stopped drinking shortly after arriving in Galway, much to Sophie's dismay. But I figured one of us needed to be responsible. We weren't hugely familiar with Galway and we were going to have to get ourselves back to Ballytiernan safely. It was the right decision, because Sophie, as I had predicted, had descended down a messy slope. It turned out her cousin Sam was a very bad influence.

I knew Sophie was not going to be impressed with my chirpiness, so I decided to ease her pain by making a big dirty fry-up.

I set the table all pretty and romantic. I got a flower from the front garden, popped it into a vase, and wrapped up the cutlery in lovely summery floral serviettes. I had the sausages, rashers, big fat mushrooms and eggs sizzling on the pan when Sophie trudged into the kitchen, groggily, like a cartoon dog, sniffing the air and following wafting food-smell lines. For the first time since she arrived, I can honestly say she looked a total mess. Her hair was all over the shop, wiry little bits poking up at bizarre angles out of her head, and her Avatar Eyes were now replaced with big black smudgy panda eyes.

'You look hot.' I gave her a gentle little kiss on the cheek. '"Get the Ballytiernan look!"' I mimicked another TV ad.

'Have I ever told you that you are the world's best housewifey?' she croaked, taking her place at the table, with a plate full of greasy, salty deliciousness in front of her.

'I'm too good,' I agreed. 'Sometimes I even surprise myself with my own goodness.' I poured her some orange juice.

She took a big glug and did a massive whopper burp.

'Classy bird,' I remarked. She waved her hand in front of her face as though to get rid of the smell.

'Burps don't smell,' I laughed.

'That one smelt of vodka,' she replied grimly.

'*Eew!* "Get the Ballytiernan-breath smell . . ."' I used the seductive British ad voice again.

'Oh Katie, don't make me laugh . . . my head is splitting.'

'Well, get these Paracetamol into you because I need my wingwoman in top form for Farrelly's trad session tonight.' I raised my eyebrows, with a big fake encouraging smile.

We flopped onto the couch after devouring the fry, and groaned simultaneously. Sasha chomped away on the leftover gristle in her bowl, purring loudly like the happiest cat in the world.

Then all three of us snuggled up together on the couch with our full bellies and snoozed for the rest of the day, with the *EastEnders Omnibus* creating atmospheric background noise.

Chapter 16

I used a lot of Sophie's eyeliner that night because, for whatever reason, I was feeling kind of punky and rebellious. There was a new Katie in town, the kind of girl who went after things and got them. And rode them. By things I meant Fred, obviously. I caked my lashes in mascara to complete the look. I glanced over at Sophie through the mirror and thankfully the panda eyes were gone. She had managed to dig out a sparkly River Island cami top I'd forgotten I had, and of course it looked way better on her anyway.

Sophie proposed a deal with me as I locked up Winnipeg.

'I get to keep this top if you have sex with Fred tonight!'

'It's not going to happen!' I protested feebly. 'I'm not that kind of girl!' Who was I kidding? When it came to Fred, I didn't honestly feel I had any control over my actions at all. I was pretty sure I was whatever kind of girl he wanted me to be. I scolded myself for not being more of a strong independent woman.

Sophie laughed at me. She had no faith in my resolve at all.

'Say goodbye to it now, beeatch!' And she pranced down the path wiggling her bum.

Tonight we were in Converse as blisters had consumed all four of our collective feet.

'I'm glad I'm not in heels today – this walk is a bitch,' Sophie moaned. We weren't even halfway to the village yet. 'You need to get yourself a motor vehicle, girl,' she said, putting on a voice that sounded remarkably like Jim's.

I could hear "Whiskey in the Jar" blasting out of Farrelly's from half a mile down the road.

I spotted Fred immediately when we got in the door. He was sitting at a table near the wall with Rory, Isabelle, and a few other lads. It was lovely to see him not working. There was something so calm and sexy about him. One of the guys he was with looked like an older version of him and I was sure it must be his brother, Seán. My childhood crush. He was still pretty rideable, but Fred was the one responsible for the butterflies in my stomach. I smiled over at him and moved in that direction, but Sophie grabbed my arm and pulled me towards the bar. She leaned in close to me, 'I think you're going after the wrong sibling, Katie. Fred's brother is *foxy!*'

Jim came over. 'Hiya, girls! How are the heads after last night?'

'Ah sure, we're getting back on the horse, aren't we?' I fake-laughed politely and ordered two drinks.

I sneaked a quick glance back at Seán. He was similar to Fred, but without the scar and crooked nose. Although he was clearly older, he was far less scruffy and rough around the edges. He seemed more of a city boy. But Fred's scruffiness was refreshing. After spending years in New York, where almost every man had tweezed eyebrows, got regular manicures and frequent back, sack and crack waxes, it was refreshing to be around a man who didn't obsess over how he looked. I couldn't have imagined that I'd be attracted to someone so totally unlike Seb. Although it seemed unfair to describe Fred as scruffy tonight. He was wearing a white linen shirt, with a white T-shirt underneath, which set off a sun-kissed glow he had gradually built up from working out in the field. I smiled to myself, thinking about the white Irish farmer torso hidden underneath.

Rory and Fred had pulled over two more stools to their table while we were getting our drinks at the bar, and Fred immediately introduced us to Seán as we sat down. Seán didn't seem to waste any time giving my blonde sidekick the mince pies. Although in typical Irish lad fashion he wasn't going to make any moves until he was plastered, if at all.

After countless tequilas and sambucas, followed by a fairly haphazard but nevertheless compelling impromptu rendition of the *Riverdance*, we collapsed down onto the stools and benches at our table. Seán was somehow still doing a somewhat accurate impression of Michael Flatley with his arms spread out and his toes pointed, legs flying. I was exhausted from my own fairly exerting moves, but couldn't stop laughing watching him.

'I still have to prank Billy Goat,' Sophie whispered, her voice slightly squeaky as it usually got when she was drunk.

'No, Soph!' I groaned. I'd been hoping she had forgotten about it.

I looked over at the table where Billy was sitting with his cronies. Of course, he was looking annoyingly conceited, with his beanie hat and ridiculous moustache, which was collecting froth from the head of his beer. It was ever so tempting to let Sophie do her worst, just to wipe the smugness off his face. But I had never been a fan of pranks. They made me nervous.

'Just a silly little prank,' she said with a wave of her hand. 'You don't have to be involved. I don't need you anyway. I have an idea. Where's Isabelle?'

'Why do you want Isabelle and not me?' I said, slightly huffy.

'Her assets are much more useful than yours.' With that she got up and headed over to Isabelle who was at the bar with Rory.

She seemed to be saying something really interesting, and they all seemed like they were having great *craic* conspiring together. I started to feel a little left out. Obviously, I knew I was being idiotic. I was taking a sip of my pint when Fred slid in beside me.

'Have you always drunk a pint of beer with a straw?'

'Yes. It means I don't have to get my hand all cold lifting it to my mouth.'

'Gets you drunk faster too, you know?' he laughed.

I nodded and shrugged my shoulders. 'Additional benefit.'

My hand was on the bench at my side. He put his hand down by his side in a mirroring manner, and his little finger touched mine. It stayed there next to mine sending tingles from my little finger down into my toes.

'Where's Luigi?' I asked. Seán was known as the Luigi to Fred's Mario.

'He's outside smoking.' He looked away. For the first time all night I saw his happiness fade slightly.

'Everything okay?' I asked gently.

He looked back around at me and sighed wearily. 'I'll tell you something, Katie, it's great having him here but . . . I'm kind of pissed off with him.'

I'd never seen him serious like this before.

'He only started smoking in the last few months, and I just *cannot* understand it.'

I looked at him blankly. I knew smoking was unhealthy but I wasn't sure why he was taking it so badly.

'Oh sorry, you probably don't know. Our dad died of lung cancer last year –he used to smoke a minimum of forty cigarettes a day.' He exhaled solemnly. 'Why would he take it up all of a sudden after years of not smoking? It's bonkers.'

I instinctively put my hand on his knee. Strangely it felt all right so I left it there. 'I'm so sorry, Fred. No, I didn't know that. I should have known. My head does be up in the clouds sometimes. I'm so sorry . . . that must be really hard for you.'

'Yeah,' he nodded. 'Don't worry. You couldn't have known. No one around here talks about stuff. Myself included.' He looked up at me and pressed his lips together in a sad smile.

I suddenly became aware of my hand on his knee, and felt like my palm was sweating or something, so I removed it and reached for the beer mat in front of me, as though I suddenly needed it for something. We were silent together for a few moments. I started absentmindedly tearing little pieces off the beer mat, and looking over at Sophie, still deep in conversation with Isabelle.

'You know what they say about someone tearing up beer mats?' he smirked.

'No.' I could now feel the edge of his hand barely touching the outside of my thigh. It was like it just grazed my skin lightly but then stayed there tentatively. I could feel goose bumps forming on my thighs and the little fair hairs there were standing up. I could almost hear my heartbeat.

'Well, I'm not saying it's true or anything, but they do say it's a sign of sexual frustration.'

I slapped his arm playfully.

'Oh . . . hang on . . .' I took hold of his forearm.

Sophie was on the move and I was grateful for the distraction. Of course I was probably sexually frustrated, in fact he was spot on, but I wasn't going to admit that. Especially considering my 'just fuck me' comment from the other night. It was just too pathetic.

'Watch this,' I said quietly, glad to change the subject. My eyes were fixed on Sophie. Fred followed my gaze.

Sophie sat down beside Billy, a big flirtatious smile plastered onto her face, and started making small talk, and fake-laughing, no doubt at his stupid innuendos.

'Why are we watching this?' Fred whispered.

I found his hand under the table and squeezed it, then quickly removed my hand gently and flashed him a sly smile.

A few minutes later, it must have been Isabelle's cue, because she strutted over to the other side of the table, like a Victoria's Secret model. Her silky hair swished mesmerisingly, and her boobs bounced lightly, drawing the undivided attention of everyone at the table. Right then she could have asked all of them to cut off their right hands and they would have willingly done it without batting an eyelid. But instead she leaned over with her hands on the table, pushing her luscious big boobies together with the biceps part of her arms. I definitely saw more than one lad cross his legs under the table.

The moment she was sure every one of them was completely hooked on Isabelle, Sophie whipped something out of her pocket. From where I sat I could just about make out what was in her hand – the salt, pepper and vinegar sachets we kept in jars on the tables of the pub. She tore them open and quickly poured them into Billy's pint. Within seconds, his pint fizzed up and exploded. It was overflowing.

Billy's reaction was priceless. He picked it up to try drink the overflowing beer – probably didn't want to lose a drop, the tight bollix – but his face contorted with disgust from the taste of it and he spat it out. Meanwhile the frothing liquid was spilling down onto his crotch. It couldn't have worked better. He jumped up and slammed the pint back on the table. He looked like he had wet himself. It was priceless. Everyone around was howling with laughter.

Sophie had sneaked away the minute the deed was done, so as not to get herself wet from the overflow. She quietly rejoined our table and gave me a sly little high-five. Sophie always got away with these things. I always got caught, which probably explained why I was never keen to get involved. She was so stealthy and sneaky no one ever noticed her, and she looked so innocent no one ever pointed the finger in her direction. She was looking very pleased with herself now, and I had to admit I was proud of her work this time.

'How did you do that?' I asked.

'Just a little concoction I discovered back in university. I haven't tried it in ages so I'm kind of thrilled it worked so well,' she said, grinning.

Bemused, Fred looked from me to Sophie and back to me again. 'I know Billy deserves that for many reasons, but is there any one in particular? Or do you guys just do that sort of thing randomly for laughs? Should I be keeping an eye on my pint?'

I laughed. 'Well, it is actually the sort of thing Sophie might do for laughs. I'm not quite the genius mastermind she is. But no, this time it was payback.'

'For what he did to Katie in here on – whatever night it was,' Sophie pitched in.

'Monday, when he smacked my ass and outrageously implied that we had . . . yunno,' I finished, slightly embarrassed.

'Yeah, I sort of guessed that was a load of horseshit,' Fred answered.

'Spot on.' I shrugged, as though it was no big deal, but I was relieved. Hurrah, he didn't think I was a slut! I celebrated internally.

'I doubt anyone actually believed that,' Fred said matter-of-factly, making me want to grab his face and kiss it. 'Come on, you're way too good for Billy!'

'Yeah,' Sophie chirped. 'As if you'd go near Billy Goat, and that hairy slug on his face.'

'Well, anyway, I'll have to get you a drink for that very impressive display, Sophie! What will ye have, ladies?'

Seán arrived back when Fred was up at the bar.

'You girls having fun?' He flashed a mouth full of perfect white teeth. There was a slight smell of smoke off his breath all right.

'Well, you've certainly been keeping us all entertained with your fancy footwork – I don't see why you stopped,' Sophie cooed.

He smiled again. 'Fred has told me all about you, Katie. But I know nothing about you, Sophie. Hang on! Let me guess . . . You are . . . an astronomer? No! A marine biologist? An animal therapist? A jam-maker?'

Sophie giggled as he charmed her with his little guessing game.

But I was absorbed in my own thoughts. It had to be a good sign that Fred was telling his brother all about me. I looked over at him as he stood at the bar and my thoughts drifted back to our steamy moment in the shed the previous night.

I was feeling like a bit of a third wheeler with Sophie and Seán anyway so I decided to leave them to it and head over to Fred.

'Ah, just the woman I was looking for,' Fred announced. 'Give this a go.' He handed me what looked like a baby Guinness shot and I knocked it back, wincing.

'Standard baby Guinness?' I guessed.

'Close, but we added a little somethinsomethin. However, if I told you, I'd have to kill you.'

'It better not be a roofie – I could do without that.'

'What do you take me for, Katie? I'm a good honest man!'

'We'll see,' I said with a smirk.

Sophie was suddenly at my side, pulling my arm towards the dance-floor area.

The band had started playing a strange trad version of the Rubberbandits' song 'Horse Outside'. I caught Sophie's eye and we laughed at how funny the song sounded played by this trad band. It worked though. I mouthed 'come on' to Fred as I danced around with Sophie and Seán. I was glad I'd worn my Converse. He shook his head playfully so I ran over and grabbed him. I didn't let go of his hand for the whole song, except to applaud at the end. But he took my hand back in his almost immediately after we stopped clapping, and nodded his head towards the back door.

My stomach lurched.

We snuck out. We didn't go near the shed this time – it was all locked up. We just huddled behind the door, out of sight. I started to shiver. He put his arms around me. I sank into them.

'So,' he said, looking at me with those Daniel Craig eyes.

For some reason I was on my tippy-toes. We weren't quite eye-to-eye as this time I was in my Converse and not the six-inchers. But going up on my toes brought his eye level closer. He dropped his head down towards mine. I rested my forehead on his, and closed my eyes. My nose gently pressed against his. I felt a contented smile forming on my face. I wondered if he could feel the thumps of my heart beating.

'What's happening with us?' he finally said softly. He pulled his head back to look at me. I gave him a soft butterfly kiss. Then he looked like he'd been struck with a brainwave. 'Oh! We should go on a date! Would you like to go on a date with me?'

'You only thought of this now?' I laughed, plonking back down on my heels, gazing up at him.

'I've no idea what I'm doing to be honest,' he said, looking into my eyes. 'I'm a rookie at this lark. I was in a relationship for twelve years, from the age of sixteen, until . . . just over two months ago. You're the first person I've even been interested in since . . . her.' He looked away and avoided eye contact for a moment.

'Oh wow . . . Well, we're sort of in the same boat then . . . well, we're in two very similar boats anyway . . . well, kind of similar boats . . .' I trailed off. I didn't really want to kill the moment. Talking about exes was a sure passion-killer. I sensed things were still a bit raw for him anyway. He wasn't even able to say her name. Were we both carrying too much baggage for these boats? Were they going to sink? If only we could both get into one boat, put all the baggage in the other one, and push it away from us with the oar and let it drift off into the endless distance . . .

I needed to stop thinking about boats.

'Want me and Seán to walk you two home?' he asked, interrupting my thoughts. I looked at my watch and it was four in the morning. The music had stopped inside and people were on the move. I was actually surprised Jim had let it go on this long. But then the only two Gardaí in the village had been inside there all night pouring pints into their faces. And he was making pretty good money for a Sunday night, and our Jim wasn't one to look a gift horse in the mouth.

'Yeah, that would be nice,' I said.

He held open the door for me and we discreetly went inside. The lights were on and people were indeed clearing out. Jim looked exhausted and was finally shouting at everyone to 'get the fuck out, the lot of ye'.

Chapter 17

'Would you like to come in for a drink?' I asked as the four of us arrived at Winnipeg Cottage after singing the whole way from the village. The sides of my stomach were in stitches, aching from the laughter, as we had been making up the words to the songs as we went along. Seán and Fred were remarkably creative with lyrics, and Sophie came up with some crackers too. It was a good distraction from the cold. The early morning light made everything look blue and it felt colder than it probably was.

The lads agreed to come in – they needed to warm themselves anyway – and so we all bundled in the front door.

Fred immediately pulled Seán into the living room to see the paintings, as Sophie and I headed for the kitchen to get some drinks on the go and pop a pizza into the oven. I could hear Seán and Fred roar laughing inside. I felt a little bit embarrassed hearing them laughing, although I knew they wouldn't be laughing in a nasty way. But I nevertheless felt a bit uneasy. I was too exhausted to go find out exactly what they were laughing at. I was too exhausted and content to care. All I wanted now was food. I tore open some Dr. Oatker bad boys and stuck them in the oven. I told my stomach to stop rumbling – the pizza would take at least twenty minutes. Sophie was more focused on drink. She baffled me. She made a big jug of some potent cocktail, and skipped off into the living room. I got four glasses out and joined them.

'Katie! What do the ladies of Ballytiernan think of this little project?' Seán took a sip of his drink and winced.

'Well, they don't know about it really.' I shrugged.

'You better hope it stays that way. They're a different breed, these ones – I wouldn't cross them.'

'Ah Seán, don't be talking shit!' Fred interjected. 'It's the twenty-first century!'

'Not in Ballytiernan, it's not.' Seán took a sweet out of the little bowl on the side table and unwrapped it. 'It's the Middle-shaggin'-Ages around here, so it is.' He popped the sweet into his mouth and sucked it. He looked at Sophie and me. 'I hit the road as soon as I could drive, and got as far away as I could.'

'What are you talking about? You only got as far as Dublin.' Fred laughed. 'He's just trying to upset you because he's offended you haven't asked him to be in one of your paintings, Katie!'

'Indeed I am!' Seán started undressing. 'Prepare yourselves, ladies – this is a hot commodity. Smokin' hot. Brought to you all the way from the big smoke.'

It would have been a bit uncomfortable to watch if it hadn't been so funny. He got his head stuck in his jumper and, instead of sorting it out, he got impatient and hastily started taking off his jeans, then lost balance and fell back into the fireplace.

By that time there were tears streaming down my face – I was in convulsions of laughter. Sophie had her camera phone out, recording him.

Fred went over to pull him out, but then let go of his hand, and Seán fell back in, a cloud of soot puffing out, smothering him. We all erupted with laughter again.

An hour later Seán was asleep in the fireplace, not having managed to ever get himself out. Sophie was out cold, spread-eagled on the couch, her face mushed into one of my lilac crochet cushions.

Fred and I were lying on the rug, talking.

'What's his name – Seb – Sebastian?' he asked, his nose crumpled.

I nodded. 'Like the lobster in *The Little Mermaid*.'

'Sebastian what?'

'I don't want to say because you'll laugh.' I smirked, although I did feel slightly guilty sharing a laugh at Seb's expense. His surname was ridiculously unfortunate.

'Well, you have to tell me now!' He grinned.

'Sebastian Lilicrap,' I muttered.

'No way! Seriously? It's kind of a flamboyant name, isn't it? If it weren't for the fact that he's your ex, I would definitely presume he was gay with a name like that. I'd even offer to set him up with Salty O'Brien, the queen of Ballytiernan.'

My face went bright red. I contemplated not telling him but it would probably pop up again and I'd eventually have to explain. Everything comes out in the laundry, as my granddad used to say.

'Actually . . . he *is* gay.' I decided to rip off the Band-Aid in one go.

He couldn't seem to find any response. Perhaps he was wondering if I was pulling his leg or if I was actually serious. So I rambled on, filling the silence. 'So that's my story. There it is. I was in a relationship for three years with a gay man named Sebastian Lilicrap. And I had no idea he was gay, even though it was right there like a big pink flag waving in front of my face. His name should probably have given the game away in the first place, but no. I was oblivious. You better not be in the closet yourself. I really don't think I could handle that.' I bit hard on my bottom lip to stop myself from crying.

'You want proof I'm not gay?' Fred grinned like a cheeky

schoolboy and pressed his boner into my hip.

I giggled and moved away coyly. 'I think I'm going to need more evidence than that,' I whispered and smiled, shuffling closer to him. I noticed glimmers on my eyelashes and realised a few tears had in fact escaped. I swiped them away.

We fell silent. Fred lifted his hand to my face and put my hair behind my ear. I kissed his lovely wonky nose and smiled. My face was flushed and didn't seem to be calming down. His hand found mine, and his fingers laced in through my fingers.

'Do you know I used to dream about holding your hand when I was a kid?' he said bashfully.

'Seriously?' My eyes widened.

'Yeah, you were so pretty and cool. Coming down from the city in your dad's Porsche – I'd never seen anything like it down here. You had such an interesting life and so many great stories . . . and you were just the prettiest girl I'd ever seen. No other girl even compared.'

'As if! I know for a fact that is bullshit!' I couldn't believe what I was hearing. Growing up I was absolutely never the prettiest girl . . . anywhere. I was a freckly red-haired girl, and I was always too tall and too skinny. I know they sound like good things now but as a kid it makes you stick out like a sore thumb, and it makes you cripplingly awkward. Boys never fancied me in school. They were always my friends but absolutely never wanted to be my boyfriends.

'Wow, you're really terrible at taking a compliment.' He looked a little taken aback.

I softened. 'Sorry. You don't really mean it though.'

'I do! I had a massive crush on you. I can't believe you didn't know it. You think I would make it up?'

'Oh.' I bit my lip, a little embarrassed. 'I thought maybe you were just saying that to get into my pants or something.' I smiled softly.

'Well, I swear it's true. Cross my heart hope to die. Pinkie swear?' He held out his pinkie finger in between us and I grinned as I linked mine through it, just like we did when we were kids. 'But if I'm absolutely honest, I wouldn't mind getting into your pants too,' he smirked.

'Cheeky!' I sat up. 'So . . . do you want a tour of the upstairs of the house?' I was trying to remember if my room was tidy. I decided to go for it anyway – I could always blame it on Sophie.

'Lead on,' said Fred.

Up we went and I showed him around.

'Ha!' he chuckled. 'So you have a spare bedroom, but you and Sophie are sharing a bed?' He raised his eyebrows.

'It goes no further than a little bit of spooning! Honestly!' I insisted. 'Don't go getting any ideas.'

'I'm getting lots of ideas. But they don't involve Sophie or spooning,' he said, gently placing his hands on my hips.

'Maybe some forking?' I suggested brazenly, biting my lip.

'Hmm . . . forking sounds good.' He pulled me in to him, his fingers grazing my thighs as they found the end of my dress and lifted it over my head. I stood there in my favourite Victoria Secret barely-there silver lace bra and pants. I hadn't worn them since New York, and it felt great to be back in them. They were fairly loose so my belly only dipped over the top a tiny bit.

He looked me up and down as his eyes darkened.

'You're beautiful,' he sighed and hooked his index finger into the waistband of my knickers. Then, as he gently kissed me, they floated to the floor.

Chapter 18

I opened my eyes, drifting gradually out of deep sleep, and focused them on the clock beside my bed. Thirteen hundred hours. I could barely move a muscle. I twitched my toes under the soft yellow cotton duvet, and it took all the effort I could muster to roll over to cuddle the pillow on the other side of the bed, as I did most mornings. I found a man there. In my fuzziness I momentarily thought it was Seb. My heart lurched with a bizarre deep warm contentment, which was suddenly replaced with overwhelming longing and sadness when I remembered he was in America and I was in Ireland. Then I was confused. Why were thoughts of Seb even entering my mind? I turned back over on my back and stared at the bumpy textured ceiling. I felt terribly guilty thinking about Seb whilst lying there beside Fred. I peeked over at him; he looked so peaceful and handsome.

Then the thought struck me. Maybe Fred would feel the same way when he woke up and saw me. Maybe he would pine for his ex and regret seeing my face. The thought of that happening was too much to bear so I quietly got up, covering myself with a throw, and hopped around trying to silently dress myself without waking him. Naturally, in my haste I tripped over my laptop cord and stumbled into my closet.

'What are you doing?'

I looked around and Fred was sitting up in the bed, chewing a mint and smirking, mildly entertained.

'What the hell? You were comatose a second ago.' I stumbled around, untangling my foot with a shocking lack of grace or elegance. I became panicked. I was growing more and more aware of my very white arse, which was very exposed in the unforgiving morning light. I grabbed the first item I could find from my underwear drawer. A pair of those massive off-white granny pants that a lady should never wear unless it's her period, and even then they should be a last resort. I quickly shoved it back in the drawer and rooted around frantically in search of something more feminine. I wondered was there a way to stand while rooting in a drawer, butt-naked, that was in any way sexy? Was there any possible angle I could position myself in whereby my ass wouldn't look hideous? I finally found a little pair of pink hot pants and said a little prayer of thanks to the God of Underwear as I hurriedly stuck my feet in and pulled them up. Relief flooded over me once my bottom was snug inside the fabric. Hot pants were always a happy option. They concealed more than most knickers and were still cute and sexy. However this little pair did have a cartoon kitten on the front and 'Paws Off' written on the back. Not exactly sexy sophisticated attire, but nonetheless it was material, which would hide my bottom.

'You going somewhere?' he enquired nonchalantly.

'Oh em . . . just getting up. Out and about. Early bird catches the worm, you know?' I said with surprising enthusiasm. I sounded like an idiot. It wasn't even early, and I wasn't going out anywhere.

'Aha! But the second mouse gets the cheese?' He winked and sank back into the pillows. 'Relax – it's a Bank Holiday Monday.'

'I like that.' I sat tentatively on the edge of the bed. 'The poor first mouse though! What a tragic outcome for him . . .'

He tugged me back towards him, and I let out a sigh as I leaned back.

'Can I have one of those mints?' The last thing I needed now after all the cruel morning daylight ass-exposure was morning breath. I popped one into my mouth.

Sasha was scratching at the bedroom door so I got up to let her in, although she was probably after food, not a front-row seat to the screening of *Awkward Morning-After Conversations* starring Katie and Fred.

He laughed at my bum as I made my way to the door.

'Bit too late for those pants now,' he remarked.

Sasha's demanding meow was followed by the sound of Sophie and Seán trudging up the stairs.

So there were three hungry creatures at the door when I opened it.

Seán winked, and with a big messy hung-over grin said, 'Nice one, bro!'

Sophie pointed at her mouth with her paw, referencing our favourite YouTube hit, *Simon's Cat*. In the videos the cat wakes Simon up in various merciless ways and once he succeeds he points to his mouth and meows, demanding to be fed. I gathered Sophie and Seán were also demanding to be fed.

We plodded down to fill our bellies with grub.

'There's chimney soot all over your head, Seánie!' Fred was laughing at Seán, who looked baffled.

Sophie took out her camera to refresh his memory.

'Oh yeah, I remember waking up there at some stage with a majorly stiff back and moving onto the armchair. My back is in bits.'

I threw together some pancake mixture and soon started flipping them on the pan.

'So, Seán, I hope despite your sore back you're still up for stripping off for the sake of my art?' I glanced around at him.

'You still going on with that project? You really must have a death wish, girl. Does Mo know about Gerry's one?'

'I don't think so, no.'

'That woman would hit the roof. And she is all sorts of evil. You might want to be a bit more careful about whose husband you go after, Katie – that's all I'm saying.'

'Okay!' I smiled cheerfully. 'Then I better stick to free and easy young lads like yourself!' I winked. 'I'll give you an extra large pancake.'

Naturally he couldn't say no because my pancakes were starting to smell like the most heavenly thing on earth, and all our tummies were grumbling expectantly.

We polished off every scrap and Sophie quickly came to life, getting very excited about styling Seán's shoot. He was starting to look apprehensive when she appeared down the stairs with a feather boa.

'Seán, daaaahling, I think you'll look just divine in –'

'Hold on, I don't know about this . . . Listen, I have to come clean. I'm not even technically a farmer, and I don't live in Ballytiernan any more, so it would be a bit of a lie to include me. I wouldn't want to taint your collection with a big lie like that.'

Fred quickly quashed his feeble objections. 'You're more of a farmer than Billy the Bollix. It's not supposed to be just farmers anyway, it's the men of Ballytiernan and you are definitely a man of Ballytiernan. There's no backing out now – we're all very excited to see this hot commodity you were telling us all about last night. It's not too late to get down and do a few press-ups if you're feeling inadequate.'

Seán moaned and ran his fingers through his hair. Press-ups did sound horrific, the state we were all in. We nursed some coffees while Sophie ran around, in and out of the back door with the energy of a six-year-old child on Christmas Day. I didn't know where she got it from. I myself was sorely tempted to drag Fred back up the stairs and crawl back into bed with him and get some long overdue man cuddles back in my life.

Sophie beckoned us outside, where she had organised the set for our shoot. It was a slightly insane creation. She had basically brought the indoors out, in a bizarre medley of farmyard-meets-living-room. There was an old standing lamp with tassels, two tall Chinese vases on coffee tables, Sasha's antique Draylon armchair (Sasha still sitting on it looking very perplexed), my granddad's old ornate antique rug which Fred and I had been lying on last night, and various other ridiculous accessories, including a side table with a bottle of whiskey on it, which Seán didn't hesitate to take a swig of.

And then there were hay bales. Sophie had robbed the hay bales from Dennis Daly's field. Don't even ask how she managed to roll them all the way over on her own. The girl was bonkers, with insane strength for a tiny person too. On her way back through she'd left the gate separating the two fields open and one of Dennis's sheep had wandered onto our set. The overall look was all bit headachy, but I was keen to get it done and return the borrowed/wandered items as soon as possible. I could always edit things out in the painting.

As I was standing in the field watching Sophie with bemused respect, I felt a shiver run down my spine. Strange, as I wasn't cold. I had this uneasy feeling that we weren't alone, and it wasn't the stray sheep that was bothering me. There was something else. We had an unwanted audience. I was sure of it. As Seán began to undress, Sophie took my camera to take test shots. She didn't seem to have any shame snapping away as Seán shuffled from foot to foot looking very uncomfortable. I was thankful for her though because I knew that if anyone would have the magic ability to loosen him up a bit it would be Sophie.

While all this was happening I went for a little stroll around the garden. My Spidey senses were tingling. I peeked around the corner at the back of the cottage, keeping my body close to the pebbledash wall, and I spotted her. A little old woman with a walking stick and silver hair in tight curls was snooping around the side of the cottage, trying to get a look at what was going on in the garden. I recognised her sour little face – she was a regular at Farrelly's Bingo Night. She always sat with Mo and never once cracked a smile.

I coughed loudly and looked back around at where she was. She was scampering away, as fast as her thin wobbly legs would allow.

Fred was really enjoying Seán's reluctance and discomfort. He had a big grin on his face as Seán shivered in the breeze, lifting a pile of hay over his head, one of the Chinese vases perfectly positioned to protect his modesty. It looked good but something was missing.

'I know what's missing!' Sophie exclaimed, as though reading my mind. 'This would look way better with both of you!' She looked over expectantly at Fred. 'Oh please, please, please!'

The smile vanished from his face. 'Eh,' he muttered. 'I wouldn't want to steal his thunder now . . .'

'Well, there *are* two vases,' I agreed.

We pushed him, and he couldn't really say no after all the stick he'd given Seán. He joined his brother, grumbling about how cold it was, grabbed the whiskey bottle off him and downed about a third of it. He got into position behind the other vase and the overall result was absolutely brilliant. They looked hilarious. The grumpy faces made it. The whole thing looked gloriously awkward.

The lads finally left Winnipeg, minus their dignity. Fred gave me a little peck on the lips on his way out the door and whispered in my ear that he would get me back. Even though it was a joke threat my tummy flip-flopped and my toes wiggled. We shut the door laughing and Sophie demanded I tell her everything about getting back on the horse, and more importantly my first time with a straight man in over three years. I told her what he said about dreaming about holding my hand when we were kids.

'That's actually the sweetest thing I've ever heard,' she breathed.

I had to admit it was adorable and, more than that, it was a massive turn-on.

I adopted an old lady voice: 'Katie, says I to myself, you'd be mad not to ride this lad.' We fell about laughing.

After dragging every inappropriate detail of the night out of me, she retired upstairs to take a shower and I got down to work on the new painting. It was all starting to look like a proper collection at last! I nestled my new scene with the Flanagan brothers right into a busy painting of Canal Street in Chinatown, downtown Manhattan. It was the biggest, and probably the most impressive painting of the old collection. So much was happening in it, as there always is on Canal Street, and the guys in the middle just added to the mayhem. But it was going to be the most spectacular of the lot, I could tell already – the madness, the awkwardness, the frivolity. I hadn't started it yet, but already in my head it was comparable to Renoir's *Le Moulin de la Galette*, except a modern-day Manhattan version – on acid.

It was a lovely quiet Bank Holiday Monday. I was content to be working away. However, despite my physical contentment – owing to a mind-blowing night with Fred – I had a slightly anxious worry on my mind. I couldn't put my finger on what it was and, oddly, Sophie was quieter than usual, wandering around the cottage in a trance, which also gave me the niggling feeling something wasn't right.

I awoke bright and early the next morning. I left Sophie in bed because, from all the tossing and turning she had been doing throughout the night, I had the feeling she hadn't slept much.

By midday I was mixing paints again, slapping them on

canvases and munching on a packet of Taytos, when Sophie arrived into the living room, her big Avatar Eyes brimming with tears. Her face looked an odd greenish colour. I sat her down immediately.

'Soph, what is it?' I gaped, kneeling in front of her, holding her knees.

'Idunnowatdadooooo!' she blubbered, and blew her nose into an already damp, snotty tissue clenched in her fist. She sobbed and gasped and I made a concentrated effort to understand the words she was mumbling. I finally managed to understand the conclusion: 'I' – *gasp* – 'think' – *gasp* – 'I'm' – *gasp* – 'pregnant!'

Chapter 19

'Pregnant? Sophie! Are you sure?'

She sniffled and nodded.

'How sure?' I asked.

'I haven't had a period for over two months now,' she sniffed. 'And I've been throwing up a lot this morning.' She looked up at me, her eyes wide. 'This can't happen now, Katie, it really can't. I mean, I'm not even sure who the dad would be. God, what am I like?'

'Oh shit.' I hadn't even thought of that. I'd been thinking: why in God's name have we been drinking so much if she had this in the back of her mind? She must have been in denial. I decided it wouldn't do any good to scold her now. 'Really? Surely it has to be Chris's. Obi was just a once-off and you used protection, right?'

'Yes! Of course! Well no, maybe not. I'm not sure . . . I dunno. I dunno. I dunno.' She buried her face in a big soft cushion and groaned. 'I think we did?' She looked up helplessly.

I tried to be a good friend and not flinch at the sight of her snot and mascara and general blubber all over my lovely cushion. The Avatar Eyes had turned into panda eyes once again.

'Okay.' I stood up. 'Before we get carried away I'm just going to pop down to the pharmacy and pick up a pregnancy test. Try to relax – it might just be a false alarm. Stick on the telly there and distract yourself.'

I exhaled as I closed the door of the cottage behind me. I was worried about Sophie. A child is always a great thing, but not knowing who the dad is could be a bit embarrassing, and she wasn't really in the right place in her life for a baby. She still seemed like a child herself.

I popped up my umbrella even though it was only drizzling, and headed off. Leahy's pharmacy wasn't too far, just on this side of the village, so I got there in about ten minutes. I shook off the umbrella when I entered and tried to make myself as inconspicuous as possible, a pretty pointless effort in such a tiny little store. Leahy's pharmacy was old, with everything crammed in together behind the counter, from hairbrushes to plasters to all sorts of pots and potions with tiny labels. My eyes scanned the walls hurriedly. I was hoping it would be old Eamonn Leahy working today – he never paid any attention to what you were buying, just glanced at it, made up whatever price came into his head, and off you went. But his wife was a different kettle of fish all together.

Just my luck, Ellen Leahy appeared from the little room behind, her white hair wrapped up tightly in little pink rollers. She looked at me over the top of her reading glasses with her thin lips pulled together in a tight smirk. She was clearly enjoying my obvious discomfort and I just knew she was going to relish telling every auld one in the village what I came in for. I hated giving her the satisfaction but I had no choice. Ballytiernan didn't offer a selection of pharmacies.

I bit the bullet.

'Hi, Mrs Leahy, could I have one of those Clearblues there, please?' I pointed to the pregnancy tests and looked at her firmly. Daring her to try and make a thing of this. I really was not in the humour.

'Of course, my dear. The pregnancy test, is it?' She stood there, her eyes boring through me, her mouth turning up at the corners.

I gritted my teeth. 'Yes, please.'

'Oh right, I see. We've had a little woopsies, have we?'

I didn't want to answer. But I hated giving her this satisfaction.

'A friend, I'm afraid, yes.' I smiled thinly back at her.

'Of course . . . a *friend*.'

What a bitch!

She took forever to unlock the cabinet, but finally she took the test out, enjoying every minute. 'I think this one is six ninety-nine,' she said slowly, still holding the box in front of her. 'Or is it seven ninety-nine?'

I snatched it out of her hands, perhaps a little too roughly, threw eight euro down on the counter, delighted I had correct change, and high-tailed it out of there.

I darted around the corner of Leahy's and *wham*, smacked into Fred, who was walking Bessie and accompanied by a little boy of about eight and a little girl roughly two years younger – I recognised them from the photo stuck to his fridge. The boy bent down and picked up the Clearblue box, which was sitting in a puddle at the kerb. I nearly died. Fred's eyes suddenly widened, but he immediately checked himself and looked back at me as if he hadn't noticed. Good thing he was a farmer and not an actor. The boy handed me the box, which I shoved hastily into my handbag.

'Hi!' I forced a wide smile.

'Katie, how are things? This is Conor and that's Emily, Evie's kids. Guys, this is my friend Katie.'

'Hello,' they chimed together.

'My Uncle Seán promised to take us to the Aquarium today but he's too hung-over to drive,' Conor told me matter-of-factly. 'So he's taking us tomorrow instead.'

'Oh, that sounds like fun!' I smiled. 'Do you like sea creatures?'

'Yes. But Emily will be scared.'

Bessie had her leg cocked against the tree and was doing her business. Emily looked on in disgust.

'Fred?' She tugged the end of his jacket. 'That's eight pisses Bessie's done since we left,' she announced with her nose scrunched.

Fred and I laughed awkwardly and I told him I had to hurry back. I waved goodbye as I briskly walked away from them.

When I arrived home, I found Sophie staring at the telly with her mouth open, in a transfixed state of shock. She had somehow found a channel showing *One Born Every Minute* or something of that nature.

'Oh my God, Soph!' I rushed over and switched it off. 'I thought you'd find an episode of *Friends* or something – what the hell are you watching that for?'

She responded with a blank stare. Her mouth was open and snot was running down into it in little streams from her nostrils. It was a pretty worrying sight.

'Here, go pee on this.' I thrust the soggy blue box at her.

'Why is it wet?' she asked, blinking slowly.

'It just fell in a puddle, it's grand, go on!'

I sat on the couch nervously as she trotted off, still a bit zoned out. I found myself biting my nails, something I hadn't done since I was thirteen.

'*Katieeeeeeeee!*' Sophie summoned me.

'Will I come in?' I asked from outside the loo.

'Mm-hmm,' she responded.

I pushed the door open and she was sitting on the loo, staring bewildered at the stick. 'What does it mean?' Her lip quivered.

I gently took the test out of her hand. There was a very clear plus sign on it. Oh dear.

'Yep, you're pregnant.' I tried to smile encouragingly.

'Congratulations?' I finished quietly.

She took a deep shaky breath and started nodding her head slowly. I was anxiously flicking the test in my hand as if it was a Polaroid picture until I realised I was probably flinging pee everywhere. I dropped it in the sink and washed my hands.

'Pity they haven't invented pregnancy tests that tell you who the father is yet.' I had the unfortunate habit of making inappropriate comments when people were upset. 'Even if it told us the race of the baby, that would do the trick.' I laughed meekly. She put her head in her hands and sobbed. Tough crowd. I patted her back.

'Maybe let's get up off the loo, yeah?' I coaxed. 'I'll go down and pop on the kettle.'

As the kettle whistled I tried to think of what to say to Sophie, how to deal with the situation. I didn't even know where to start. I mean, if I was really honest, I was a teeny tiny bit excited; it would be nice to have a little baby around to play with. But the issue of the father made it all a bit tricky. It cast her as a bit of a slut, and Sophie really wasn't that – she never had been – maybe a flirt or a tease but never a slut.

Sophie followed me into the kitchen like a lost kitten. She stood in the middle of the tiles, her arms by her sides, rather hopelessly. She slowly looked up at me, gradually coming out of the trance she had been under for the past few minutes.

'What will I say if people ask who the dad is?'

'Just tell them you're not ready to talk about it yet, I suppose. It's none of their business anyway. Also I'd say people will just presume it's Chris's. So they mightn't even ask.'

'Oh God, what if they start congratulating him? That could be so awkward. And then what if he gets all excited about it and then a little black baby pops out?' Her large watery eyes looked like they were about to fall out of her head with exhaustion and exasperation.

Shit, this really was a mess. If only there actually *was* a pregnancy test that told you the father or the race. That could be an amazing new invention, I thought. Then Jeremy Kyle would be out of a job. But with technology today it must be possible! I reminded myself to copyright it later, and make a billion dollars. But now wasn't the time for that.

Who was it though? And would he want to be involved? I was fairly sure Chris would act like a dickhead about it. And Obi, as much as I liked him, I wouldn't exactly peg him as father material. Him and Sophie would make a very cute baby though. Obi was tall with chocolate-brown skin and dimples. All that with Sophie's big brown eyes would just be a recipe for cuteness overload.

'Maybe . . . I'm just going to pretend it's not happening.' She spoke softly and smiled a slightly deluded, manic, determined grin.

I cautiously handed her a cup of tea. 'In two weeks or so you'll be like three months along – that's when you start telling people. And you'll start to show at some point. You can't ignore this, Soph – in fact, you should probably go see your GP soon.'

Her face fell. 'Well, aren't you just a fountain of facts,' she muttered dryly. She slumped into a chair at the table defeatedly. Then she looked up at me, the crazy look back. 'Well, I'm only small. So I'll just have a teeny tiny baby and no one will see the bump because I'll dress to disguise it. And then the baby will be so small I'll hardly even notice labour – or I won't notice at all! It'll just plop out one day when I sneeze. Or into the loo when I'm trying to squeeze out a poo.' Her eyes went dark and cold, and she lowered her voice. 'And then I'll flush it. Like that lady in China.'

'Oh my goodness, don't even say that! That was absolutely horrific!' I stared at her in horror. I knew she wasn't really serious but she needed to pull herself together and start talking sense.

'I know, I'm sorry. I can't believe I even said that. That's so horrible. I would never do that. Obviously.'

We went quiet for a few minutes and she started to look normal again, if a little bit lost, as she stared into her half-empty teacup.

'Sorry, Soph.' I gently held her hand. 'But you know what? I know maybe it seems like the end of the world right now, but I think this is actually going to be a good thing. Imagine! A little baby to take care of! Imagine it was Obi's! We've always wanted mixed-race babies! Remember I used to dare you to go up to black men on the street and ask them if they wanted to have a mixed-race baby with you and you could call it Mixie?'

She cracked a smile despite her solemn mood. I just couldn't help laughing at the memory, and Sophie eventually joined me. 'But I never actually did it, did I?' she giggled.

'No, you chickened out,' I sighed, still smiling.

'I'm glad. It probably would have been considered racist.'

'True,' I agreed. 'We were kind of stupid.'

'And ignorant.' Sophie nodded.

A shadow of a smile still remained on Sophie's face as she rested her chin on her fist. She still held onto my hand with her other hand. It looked like her brain was working overtime. I could practically see the cogs turning frantically.

'All right, I do feel a bit guilty for not being happy about it. There are people who would give anything to be pregnant right now.' She sniffed. 'But honestly? I just don't think I'll be a good mom. I mean, for God's sake, I can't even provide the little zygote with a definite dad.'

We both laughed.

'Shut up!" I said. "This baby won the jackpot with you as its mother. Things may seem all over the place now but you'll find your feet, Soph, you always do. You'll take to motherhood like a fish to water. Come on, you've always had to be the best at everything you did, why would you stop now?' I gave her hand a squeeze.

We were silent again for a while and gradually she seemed to calm down a bit.

'So are you going to go back to New York?' I finally asked, blowing my tea.

'I don't think I should really. No. Well, eventually yes, but right now I think I'm going to need my mom. Looks like I'll probably be moving back to Dublin for a while.'

'You're welcome to stay here for as long as you need. Even when the baby comes. I could help! We could be like a modern lesbian family.'

'Ballytiernan is definitely not ready for that,' Sophie chuckled.

'Shag Ballytiernan. This village needs us to bring it into the twenty-first century. I think they'd secretly love it. They'd love the gossip. Come on! Stay here and let's be single moms together. Ballytiernan's first lesbian family. I'm pretty sure we'd make the front page of the *Ballytiernan Weekly Echo*.'

She smiled at me sombrely. 'Thanks, Katie, but it looks like I'm going to finally have to grow up and take some responsibility now. I'm going to Dublin tomorrow. See the GP and go forward from there.'

I knew she was right. She needed to go and see her parents and figure out what to do. And I was glad she was accepting reality.

'Katie! Shit!' Sophie gasped. 'I'm so sorry I won't be here for your birthday on Thursday. I know you never want a big deal, but I was going to make you a nice dinner . . . oh, and I have a present for you upstairs.'

'Don't be silly, Soph, that's the last thing that should be on your mind right now!'

She gave me a massive hug, as though I was the one who needed it and not her. I could feel her body weaken and she quietly started to sob again.

'I don't know where I'd be without you,' she said. 'I'm so glad I was with you finding all this out. No one understands me like my best friend.' Her eyes were like massive puffballs and I stroked her back.

'You're acting like a real emotional pregnant lady now! See, I told you you'd take to it like a fish to water!' I winked coyly and then we were quiet again for a while except for the sounds of us slurping the ends of our cups of tea.

'Are you going to tell the might-be dads?' I asked apprehensively.

'What do *you* think?' Sophie leaned towards me with her elbows on the table, hopeful that I would have the right answer.

'Well, you could tell them like that. "Congratulations! You're going to be a Might-Be Dad!"'

'Could you imagine their faces? Goodness, it's a big rotten mess I'm in.'

'I suppose it is a bit messy. But I can't tell you what to do. It's such a tricky situation. If you tell Chris, you're going to have to tell him he might not be the father, and that opens a whole other can of worms, especially if you tell him who the other possible dad is. And if you tell Obi . . . well, that's a big thing to tell a guy you don't really have much of a history with . . . especially if you're only fifty/fifty sure that it's his.' I took a breath and drank a gulp of tea. This wasn't particularly helpful. But I didn't know what was the right thing to say. 'So can I ask you a question?' I looked at her seriously and she nodded. 'Well, who do you really want the dad to be . . . and second question, deep down, who does your gut tell you it is?'

Instantly she replied, 'Obi.' Her mouth fell open. She looked like she couldn't believe what she had said. 'I mean, I don't know.' She twisted a loose blonde curl around her finger. 'I mean, neither of them really. If some magical super-dad could come along and claim my baby, and help me raise it, that would be fantastic. But if I had to pick . . . well, Chris is such a dick I don't want him in my life any more. Obi is less of a dick. Jeez . . . I have one lucky baby inside me.' She laughed. She rested her chin in her hand. 'And, yes, if I was to give you my best guess as to who the father was the answer would be Obi. Technically, I was probably more careless with him. With Chris, we were in a routine. I always made damn sure to strap him up or to obsessively take my pill on time. The thought of having a child with him terrified me because he was so unreliable. With Obi, I sort of threw caution to the wind a bit. I was super drunk. I don't really remember the condom part of the sex so I suppose if I don't remember it, it's possible it didn't happen. And I've been off the pill for the past while because it's making me fat. I know what you're thinking. This will make me a lot fatter, right?'

I nodded. That was exactly what I was thinking.

She smiled knowingly. 'I get the irony. It's funny though, I really never contemplated having anything at all to do with Obi. He's always just been one of Chris's mates. But he is different, you know. He's texted me a few times. It's weird, nothing too forward or intimate or anything, just asking how I am and stuff. I dunno, I think maybe he cares about me a little. Hmm. I guess I'm just not used to that. Chris hasn't even tried to get in touch since I left. With him it's always out of sight, out of mind.'

I didn't want to be smug about it (especially considering my history with Seb, I was hardly one to act the know-it-all about men) but I knew all along that Obi was different. I just got a good vibe off him, despite his Geordie accent. Or maybe because of it. The accent was endearing really, and it always surprised people in the States, coming from a black man. That was entertaining. He was a barman in one of our favourite Brooklyn bars, and was always making everyone laugh. He just seemed like he was the genuine article, as my mother would have said.

'I really like Obi.' I nodded, trying to suppress my smile. He would be so much better for her. And a way better daddy!

'Yeah.' With a big yawn, she stretched her arms out and

then threw her hair back and grabbed it all up in a big clip. 'I'm done with Chris. He has exhausted me to the point where I just don't want to know anything about him any more. Even if he does happen to be the father, that would be the extent of our relationship. Honestly, I would even contemplate raising the kid in Ireland without him in the picture at all. I think it would be better for the kid not to have him around. He's just poisonous.'

It was a relief to hear her talking sense about Chris. It was the first time she'd actually acknowledged the truth, which was that he was a total shit. For such a long time she'd convinced herself he was right for her and that deep down he loved her as much as she loved him. He had her brainwashed. It got to the point where it was embarrassing for her because everyone except her knew what he was up to. I hated him. He almost made Seb look like the perfect boyfriend by comparison.

Seb never forgot anything. Anniversaries, birthdays – you name it, he had a thoughtful present and a lovely bunch of yellow roses waiting for me when I got in the door. My heart started to ache thinking back to how wonderful he was. He was perfect. No, Katie! He was *gay*, I reminded myself. *Gay. Gay. Gay.* Not perfect. *Gay.* But maybe that was what made him perfect. He never, ever looked at another girl. He always made me feel like the most important person in the universe. There were never any games or bullshit.

He was kind of making up for it all now though, I reminded myself with a sigh. If only he would let me know where he was and that he was okay. Just because he broke my heart into a million tiny pieces didn't mean I had stopped caring about him. Even if he could let someone else know he was okay and to pass on the message to me it would have been something. Now that he'd disappeared I couldn't help feeling a bit guilty about leaving so suddenly and not returning when he might have needed me most. Where was he?

Well, as it turned out, the suspense would be over soon and it was about to snowball into a very complicated Seb situation. One to almost rival Sophie's baby situation.

Chapter 20

I strolled around a completely silent Winnipeg Cottage on Wednesday afternoon, wondering what to do with myself. Sophie was travelling across Ireland on a bus to Dublin.

'Just me and you, Sash,' I said as I spooned a half tin of tuna into her little bowl. She purred loudly in appreciation, making me feel somewhat less alone.

Then, just as we were getting used to being back to our quiet little twosome, the doorbell rang – a long loud buzz. I bristled. Why couldn't people simply press it lightly once and see what happened? I wondered this as I plodded out to the door.

It was Frank Coffey.

Frank was a 500-year-old, slim, withered character with no more than three teeth and was never seen without an ancient New York Yankees cap and always wore a pair of denim dungarees. He was without doubt the oldest inhabitant of Ballytiernan, although five hundred years might be a slight exaggeration. I had made him many a sambo in Farrelly's and we were quite good pals while I worked there, but I was surprised to see him at my door. I hadn't even thought he knew where I lived.

'Katie, I'd love to come in, thanks!' he said brightly, somehow momentarily tricking me into thinking I'd invited him in.

I stepped aside, confused. He bustled past me and into the kitchen. I still hadn't uttered a word but he didn't seem to be even slightly bothered by this.

'I've given it a lot of thought now,' he announced. 'Spent several nights mulling it over in the aul' noggin, humming and hawing, toing and froing. A long long time contemplating – too long, you might even say.' He sat down at the table with a dramatic sigh. 'I'd love a cuppa tea, thanks, Katie my dear – you're an angel of God sent down from Heaven by the Master himself.' He blessed himself.

I forced a smile and headed for the kettle. As soon as my back was turned from him I caught Sasha's eye and we both looked at each other with wide eyes and furrowed brows. I was going to ask him to continue, but I didn't think he was going to need prompting, so I got out two cups and awaited his explanation.

'I've decided I'm going to help you with your project,' he announced, his chin protruding smugly. His lined lips were pursed together in a pout.

I cleared my throat. 'I'm not exactly sure what you're talking about, Mr Coffey.'

'Your paintings, of course. Don't play all innocent with me, madam. Sure the whole village knows what you're up to in here. Word has been travelling, and sure didn't it reach aul' Frankie's ears as quickly as anyone else's. Anyway. I'm going to be one of the models.' He pronounced 'models' like 'mod-elles' and gave a little flourish of his hand. He continued. 'And in return I suppose I wouldn't . . . object to your . . . services . . . so to speak.' He ran his tongue along what remained of his teeth and moved his eyebrows up and down.

I felt my fists tighten and had a worrying feeling I was going to want to clobber this little old man. As I was fairly sure that hitting an old person was morally a grey area, I made a mental note to restrain myself.

'I've spoken about my intentions at Confession and myself and Father Stout concluded it wouldn't go against my beliefs and morals, as money wouldn't be exchanging hands. It would just be two mutually consenting adults who find each other very attractive enjoying each other's company in private.' He grinned at me, delighted with his conclusion. 'I've always known I'd be a model some day. I'm like a fine whiskey, you see. I've only ever improved with age. And would you believe it's all natural? All my own joints. All my own teeth. Can you believe I don't even need dentures at my age? These are my own natural God-given teeth. Can you believe that?' He smiled again, displaying all three of them proudly. Two of them were almost completely brown, the one at the front slightly more yellow than the others. That one had a chip across the bottom. It was more of a half-tooth really.

'The only thing I do need a bit of help with, I'm not afraid to say, is . . . well . . . that department.' He nodded down at his crotch and looked back up at me, raising his eyebrows again.

I shuddered.

'I'm sure a fine young thing like yourself and the right, well, stimulation so to speak, and I wouldn't be a far cry from the stallion I was in my heyday.'

'Wow! Okay, that's enough, Mr Coffey. I'm afraid I have to stop you there,' I interrupted firmly. 'I am absolutely not in that line of business. Yes, I am an artist, but I am not a prostitute.'

'Oh, of course not!' He nodded, winking exaggeratedly. 'No, no, of course you're not a prostitute. *Escort* is the word we use nowadays.'

'I am not an escort!'

'Oh yes, sorry, that's not the right word either. You enjoy the *company* of the men you work with.'

'I don't sleep with my models.' I obviously decided to omit the exception that was Fred. He opened his mouth to protest. 'I'm not going to have sex with you!' I shouted.

He finally stopped for a second, momentarily shocked.

I squeezed my hands together behind my back.

'It's because I'm a few years older than you, isn't it?' he then resolved bleakly. His face dropped and he looked crushed.

I felt like I'd stepped on a puppy.

I closed my eyes tightly and put my fingers on my temples. My head had started pounding. I sat down and took a big mouthful of tea. My eyes started to sting with tears. Was this what people thought of me? Was there a big game of Chinese Whispers going around Ballytiernan, spreading outrageous rumours about a brothel in Winnipeg? I buried my head in my hands for a few minutes, coming to terms with it all.

When I looked up at Frank he was quietly fiddling with the tassels on his little cravat. Now, for the first time since he arrived he looked like a sad, lonely old man and I felt awful about that. He hadn't touched his tea. I nudged it towards him.

'Listen, Mr Coffey. It's not you, or your age or anything. I'm just honestly not in that business. I am a good girl and I'm sort of . . . in a relationship. So you see it would be unfair on . . . him, if I were to get up to that sort of thing. Whether or not I wish to.' I didn't really know what I was saying, or if it was helping the situation. 'You're a lovely man. You've just misunderstood the situation.'

'So do you not paint naked men?' he asked.

I paused, unsure of what to say. 'Well, yes, I do. I do paint naked men, as part of a project. A collection.'

'And you don't want me involved?'

'Of course . . . I want you involved, if you're interested. But you have to understand I won't be compensating you with any . . . services.'

'Aw, I dunno . . .' He had visibly lost his swagger.

I felt a pang of guilt for having shouted at him, and felt it was probably my responsibility not to leave him feeling like this. I internally sighed.

'Can I call you Frank?'

He nodded.

'Frank, you're a very attractive and distinguished gentleman. I'd love if you would be in one of my paintings. I'd really be delighted.' I nodded enthusiastically as though agreeing with myself.

'Really?' he asked, brightening slightly.

I nodded even more effusively. I was starting to feel like a nodding doggy on a dashboard.

Before I knew it I was putting my camera around my neck and heading out the door to go to Frank's house. Frank was certainly going to add a new element to the whole thing. Bring it in a different direction. But maybe that wasn't a terrible thing. The Don McLean song about Van Gogh sprang back into my head, where he talks of weathered faces lined in pain. I found faces with lines fascinating. They had stories and memories, love and pain etched into them. It was a beautiful part of the life cycle. The end of the story. I wasn't sure I wanted to see it in its full nakedness though.

Frank had insisted we do the shoot at his house as he had some great ideas for set-ups and even props. It was safe to say I was feeling more than a little bit apprehensive. Frank, on the other hand, was rather excited. He was behaving like a child on his way to Disneyland. He did have remarkable energy for his age. Then something worrying struck me. Maybe he thought he still might be in with a chance of sympathy sex or something, I thought wearily. I shook off my apprehension. No, he was just excited about being a model for a day, I told myself.

Every square inch of Frank's house was covered in trinkets

and other junk. Aladdin's Cave popped into my head. It was actually surprisingly inspiring. It was simply very original, in a haphazard, unintentional way. There was a collection of miniature lorries lined up in a row on the mantelpiece. That was the most organised it got. After that it was basically chaos. A bone-china teapot sat perched precariously on an unused ornamental ashtray. An old tribal horn was leaning against a stack of dusty encyclopaedias, and doubling as a vase for cheap pound-shop plastic flowers. There was a life-size sculpture of a cat sitting in the fireplace and it appeared to be an exact replica of the real black-and-white cat that was roaming around the clutter. But, unbelievably, that was not the creepiest thing in the room. The random assortment of taxidermy woodland creatures dotted around the room all seemed to be staring at me. That was the creepiest thing. And they made me overwhelmingly uneasy. I couldn't decide which one topped the creepy list. Probably the owl, which somehow looked like a sleazy old pervert. Or actually, the swan. The swan looked demented. Its eyes were like little black balls of evil. I tore my gaze away from the demented swan and followed Frank out of the living room – stepping over a gramophone seemed to be the only way through. He went via the kitchen out into the garage. I followed, trying not to inhale all the dust.

'I was thinking we could do the shoot in here.' He stopped.

'Oh. Well, it's very dusty,' I muttered from behind my hand. 'And I'm having trouble seeing anything. We'd need a bit more light in order to get a good shot.'

'Aha! At your service, madam, don't you worry!'

He ambled over to the rusty, steel garage door and started winding an old rickety handle.

'*Let there be light!*' he bellowed theatrically.

The garage door screeched upwards slowly as sunlight gradually crept in, illuminating all the dust particles. The garage gave me a very claustrophobic feeling; I was getting a bit panicky as the dust gradually filled up in my lungs. As soon as the door screeched to a point where I could bend down and get out without having to attempt a very awkward limbo, I darted for freedom. I gasped from the other side.

'Sorry, Frank, just couldn't breathe in there.' Suddenly an idea popped into my head. I stood breathing in the fresh air until the door had completed its journey.

'We'll let this place air out for a little while and maybe you wouldn't mind introducing me to all your taxidermy animals, please, Frank?'

He beamed. 'Oh yes, they're wonderful, aren't they? My brother and I spent over fifty years collecting them from all over the world. It was a great hobby for a long time, although when eBay came along it became almost too easy. Took the fun out of it. Anyway the brother died last year so they're all mine now!' He seemed thrilled about this. He reminded me of one of the characters from Martin McDonagh's *The Lonesome West*. I imagined his brother and himself went on at each other like the two brothers in the play, tearing at each other's throats all day long until one died.

I held my breath as we went back into Aladdin's Cave to meet its inhabitants. As we passed back through the kitchen he stopped to take something down from the wall behind the door.

'Oh, you have to see this.'

I automatically gagged as he displayed a case full of mounted taxidermy insects, massive ones that looked like they came from somewhere deep in the Australian outback.

'Aren't they delightful?'

I nodded. I could sense he was about to launch into a detailed description of each one so I quickly asked if we could take a look at the animal ones.

How he didn't cause a landslide when he climbed on top of a jam-packed oak cabinet, to get a very pretty but creepy stuffed duck, was baffling. Frank was delighted to tell me that his brother and himself had named the duck Proinsias when they acquired him in Sligo in 1999.

'Can we use him in the shoot?' I was getting excited about the idea of using taxidermy animals in one of the paintings. Although people probably wouldn't know they were taxidermy unless they looked closely, and even then perhaps not. But I liked the idea of challenging the viewers to decide these things for themselves. Also, I thought it would be best to run with the theme of Frank's eccentricity. However, I was going to try to convince him to keep most of his clothes on, or else it was probably going to look a little too weird, now that animals were involved. I wasn't all that keen on becoming a freaky fetish bestiality-porn artist.

Frank stuffed the duck under his spindly little arm, patted its head and tickled it under its chin.

'I think the fox would be great too.' I pointed at the fox perched on an armchair in the far corner of the room. This was as close as I wanted to get to the thing. It was making the most terrifying face. His ears were pulled back, the eyes were protruding ferociously and his Jack Nicholson grin revealed a vicious set of pointy fangs.

'Excellent choice. Not everyone loves Pussy – he looks fierce but he's a softy really.' He picked up the fox and we headed back to the garage.

The dust had calmed down a bit by now and we set about organising ourselves.

We brought out some of the other dead animals and arranged them around the space. Then I got Frank to stick the duck back under his arm and a badger under the other.

'I absolutely love your dungarees, Frank, and your hat, so it would be great if you left them on in the shot.'

'You don't want me in the nude?'

He pronounced nude the proper way, like *new-d*, and I couldn't help laughing. I hadn't heard it said like that in a really long time. He looked offended.

'Well, none of my models are completely in the nude, Frank,' I lied. 'You have to leave something to the imagination.'

'Oh yes, the ladies like that, don't they? In my experience they have very active imaginations.'

I nodded in effusive encouragement. I made a mental note to gag later. 'You can put the strap of the dungarees down on one side of you want to be really risqué. The ladies might like that.' Oh man, any self-respect I once had was depleting rapidly.

Now it was really starting to feel like I was directing a weird geriatric porn shoot.

Chapter 21

I was sitting at home with a big mug of tea and a box of chocolate fingers two hours later, wondering if that had really all just happened. I scanned through the photos on my camera and yep, there they were. Frank's big gummy grin was offset quite comically by the blank staring faces of the odd, lifeless creatures clutched under his arms. The others were dotted around him in strange attack poses, but mostly their faces still looked blank. Except for the fox. That fox's face was scarier than anything Stephen King could have ever imagined. I debated leaving it out of the painting but then I didn't want to disappoint Frank by not having 'Pussy' included. Also it contributed to the emotionally mixed-up energy that was somehow infiltrating the collection. And I was liking it. I didn't want the audience to know immediately how the piece made them feel. Like the Mona Lisa, which has the effect of leaving the viewer unsure of her mood. Frank and the animals gave a similar vibe. He was so confident and the animals looked calm, but when you looked closer, were they dead? Were they trapped in those positions they were in? And Frank himself, when you really looked at him, you saw his vulnerability. I hoped I could do it justice in the painting.

There was a lot that could be done with this, and I knew I had a challenge ahead of me if I was going to capture everything that was going on, and every story that was being told.

I nibbled both ends off a chocolate finger, dunked it into my tea and sucked up the hot liquid through the biscuit like a straw. Then I ate the biscuit. An old classic trick. Absolutely delicious. The warm chocolate and biscuit melted on my tongue. I told myself I could do this, and make something really great of it. I savoured the taste as I took my phone out of my pocket. As I expected there was a message from Sophie.

Back in Dub now and just had the mother of all conversations with my parents. Told them every detail of the whole sordid affair. Just wasn't bothered trying to hide anything from them – it's too exhausting as it is! The good news is they still love me, and they're going to help me. Bad news is I took six more pregnancy tests and nothing has changed. I defo still have this little zygote dude growing inside me. Bummer.

I sent her a quick encouraging reply and then I eagerly got to work on little old Frank. I loved the direction the project was now taking. It was becoming more about characters, which was the original intention. I wanted to capture the characters of the village, and their little quirks and stories.

I was really enjoying sketching the outline of the painting and doing little rough drafts of the animals. Every time I did a sketch of a creature I stuck it on my wall. Slowly I was becoming more comfortable with them, and developing methods to portray the lifelessness. The glassy eyes took a bit of mastering but I was getting the hang of it. My habit had always been to put as much life as possible into eyes so this was new to me. I then took them off the wall and started sticking them onto the canvas in the positions I wanted them in. One was crossing the road, another was waiting at traffic lights, others were in Frank's arms or by his side. It was already making me laugh. I knew it would be a bit creepy, but I liked that. I was lost in its strange little world.

After spending a few hours working away on the animals, I stretched out my arms and took a stroll around the cottage. It was dark and quiet. I flexed my bulging fingers. They often swelled up at night if I worked for a long time. I never knew why. My Claddagh ring was wedged in between the swollen folds of my fingers. I squeezed my hands, forcing them into fists and the skin tingled. I ran them under cold water and then splashed water on my eyes, which felt like they were going crossed. I ambled into the kitchen, flicked on the light switch and the bulbs flickered. Sasha blinked up at me, baffled as to why I was waking her from her sleep. She was curled up on top of the clean folded clothes I had taken out of the drier but hadn't made it as far as the hot press. Begrudgingly I left her there, and popped on the kettle.

I felt refreshed when I faced the painting again. It was closing in on eleven o'clock, but I was nowhere near ready to pack it in for the night. The night-time was always my best time to work. It was when I really came alive and buzzed with inspiration. I liked the thought that the rest of the world was sleeping while I was creating. I felt like Santa Claus working away through the night – then the world would be delighted with the results of my labour. However, the natural daylight was obviously not on my side at this hour. The yellowy glow of the old-fashioned hanging lightshade wasn't the best lighting for an artist, and often in the morning I would be shocked by how different it looked. But, despite all this, I painted avidly into the night, knowing that I might well have to repair it all in the morning light.

I set to work on Frank now, with a fresh burst of energy. I was doodling in little wispy white curls on his chest and his small pink nipple, which was proudly displayed on the side where he had dropped the strap of his dungarees, when I heard the doorbell chime.

I hurried out into the hall, a little pathetically eager, thinking it was Fred. I couldn't see anyone through the glass windows at the side of the door. That was strange. Well, it's definitely not Fred, I thought with a sigh. Who would be calling at this hour anyway? Maybe I had imagined it. I chewed the inside of my mouth as I approached the door. I peered through the glass. Nope. No one there. I reached for the door handle, feeling like the dumb blonde in the scary movie that gets killed first. I thought to myself that this was the part of the movie where you were shouting at the screen, telling her to keep the door shut and phone the police. Then she would open the door anyway and you would conclude that she deserved to die because she was so stupid. But, come on, this was Winnipeg, not Wolf Creek. I timidly opened it and peered out. Nothing. See. Safe lovely Winnipeg. The cool air felt nice on my flushed cheeks.

I peeked out a little further and noticed something sitting on the doorstep. My brow furrowed curiously as I picked it up. It was a fruit loaf. It looked delicious through its clear plastic bag. How sweet, I thought. Someone had made me a fruit loaf. There was a note with it. I closed the door and hurried into the kitchen. What lovely person would make me a fruit loaf? I wondered. I flicked the kettle on again. Sure I would simply have to have a piece, and I couldn't do that without a cup of tea, could I? I popped the loaf down on the table and unfolded the note. It was a straightforward white A4 page and on it was a typed letter. It simply said the following:

Ms. McKenna.

I am formally issuing you with an order to cease and desist. This is in regard to your activities involving nudity, art and shamelessly lewd sexual behaviour. Unchaste individuals are not accepted around here. You have caused enough harm now and must stop these activities immediately and are warned not to take them up again. I hope I will not have to pursue this issue herein. Should you do as you are told we can remain a peaceful community, and no further action will need to be taken.

Regards.

PS. I would like to present this fruit loaf to you as a peace offering.

I read the letter over and over, trying to digest what it was saying. I scratched my head. I was unsure how to deal with it. I wasn't sure if I should have felt scared or threatened, but I wasn't. Some sexually frustrated, prudish aul' one just didn't seem like something to fear. I had an idea it was probably from Mo or Blue Rinse Lady. I took out my phone and sent Mac a text, enquiring after her sister's health and asking to see her as soon as she got back. I decided to put it out of my head until then.

I stood up from the table, still holding the note, and picked up the fruit loaf. I popped the note into the drawer below the cutlery drawer, on top of take-away menus and fliers. I walked over to the bin and pressed the metal lever with my foot. I dropped the fruit loaf into it and let the lid close firmly over it. I dusted my hands off. I had a slight regret about wasting the fruit loaf but I decided it was wisest to steer clear of cyanide desserts for now. But I wasn't going to let it bother me. Whoever wrote the letter was just bored with their life and had nothing better to do.

I, on the other hand, had something important to do. Little old Frank and the dead animals weren't going to paint themselves. Snow Patrol were blasting out of my iPod dock when I went back into the living room. They were singing 'Spitting Games'. I was lost in Frank's little world again before I knew it.

I thought I had forgotten all about the letter but when my

phone buzzed at midnight I almost jumped out of my skin. Could whoever had written it possibly have my number? How did they know I was still awake?

Of course it wasn't them ringing anyway. Instead, bizarrely, it was Jules' name that popped up. Jules wasn't my favourite person. She was very much a fair-weather friend, and a total sly bitch. The misery-seeking cow who rang Sophie when Chris cheated on her. What bad news did she have for me? She was one of the New York gang, but she was from Cornwall or somewhere posh in England. She liked to pretend she was a hipster though. Some of the others liked her for some reason so I tolerated her. One of those types – we all know at least one. Anyway she was calling me for some reason and before I even know what it was I was already feeling apprehensive. It wasn't likely she was ringing just to catch up. With Jules there was always a motive. I reluctantly slid my finger across the screen to answer.

'Hello?'

'Katie? Hello? Are you there? I can't really hear you very well. The line isn't good. Oh my God, you really must be in the absolute middle of nowhere!'

I could hear her perfectly. Every syllable was completely audible in her annoying high-pitched voice.

'Anyway, I just felt I had to ring you. I have a bit of news, I suppose you could say. Seb has come back to New York, darling. Are you there?'

'Yes.' I held my breath.

'Anyway, there's something else you should know. I thought I should ring, as I said. In case you heard it from someone else or found out some other way, Are you still there?'

'Yes, Jules, I'm still fucking here!'

'I can't really hear you, darling. Anyway. I suppose I should just say it – just in case you can hear me.'

Someone really needs to invent a phone you can stick your

fist through and punch the person on the other end hard in the face, I thought. Sadly it had not yet been created and my fists would have to find something within their reach to punch. I was really on a roll with these invention ideas though. Pity I wasn't an inventor, I thought.

'Anyway, babes, I hate being the one to tell you this,' Jules continued.

As if! She lived for moments like these. I knew well that the only thing she was devastated about was that she couldn't tell me to my face and enjoy my pain, the sadistic cow.

'He came out with us last night. No one expected to see him there, but there he was, out of the blue. In great form. Oh, sorry, babes. Anyway, long story short, darling, he hooked up with Erica's friend from uni, this gorgeous Colombian chick called Natalia. So yeah, it's weird. He must have like decided he's not gay any more? Maybe it was just when he was with you or . . . I dunno, but like, don't be upset, honey, you're so much better than him. I hope you're okay.' She paused.

I could sense her anticipation: she was praying I'd burst into tears.

'I really can't hear anything you're saying, Jules,' I said loudly and hung up.

I gently put the phone down and composed myself. My stomach was churning like a cement-mixer and there was some disgusting bile forcing its way up my throat, but I was determined to overcome it. I swallowed, tilted my head back and shook it lightly, to get rid of the mounting tears in my eyes. So fucking what if he scored a girl? So what if he wanted to humiliate me even more than he had, more than I thought possible? Yes, maybe I was so unsatisfactory a woman that he went gay and then decided to go back straight at the mere sight of a Colombian sexual goddess, probably a real woman with big boobies and an ass that just wouldn't quit. That was not me. But I was fine with that. So fuck you, Jules.

I had just about recovered when my phone started buzzing again. I flinched. If it was Jules ringing back to rub salt in the wound I had just mended, I would mill the thing against the wall. I approached it with caution. Jim's name was flashing on the screen and I groaned. What could he want? I really ought to just run down the field and throw this phone in the stream.

'Hi, Jim.' I could have tried a little harder to sound enthusiastic but I really couldn't be bothered.

'Katie! Hubes isn't well.' He breathed heavily into the receiver.

I had to instantly feel sorry for him despite the creepy sound of his deep breaths. He did love his dogs and Hubes, despite being mischievous at times, was always a cheerful and sweet dog.

'Aw, that's really terrible, Jim! What can I do to help?'

'Well, I have to drive to Galway straight away to get her to a vet that works after hours. The bar is packed with geriatrics. It's completely black with them. The regional ladies' bingo clubs have organised a blind date night with the gentlemen's poker clubs and the place is absolutely mobbed. They've come from all over the west of Ireland, maybe even further. They're staying at the Oak Inn and Bernadette Reilly's B&B. Tonight they've descended upon Farrelly's.' He gasped. 'And it's only Fred working. Well, it was Fred and myself and we've been running around the place like headless chickens. We still are, but I can't leave Hubes in this state. Is there any chance you could help out, Katie? There's no way Fred could manage it by himself. I'm so sorry to ask, I know you're not officially working here any more. But didn't Cormac head off at the weekend – to Thailand if you don't mind – with a group of friends, so he says, but I've never seen him with any friends. Anyway, God knows when I'll see him again.'

'Jim,' I interrupted. 'It's nearly twelve thirty – shouldn't you really be closing soon?'

'Well, they've come all this way to my pub – it's great for

business really. I told them I'd stay open as long as they wanted. Lock-ins are where I make all my money these days. Why do you think Farrelly's is the only pub to have survived around here? I'm not ready to lose this pub, Katie, I need this business. I'm begging ya, Katie – you're quite handy behind the bar and I'm really stuck and you know I can't leave Hubes in this state.'

'Of course, Jim,' I assured him. 'I'll leave now. Go get Hubes some help. Give her a cuddle from me.'

'Thanks, Katie! Ah, you're an angel! I really appreciate it. I'll send George Best out to collect you.'

He hung up and I immediately started faffing about. Crap, I looked like a demented, homeless artist. Fred had seen me looking pretty terrible but still – that didn't mean I should make a habit of it! I ran upstairs, taking off my jumper and my pyjamas pants as I went. I blotted on some lipstick in a desperate bid to look fresher. I now looked like a nudist, demented, homeless artist with badly applied lipstick. There was only one thing that would make me feel good right now. The only thing in my closet that ever truly made jaws drop. That was my skin-tight black leather trousers and black corset combo. Maybe it was a bit extreme. It was probably a bit too defiant, considering that less than an hour ago I had received a warning that unchaste individuals would not be tolerated. This was definitely the most unchaste outfit I owned. In fact it bordered on being dominatrix. But I was feeling ballsy and determined to shove my sexuality in Mo's face, or Blue Rinse's face, as opposed to hiding it away. In fact, maybe I would just become a total slut and see how they liked that. I had never in my life responded to threats. If anything, they made me even more rebellious. I sleeked my hair back into a wet ponytail, using water and Vaseline. I then put on a megaload of eyeliner and an extra layer of blood-red lipstick. I looked like a Charlie's Angel (in my own less impressive way). Although it was sad that poor Hubes wasn't well, this was an opportunity for me. I would get out and put on a brave, resilient face. Anyway, although I had been blissfully enjoying my night of painting, perhaps I needed to get away from the paint fumes and naked men of Winnipeg Cottage for a while. Real people out in the real world had their merits too.

I quickly gathered my things, applied another lick of mascara, petted Sasha's head and told her to look after the place, and briskly headed out. I chewed the inside of my cheek again as I sat in the back of George Best's car. The taxi driver not the footballer.

I hadn't spoken to Fred since the whole pregnancy test/puddle fiasco. Not even a text. I couldn't tell him the whole story. It was Sophie's secret for now. However, I obviously didn't want him thinking that the pregnancy test had been for me. God knows what conclusions or suspicions that would lead to. I sort of hoped he'd thought it through and realised it might have been for Sophie, without me having to tell him. Anyway I decided not to discuss the subject at all. Perhaps I would just drink a lot and then he would get the message that I was not containing a baby.

'Penny for them?' George asked, looking at me in the rear-view mirror. We were whizzing along the road into the village at George's usual perilous speed.

'My thoughts are worth more than a penny, Georgie!' I snapped out of my trance and smiled at him. 'You couldn't afford them.'

Chapter 22

Jim was right: Farrelly's was completely mobbed. How did they have the energy to still be going after midnight? Ecstasy was my best guess. OAPs filled every corner and square inch of the pub – not just bingo ladies, but also auld fellas trying to pick up some hot available widows. And the flirtation was outrageous. Frank was the first person I saw as I came through the door, and he flashed me his big fabulous grin and winked at me knowingly, then got back to flirting with some very keen lady close enough to his own age.

I nipped in behind the bar, an empty wineglass on every finger, having swept them off a vacated table. The occupants were up jiggling around eagerly, trying not to pop their hips out whilst dancing to Daniel O'Donnell. I placed the glasses down on the glass-washer tray and greeted Fred with a light breezy kiss on the cheek. His hair was sticking up all over the place. He looked adorable. He seemed to appreciate the kiss but I didn't really stop to think about it. About ten orders were shouted at me the second I looked out at the punters. I tried to focus on what they were asking for but I could feel Fred's eyes checking me out as he restocked the wine. We worked silently together, weaving around past each other to get what we needed. It felt electric but we said nothing. Just worked. Pulled pints, poured wine, shook up mixers. He would reach around me for the ice bucket and I would feel his breath on my shoulder and his arm would graze mine.

'I'm glad you're here.' During a very brief calm moment, Fred's eyes finally locked on mine, and my tummy lurched. 'I need to check the Gents' loo – can I leave you on your own for a second?'

'Sure. Is everything okay?'

'Old Mr Healy, who lives over near you actually, has set up a little office in the Gents'. I believe he's dealing Es, Viagra, and God knows what other aphrodisiac drugs. I need to shut the operation down before things get out of control.'

He swiftly headed off towards the loo, where there was a queue of auld fellas and the occasional giddy lady spilling out along the wall. There had never been a queue for the men's toilet. I knew there was something behind this energy they all seemed to have.

Goodness, old people could put away their drink. As the night wore on, I did my best to use distraction tactics to slow down the inevitable messiness, and it mostly worked. Between the two of us we managed to convince them they were having more booze than they really were. Ginger ale and non-alcoholic Becks with the labels torn off came in very handy. But nevertheless they were still a rowdy bunch.

Things were starting to calm down at about two thirty-ish. Luckily the pensioners seemed to know their limits, or else their weekly allowance had run out. So Fred and I started to relax a little and decided to hold a few 'staff meetings', a regular ritual where we did a round of tequilas, when things got quiet. Just to keep ourselves going. Just then Terry wandered up to the bar with a big Cheshire Cat grin on his face.

'Terry,' I smiled. 'Great to see ya, pal. I saw ya over there flirting with that saucy minx, Ms O'Toole! I think you're in there like swimwear, you stud. She seems well interested!'

Terry raised his eyebrows and glanced away bashfully, but he was clearly delighted with himself.

'Guinness extra cold?' I suggested.

'Well now, Katie, I actually came over to offer you a little something! My own home baking if you don't mind! I'd be devastated if you didn't take one after all the pints you've poured me over the years.' He produced an old Quality Street tin and took off the lid.

'Over the years? I wouldn't quite say that Terry,' I laughed. I peeked into the tin. I was feeling a bit peckish as it happened. 'What are they?' They looked sort of like cupcakes because of the gloopy icing swirled on top. It was all a bit messy and stuck together, but they had a certain home-made charm about them.

'Terry's Special Fairy Cakes!' he beamed. 'Go on, Fred, there's one in there for you too!'

I had a sneaking suspicion they were brownies of the illegal variety. I looked at Fred and he seemed to be thinking the same thing.

'There isn't anything unlawful going on here now, Terry, is there?' Fred asked with one eyebrow raised.

'Would I do something like that?' Terry winked – he couldn't seem to wipe the smile from his face, even though he was pretending to be serious.

I shrugged, stuck my hand in, chose one and took a big bite. It was sticky. I licked the icing off my fingers and smiled at Fred. My suspicions were confirmed. But whatever. It was a tasty treat and I was feeling a bit reckless.

'Mmm! Terry, these are yummy! Did you really make them?' I said, before shoving another mouthful into my face. Terry nodded.

Fred was looking at me with his eyebrows raised, a slight smirk forming in the corners of his mouth.

'You have a bit here.' He pointed to the side of my mouth.

'Yeah, I'm saving it there for you – you can lick it off whenever you like.' I struggled not to laugh at myself. He knew it was a joke, but he very stealthily leaned over and licked it off. Then stood back as though nothing had happened.

'*Woop!*' Terry cheered. 'Get stuck in, Fred! Good man!' Then he got caught up in flirtatious conversation with Ms O'Toole who had wasted no time finding him again.

'Tastes good on you,' Fred said quietly to me and smiled.

'Well, it's my birthday in a few hours, so it's sort of fitting that I'm having some cake,' I casually informed him, as I washed the cake down with a gulp of Strongbow cider through a straw.

'Your birthday?' Fred asked.

'Yep.' I shrugged. 'And who would have thought that Terry would turn out to be the very thoughtful person who made me birthday cake, even though he didn't intend to . . .'

Fred nodded as I put the rest of the cake into my mouth and licked my fingers clean again. He took a couple of shot glasses out of the glass freezer, took the tequila off the shelf and poured.

'Happy Birthday, Katie!' he said quietly, looking straight into my eyes and we clinked glasses and knocked them back. I had finally become sophisticated enough to not need a lime after the tequila. Or else I just couldn't taste the tequila.

I hadn't really thought about my birthday a lot. I never had made a fuss of it, not since I was a child, and I presumed that this year it would be particularly low-key given that I didn't exactly have a circle of close friends where I was now living. I was hardly going to go around telling everyone my birthday was approaching and that I wanted to do something big for it. The thought of doing something like that made my cheeks burn. I just sort of thought the day would pass like any other. Maybe I would get a phone call from my mother telling me every unwanted detail about the day I was born.

Ms O'Toole was leading Terry away – the woman was keen! – when Terry turned back to us, his face momentarily perplexed. Like he couldn't remember why he was standing there at the bar.

'Oh yeah!' he announced. "Freddie, have one! And Katie, have another!'

I happily stuck my hand in and helped myself to another.

'Go on, Freddie! You have to give them a go! Live a little – you won't start putting on the belly for another few years.'

'Can I put a couple aside for later please, Terry? I had a big dinner earlier.'

'Go on then.' Terry seemed unimpressed.

Fred picked two and Terry moved off with his lady friend.

Fred rang the bell and shouted, '*Last orders!*'

I moved down the bar, expecting a crowd to gather to get the last drinks in, but the few remaining OAPs were all too drunk and oblivious.

I noticed Sheila, the sweet old lady with the pink bow, sitting along the wall with her husband Liam. They were huddled together. Liam was reading a book aloud and Sheila was giggling and clutching his arm. I moved towards them to see if I could hear what they were reading.

After wandering over as stealthily as possible, I finally arrived within earshot and when I heard what Liam was reading I only just managed to stifle a snort of laughter.

I hurried back to Fred as quickly as I could and grabbed him. 'You have to come see this.'

When we made our way back over Sheila's hand was wandering under Liam's belt buckle.

'Shit, Katie, I don't *want* to see this!' Fred whispered and turned around.

'No, listen to what he's reading to her!'

We fell silent.

Liam's voice was deep and hushed. "'*Come on, you big sexy ride! Give it to me!' I explode like a . . . a whale . . . and you gather yourself around my big . . . lad, like a barnicle clinging onto a rock . . . he-he . . . I then do the ejaculation bit! Then I lie there on top of you like a beached whale . . . Jesus!"'*

Fred's mouth fell open into a big silent laugh.

'The cover says *Fifty Shades of Green*,' I whispered. 'It looks like a self-published knock-off of *Fifty Shades of Grey!*'

'Oh my God, I heard a rumour that was going around.' Fred pulled me back behind the bar and we collapsed laughing.

'Hey, you two!? Can I get my last order in or what?'

Fred served the grumpy gentleman.

I was wandering around, my brain feeling all lovely and bubbly, slowly and cautiously picking up more empty glasses, when I found an OAP travel pass on the ground near the men's loo.

'What's this important misplaced item?' I said aloud to myself, my brows deeply furrowed as I investigated the card. I squinted at the photo of the man – Dermot Duffin, a chubby old chap with pink cheeks and a few feathery strands of pure white hair pulled across his head in a comb-over. I did a quick scan of the bar to try and locate him and return it, but I couldn't seem to focus my eyes. It was as though a tequila-and-brownie-induced blurry haze was impairing my vision. And my brain was all of a sudden working much more slowly than normal. To add to the difficulty, the old people were all starting to look very alike: small, wrinkly and with wispy white hair.

I stuck the pass in my pocket and glided very smoothly over to Fred.

He smirked.

'You've been wandering around for twenty minutes and you collected three glasses! And you're cradling them like they're made of precious gold dust or something! I knew this would happen! You've become useless since having those

Terry's magic fairy-cake things,' he scolded.

I could feel my eyelids blinking slowly, but I maintained a very sombre expression. 'I'll have you know I am actually on a very important mission,' I said with a slightly English accent, sort of in the style of James Bond. I stared at him intensely so that he would get the severity of the situation, then I squinted my eyes because I felt like I was being too stare-y. I explained my dilemma, like it was a top-secret investigation. He looked at the photo, moving it closer to his face and then far away, peering at it like an old fella himself. I came to the conclusion he was probably making fun of me, so I stuck my hand on my hip, ready to get all sassy with him.

'Nope. I don't recognise the chap, Bridie,' he concluded. We had decided earlier that we were honorary OAPs ourselves for the evening and my name was Bridie, or Betty or Kitty, whatever came into Fred's head in the moment, and his was Paulie or Dickie, or whatever tickled my fancy. At this stage, after what felt like a triple shift, we were both feeling fairly silly and perhaps giddy with exhaustion, never mind my additional giddiness enhancement.

'This is a very serious mission, Miley,' I insisted. 'It would be very tragic altogether if he couldn't get back to wherever he's from without his *old person bus thingy* and was stranded in the wilderness of Ballytiernan! We couldn't let this happen. How could we live with ourselves? *How?*'

'Dermot Duffin . . . that name is familiar to me though, Patsy. 'Tis indeed to be sure,' Fred mused.

After a few minutes, Fred spotted a potential candidate, a chubby old gent in the corner, sitting near Terry, and despite my blurry vision I was pretty confident it could be our guy. We briefly deliberated and came to the conclusion that he looked exactly like Dermot Duffin. A little less hair, but probably the photo was taken a few years ago. We decided that there was a one-hundred-per-cent chance it was our guy. Just in time to help us with our objective, Terry was wandering towards the bar using all his concentration to put one foot in front of the other, clinging to anything he could grasp.

'Don't serve him,' Fred whispered, although I didn't think the whispering was necessary – Terry was so plastered he wouldn't have heard if Fred had used a megaphone.

'*Terry!*' I shouted, hoping he could lip-read, when he arrived at the bar. 'Look, I found your friend's travel card!' I thrust it at him. 'Can you do me a big favour and make sure it gets back to him? Go on, off you go! Do that for me, will ya, buddy? It's very important.'

Terry looked confused but, shockingly, he seemed to understand the request as he took the card and staggered off back in the direction of his friend.

Fred rang the bell and shouted '*Bar closed!*' Then we had another round of well-earned tequilas.

Terry's friend arrived up at the bar, looking very cross.

'Hello, sir, another Smithwick's, is it?' I offered, reaching up in slow blurry motion for a pint glass.

'What are you doing? We just rang the bell – bar closed.' Fred laughed, grabbing my hand before I got hold of a glass.

'You saying I look like a fat ugly old bastard?' Terry's friend spat.

I blinked.

'Em, excuse me?' Fred cut across.

'You two thought this was my travel card. This looks nothing like me. This lad is a *fat ugly bastard!*'

'I'm extremely sorry, sir,' I said as I struggled to hold in my laughter.

'Yes,' Fred nodded very matter-of-factly. 'We're very drunk, I'm afraid.'

I disguised a snort of laughter as a cough.

Fred proceeded: 'Our vision must have been impaired by the alcohol. Yes, on second thoughts, you're right – it looks nothing like you.'

The man threw the photo of his doppelganger across the bar, narrowly missing Fred's face, and stalked off. We fell to pieces laughing, both of us crouching down behind the bar.

I grabbed Fred's hand. 'It looks exactly like him,' I squealed, my voice reaching an octave where not much sound actually came out of my mouth. I attempted to wipe the tears from under my eyes with my other hand without destroying my mascara.

'Am I touching my face? It doesn't feel like I'm touching my face?' I looked at him, confused but nonetheless content. Even if I did feel a little out of control, I felt so safe with Fred it wasn't worrying. 'Is my face covered in mascara? It feels a little strange.'

'Don't worry – you still look lovely,' he teased. 'You actually look a bit like Sandy from *Grease* in that outfit. "*You're the one that I want*," he sang in a mock deep voice.

We both fell apart laughing again. He wiped a blob from under my eye and placed his hand gently on my face. It felt so nice there; I could have put the weight of my whole head into his hand and fallen asleep right there. I didn't do that. My head did fall a little though, and my shoulders sagged a bit. I looked into Fred's clear blue eyes and all my pent-up thoughts came spilling out of my mouth.

'So I told you how I turned my ex gay, right? Well, it turns out he's not gay. Or he was but he's not any more. He's hooking up with a Colombian girl. Isn't that nice? I still haven't heard anything from him.'

Fred looked back at me. He seemed unsure of what to say.

I shook my head, embarrassed. 'Sorry. Why am I saying this? You don't want to hear about my ex-homosexual ex-boyfriend. Of course you don't. What the hell is wrong with me? I must actually have some sort of retarded defect or something. I don't have a clue why you're even interested in me. You probably won't be after now. I'm self-destructive. And I'm damaged goods. And I'm a temporary-gay-converter.

You should probably make a run for it now or you'll become gay too.'

Fred laughed gently. 'Katie, we're all damaged goods in one way or another. And I'm willing to take the risk of being turned temporarily gay. I have a hunch you might be worth it. Now shut your beautiful mouth and I'll tell these people to kindly piss off.' And he stood up to do just that.

Chapter 23

I awoke the next morning in my bed. I had absolutely no recollection of how I had got there. I looked under the sheets and I was still in the clothes I had worn to Farrelly's. Minus my jeans. At least my knickers were on, even if they were my old blue World Cup knickers with ITALIA written across the bum. Nice. I rolled over and buried my face in my pillow with a groan. Nice way to wake up on my birthday. I peeled my head off the pillow about an hour later because my body was craving water and it wasn't going to let me lie there a moment longer without it. My eyes focused and I noticed on the pillow beside me a little scrap of notepaper.

Written on it in neat, functional handwriting were the words 'Happy Birthday, Funny Girl. X' I smiled, my tummy fluttering, despite its delicate state. My birthday wasn't turning out too bad after all. However, I had to remind myself not to forget about The Fear. What had I done/said the night before that could possibly haunt me? I guessed it mustn't have been too disgraceful if Fred had referred to me as 'Funny Girl' in his note, as opposed to 'Vile Hideous Vulgar Girl'. I was hopeful anyway.

I dragged myself down the stairs, making a beeline for the sink, shakily poured myself a pint of water and hurried back up the stairs as quickly as I could before my legs gave way underneath me. I flopped back down onto my bed and rolled over onto my tummy, propping myself up on my elbows.

I scrolled through the contacts in my phone, found his number and tentatively pressed call.

I held my phone up to my ear and mashed my nose into my pillow, face down.

'Hello,' I muttered when he answered.

I could hear him chuckling.

'What happened?' I asked, using my most innocent voice. I was hoping he would go easy on me.

'Well, you, madam, were a little bit . . . inebriated.'

'A little bit? Are you going easy on me?'

'I am,' he confirmed.

'Did I do anything embarrassing?' I was still talking into my pillow.

'You were charming.'

'You're lying.'

'I'm actually not. You happen to be that rare breed of adorable drunk. However. You want the truth? You weren't a very good drunk bartender. In fact, you were terrible. You completely lost any capability to do the job properly. I had to fire you. I demoted you from bar staff to bar patron and even had to refuse you drink in the end. I actually ended up barring you for life.'

'You did not!'

'I did. But then I revoked it. The only reason you got away with any of it was because whenever I went over to you, you were so full of happiness and affection it was impossible to be mad at you. Also you were completely oblivious.'

'Well, I am lovely,' I joked smugly. 'How did I get home?' Oh God, fuzzy memories were coming back into my head. 'Hang on – did I throw beer mats at your head?'

'Yep. You were throwing them like frisbees. I had to confiscate them.'

'Sorry.'

'Don't worry, I'll get my revenge. Anyway, somehow you still managed to charm everyone.'

'It's a special ability I have,' I mumbled. 'Did you take me home?'

'Of course. Have you been downstairs yet?'

'Em . . . yes, why?'

'Did you not see what was on the table?'

'No. What is it?'

'Never mind, you'll see later. Okay, I gotta go. Bessie is staring at me begging for a W. A. L. K.'

'Oh, one more question! Why am I half-naked?'

'Well, you tried to undress yourself. And . . . you also tried to undress me. Both attempts were unsuccessful.'

'Why?'

'You fell asleep.'

'Oh.'

I hobbled down the stairs, eager to see what was on the table. I was hoping it was something lovely like a present, maybe a steaming hot full Irish breakfast (most unlikely to be hot by this time), but I was slightly worried it could also be the revenge he was talking about. Something scary, like a lizard or the head of a horse. Fred didn't seem like the psychotic crime-lord type though. And I didn't think throwing beer mats warranted that sort of revenge. Thankfully it was the former – something lovely. A massive beautiful bouquet of flowers. I didn't know how I hadn't noticed it earlier. It was enormous. The whole kitchen smelt like the Botanical Gardens. In front of the flowers was a box of Ferrero Rocher with a red ribbon around them. I must have mentioned they were my favourite chocolates. How had he done all this before I'd even woken up? He must have robbed my keys on his way out last night and returned them in the morning with the flowers and chocolates. Sure enough, the keys were in their usual place in an antique ash tray near the telephone and there was another little note underneath them: '*Borrowed and returned before you even noticed. I got skillz. You can just call me Mr Perfect. Let's have dinner tonight. I'll pick you up at 8 for some of Ballytiernan's finest cuisine, or maybe if you're really lucky we'll venture further afield.*'

Well, I wouldn't be calling him Mr Modest anyway, but Mr Perfect seemed fairly accurate, the way things were going so far this morning. And the prospect of what was to come had me all giddy and excited already. Within minutes I was skipping around the kitchen, having forgotten all about my hangover, and singing '*Happy Birthday to me, Happy Birthday toooo meeeeee!*'

The kettle bubbled and I popped some bread into the toaster.

'Sasha? What did you get me for my birthday?'

Sasha looked up at me. I had interrupted her in the middle of scratching the press containing the tuna tins.

'*Meaoooow!*'

'Okay, okay, I get it.' I opened a can of tuna. 'Here you go, you selfish little madam,' I muttered, plopping some into her dish. 'Do you even care that it's my birthday and I haven't even had my own breakfast yet? No, you don't. Do you?'

She didn't deny it, just tucked into her brekkie nonchalantly. I suddenly remembered the little box and card on the dresser in my bedroom. Sophie had left them behind for me.

'Haha! Whatever, Sash, it's my birthday and I'm getting pressies because I'm special! Don't look at me like that, Sash – stop player hatin'.'

I galloped up the stairs two at a time and tripped at the top. I pretended it didn't happen, chose to ignore the thump on my knee and rushed into my room. I grabbed the box first – when no one was watching I didn't have to go through the polite formalities of opening the card before the present. I opened the box in a little too much of a rush, and a silver and gold bracelet fell out onto the wooden floorboard with a clang. *Oooops!* I picked it up gently and gave it a rub. It was gorgeous, a charm bracelet with one little charm of a cow hanging off it. It was really delicate and pretty. Even the cow was somehow dainty. I slid it onto my wrist and admired how lovely my arm looked with it on. I even looked in the mirror to get the overall effect of how lovely I was, with my lovely arm with my lovely bracelet on it. This was textbook Sophie – she would forget the most important things in her own life, condoms and such-like things, but she wouldn't ever forget to get me something wonderful.

I skipped back down the stairs to the sound of my phone buzzing. It was my mother. I answered. Bracing myself for what was coming.

'HAPPY BIRTHDAY TO YOU, HAPPY BIRTHDAY TOOO YOUUUUU, HAPPY BIRTHDAY, DEAR KATIEEEEEEE!' my mam and dad wailed down the phone.

I held it away from my ear, and even Sasha jumped lithely off the kitchen stool she was perched on and trotted swiftly out of the room. She had the right idea. What was coming was even worse.

'Hi, guys, thanks! *Thank you!*' I interrupted before they could launch into 'For She's a Jolly Good Fellow . . .'

'Katie, on this day thirty years ago – or twenty-nine years ago – sorry, love, I keep thinking you're thirty. I'm just bracing myself early for having a thirty-year-old daughter. It's going to be very hard for me, you know. Anyway! On this day twenty-nine years ago you were forcing your way out of me, arse first, causing me the most agonising pain I have ever experienced in my whole life. And then I did a poo, a smelly one, and then I had an orgasm. Pain, shame and pleasure. And then there you were, and it was only the beginning of it all!'

You would think this story would disgust and horrify me beyond belief. However, I had heard it every year for as long as I could remember and I had gradually somehow developed the ability to zone it out, and detach myself from what she was actually saying.

'That's lovely, Mam, thanks,' I said when I sensed it was the end of the story.

'Anyway, petal, your father has transferred two grand into your account – is there anything else you'd like?'

My parents had always thrown cash at me like it was skittles around my birthday. They had always had so much of it. I wasn't complaining though.

'That's more than enough, Mam.'

I spent my birthday lazily watching the *Sex and the City* and *Gossip Girl* boxsets and reminiscing about my old life in New York. I then took a delicious bubble bath, put on a face mask and this hair-restoring goop that Sophie had left behind in my bathroom. I shaved my legs! The whole works. I emerged from the bathroom smelling like a meadow of roses and coconuts, if such a thing were to exist. I popped a Ferrero Rocher into my gob and combed the tangles out of my damp hair, feeling utterly content. Even my hangover had eased off to give me a break on my special day. I slid into a delicate cream silk-and-lace, above-the-knee dress and draped a light, off-the-shoulder, cream jumper over it. I was feeling brave so I cut a few ringlets of my hair to create a bit of a fringe around the front. I looked in the mirror at my fringe and laughed at myself. I looked like one of those curly-haired dogs whose hair flops down in front of their eyes. A Labradoodle or something.

At seven thirty the doorbell buzzed loudly. Shit, he's early! I was pretty much ready so I wasn't sure why I was panicking. I just was expecting a bit more time to admire myself in the mirror – not too much, however, or I would find things to criticise. I ran down the stairs in my bare feet. I hadn't sorted shoes yet. Well, he would have to understand, given that he was thirty minutes early!

I opened the door with a big smile only to find an Asian

man standing on the step, his lorry parked behind him and in his arms was a massive bouquet of yellow roses – there must have been over thirty roses with white-and-green garnishing of leaves and herbs. The man's head only just peeped out over the top of it.

My heart stopped in my chest for a second that felt like five minutes. I stared at him. I couldn't breathe never mind say anything.

The only person who ever sent yellow roses was Seb.

'Hello, madam, a delivery for Katie McKenna.'

'Yes,' I blinked. 'This is . . . m-me.' I stumbled over the words.

He fumbled to extract an electronic signing thing from his back pocket and held it out in front of me. I looked at it, still frozen to the spot.

'Please sign, madam – I come all the way from Galvay this evening,' he begged, pronouncing Galway with a 'v' instead of 'w'.

'Oh sorry, of course.' I pulled myself together and scribbled a signature. I then somehow managed to take the flowers off him and carry them into the kitchen. I lost a few leaves and petals on the way, trying to get it through the door and down the hall. I went back to shut the door.

I was still in shock. It was definitely him, wasn't it? I went back into the kitchen and opened the little envelope sticking out of the top.

Katie, my love,

I can't begin to describe how sorry I am for what I have done to you. It torments me constantly thinking of how I have hurt you. I love you still, Katie. My life is empty without you. I cannot justify what I have done. I can only say that I can't make sense of any of this, of how I feel and why. I hope someday you can forgive me. Another surprise will arrive tomorrow. I hope you will find it in your heart to accept it, or

at least give it a chance.
  All my love,
  Your Seb

A steady stream of tears flowed down my face. What was he doing to me? After all this time? Why couldn't he just leave me alone? I had just started to feel really content with my new life. I was going on a date, and then this happened. My make-up I had spent about an hour applying was ruined, and Fred would arrive any second. And he would find an obnoxiously large bouquet, which dwarfed his one – I hadn't even thought that would be possible. Trust Seb to be the most extravagant. I didn't have time to process everything.

I rushed upstairs, thinking fast. I dabbed my eyes with cold water – the redness wouldn't go away but I did my best at repairing the make-up and recovering myself. I covered my red nose in powder and looked almost normal. If a little traumatised. I then went downstairs and hid the yellow flowers behind the couch. It was almost a metre from the wall with them behind it, but hopefully we'd leave so fast Fred wouldn't notice. I made a firm promise to myself that I would put the whole thing out of my head, so I could actually enjoy this evening. I was not going to let Seb mess with my head and ruin it all on me.

With five minutes left, I ran upstairs for one last inspection and to put on Cinderella's glass slippers, and I would be ready for my prince. Well, I didn't have glass slippers, but I did have a cute pair of patent white brogues. I clicked my heels together and the doorbell chimed. I smiled.

'Where are we going?' I asked and I couldn't stop a massive grin spreading across my face as he informed me that it was none of my business.

We were in the back of George Best's car. There was a light smell of Fred's cologne mingling with my spicy Moschino

Glamour perfume. We looked at each other across the back seat in the dim evening light. His eyes were dancing. I was pretty sure I was blushing slightly. I bit my bottom lip, to prevent myself from giggling. I didn't want to ruin the moment by being a dork. I tore my eyes away from his and looked to the winding road that preceded the motorway. As usual George's cab was barely touching tarmac at parts, particularly when taking corners. I was sure my side lifted off the ground at least once. I clung on to the seat, really hoping we didn't crash and die. This really wouldn't be a good time to die. Especially before tonight, which I just knew was going to be magical. Dear God, please let us survive this cab journey so I can have a lovely evening with Fred and lots of wonderful sex. Forget the sex part, God – pretend you didn't hear that. I tried to distract myself from thoughts of a gruesome car crash, which seemed all too possible. I made a mental note that it just wasn't worth taking rides from George Best any more. Even if he was the only cabbie in Ballytiernan.

'Galway?'

'You'll see.' Fred squeezed my hand.

There weren't many other options. Galway had a lot more to offer than the small towns near us. But he could have taken me anywhere and I would still have been excited. It was my birthday and I was being swept away by a wonderful man who was holding my hand, sending little electric pulses right to my toes. And I wasn't thinking about Seb and his what-the-fu*k reappearance in my little world.

The taxi came off the motor way as I predicted at the Galway exit but instead of continuing into the town, we pulled up outside the G hotel. I looked across at Fred, my eyes widening.

'Seriously?'

He smiled and said nothing as he stepped out of the cab. Moments later he was opening the door on my side. I looked out at him, unsure what to say. All I knew about the G was it was uber swanky-pants, the type of place where getting into the swimming pool is like sinking into a tranquil black lagoon with twinkling underwater lights and you can watch a flat-screen TV from your bathtub, which is probably filled with champagne if you request it. Like what you'd find in a famous basketball player's LA mansion on *Cribs*.

He escorted me into the ostentatious lobby reception area and straight through to the restaurant. I patted down my curls self-consciously. Fred spoke to the host and I was guided to a table while he disappeared off somewhere. He reappeared a few minutes later and sat in front of me. He placed a room key on the table beside my fork.

'That's your one,' he smiled.

I wrapped my feet in around his legs under the table. I was simply infatuated. My eyes stayed glued to his magnetic crystal-blue eyes. There was such clearness in them. Something about his nature was spelt out in his eyes – honesty and an openness which was so refreshing and engaging. Anytime I opened up about anything to him or told him anything about my life I felt like he was really listening, like one hundred per cent, and was completely interested in everything I was saying.

Our composure didn't last long. Before we knew it we were abandoning our half full plates and making a beeline for the elevator. The food was undeniably delicious but I was only really hungry for one thing. Even in the elevator I had my body pinned to his, and my hands were travelling up his back under his shirt. We only just got in the door of our room in time because I couldn't have held off any longer. We tore each other's clothes off in a mad frenzy.

I woke up on a cloud. The softest material was wrapped around my bare limbs. I slowly opened my eyes and a strip of soft light was flooding in through a gap in the heavy curtains. My gaze lazily drifted over to the man beside me. He was on his side. I took him in as I lay there, my eyes lingering on his lower back and then up to his broad shoulders. I momentarily contemplated waking him to tell him he had a lovely back. One that I wouldn't mind pouring tequila all over and licking it dry. I decided it probably wasn't a good enough reason to wake him – maybe I'd tell him another time. After a few minutes I started to feel that maybe it was weird that I was staring at him for so long, so I turned over and found another comfortable position on the loveliest mattress of all time – it would have been impossible to find an uncomfortable position. I began drifting into that wonderful half-dreaming state where you can guide your dreams and enjoy them while being semi-conscious.

As I was dancing in and out of this lovely state of being, I felt a hand moving down the side of my back over my hip, pausing gently on my upper thigh and then moving slowly back up and wrapping itself around my stomach. I gradually realised it was not a part of the dream – it was Fred's arm in the real world, and it was wrapped around me. His hand lingered on my lower stomach area and I softly moved myself backwards into his lap and rested my body against his. You just can't beat a bit of spooning. We were connected at every point; even my feet lay on top of his feet.

'Hi,' I whispered.

'Hello.'

We lay like that for another hour or so, floating in and out of sleep. His hands wandered every so often and I let them. Eventually I decided I couldn't ignore the thing that was poking into my back for very much longer so I dragged myself up out of the bed.

'Where you going?' He found my hand and held onto it.

'I need a shower.'

'Oh, okay.' He let go of my hand.

'Well? Aren't you coming?'

'Oh . . . well, I suppose it would save water if we showered

213

together,' he agreed with a serious face. 'We're only being ecologically aware,' he added as he scampered after me with a cheeky smile.

The taxi back to Ballytiernan was a proper Galway taxi, from a proper taxi company. It took twice as long as George Best did, but I felt less nauseated and the lack of fear for my life was a nice change. I had buckled myself into the middle seatbelt and rested my head on Fred's shoulder for the whole journey. I gazed out at the fields and hills as they passed by at a nice normal speed. I was finally starting to feel a sense of real love for this land. I used to feel like land without buildings, lots of people and action was, well, perhaps it was beautiful, but it wasn't for me. It wasn't where I thought I belonged, where my heart was. Now I felt so completely different. There was nowhere else on earth I would have preferred to be at that moment, and it was as though I could feel my soul gradually becoming entwined with this part of the world. I was falling for it. And a massive part of this change within me was to do with the fact that here was where I was falling in love.

The taxi pulled up outside Winnipeg and I looked over at my companion.

'Thanks so much, Fred. I really couldn't have dreamt of a better birthday.' I smiled at him, but he wasn't looking at me.

'Who is that?' He was looking past me, out the car window, towards the cottage. His brow was furrowed and his mouth slightly open.

I looked around and my lower jaw fell open into my lap. I got that sudden hideous feeling, like my stomach had fallen out of my ass. The long skinny frame of a man was sitting on the doorstep with his head down resting on his arms, which in turn were resting on his knees. Possibly sleeping. I knew immediately who it was. But I just couldn't believe he was here, at Winnipeg. At my cottage.

'It's Seb,' I said quietly.

'Okay,' was all he said. He sounded shocked and there was a touch of frustration in his voice, understandably.

'Sorry, I don't know what's going on. I didn't know he would show up like this. I can't believe it. I swear I haven't seen him since we split up.'

He said nothing. I didn't want to get out of the cab and leave Fred but I couldn't invite him in. It would be too strange. I guessed he was thinking the same. He seemed torn but resigned. What choice did he have? He turned his head away from me and looked out the window on his side of the car. There was nothing to look at only a hedge and a field, but he was avoiding eye contact, maybe so I couldn't say goodbye and go. I played with the handle on the car door on my side, unsure what to do. He really was doing a good job of pretending to study the hedge with stern interest.

'Well,' I broke the silence, 'I'd better go . . .'

I couldn't even give him a kiss goodbye with Seb sitting there on the step. Also I wasn't sure if he would receive it well. It was tragically awkward. The whole thing was a terrible way to end our first proper date, which up until then had been entirely perfect. I opted to just gently touch his hand with mine and give it a soft stroke with my fingers. He didn't object. I looked up into his eyes one last time before getting out, pleading with my eyes for him to understand the position I was in and how hard this was for me. He smiled slightly, and then reached his hand up to the side of my face. He leaned forward and planted a soft kiss on my lips.

I silently got out of the car and closed the door. It pulled away almost immediately.

I stood still for a moment before timidly walking up the path.

Chapter 24

I kicked him to wake him. Not like a karate kick, but not overly gentle either. He groggily looked up at me. I said nothing but my eyes bored into him like lasers, piercing through him with every ounce of energy and anger and pure disgust I had built up inside me.

I unlocked the door and left it open behind me for him. Call me a softie, but I just couldn't bring myself to slam it in his face. I had imagined what it would be like to see him again. But I never thought it would be like this – that he would just arrive on my doorstep in Ballytiernan. But all the same, I had thought long and hard about all the things I would say to him, all the unanswered questions in my head. I knew deep down though that I was scared to ask them for fear of the answers.

I had imagined shouting at him, slapping him hard across the face. I had thought about how satisfying it would be. But when he was there in front of me in the flesh, standing there in my kitchen, so broken, so vulnerable, his eyes devastated and lost, my overwhelming urge was to hug him.

Everything else disappeared in that moment. Tears silently streamed out of my eyes and down my face. My shoulders, my whole body shook as the emotion poured out of me. I was scared to open my mouth. I couldn't even look at him, be there with him without it all spilling out of me like a river bursting through a broken dam. I had blocked it all out and pursued a whole other life with such conviction that it surprised me how much tension was cooped up inside me. Having him there in front of me simply tore me down.

He timidly approached me and wrapped me in a hug. He was trembling. I melted into his embrace and our knees seemed to buckle at the same time and we sank down onto the wooden floorboards, and sat there wrapped in each other, both defeated.

For a long time my heart felt too heavy to form words or thoughts, but finally I took a big shaky breath and spoke.

'Why, Seb? Why did you do that to me? What happened to you – what happened?'

He looked at me. His dark brown eyes looked completely exhausted, they seemed to be protruding out from deep grey circles. His cheeks were hollow and the usual creamy, warm caramel glow had left his complexion and had been replaced by a yellowish hue. As I allowed myself to properly examine him, I realised he looked totally different. I had never seen his hair ungroomed before. He had always been one of those people whose hair, even when they've just woken up, seems flawlessly styled. Now he looked like one the boys from *Oliver Twist*.

'I just don't know, Katie,' he said, his shoulders collapsed. 'I've been in a really bad place. I don't even understand it myself. But I've been trying . . . I promise, Katie. And I'm going to do whatever it takes to get my life back and make it up to you. I need you more than ever. You have to help me.' He clutched my hand; he seemed terrified of what my reaction might be.

It was overwhelming. I tried to focus my thoughts on what I needed to say but my brain was like mush. It felt like all the horses of the Kentucky Derby were stampeding through my head.

'Where have you been, Seb?' was all I could come out with.

'I've been all over. After what happened, after you left, I hit rock bottom. I tried to ignore everything in my head – severe fucking depression – bi-polar, that's what they say I have. One minute I was like the most devastated guy on earth, contemplating throwing myself into the Hudson, the next I was out partying like crazy, meeting guys, experimenting, discovering myself or whatever . . . I took way too many drugs. I wore a ballet tutu for three days straight, Katie, and it felt like all I did was twirl and throw vodka shots down my throat. And then one day . . . I'd forgotten you had left. I was on a strange trip. I couldn't remember what had happened, and I bought fifty magnolia cupcakes and brought them back to the apartment for you, and when I realised you weren't there I ate them all, all fifty of them – it took me a couple of days, but it was all I ate. Days passed and I didn't leave the house. Sorry, I'm finding it hard to filter out what is irrelevant . . . I suppose you don't need to know any of that. Then where did I go?' His eyes glazed over for a moment and then he snapped back to reality and looked like he was searching the depths of his brain. 'Oh yeah. I got on a Greyhound bus for about eight hours and ended up at my mother's house. I told her and my whole family that I was gay. They said I wasn't, that I didn't have to be and if I loved them I would choose not to be. I sort of expected that a bit, well, I should have anyway, but nevertheless it knocked me back when they said that. At first I fought with them. I tried to leave but they wouldn't let me. My Uncle Noel and Megan's husband Pete – they forced me to stay there. I got really upset then, I started to hurt myself.' He lifted up his top and his stomach was covered in scars, deep wounds and small gashes everywhere.

I gasped. I reached out and touched his stomach gently. I had a sudden urge to kiss the distressed skin but I stopped myself. I sat there speechless, waiting for him to continue.

'Then they sent me to this religious place in – in Utah, I think. It was like a hospital or an institution, but it was run by some sort of monks. They told me there that they would cure me. I think maybe they did cure me.' He paused and wiped his nose in his sleeve.

My mouth was hanging open, horrified. This was sounding like an absolute nightmare. I had known Seb's mum was religious but I never thought she would have reacted like that. She had always seemed so loving and supportive, and she was so nice to me when I met her. I would have thought that maybe she would try to understand his situation, put aside her differences and resolve to stand by his choices, instead of just a flat refusal to accept them.

He looked up at me with a sort of demented hope in his dark eyes.

'I'm trying, Katie, and I think I can get back on track. I miss you so much.'

'You can't just decide to be straight, Seb.' I avoided his gaze – it was making me uncomfortable. He was looking exasperated, and I felt like I wasn't helping by saying this, but I couldn't go along with his delusions. 'It's not something you can be cured of and you know it.'

'I just need time. We need to get back to where we were when we first got together, when it was exciting and romantic. You've always been the only one for me, KitKat.'

'Stop, Seb.' I didn't allow myself to look at him. I didn't want to let myself believe anything he was saying because he looked so broken and unstable. It was too difficult. 'You're hurting me.'

'I never want to hurt you again. I'd marry you, Katie. I would. Tomorrow if you'd have me.'

'I said stop, Seb. Please.'

'Sorry.'

We sat in silence together.

'Please don't make me leave,' he finally muttered softly.

I was exhausted by this stage. 'You can stay awhile,' I sighed. I wasn't sure if I regretted saying it, but I couldn't kick him out. I would never forgive myself if anything happened to him.

I stood up and flicked on the kettle. Seb was still on the floor. He looked unwell and his body was still trembling. He wasn't wearing enough for the Irish summer; he was dressed for an American summer's day, in a small T-shirt and loose khaki shorts that seemed to hang off his skinny frame. I grabbed a throw from the living room and draped it around him, made tea and then held my hand out to pull him up off the floor. He stood up shakily.

I put his rucksack on my back.

'Come on,' I said and he followed me silently up the stairs.

I put him in the spare room, sat the tea down gently on the faded wooden table by the bed, and pulled the layered linen curtains across the window, leaving the room steeped in a muted dark evening glow. It looked peaceful. Seb sank into the soft floral sheets, succumbing to the quietness willingly.

I shut the door behind me and without thinking I wandered across into my own room. I climbed under the covers and curled up into the smallest ball possible. My eyelids fell heavily closed.

Chapter 25

I awoke with that shaky breath you get from the exhaustion of a long bout of crying. My bedside clock blinked 7 a.m. at me. I had been in what seemed like a heavy sleep for about twelve hours. However, physically and mentally, I felt like I hadn't had a wink of sleep. Compared to how wonderful I had felt waking up the previous morning, the reality of this morning was grim and depressing.

Seb had somehow managed to get into the bed beside me without waking me. He was now in a deep slumber with one arm draped around my waist. I stiffened.

I tentatively stretched out my only unobstructed hand and jabbed my phone: it flashed a missed call from Fred. Shit. My throat was so tight I could barely catch breath and my heart felt like a big lump of lead in my chest. Just last night I had been in bed with Fred. And here I was in bed with my ex. Fred's arm had been exactly where Seb's was now on my waist. I slid out from under it swiftly. We weren't doing anything serious but still it felt very wrong. It felt like we were back together but it was fucked up. And also I felt like a doormat for letting him back into my life so easily. But what could I do? He was so troubled and he needed help. I didn't think he had anyone else to turn to.

I shuffled out of the bedroom, had a long shower where I stood under the water staring straight ahead of me until I was a giant wrinkly prune, and then I wrapped my fluffy pink dressing gown around me and retreated down to the living room to do some sketches. I desperately hoped to lose myself in a nice easy sketch. The sounds of my thoughts would quieten down as I worked and eventually there would be no voices in my head. Just silence.

I began a detailed study of the sheep in Fred's arms from my original painting. I hadn't done much preliminary sketching for that one and it seemed that the sheep suffered most from my lack of preparation. He wasn't quite as perfected as the various men in the collection. It didn't help that I wasn't hugely experienced with sheep. I also had work to do on Frank's taxidermy animals for the same reason, but I just didn't have the fondness for them that I had for the little sheep. As I numbly chewed on a banana, I did a few rough sketches and my technique gradually improved throughout the early morning. The voices in my head did quieten down too. As the light gradually got brighter, streaming in through the window, I was becoming more and more accustomed to the sheep's little face and I felt ready to fill it in properly in the original painting. Everything else about the painting seemed finished and it was just waiting for that one last detail. I worked on it until the sheep was full of life and character. He was almost stealing the show from Fred. He was charming and sweet and I felt so at peace completing him.

Then it was done. My first painting of the collection was completely finished.

I signed it and stepped back. In a few weeks I would varnish it and that would be it. Now I had to exercise restraint, hold back and leave it alone, or else it would never be dry enough to varnish. This was always my problem. I always found fault the more I looked at something.

The hands of the big old clock on the wall clicked gently together at the top signalling midday. I had been painting for over four hours.

I lifted the canvas gently by the corners and shuffled round to the side of the couch. It would dry quickest there beside the window. I was standing in the middle of the living room, taking it all in, when I heard footsteps coming down the stairs. I didn't move a muscle. I could hear him going into the kitchen looking for me, then I heard him drift back out into the hall. He gently pushed open the door of the only place left to look, and peeked his head around.

'Hi,' he croaked. His shoulders were hunched, his eyes sleepy, hair all over the place. I said nothing.

He wandered into the room silently, taking everything in. He stopped near me and his long slumped frame seemed to perk up a bit. For the first time since he arrived his eyes showed signs of the sparkle of the Seb I used to know and love.

He breathed in. 'Katie.'

I looked up into his eyes properly; they were gradually coming to life. They were wandering around the room almost as though they suddenly had a life of their own. His head merely followed them, and his body numbly followed it.

'You know, I always knew you were capable of this.' Standing there amongst my paintings just seemed to breathe life into his soul. 'You had this potential to create masterpieces but I never saw you get there. Not while we were together. Something always hindered you. *This* is the brilliance you were destined to reach. These are simply spectacular. Now I know why you were meant to come here, Katie. It's like everything happened for a reason. You've become a master.'

'Ah, come on now!' I laughed.

He was getting a bit too American on me. He had always got this way about work that inspired him. But when I thought about it, although he always encouraged me and told me I had great talent, he had never got this excited over my work before. As it happened, this time his encouragement was much less sought-after. I simply didn't yearn for his approval any more. It wasn't like back in New York when I was so desperate for him and his peers in the business to rate me.

'It's just a bunch of farmers, Seb – let's not get carried away.'

'No, Katie. You mustn't do this thing you do. You always make little of your work and your ability. This time I won't have it, because this time you have risen above anything you ever did before. You're like a new person. You have not quit because you got bored or lost faith. You have persevered and created a collection that will truly captivate people. Each painting tells so many stories – they are so complex – just look! This teenage girl with braces in the foreground here, she is looking at the man on the tractor as though she's never seen anything like it before, and her mother is pulling her away. It's brilliant. And I just adore these guys.' He pointed at Seán and Fred. 'They know they are being watched and they are so uncomfortable, and look at these Manhattan school kids, crossing the road in front of the boys – they are so excited! I can almost hear the sound of their laughter. It is a beautiful moment you have created. They are a series of beautiful moments.'

He shook his head again. He looked at them all again, separately.

'Is this the lot?' he asked.

I hesitated. There was a time I would have killed to hear him say all this about my work, but I wasn't that artist any more. I painted for myself, not for anyone else and certainly not for Seb. In fact I liked that it was removed from him. It was my own thing. My new life without him. But he was trying to be nice and I had to reluctantly accept that.

'I have one more beside the couch.' I pulled out the final

canvas. The only finished one. Fred and the sheep. He nodded, and then shook his head.

'The detail in this . . . it's really gentle, done with such care and attention. You put the most passion into this one, I think. Who is he?'

I paused. 'That's Fred. He's . . . a very old friend.'

Seb seemed to sense my awkwardness, and maybe that I wasn't telling the full story. He looked away, not wanting to push it.

'Joanna Lenoir is just going to go crazy for these,' he said.

Okay, now he was losing the run of himself, I knew there was no way Lenoir would ever even sniff at my work. She was the head curator of the department of Modern and Contemporary Art at the MMA and totally brilliant and revered. She was known for her dedication to new work by innovative young artists and she was credited with discovering a lot of the most successful new artists in Manhattan. I had heard so much about her from Seb over the years – he had so much respect for everything she did there. He had spent a few months working closely with her on two connected exhibitions and I didn't hear the end of it.

I smiled at him. His enthusiasm was infectious. But it was also a bit infuriating. For some reason it was simply unwelcome. I didn't want this from him now. It was like he thought he could take away the pain of what he did by blowing my trumpet. So a niggling part of me was reluctant to go along with this optimism. On top of this I struggled to believe so highly of my own work and I felt it was all likely to end with me broken-hearted. Every time I was close to finishing a collection I got this vulnerable feeling and automatically went into self-preservation mode. I never allowed myself to get excited any more because so many times I'd been crushed and ended up with an apartment full of rejected paintings. And paintings are the worst thing to have lying around the house unsold or unappreciated because they are massive. They only served to remind me of the rejection, and gradually take little chips out of my optimism.

'Seb.' I said. 'Please don't go winding me up like that.'

But he shook his head, refusing to back down this time.

'I mean it, Katie. Have I ever given you false hope about your art before?'

'About my art, no, but you really can't talk about false hope.' Even though I knew he was trying to be kind, I couldn't help feeling annoyed. It felt like he was being condescending.

'Come on, Katie.' He shrugged his shoulders and raised his palms up in exasperation.

He was making it seem like I was being unreasonable, but I just wasn't ready for all of this yet. This friendliness, encouragement, familiarity. It felt wrong. He had been gone this whole time, since I started this collection. What right did he have to breeze back into my life and inundate me with praise and support?

'No, you come on, Seb. There was an abundance of false hope in our relationship. You were straight, then you were gay, now you're straight again.'

His eyes fell to the floor.

'Why did you score that Colombian chick?' I faced him, daring him to look away from me.

'I didn't want to mess you around, Katie – I wanted to prove to myself that I could be straight so that when I came here I could make a commitment to you and not let you down again.'

'This is so messed up, Seb.' I shook my head. 'Hooking up with a Colombian sex goddess is not the way to prove to me that you're ready to commit to me again. It's fucked up. Anyway, you're gay. You said so. That's what you said, Seb. You can't just decide you're not any more because your mother doesn't want you to be. It's not fair to me. You're gay.'

'I'm not.'

'You are!' I shouted.

'I'm fucking not!' He raised his voice to meet mine.

'Yes, you are, you're a big fucking pink flowery quee–'

He suddenly lunged towards me and locked me in a passionate kiss. Old feelings flooded back into my heart and gut and core without warning or authorisation and I melted into it. It felt like my soul was entwining itself with his. It was a typical amazing Seb kiss, his soft lips gently but firmly pressing against mine, slipping me a little tongue, not allowing me to second-guess it. I immediately wanted to grab his hand and run upstairs with him. He broke off the kiss, leaving me red-faced and panting. He smirked at me.

'*Queer!*' I finished defiantly.

I couldn't stop my heart racing though, and he knew the effect he had on me. I was so sorely tempted to fuck him just to see if I could get a feel for whether he was really turned on or if he was just a gay wolf in straight-sheep clothing. But no. I would definitely be cheating on Fred if I did that. Things weren't completely official with him, but he was basically my boyfriend now and I knew it would undoubtedly hurt him. Moreover it would make me an absolutely terrible slag of a person.

'Listen and let me explain, yeah?' He frowned at me, walked towards the table and sat down with a thud. 'God . . . well, I'm glad to see you're still the same stubborn leprechaun I know and love.'

I shot him a warning glare.

'I'm bisexual,' he said, staring straight into my eyes, almost daring me to interrupt him with my scepticism.

I just couldn't help myself. 'Bisexual is not a thing!' I took fast steps towards the table and jumped onto another chair, landing in a crouching position, with my feet on the chair and my bum sitting on the heels of my feet. 'Everyone knows that. It's just a synonym for denial!' I knew I was being unfair. I didn't really believe this. I had read an article about it once but I didn't really agree. I just wanted to press his buttons. I felt like having it out with him, being irrational, arguing for the sake of arguing.

'Will you let me talk?' He stared at me. 'I have come to realise that I fall in love with a person rather than a gender. I first felt attracted to a boy when I was eleven years old. He was my neighbour. I also liked girls so it was a real shock when I found myself attracted to a boy as well. He was fourteen and he was very decidedly gay. He said his mother had known he was gay practically since he was born. He just came out of the womb gay. He convinced me it would be okay to be gay, said it had been about as inconvenient for him as a toothache. We became very close very quickly and one day we were sitting on my bed and we kissed. My mother walked in and she hit the roof. She sent him home and sat down with me and asked me to promise never to let it happen again. So I didn't . . . for six years.

'When I was seventeen I met another boy, Bruce. We were crazy about each other. He was very serious about our relationship and wanted to go public. I knew by then I was bisexual because I had had girlfriends and was having the normal teenage boy reaction when I saw a naked girl, but then I had a very similar reaction when I saw a boy. But Bruce convinced me to tell my mother. I told her that I was bisexual and she cried. She said it would kill her if I ended up with a man. That I was her only son and the only thing she wanted from me was to see me happily married to a woman, with kids and a normal life. She said that when she died she wanted to know that one day we would be reunited in heaven, but if I chose boys I was turning away from God, and therefore choosing not to go to heaven. She was so upset, Katie – I couldn't hurt her like that.

'Breaking up with Bruce, letting him go, was one of the hardest things I've ever had to do. But my loyalty has always been to my mother: the woman raised me on her own, and struggled so hard to give me a good life. I owe everything to her. I knew anyway that I could be happy with women, so that other side to me wasn't worth losing my mother over. I felt like I was being selfish if I fooled around with boys, when I could just as easily have stuck with girls. I did feel like I was always suppressing a big part of myself, and in a way I felt like I was living a bit of a lie. And in Manhattan where the gay culture is so appealing, it was particularly difficult to stay away from it.'

I was dumbfounded. I had been so unaware of this part of his life, and it seemed so huge and overwhelming, I couldn't believe he had kept it from me. I had thought he'd shared everything with me.

'But when I met you, I cannot tell you how amazing it felt. I remember the day I first laid eyes on you. I was standing in front of Picasso's *Head of a Woman* at the MMA, completely lost in its beauty and originality, and then the real head of a woman stood right in front of me, with a big mop of curly red hair completely blocking my view of the painting. I thought, this bitch better move out of my way, but you didn't. You stayed there; you seemed just as mesmerised by it as I was. I coughed to get your attention and you seemed to snap out of your trance. You looked around at me and said in a thick Irish accent, 'God, sorry! Look at the state of me, standing here right in front of you like an eejit.' I could hardly understand a word you said but I was immediately infatuated. You completely changed my world. You must have noticed how incredibly happy I was with you. I had a real soul connection with a woman, I was so attracted to you on every level. You were ambitious, sexy, creative and incredibly talented. These things are huge turn-ons for me, especially talent and ambition, and you had so much of that when we met and you had just graduated from college. You were just so vibrant. I was captivated.'

'So . . . what happened?' I softly pressed. I had a feeling I wasn't going to like the next bit but I needed to hear it.

He sighed and continued. 'Well, you must have sensed connections seemed to break down between us towards the end and we were slowly drifting apart. You were less motivated and you had lost your ambition and, trust me, I hate myself for this, but I just found my affection wandering. Maybe I should have supported you more, tried to get you back on track, but you seemed so uninterested in anything. You spent all your time at the B-Cup coffee shop –'

'I *worked* there!' I could feel myself getting upset by these accusations. It was tough being an artist and never getting any recognition and, yes, I had become complacent, but it was to protect myself from the ongoing torture of constant rejection.

'Yes, I know, but I didn't see you as much then and . . . come on . . . you must have felt the drift. We hardly spoke.'

The anger fell out of me and was replaced by sadness. There was no use fighting it; he was right. I was lost then. As sad and hard as the death of my granddad and my relationship was, there was a very clear silver lining. It brought me clarity. The move to Ballytiernan brought me focus I hadn't had for a long time. Before I left New York I hadn't been myself. But he shouldn't have been so quick to look elsewhere. He could have been a supportive boyfriend. Weren't you supposed to ride the highs and the lows in relationships?

As much as I loved Seb it was slowly dawning on me that he wasn't as reliable or patient as I had thought he was. He was a New Yorker, not a whole lot better than Jules or the rest of my Manhattan gang. He lacked loyalty. He had that same thirst for constant change and adventure that everyone in Manhattan seemed to have in abundance. On one hand it was great but, on the other, everything seemed so fleeting, especially relationships.

Despite his efforts to win me over, it dawned on me there and then, as clear as day, that I would never have had a solid relationship with him. It was also so appropriate that he was bisexual. It suited him. He was just generally a flighty, never-satisfied-with-one-thing type of person. He was full of passion, but it didn't ever last long before he was on to the next wonderful thing. Infatuated with it. He had always been like this – all of our friends had been surprised our relationship had lasted longer than a few months. They'd all put bets down on it failing after a few months because he had been a notorious player before then. I now guessed that the only reason it had lasted as long as it did was because he desperately wanted to please his mother. I couldn't help feeling like a chump.

'So if you're *all of a sudden* bisexual now, and you apparently have been all along, why did you tell everyone you were gay?' My eyes narrowed.

'Well, I met someone. Just before we broke up. And I was so tired of living with a secret. I just wanted to be myself for once, to feel free. So I decided if I told everyone I was gay this time, they would be forced to accept it. I suppose I was thinking particularly of my mother. If I told her I was gay I thought maybe this time she would, I don't know, feel sorry for me. Want me to be happy. You know? I thought if I was firm this time, spoke with conviction and certainty, she wouldn't be able to talk me out of it or refuse to believe it. Obviously I expected too much.' Now his eyes filled with tears and his breath became strained. His voice broke and he began to sob softly as he spoke. 'I just want her to accept me, Katie, the way I am, and accept who I choose to love, regardless of gender. Why can't she just do that? Is it too much to ask?'

He blinked back his tears. He roughly rubbed his eyes with his knuckles.

'Be careful with your poor eyes,' I scolded. 'Don't be so rough with them.' I handed him a tissue. 'Dab them gently, Seb.' It was strange how easily we could fall back into this sort of relationship, where I had the constant urge to mind him and look after him.

He nodded. When he had calmed down and got his breath

back, he continued. 'When all of that happened at my mother's house, it was like the straw that broke the camel's back. I had to decide once and for all, I had to choose between my family and my sexual freedom. I chose my family. It's not enough of a reason to lose them, and I need to stop thinking about myself. I've tried it both ways and I know what I want now. I want to commit to something, forever, and put all that behind me. I want to bury it. I mean, at the end of the day I can be happy with a woman. I can be happy with you, Katie.' Despite him having nearly rubbed his eyes raw the tears were welling up again. 'You're the only woman I've ever really loved. I was so relieved when we found each other. My soul felt peaceful. It was like finally the pieces of my little puzzle slotted into place, after years of it being so disjointed.'

I shook my head miserably. All I knew is that I didn't want to go back there. It felt like beginning a marathon. It all just seemed like everything was a lie now, and him talking about it like this just made me incredibly sad. Although he seemed totally sincere, it was tainted.

'Please, Katie,' he pressed before I could say anything, 'we could be so happy, I promise. Like before.'

'It's not good enough for me, Seb.' I finally found my voice. 'I want to be with someone special, and to be someone's special someone. Not because it would make their family happy, but because they truly love me. I don't want to have constant doubts about whether you really want to be with me or if you are just settling for me. I want to be swept off my feet. I want a fairy-tale romance. I deserve it.' I was crying now. I wasn't sure why exactly. I just felt that if he could cry then so could I. 'I deserve a happily ever after,' I blubbered. 'I deserve Prince Charming! I'm a princess!' Oh God, I was practically wailing now. There was mascara and snot coming down my face. Yep. I was only a tiara away from being a perfect princess. Any prince's dream bride. Where are you, Harry? I thought wistfully.

'Please. Just give me some time, here away from New York. We can get to know each other again. I'll show you how special you are to me. I can be your prince.'

A tiny part of me wanted to give in. It was tempting to just pick up where we left off. He made it seem like it would be easy. But Fred! A vision of his wonderful wonky smiley face appeared out of nowhere in the frontal lobe of my brain and I felt awful for almost having forgotten about him. He had swept me off my feet at every opportunity. He was sexy, wonderful, everything I could have wanted. There was no question about it. Why was I even entertaining the idea of anything else?

'Seb, I'm seeing someone now,' I said directly. There was no other way to say it and I couldn't go any further without telling him.

'Oh.' He stepped back. He looked shocked.

This nearly made me laugh. I wasn't a spinster. Had he expected me to be sitting there in Ballytiernan twiddling my thumbs, waiting for him to change his mind and come find me? I rolled my eyes before I could stop myself. I was losing my patience.

'I'm sorry, Seb, but what did you expect?'

'How serious is it?'

'Well, I really like him. What do you want me to say? Yes, it's pretty serious.' I folded my arms and blew the stray curls off my face, to demonstrate my exasperation. There was a big one stuck to the snot/mascara residue, so I defiantly released it with my hand and stuck it behind my ear.

'Okay, I get it. I'm sorry. But you and I, we have a history together. Surely you don't want to lose what we have? You've only known this guy, what, like a few months?'

'How arrogant of you! And actually – I've known him since I was about four or five. Maybe even earlier.'

He was stumped. He started pacing the room.

I couldn't stop myself making a dig: 'I was friends with him way back when you were kissing your first *boyfriend*!'

'Fine! Fine. You've known him a long time, I get it, okay?' He scratched his chin, still pacing, and then came to a stop in the middle of the room.

'There's a flight from Shannon to New York on Wednesday, four days from now and I'm booked on it. Please give me until then to try and win you back. Just let me stay here. Then after that I'll leave you alone to get on with your life as you choose.'

I looked at him. He was asking a lot. What would I tell Fred? This wasn't good timing. This should have been like the honeymoon period, when Fred and I should have been spending every waking minute shagging. Building a bond, making a connection, which would determine whether the relationship would really work out. Now my ex wanted to stay at Winnipeg, like a big inconvenient pink elephant.

'Okay,' I sighed. As much as I wanted to, I just couldn't kick him out and I hated myself for it.

'Thank you, Katie.' He wrapped me in a big hug.

At that moment the doorbell rang. I jumped. Who could it be? I looked over at the window and through the slits in the blinds I could see Fred's truck. My breath caught in my throat. There was a worryingly good chance he could have seen into the living room on his way up the drive and seen Seb and me embracing.

I stood there, frozen to the spot.

'Will I get it?' Seb asked.

'Good God, *no*! Don't go near that door. You stay here and be quiet. Please.'

Chapter 26

I closed the door of the living room firmly behind me. I could feel my heart thumping against my chest as I walked towards the front door. I was suddenly all too aware of how this was going to look. I was still in my dressing gown and slippers, and had just been hugging my ex-boyfriend. Oh shit. I bit my lip hard and opened the door.

'Hi.' Fred stood there with his arms folded, his face red from the wind. The trees were blowing aggressively behind him. The weather was getting bad even though summer wasn't nearly over.

'Hi, Fred,' I said.

It felt like I should ask him in but I couldn't do that. It would have been so horrifically uncomfortable. So we stood there, with what felt like a vast distance between us, looking at each other in silence. I didn't know what to say.

'So he's still here then,' he finally said through gritted teeth.

'Yes,' I said quietly but the wind blew loudly, making my words inaudible. It sent a chill down my dressing gown and I gripped it tightly around me.

'What?' he said loudly, rubbing his hand across his stubble. His hand fell down by his side in a tight fist.

'Yes,' I said again, reluctantly louder. It sounded like an attack and that was the last thing I intended it to be.

'Okay.'

He looked really pissed off. It was like he wanted to talk to me but the wind was making it impossible. Also the fact that I hadn't invited him in wasn't helping the situation. But I just couldn't. Not right now. I couldn't look him in the eye. I was brazenly betraying him, after everything he had done for me to make me feel so special on my birthday.

I reluctantly met his eye and he silently said everything in those few seconds, his eyes red and intense. He turned on his heel, walked over to his car quickly, slammed the door shut and sped off.

Even though I'd only just showered a few hours ago, I ran myself a bath. I didn't want to see Seb for a while, but it was a cottage not a mansion so there were only a few places I could go where he wouldn't follow like a needy puppy, and thankfully the bathroom was one of them. For starters there was a lock on the door.

I knew I wasn't going to really enjoy the bath. I couldn't get the vision of Fred's gutted, angry face out of my head. I didn't deserve to enjoy the bath. Why had I let him walk away without finding a way to talk to him? I should have just invited him into the cottage and dealt with the awkwardness that would have ensued. It was cruel to have let him stand there in the wind.

I sat in the bath until the water went cold, until my feet started to go blue. Blue was an appropriate colour for me; I wanted to stay there until I went completely blue. I emerged out of the bathroom twenty minutes later, even more shrivelled, but cleaner than I'd ever been in my life. Being clean didn't make me feel any less shit though. I padded into my room in search of slippers and noticed my phone flashing, over at the wall where it was charging. It had a missed call and voicemail from Fred. I called voicemail. His voice sounded composed and direct.

'Katie. When I called around I was a bit . . . flummoxed, I suppose, that your ex was still there, staying with you. I don't really understand what's going on now and where I fit in, or if I fit in at all.' His voice cracked. 'Anyway, I just realised I didn't even actually say what I called over to tell you. I think it might be important, so just call me.' And he hung up.

That was it. He didn't sound very friendly. That was absolutely understandable though. The phone had no signal when I tried to call him back. Typical. Ballytiernan was always patchy at best for reception. After ten minutes of walking around the room and pausing in various positions, trying to get those precious few bars of signal, I gave up, stuck my phone in my pocket and followed my nose down the stairs.

There was an incredible smell wafting out of the kitchen. It smelt like rich tomatoey pasta yumminess and my stomach was growling in approval and anticipation. My stomach was never good at picking up on the overall mood I was feeling. No matter how awful circumstances were, my appetite always had its own opinion. It didn't much care about ex-boyfriends – new boyfriends – angry boyfriends. If it was hungry it was hungry. And food was food. And food that smelt good made my tummy go crazy. Boy, was I hungry! I apologised to my stomach – all I'd given it all day was a banana. And because I had been so cruel to my tummy, it was my duty to let Seb play the perfect little househusband. In fact, my stomach firmly demanded that I go along with this charade until it had its fill of what was in that pot. Then I could deal with the disaster that had become my life.

I loaded the big flavoursome meatballs into my mouth as though I hadn't eaten in months. I had to confess, one thing I really missed about Seb was his cooking. He had learnt how to cook from his Puerto Rican mother and, although I knew it wasn't really true, her recipes convinced me that Puerto Rico was the most delicious place on earth, full of very happy chubby people.

After devouring more than the capacity of my stomach, and expanding accordingly to accommodate the food mountain, I dug the phone out of my pocket to call Fred. I left Seb to wash up the dishes. He wouldn't let me near them, so I wasn't going to put up too much of a fight.

I finally found signal outside the front door. He answered after the first ring.

'Hi, Fred, I'm sorry, I'm so sorry – about everything. Sorry I missed the call – I was in the bath. Sorry. And em, Seb is still here . . . he's just staying a bit longer . . .'

'That's great, Katie, but I don't really want to talk about it, to be honest.' His voice was strained. 'What I called around to tell you – Billy Hanlon was in Farrelly's last night. He's still making out he slept with you. Word is out about the paintings and the whole story seems to have really grown a skin. They don't think you're just painting the men. They say you're offering services in return. I didn't bother correcting them or anything. Sorry, I just wasn't in the humour for any of it.' He sounded exhausted and reluctant to continue. 'Billy said that Frank Coffey hasn't had that sort of stimulation since he was in his thirties. Apparently he'd had better but certainly wasn't disappointed. I wanted to hit him, Katie, I really did, but I just don't know . . . I suppose you're not my girlfriend . . . really . . . so . . .' He took a deep breath, allowing me a space to interrupt but I was lost for words – my brain felt numb. 'Anyway, he then said Gerry was in the doghouse. Mo has found out. Apparently she's outraged – mortified. And she really has it in for you. She's known to be a bit loopy, Katie. Well, more than a bit. Apparently she poisoned a whole flock of sheep once because they kept wandering into her field. Anyway, maybe it's nothing to worry about but . . .' He stopped and went silent.

I immediately thought back to the fruit loaf. My head was pounding all of a sudden and there were very aggressive cramps in my stomach. It was like someone was repeatedly punching me in the gut. I shouldn't have eaten so much pasta. At least it wasn't fruit loaf though. I silently blessed myself and said a little thank-you to the Saint of Poison Prevention whoever that might be.

'I'm not so sure a bored middle-aged woman could really be all that dangerous,' I responded, trying my best not to sound terrified. I massaged my stomach with my free hand. I really didn't want to sound like I needed comforting. I didn't think he would be overly sympathetic with me right now if I made a drama out of it. Besides, there was no way I was going to leave Ballytiernan just because of one sad jealous woman. 'What's the worst she can do – throw her cupcakes at me?'

'Sorry. I don't know why I'm even worried about you. You have your ex there to protect you anyway.' He sounded exasperated.

'Sorry, Fred,' I said softly. 'I'm really sorry, okay? I don't want you to be worried about me. I'll be okay. And there's nothing going on with me and Seb – he just needs a friend at the moment.'

'Okay. I just don't know where I stand. That's not what I wanted to talk about anyway. You can ignore what I'm saying if you want but at least I'll feel better that I've said it. I think you need to be careful.'

'Thanks, Fred. I'm so sorry if I'm hurting you. Maybe I do deserve the wrath of Mo.'

He said nothing.

'Thanks,' I repeated. 'I'll be careful. And I'll explain everything when I see you . . . about Seb and all that . . .'

'All right, well, goodbye, Katie, take care,' he finished and hung up.

I couldn't comprehend any of it. My head was fried, and I wasn't really sure whether the knots in my stomach were because of Mo, or because of the situation with Fred and Seb. Or maybe they were knots of pasta. I really didn't want to talk about it with Seb because he would just want to stay at Winnipeg longer to protect me and that wouldn't help my situation with Fred. I did my best to put it out of my head for the rest of the day – there wasn't a lot I could do about it right now.

Seb and I then vegetated on the couch in a food coma, watching re-runs of *Jerry Springer*, like the good old days. It was a good way to distract myself from all the mayhem that was rumbling around in my head. I didn't want to think about it any more. I wanted to do what I do best – go back to ignorant oblivion. I mean, how dangerous could a bored café owner be? Right? Good. Forgotten. For now anyway. I'd get back to stressing about it tomorrow.

Watching Jerry Springer was always our favourite thing to do when we had some free time together. We would pretend to be the audience. We'd boo the bad guys and applaud when someone said something like 'You gotta grow up and be a man, you got eight babies who need their daddy!' We'd clap and shout '*Yeah! You tell him, Kay-Cee!*' Then we'd gasp dramatically when someone made an outlandish accusation. '*Oh no, he didn't!*' Or if we really got into it, we would pause the television, and get involved ourselves. We'd pretend to be a family member, or a pimp or a hoe, who had some twist to bring to the tale, which would accordingly provoke gasps from the audience. Well, we would do the gasping ourselves. It was always a fun way to spend an evening, and as always my sides were hurting from laughing as I dragged myself up the stairs to bed.

I insisted firmly that Seb stay in the spare room and he dutifully obeyed. As I lay in bed staring at the dark ceiling, I realised it was fun with Seb, really fun. But it wasn't the same kind of sexy, butterflies-in-my-tummy kind of fun that I had with Fred. It was starting to feel more like I was hanging out with my gay best friend.

Deep down I knew that it was a huge mistake to let Seb come between Fred and me.

I couldn't sleep. The evening with Seb brought back all those familiar happy feelings. My stomach sank. I hated that I liked being with him. It was the comfort of it, the fun. And then the fact that I had been rejected for so long, and now he wanted me back. It eased away all the self-doubt that had plagued me. I willingly soaked up the reassurance. I knew it! I told myself. What we had wasn't a lie. The three years hadn't been a lie, and I hadn't been a fool. Maybe I was being even more of a fool for letting him back into my life, but I couldn't help it. He was infectious. He was slowly worming his way back into my soul. And I was letting him.

Shit.

Chapter 27

The storm had passed the next morning and I awoke to the sound of birds chirping outside my window. They were probably wondering where the lovely old man who used to feed them had gone. I told myself I should try to be a better nature person. I leaned over to open up a little gap in the curtains and then I flopped back onto my bed to begin the process of talking myself into getting up. I gazed at the birds. I wished I could be as chirpy as they were. I eventually forced myself to sit up; that was a start anyway. However, as soon as I caught sight of myself in the mirror at the end of my bed I sank back down into my bed again. *Gah!* One step forward, one step back. My face looked exhausted and haggard. I buried it in the pillow and decided falling back to sleep was in actual fact a much better idea. But I couldn't. I flopped around in the bed like a fish caught in a net.

Right. I needed to see Fred. I needed to explain everything to him and beg him to understand.

I arrived at his door an hour later with my big, blue, woollen, winter, bobble hat on, even though the weather was quite nice, because I was having a horrendous hair day. I didn't want to inflict the sight of it on anyone. He didn't answer. I peeped in through the letterbox.

'*Fred? Bessieeeee?*' I called.

Nothing.

I set off around the side of the bungalow and across the field in search of them. I spotted the pair of them rounding up the sheep and made my way over cautiously. I knew he could see me coming and it was the longest walk of my life.

'Hi,' I said eventually as I arrived at his side. He didn't say anything. 'You can tell me to piss off if you like.' I was scared to look at him.

'Well, it's going to be really hard to take you seriously with that hat on.'

I thought I saw a hint of a smile.

'But why don't you clarify for me what's going on over there at Winnipeg, and then I'll decide whether to tell you to piss off or not.' He wasn't really smiling, but his face was softer, like he didn't want to be annoyed with me, or to argue. He seemed to want to give me a chance to explain. He was so solid and stable compared to Seb. No drama or bullshit.

'Nothing's going on.' I looked him straight in the eye. 'Honestly. He's just staying with me for a few days. He's in a really bad place and has no one else to turn to.'

'Okay, that's your choice. Given what you've told me, I really don't see how he has any right to lean on you. But if you want to help someone I can't blame you. As long as that's all it is.'

'Yeah, you're right . . . but I feel bad for him.' I fiddled with the cord on my anorak.

He looked sceptical. 'So is that it? He's just staying with you. Nothing else? He's not trying to get back in there with you? No kisses, cuddles or anything?'

I paused. I was stuck. Literally stuck. The storm from the day before had made the field all sludgy and I was wearing a pair of Converse. My feet were slowly sinking into the mud. I pulled them out and found a firmer piece of grass to stand on. He was still looking at me, waiting for my answer.

The problem was that I didn't know how to answer.

'Katie? Have you slept with him?' His clear blue eyes were pinned to mine, and as much as I wanted to, I couldn't look away.

'No!' I exclaimed. 'Well, not technically. He slept in my bed but nothing happened.'

'What the fuck? Did you kiss him?' He looked completely exasperated, and I felt like a total idiot.

'Just once . . . but it was he kissed me,' I said quietly. Without realising it, I had tied about five knots into the string of my anorak now. And pulled them tight. I would probably have to cut it off later.

'Is he not gay any more or what?'

'He is . . . well, no. Not technically, no . . .' Why did I keep saying *technically*? Why couldn't I find proper words to articulate what was going on? Because I felt guilty, that was why, and it was messing with my head. 'He says he's bisexual.'

'So is he trying to win you back or what?'

'I'm not sure . . .'

'What's wrong with you? Is one man not enough for you or something?'

'No, I just . . .'

'Was I not good enough? Was Friday night not enough? I did my best to make you feel special, because I thought you really deserved it. What more could I have done? Please, Katie, tell me, because I have no fucking clue any more. You know, I really thought you were different. When I met you I really wasn't looking for someone, you know? I had just come out of . . . something that really . . . hurt me. Okay? But I liked you a lot so I gave it another shot, and I just got trampled on again. I give up.'

'Fred, please!'

'What are you doing here, Katie? What do you want from me?'

'I don't know. I just wanted to explain what was happening. For it to be okay with us,' I said feebly.

'Well, at the risk of sounding like a thirteen-year-old: do you want to be my girlfriend or not?'

'I guess I do but . . .'

'But what?'

'I need to work things out with Seb right now . . .'

Damn. I should have prepared myself for that question.

He stepped away from me.

'Okay, well, if it's all right with you, Katie, I'm going to have to kindly ask you to piss off now.' With that he tied up the pen where the sheep were happily having their dinner, and him and Bessie set off back towards the bungalow. I watched them walk away, my feet slowly sinking back into the mud.

I did want to be his girlfriend. I did.

Chapter 28

I had fucked things up big time. As I walked through the fields between Fred's lovely bungalow and my cottage, every step filled me with regret until I was about to burst. I didn't bother crying; I didn't feel I deserved to feel sorry for myself because really it all was my own doing. Why was I so self-destructive? How had I handled things so badly? How had I allowed Seb to come between Fred and me? When I thought about it, I realised Fred had become the best thing about Ballytiernan – he was the main reason I was so happy there. He inspired me to start painting again, even if it was unintentional; but most of all, he made me feel special and important. Had I really just had a massive fight with him? I trudged numbly through the mud and rain towards Winnipeg. I couldn't bring myself to look back at his bungalow. Would I ever be welcome there again? The wild landscape that surrounded me for miles and miles all of a sudden felt like a big lonely abyss without him. I didn't want to be there any more, but I didn't want to be anywhere else either. I didn't want to be in New York, I didn't want to be with Seb. I wanted Fred. I could feel my heart screaming at me for being so incredibly foolish.

I didn't want Seb.

Yes, I had felt obliged to help him, and I hadn't been able to bring myself to say no to him because of how vulnerable he was, but why was my loyalty to him destroying my life? Seb needed to get out of my life. Everything he was doing was only serving his own needs. There was no consideration for what was best for me.

I had to make him realise that in order to help him I was sacrificing my own happiness, and it just wasn't fair on me. I needed him to see that it was never going to work out with him and me, because even if he insisted he wasn't gay and even if he swore to love only me forever, I didn't love him any more. The fact of the matter was that I was in love with Fred. Was I in love with Fred? Holy sweet Baby Jesus in heaven, I was actually completely in love with Fred. And I had walked away from him. I had messed everything up, basically because I was an imbecile. I had a sudden urge to slap my own face really hard, but I didn't because I was not yet that crazy. Although if things continued the way they were going, I wouldn't be far off. Maybe I would even do the removal job on the aul' ear. Maybe I really was becoming Van Gogh after all. It wasn't nearly as beautiful and profound as I'd thought it would be.

I didn't know how I was going to fix things with Fred, but if I was to have any chance, Seb had to go. It was going to be tough but it had to be done.

I marched into Winnipeg ready to confront him and insist that he go away and leave me to recover my life at once.

'Sebastian,' I announced with a strong sense of clarity and determination in my voice as I took my coat off in the hall, and 'commanded the space', as my old drama teacher in school used to tell me to do.

'Katie!' He rushed out of the living room so fast I almost jumped out of my skin. 'I have amazing news!'

'Katie!' Mac appeared behind him, her head peering around his left shoulder. 'He has the most amazing news!'

I blinked. This wasn't what I had planned. Why was Seb so jolly? This was supposed to be a serious sombre moment where I reclaimed my life and told him to shag off out of it. And why was Mac here?

'Mac! You're back!' I hugged her.

She was beaming. Her and Sebastian both seemed to be radiating delight.

'You are going to *love* me!' Sebastian's eyes were sparkling.

'No, I don't!' I exclaimed. I was totally flustered.

'What?' He looked momentarily confused but brushed it off in his excitement. 'Last night when you were in the bath, I took a load of photos of your paintings. I know I shouldn't have, blah blah blah! But I sent the photos to Joanna Lenoir. It's ten a.m. over in New York now, and she literally only just arrived to work and she has *already* replied. That is record time. Well? What do you think? Do you want to know what she said? Will I read it to you? Oh my God, you are going to die with excitement and happiness.'

I blinked. Then I furrowed my brow. I wasn't excited, I was angry. Well, as it gradually dawned on me what he was saying I was a teeny bit excited, but I wasn't about to die from it. I rooted my muddy Converse to the floor to maintain some of the clarity and conviction I had come in with. He wasn't going to win me over again with his tricks.

'Go on, read it to her, darling!' Mac urged.

'What does it say?' I kept my voice frosty.

'"*Dear Sebastian, hope you're getting better blah blah . . . glad to see you have not lost your eye for incredible artwork.*"' He lifted his head out of his phone and raised his left eyebrow up in a massive arc like The Rock. He continued. '"*It seems you have made quite a discovery. I need to see these pieces in person – there seems to be something very special there all right. Tell me more about the artist, and where the idea for the collection came from. Also can you please arrange for them to be couriered here so I can have a proper look?**

Then we can talk about bringing the artist over here for a meeting, if indeed they are as spectacular in the flesh as they seem . . .'" He looked at me again, his mouth and his eyes wide open.

Mac was nodding in the background. 'Of course they are,' she whispered. She squeezed my shoulder as she brushed past me into the kitchen. I could hear her flick on the kettle.

Seb was practically dancing on the spot. 'Oh my God, Katie, can you believe it? I knew she would love them! She might even rehire me after this! You are going to be a huge success with this collection, I can just feel it!'

I was completely dumbstruck. This was incredible. For years I had dreamt of this kind of reaction to my work, but I had never really believed it would actually happen. Even now I was scared to believe it. It just didn't seem possible. He handed me his phone with the email and there it was, in black and white.

'Wow.' I sat down in Sasha's armchair and reread the email five more times. 'Are you sure you sent her the right pictures?'

'Shut up, Katie, of course I did!'

As he said this the doorbell rang. My brow furrowed because I wasn't expecting anyone, but Seb jumped and clapped his hands.

'Yay, it's here already!'

'It is? What is?' I was completely bewildered now.

'I hope you're hungry!' was all he said, accompanied by a chuffed little wink. He scurried off to the door excitedly.

My head was reeling. I hadn't said anything I'd intended to say, which was a bit frustrating, but, good God, this thing with Joanna Lenoir could completely change my life. Did I want my life to change? I supposed it wouldn't have to change massively if I didn't want it to. I could still live and paint in Ballytiernan – after all, this place had inspired me more than anywhere else. But the opportunity to exhibit in the MMA would give me the sort of exposure artists of my age would cut off their left arm for (unless they were left-handed).

Seb arrived back with two big brown-paper bags that smelt divine. He opened one and started taking out a range of little boxes of Chinese food.

'I'm off!' Mac announced. 'I just popped in to say hello, pet. I'll leave you to your dinner.'

'Mac, stay! It looks like we've got loads here!'

'Really?' Seb looked flustered. 'Oh, it's just . . . I've only got two spring rolls . . .'

I looked at him. It was unlike him not to want to share.

'Don't worry, my dears – that Chinesey stuff never sits right with me anyway.' Mac grabbed her handbag and jacket.

I walked towards the door with her and Seb stayed behind.

'How did everything go with your sister, Mac?'

'Not good, I'm afraid. She hasn't got a clue what's going on. It's probably for the best, to be honest.' She paused. Her voice dropped. 'What's going on here, Katie? What about Fred? I thought you two were looking very cosy before I left. And that lad is . . . he's lovely but . . . he's a bit *fluffy* if I'm honest with you. You know?'

'Mac, it's a mess. Fred is, well, he's amazing and he took me away for my birthday and everything was great . . . he was wonderful . . .'

Mac raised her eyebrows and a smirk crept into the corners of her lined mouth, as she stuck her arms through the sleeves of her jacket.

'But then Seb turned up and . . . well, it's . . . I've been an idiot and he needs to go. I need to get rid of him and make it up to Fred.' I furrowed my brow and almost choked on the lump on my throat.

Mac looked at me sympathetically. 'Don't worry, love.' She wrapped me in a hug then pulled back and looked at me. 'Just be careful. I think that fluffy lad in there has a different view on things . . .'

'Don't mention any of this to Fred, please.'

'Of course not. And I'm thrilled for you about your paintings! Good on you, girl! I'll see you soon, all right?'

'Please, I'd love that.'

When I arrived back in the kitchen Seb had my granddad's old candelabra sitting on the table and was lighting the candles.

'Can you get cutlery, darling?' he instructed.

I flinched at him calling me 'darling', but silently did as I was told. He had also dug out one of my granddad's jazz CDs and had popped it into the little CD-player in the kitchen, and as Etta James came on he joined in: '*At laaaaaaast . . .*'

I walked slowly back to the table, feeling very apprehensive about what was happening. I placed the knives, forks and spoons on the table carefully. The cogs in my brain were turning and I was realising this wasn't right. I needed to say something quick. I needed to get everything off my chest. Everything I'd been thinking about the whole way back from Fred's place.

Seb opened the second brown bag and produced a bottle of Dom Perignon champagne.

I gasped. 'Seb! What are you doing? That is not necessary!'

'Katie, it feels like my life is finally coming back together again. I feel like myself again, and I owe it all to you. You were so good to let me stay here, and give me a second chance. There aren't many people who would have been so forgiving in your position. I'm just so lucky to have you. Last night watching *Jerry Springer* on the couch together felt just like old times – it felt so right.'

'Seb . . .' I was really hoping he would notice how uncomfortable I was and that I didn't share whatever it was he was feeling. But he was lost in his own happiness.

He rambled on, full of delight and enthusiasm. 'And now, I just know you're going to be such a huge success, and I'll get my old job back, maybe even move up to a better position! And we can go back to New York, get a great new apartment and start our life together again . . .'

Oh dear, he was deluded. He was totally getting carried away. All I could do was stare at him. I started to slowly shake my head but he didn't seem to notice. Before I could decide what to say to bring him back down to earth without completely crushing him, he jumped up out of the chair his bottom had barely been sitting in for two minutes.

'I wasn't sure when would be the right time to do this, but I think this has to be it . . . now . . . here . . . Katie, I need you in my life, you are everything to me . . .'

It was like watching a car crash in slow motion. I felt powerless to stop the disaster unfolding in front of my eyes. He dropped down onto one knee. My mouth was agape – how could he not see the horror that was undoubtedly etched all over my face? Then he actually proceeded to take a little dark-blue velvet box out of his pocket. I couldn't believe what was happening. I was completely shocked and speechless. Inside the box was the most beautiful vintage diamond ring I had ever seen. It was so incredibly beautiful, the kind of ring no girl could ever say no to, but that I certainly couldn't say yes to.

I could feel my heart pounding violently against my chest and hear it loudly in my ears: *Thump – thump – thump.* I was doing my best to shake my head because no words would come out of my mouth. My vision was getting blurry and little blue dots were appearing in front of my eyes.

Then black.

I came around and I was lying on the kitchen floor with a cushion under my head. Seb was staring at me, completely panic-stricken.

'Oh, thank God! Are you awake?' he exclaimed. 'Your eyes have opened but you're still not saying anything. Oh God, say something! I wasn't sure if I should put a spoon in your mouth to hold your tongue – is that something you're supposed to do? I've heard something about a recovery position, should I do that? Or maybe I should have done CPR! Or the Heimlich manoeuvre? Or is that just for when someone is choking? Oh, I'm the worst person in a disaster – I have no clue about first aid. Please say something, tell me what to do? Should I lift your legs above your heart?'

'Calm down, Seb, I just passed out, that's all. I'll be fine.'

'Oh, okay. Phew! Shit, Katie, you really scared me. One minute everything was going so beautifully and then the next you're lying on the floor and it's a total absolute disaster.'

I sat up slowly and took Seb's hand in mine. It was a lot cooler than my clammy one.

'Seb, it was always going to be a disaster anyway. That's probably why I passed out. It was just too much for me to handle. I am so, so sorry, Seb,' I looked into his eyes with every bit of sincerity I had, 'but you know I can't marry you. I don't love you. I can't move back to New York with you. I'm happy here. I'm happier than I've been in a really long time and for the first time in my life I feel comfortable with who I am and where I am. You're not the guy for me, Seb, and I'm not the right girl for you.' A tear slid down my cheek and landed on my hand, which was still clutching onto his. 'Seb, it's over, like properly over.'

I leaned towards him and kissed his cheek gently. He nodded.

Chapter 29

When the reality hit me that my paintings would have to be shipped to New York for Joanna Lenoir to look at them, I had a mild panic attack. They weren't finished! What had Seb been thinking? I spent the next few days like a frantic hermit. Locked away from the world, obsessing over every little detail to get them finished on time, forgoing the unimportant things in life such as showering and eating.

Seb actually said he was glad I wasn't marrying him because I had turned into a lunatic ginger version of the Crazy Cat Lady from *The Simpsons*. He said I was basically freaking out and throwing cats at anyone who disturbed me. By cats he meant paintbrushes, of course – I would never throw Sasha – and by anyone he meant himself, as there no longer existed anyone else who gave a shit about me in Ballytiernan. Fred had stopped answering my calls and, even though I looked horrendous, I'd taken a break on the second day of hermitage and braved the outside world to go to his house, but there was no one there. This didn't help my temper. My stress levels were off the charts and I kept thinking of Fred too. And I couldn't help taking it out on Seb a little. It was his fault I was sending my work to New York, even though it was obviously an amazing opportunity. And it was also his fault that Fred wasn't speaking to me. And he was also just the unfortunate person who happened to be in the firing line at the time. And my paintbrushes seemed to be like heat-seeking missiles whenever he was around.

I think Seb was glad that he would be leaving on Wednesday. I had become so smelly and insane. We had arranged to have the paintings couriered over on Wednesday on the same flight that Seb would be on so that he could meet the package at JFK and accompany it to the MMA.

With only two days left I could almost leave them alone, without crying. So I signed them and finally I took a shower. It felt so amazing to be clean. There was simply no point in trying to comb my hair though; it had basically become one disgusting dreadlock. However, when I realised how little time I had left to actually dry the paintings before they would be wrapped up in bubble wrap and shipped over, my dreadlock became the least of my worries. You would think drying would be something I could have no control over but I quickly became obsessed with mastering the sun. First I went at them with a hairdryer but I soon realised how futile that was, as it was only drying a tiny patch at a time. So I took them all out, one by one, to the sunniest corner of the outside of the house. And ran back and forth with them every half-hour (any drop of rain and I almost had a hernia). I enlisted Seb to help, doubling my efforts. He wasn't the friendliest assistant ever. I've never seen someone roll their eyes so frequently – I was convinced they were going to get stuck at the back of his head if he kept it up.

I admit it wasn't my sanest few days, but by Wednesday the paintings were as dry as they were going to get so I made my peace with letting them go. It wasn't easy but thankfully Seb was still there to coax me into releasing my vice-like grip on them.

As soon as they were packaged and gone, Seb gathered his

things and set off down the windy road towards the village to catch the bus to Shannon. He gave me a big hug before he left and told me that he was glad I'd made the right decision for both of us. In the lead-up to the shipping of the paintings, he had experienced a whole new 'bat-shit-insane' side to me that he'd never seen before, and the single-dreadlock look was 'not hot'. He still hoped I would stay in touch, and we could find a way to be friends, because he didn't want to lose me completely. I had to agree. I didn't want Seb totally gone from my life. Even though he wasn't the man I loved, it would be a hole no one could fill if he wasn't in my life. There were things about me only he would ever understand. I definitely didn't need him if I ever had an accident though!

I spent Wednesday night pulling a comb through my hair. It honestly took about six hours to untangle it. I felt like I had been scalped by the time it was back to normal. I rewarded myself with some jam doughnuts and tea for a very late dinner, and fell asleep in front of the TV.

The next day my life felt jarringly empty without my paintings. I had rung Fred's phone three times and left him two voicemails and sent two text messages. Nothing back. I had been stalking his Facebook page but that was a bit of a fruitless endeavour. And it was only making me pine for him even more. I guessed I would just have to come to terms with the fact that he didn't want to talk to me. I couldn't force him to talk to me. Maybe he had just come to the conclusion that I wasn't worth it.

I wandered around the cottage, sitting down occasionally on various chairs and couches, trying to figure out what to do with myself. Where to from here? Sasha observed me, looking mildly concerned. 'Sasha, what should I do?' I looked over at her desperately. She was probably just relieved that her living room didn't smell of paint any more. And even though she acted all cool and aloof maybe she was secretly glad to have me back to herself, with no men or paintings around to distract me.

I was feeling quite uneasy now that my paintings were gone. I was definitely suffering from empty-nest syndrome now that my babies had flown off to greener pastures. I hoped they would do me proud. I started to wonder where they were now – had they arrived at the MMA by this stage? God, what if the photos Seb sent were totally misleading and she actually hated the real things?

My thoughts were interrupted by the buzz of the doorbell. 'Please be Fred, please be Fred, please be Fred,' I prayed as I walked to the door, clutching my two hands together in a sort of prayer-like clasp.

I opened the door.

'*What?*'

It was Seb.

'I thought I'd got rid of you!' I said aloud without really intending to, but I just couldn't keep it in. I really had thought that he was finally out of my hair.

'I know, I know, please don't hate me! I missed my flight! *Ooops!* I thought it was eight p.m. when in fact it was eight a.m. I'm such an idiot! I slept on a bench at Shannon Airport, surrounded by *craaazy* Irish people – your people don't travel well – the grumpo-meter was off the charts in that place. Please don't make me go back there. The next flight they could get me on is Friday. Please! I can't go back there. Can I take a shower? I stink! That bus journey to and from Shannon – *twice* in the space of twenty-four hours, God help me!'

'Fine.' I rolled my eyes. 'Go take a shower. You *are* a smelly bastard. My flowers are practically wilting from the smell of you.' I pointed to the pots of flowers at my front door. They were wilting, but probably because I was terrible at taking care of them. I looked at them, feeling a bit guilty.

Seb rushed past me and up the stairs to the bathroom. I went to the kitchen and came back with a jug of water for the flowers. I watered the parched soil in the pots and went back inside. I had barely shut the door when the bell rang again! What is going on here? I thought I was finally on my own?! Who could it be at my door this time?

Well, I certainly was not expecting it to be Mo Brady.

Sasha and I were pretty freaked after Mo's threatening visit. She seemed fairly demented. Maybe she was angry that the fruit loaf hadn't done me in. As it turned out, I was now absolutely delighted that Seb was upstairs in the shower. Sasha and I obviously weren't damsels in distress but I was starting to get the feeling Mo wasn't to be taken lightly. Having a man in the house was certainly helping me to remain calm. I was in the middle of saying a quick little thank-you prayer to the God of Flight Mix-Ups when my phone started buzzing. I pulled myself up off the ground in the hall and followed the noise into the kitchen. Sasha veered off into the living room for a snooze in her queen chair after all that stress.

When I saw what number was flashing I froze. It was a New York number. I nearly peed my pants right there.

'Hello?' I held my breath. I didn't feel emotionally stable at all right now.

'Katie? It's Joanna Lenoir at the MMA. I got your number from Sebastian, I hope you don't mind.'

'Not at all, Joanna!' My voice came out a little squeakier than I would have liked, but at least it did come out. That was something to be grateful for.

'Well, I just wanted to let you know that I really love the pieces you sent over and I'm very interested in meeting with you. Would you be able to come over before the end of this week? I can clear Friday evening for you? We can go for a dinner meeting. Sebastian can come along too. Do you think you'd be able to get here by then?'

'Yes! Absolutely! That's amazing! Thanks, Ms Lenoir, I'm

really looking forward to meeting you.' I couldn't believe I was speaking so coherently. Go, me! It was definitely personal growth if I sounded this normal when it was like a Cinco de Mayo carnival mixed with the Texas Chainsaw Massacre inside my head.

'Yes, likewise. My assistant will email you and arrange to book you a flight. Great, see you Friday then.' And she hung up. God, she was impressive – all business, no 'goodbye' bullshit. Just like a badass businesswoman in the movies. I stared at my phone again. But this time I wasn't begging it to ring, I was thanking all the angels and saints in heaven for how wonderfully lucky I was, and I was thanking my phone for being the carrier of this great news. I even rewarded it with a little kiss. No one was watching. Sasha was in the next room. Speaking of whom, I decided to run in and hug her. She deserved to share in my happiness; she had shared in so much of my sadness and more recently, my terror. Sasha didn't seem to enjoy the hug as much as I did. She never really enjoyed hugging if it was forced upon her. Things had to be on her terms for her to approve, but she went along with it because she could sense how delighted I was. She was a good little cat really.

By the time Seb came down the stairs I had completely lost the plot altogether. I had put all thoughts of Maniac Mo out of my head now. By this stage I had progressed to the screaming and crying stage of ecstatic excitement. Through my hyperventilation I tried to tell him about the phone call. He eventually understood what I was saying – it took a lot of gestures and guesses and nodding but we got there in the end and he joined me in jumping around clapping and screaming. Sasha wandered into the kitchen to see what all the commotion was about. When she realised it was just two jumping lunatics she retreated. She didn't entertain such idiocies. I knew she was happy for me though – I could tell by the way her tail wiggled as she walked back out the door.

Chapter 30

Sebastian was not happy to be back at Shannon airport. I on the other hand was overjoyed. Not only was I escaping Ballytiernan and Mo and the torturous isolation, but also I was an important artist being flown to New York for God's sake! Lah di dah!

I could see what he meant by the grumpo-meter. But in fairness to the cranky people at the airport, it *was* crazy o'clock. Our flight was departing at eight a.m., so we had got George Best to take us to the airport in the death cab, as there were no buses at five a.m., much to Seb's enormous relief. Despite the lack of sleep I was bright as a button. I was so smiley the other passengers were looking at me like I needed to be sent to a mental institution and not on a plane. They all looked so glum. But then I was not flying Ryanair, like a good lot of the people there were, the poor souls. I was flying on a transatlantic airline where I would even get offered a meal without having to take a mortgage out on Winnipeg. I could feel their pain but I still couldn't lose the spring in my step! I hadn't really missed New York like I thought I would have, but nonetheless I couldn't wait to get back there. What a weekend this would be!

When I had rung Sophie to tell her all the news, I had been surprised that her Irish phone was out of service and when I tried her New York number it rang. She was back there! She told me that she had decided to go back for a few months. The doctors told her not to let her pregnancy take over her life, so they came to the decision that she would go back to New York and try to get her life back together and live normally until the third trimester. Then she would come back to Dublin to give birth. She had a doctor in New York who would look after things and communicate with the Dublin one.

So I made plans to stay with Sophie. This was a perfect arrangement, as going back to the old flat with Seb would have felt very strange. And I really couldn't wait to see Sophie again.

'I think you're gonna fall in love with Manhattan again and want to move back,' Sebastian predicted smugly as we sat at our departure gate.

'Hmm . . . I just can't see it happening,' I retorted. 'Honestly? I'm not ready to give up on Fred. Yes, I know he's not answering any of my calls, but I don't know. Maybe if I keep ringing . . .'

'That is really pathetic.' Seb looked at me patronisingly.

'Fuck you, Seb! This is all your fault!' I narrowed my eyes so much they were nearly closed. How dare he comment on this? He was supposed to just sit there feeling guilty for ruining my life!

'You can blame me all you like,' he stated calmly, not lifting his face from his magazine, 'but deep down you know it was your own issues that allowed you to drift away from him. You were scared to commit again, and when I showed up it was an easy way of deferring that. Face it, you weren't ready to fight for him because you were scared of what that would mean. And now you've realised what you lost and you want to blame me. Yes, I will take part of the blame. But not for the reason you think.' He finally lifted his head and fixed me with a firm look. 'I accept that by hurting you the way I did I damaged you. I know I handled everything really badly and it resulted in you being broken somewhat. I do regret it. But I have apologised for that plenty of times so, really, I think I can wash my hands of any guilt there. It wouldn't be healthy for me to hold onto it.'

I stared at him. Since when did he become so cool and collected? All of a sudden he was the expert on issues and guilt and all that crap! A right little psychiatrist, he fancied himself! The smug American prick.

'Well, aren't you just marvellous!' I remarked sarcastically.

'I am,' he grinned. 'Anyway, I think you should forget about this Fred bloke. He sounds like a drag. A farmer! When have you ever been interested in farmers? Imagine spending your life stuck on his farm? What would you do with yourself? Sit around doing paintings of his sheep for the rest of your life? Get your kicks going around the fields naked on his tractor? Getting off on the vibrations? I can just see you – over the years, becoming a demented horny old lady.' He did an impression of an old lady on a tractor having an orgasm.

A few heads nearby turned to look at him. I hated that his impression was so funny so I tried my best not to laugh.

'It's none of your business what I would do with myself! Or how I'd get my kicks! And anyway you've seen how happy I've been since I got there! I've felt more inspired and content than I ever did in New York. I actually wouldn't mind painting sheep anyway. Sheep are nice! Nice *non-judgmental* creatures.' I thought about the sheep in Dennis Daly's field, who kindly decided not to judge me for my original freak-out when I first arrived in Ballytiernan. 'Unlike you! You could learn a thing or two from sheep.' I jabbed Seb in the chest. 'Anyway. You just want me to come to New York so I can be your fag hag. Well, I'm sorry, but just because I have curly red hair does not mean I am going to become the Grace to your Will.'

He smirked at me. '*Touché*. I'll miss you though, Redzer.'

Chapter 31

I inhaled the lovely warm polluted air as we exited JFK. Thanks to the time difference, it was only 10 a.m. when we landed, so I had the whole day to find something nice to wear to dinner. Sophie was at work so I dropped my bags off with the doorman at her apartment. He told me how lovely and long my hair was since he had last seen me. I figured the dreadlock must well and truly be gone or he wouldn't have mentioned my hair. I thanked him for agreeing to take care of my bags and slipped him five bucks. Actually it was probably for the tip he said it, but no harm. I was happy, he was happy. Seb headed off to his own place, which I was keen to steer well clear of.

I spent the evening wandering around Manhattan and it was strange; it really felt as though I'd never left. I still had plenty of my parents' birthday present to spend so I strolled up Fifth Avenue in search of something pretty. I wandered into Anthropologie and immediately found something. I always did in Anthropologie. It was an exquisite piece with wonderful prints, like a real piece of art. Even though the patterns were Indonesian style, it reminded me of the famous Ukiyo-e Japanese prints, the way the design seemed to have such movement. It was from the Jen Kao collection and it would be perfect for my meeting with Joanna Lenoir. It had three different prints running through it with a blue floral, swirly pattern at the top, then a geometric block pattern at the waist and then a delicate red mosaic-style pattern at the end. Zigzag lines separated the different prints, kindly giving me curves in all the right places. It just seemed to be made for my figure. I decided I didn't need Fred after all: I was in love with a dress.

After spending the afternoon strolling through Central Park, I made my way back to Sophie's apartment to let her beautify me.

I took the elevator to the fifteenth floor. Looking out the window of the elevator, I couldn't stop the giddy feeling that was infecting every part of my body. Of course, in the line of business Sophie was in, her building was bound to be spectacular. There were glass windows everywhere, even in the elevator. So you got an incredible view of the city as you travelled up the side of the building. It was a little nauseating if you had an unsettled stomach. I had several memories of almost throwing up in it after nights out. It was better than my flat though which had no elevator at all and required climbing six flights after a night out, leading to many a bruised shin.

I attacked Sophie with an enormous hug the minute she opened the door to her apartment, practically mowing her down in the process. She stumbled backwards from the blow, laughing.

'Oh sorry, Momma – sorry, Babba,' I said, hugging her tummy, gently this time. 'How are you?' I couldn't help smiling. She looked particularly radiant.

'We're doing fine!' she beamed. 'It feels strange saying that, but actually the doctors say it's good to talk about 'us' and 'we' like that. Especially seeing as it's just the baby and me for now. I think it's supposed to make me feel less alone or something. Like we're a team, I guess.'

'Well, you're both lucky to have each other!' I chirped. It was nice to see her so positive and happy. I had been pretty confident she would take to it all well in the end, but it was a relief to see it all the same.

'So have you told anyone over here yet?'

'No, I'm not ready to at the moment,' she decided firmly, but then her face fell into an unhappy little pout. 'People are just starting to think I'm getting fat though.'

'Of course they don't! You're not showing at all – you're still tiny!'

'Look.' She pulled up her shirt and she did have what looked like a muffin top flowing out over the top of her jeans.

I tried not to laugh. It was funny though; I'd never seen her with overflow like this.

'Oh yeah.' I nodded. 'It does look a bit like you ate all the pie.'

'You're not helping, you cow!' She glared.

'Sorry. You just need to dress a little bit more tactically. Come on, you're usually good at this stuff. No more jeans, okay? Loose dresses and that sort of thing would be better, right? It's a good excuse to get yourself a nice little Diane Von Furstenburg wrap dress! In fact, I'm going to get you one tomorrow, as a maternity present.'

'Really? No way, Katie, they're way too expensive.'

'Don't be silly. I'm minted. It was just my birthday and I still have loads of my parents' present to spend.'

'God, are they still throwing mountains of cash at you on your birthday?'

'Yep. Well, now it's an online bank transfer. I considered not accepting it. I'm getting a bit too old for handouts. But then it's my birthday and they want to give me something. It's pocket change to them anyway, and I never ask them for anything otherwise. Anyway, tell me everything! What's your plan, Stan?'

'Well, believe it or not, I'm not doing too badly. My

company's maternity package is actually pretty amazing. Because it's a German company, they basically go by German standards, so I'll get a year's paid maternity leave!'

'What? That's amazing, Soph! Wow!'

'Yep.' She grinned. 'Who knows, maybe I'll even pop out a few more if I get used to all the free money! So anyway, I'm going to go to Ireland for the year so my mammy can help me. Well, maybe not the full year, depending on how I'm getting on.'

'You'll become a lady of leisure,' I laughed, knowing full well Sophie would get bored out of her tree being a lady who lunches.

I quickly jumped into the shower and then we continued our catch-up as Sophie got to work on making me look all fabulous and glamorous.

I hailed a yellow cab outside Sophie's building at seven thirty. She had somehow managed to restructure my curls into bigger, looser ones using some magic curling-wand contraption. She called them Marilyn Monroe curls. And she created this cool subtle Aztec look with the make-up, which really worked well with the dress. Cruising through Manhattan from the Lower East Side up to the Upper West Side, even though I'd done it a million times, felt like an adventure. The summer was winding down and the days were getting shorter, so the sky was a rich blue colour with an orange glow from the streetlights. We drove through Central Park and I watched all the happy couples strolling around in the warm autumn evening air, the park stretched out for miles around them, but nevertheless the big skyscrapers loomed like big walls around the edges of the park, watching over everything. They made sure you never forgot where you were. It all felt so far from Ballytiernan. New York was always so romantic in small doses, but it was often a different story if you lived there. I had to remind myself of this, because I was really wondering why I was so determined to stay away from this magical city. I just couldn't stop myself thinking maybe I was crazy to be leaving this place, especially now that I had such a great reason to stay. There wasn't a lot for me in Ballytiernan, especially if Fred never gave me a second shot. I had been so content cuddled up in my cozy little Ballytiernan bubble, I hadn't really realised what I was missing. Was I letting myself grow old there, when I should still have been enjoying my youth in the city? I bit my lip and told the uncomfortable feeling in my stomach to piss off.

I shook even more life into my curls as Sophie had instructed me to, 'for dramatic impact' as she had informed me. I reapplied my lipstick with my hand-mirror, and as I drew nearer to the Upper West Side the sorrowful feeling in my tummy was gently pushed out and replaced by fluttering butterflies. I clicked together the heels of the red strappy sandals Sophie had loaned me and felt like Dorothy on her way to Oz.

The cab pulled up outside the restaurant, on 77th street and Columbus Avenue. It was a typical trendy Manhattan place called Dovetail, where the décor was modern and stylish but it still had the traditional New York redbrick walls. I was escorted to a table in the back, away from the crowds, but still in good people-watching proximity. It was the perfect spot where you could get the buzz and the vibe of the place but couldn't be overheard.

Seb was there already.

'Is she coming?' I mouthed, slightly panic-stricken. I couldn't manage to shake the paranoid niggling feeling that she would realise what a mistake it was and pull out last minute and have my paintings burned before anyone else could lay eyes on them.

'Of course,' he whispered. 'She's always a few minutes late. Anyway, we're ten minutes early! Very un-cool. But it would be even worse for us to be late. So better safe than sorry. You look unbelievable, by the way!'

'Thank you, darling,' I said, employing an elaborately gracious air.

Joanna hadn't even arrived yet and already I could tell she was a very important, respected customer. The waiters were practically fawning over us. All I'd had to do was mention her name at the desk and I was practically carried to my seat in a king's chair. Not quite, but not far off either.

The whole restaurant seemed to stop and take notice when Joanna walked in. I felt my mouth go dry.

'Sebastian, Katie, wonderful to see you both. Katie, it's a pleasure to meet you.' She did the two-cheek kiss thing.

I always paused after the first cheek, unsure whether the person was a two cheek-er or a one cheek-er, but I got the impression pretty quickly that Joanna was a two cheek-er so I prepared myself for that, thankfully. She was the ultimate power woman: six-inch Louboutin heals, expensive-looking black dress suit. Very chic. Displaying her keen eye for design, she had added little creative touches such as a captivating turquoise stone neckpiece. I immediately felt too colourful. How could I have forgotten everyone in Manhattan wears black?

'Mr Tobago is on his way. He'll be here shortly.' She immediately registered our confused looks. 'Oh, I didn't tell you about that, did I? Oh my goodness, sorry, darlings.' She had a posh English accent. I wondered if she was actually English, or if it was put on like Madonna did for a while. 'Let me quickly fill you in before he gets here. He is a hugely important and influential art buyer and promoter. You would be so lucky to have him on your side. If he likes you he could buy the whole collection and even fund the exhibition. Dame Judith Palmer and her people are also interested in looking at them – which would obviously give you great publicity, but she would only buy one or two, she never buys a whole collection. So I think if we can get Mr Tobago to play ball it would be the best position to be in. Dame Judith might come to the opening exhibition anyway if we don't make it public that the collection has been purchased. The same goes for David Letterman. And he might even have you on his show if we really push for it. Martin Stevens also showed interest – your work is right up his alley, darling. We might be able to get him along for the exhibition too. He would almost certainly come if we auctioned them. But it would be a big decision to go in that direction – it might not work in your favour as a new emerging artist.'

My head was literally exploding. My mouth was hanging open like a simpleton's at a university algebra lecture. Seb nudged me hard in the ribs and I snapped back to life.

'Oh yes, yes, of course! That sounds like a very good plan indeed!' I cooed. Oh God, why was I now adopting a hint of a faux English accent? Get it together, Katie, I warned myself.

'Mr Tobago always likes to meet artists before agreeing to put his weight behind something.' She nodded. 'So this is why I invited him along this evening. It's very important to leave a good impression. He goes for the personality of the artist almost as much as he values the individual pieces. I do have a feeling he'll like you though.' She smiled warmly. 'If I remember correctly his mother was Irish, or was it his grandmother? Either way being Irish puts you in a good position. I think it's why he has such an interest in what you've done with the collection. He doesn't look Irish though,' she lowered her voice, 'he's brown-skinned. Very handsome though.'

I could feel Seb beside me looking back and forth eagerly from Joanna to myself as though he was watching the final of the Wimbledon Grand Slam. He was nodding with her in loyal agreement and then nodding back at me in exaggerated encouragement. His expressions were so flamboyant! How could I not have seen it in the past? Maybe this was his work persona. I wondered had he even noticed her derogatory 'brown-skinned' comment. He was half-Puerto Rican himself.

It was very strange that he faithfully nodded along with everything she said even if it was offensive towards him. I didn't like this side to him at all. Even if his skin hadn't been brown, he certainly had a brown nose from all that time he was spending with his head in her backside.

I twisted a curl around my finger as they proceeded to discuss my work. It was a strange feeling. Occasionally I felt I had to agree, but I was not in the habit of applauding my own work so I just smiled occasionally and said, 'Thank you'. It did give me such a thrill though to hear Joanna Lenoir getting so passionate about my collection. It felt remarkably like a dream. Stuff like this just didn't happen to me in real life.

'Your figurative work reminds me of the work of the great Lucian Freud,' she cooed.

I nearly died. She couldn't possibly be comparing my work to someone so wonderful.

'But to go a step further – there is another dimension to your art. This complex figurative work is then merged with breathtaking cityscapes.' She sipped on her Cosmopolitan. 'It's just so refreshing to see a modern young artist who is not lazy. It is so clear that months, even years of work and passion has gone into this collection.'

She wasn't wrong. I had spent years doing the cityscapes. I had really taken my time with them, and been sure to get them as perfect as I could. Then the figurative work had totally consumed me since I arrived in Ballytiernan, and I had enjoyed not rushing them. Well, except for at the end, but thankfully they were almost done by then.

She continued. 'So much modern art these days is so minimal, it looks like they did it in an hour. Especially with young artists. Sometimes it seems they don't have the patience or attention span. I really want people to appreciate new work that takes true talent and dedication. The kind of commitment that is reminiscent of the old masters. Just think about Michelangelo painting the Sistine Chapel – it took him over four years – most of it spent lying on his back! And the monks who went blind while creating the Book of Kells in Ireland. I'm so glad to see you Irish haven't lost your work ethic.' She smiled at me, a twinkle in her eye, the sort of look that made me feel important. Then she spotted someone coming into the restaurant and stood up.

'Oh, here he is! Mr Tobago, it's so great to see you!' she beamed.

I don't know what I had expected, maybe some rich fat old guy with a big twirly moustache. But Mr Tobago was gorgeous. He was tall with broad shoulders and rich smooth dark skin. He was incredibly handsome. He reminded me a bit of Princess Diana's boyfriend Dodi Fayed. He had a big white-toothed smile and greeted me with a very gentle, respectful one-cheek kiss. He smelt of coconut and leather. My knees weakened. Goodness, could this handsome rich stranger really be giving me weak knees? Could I really have moved on from obsessing so single-mindedly over Fred this quickly?

'I'm so sorry to keep you waiting, guys.' He flashed his lovely smile. He spoke with a soft general American accent and thankfully he didn't seem to want to rush into art talk straight away. 'This place does an excellent tasting menu. Shall we just order that and we can all try a bit of everything?'

'Suits me,' I chirped. 'I can never decide on one dish. And then I always make the wrong choice and end up with food envy.'

He smiled at me, his eyes holding my gaze.

'Is that settled then?' He looked around.

Seb was nodding eagerly again like a puppy on a dashboard. He was going to have to cool it with the nodding or he would end up with a sore neck.

'I'm not all that hungry, Mr Tobago, but it sounds like a great plan,' Joanna agreed.

'Joanna, you know you can call me Terence – please, everyone, call me Terence. Mr Tobago is my dad and he hasn't got any interest in art or good food so you're talking to the wrong guy if you're talking to him.' He chuckled softly. 'Although I can't claim to know a lot about art myself – I just know what I like.'

He winked at me jokingly and then turned to a waiter and discreetly ordered for all of us.

Then he turned back to me. 'Katie, it's really wonderful to meet you.' He looked serious. 'I am already a huge fan of yours. I just can't believe you're so young. You paint with such skill and expertise.'

'Goodness, thank you.' I was so glad the restaurant was dimly lit because my cheeks were burning.

'Where in Ireland are you from?'

'I'm actually from Dublin but I'm living down the west at the moment.' Oh shit. I was lost in his eyes. They were deep brown, almost black.

'My mother was born in Listowel, County Kerry,' he informed me.

I found it hard to believe. He just looked like the farthest thing from a Kerryman. He continued speaking and we all hung on his every word. 'She lived there until she was sixteen and then moved to New York. I sometimes think it's such a pity – I would have loved to have grown up there, but then she would probably never have met my father . . .'

We were all captivated. Terence Tobago spoke with an air of sophistication, but also with a hint of passion in his tone. I was so thankful he was there, because for some reason Joanna made me feel uncomfortable. She was so brilliant and impressive, and so kind about my work, but she still seemed very serious and stiff. When she smiled it was large and toothy but she couldn't seem to hide the fact that it was forced, and she didn't enjoy it. I resorted to laughing even more to fill her silences. I knew this just made me seem like a giggling fool.

Seb was totally useless. I definitely wasn't a fan of 'work Sebastian'. He didn't have any opinions of his own. He just stroked Joanna's ego with his constant fawning and nodding. He only just stopped short of applauding when she spoke. It was embarrassing, but she didn't seem to find it annoying at all. I wondered if all her work colleagues treated her like this, and whether I would be expected to also. But, despite Joanna and Seb, Terence made me feel so relaxed. He was normal, funny, and even a bit goofy at times. He even got Joanna to loosen up a bit and somehow she managed to crack a few almost genuine smiles for him.

After the meal, Joanna confirmed that I would come into the gallery tomorrow and meet her there to go over some things. She wanted to show me some ideas she had for the exhibition. I promised I'd be there by noon. Terence added that he didn't want to be left out; he wholeheartedly wanted to be involved in what we were doing.

I still couldn't believe all this was about my work. I kept wondering if I would wake up back in my bed in Ballytiernan, laughing at myself for having such an outlandish dream. I kept pinching myself repeatedly, so much so I was sure I would have a bruise.

So we all concluded we would meet at the gallery at about noon on Saturday and once everything was sorted Joanna scooted off, but not forgetting lots of cheek-kissing first.

Terence got up to go the loo and, as soon as he was out of earshot, Seb turned to me.

'That man is divine. Oh, what I would do to him!' he said dreamily.

'Keep your urges to yourself, please.' I put my hand up in front of his face. 'I'm not ready to be your fag hag just yet. Anyway, he's not gay.'

'That hasn't stopped me before. It's a challenge, isn't it?'

'Seb, I told you! You can't talk to your ex-girlfriend like that. It's just wrong!'

'Yeah, whatever. Any hole is a goal, darling.'

'Seb!' I slapped his arm.

I wasn't sure why I was being so hard on him – I actually wasn't really disturbed by it at all. I was so over Seb that it didn't matter any more. But still I thought he should have more respect.

'I'm surprised you even know what he looks like seeing as your head has been so far up Joanna's ass for the whole evening.'

'My head is nowhere near her ass. Terence's ass – now I'm much more interested in that.'

'You're definitely not his type, Seb.'

'And who is? You?' He looked at me. 'You like him, don't you?' His eyes bored through me, his eyebrows raised.

I said nothing. I begged my cheeks not to go red.

'You do!' he insisted. 'But what about your Irish chappie?' He narrowed his eyes now in a really annoying, smug way.

'He won't return my calls – thanks to you.'

'Well, you might be thanking me for real when you've married your rich art-investor husband and are pooping out lots of his beautiful babies!'

I laughed. 'Women don't poop out babies. Don't tell me you've forgotten what a vagina is already?'

Babies. I really didn't see that kind of a future with Terence. I saw that future with Fred, and thinking about that alternative made my heart pang with longing. Terence was lovely and charming and funny but he wasn't really my type. He was too perfect. Too smooth, clean-cut. No matter how fabulous Terence was, the truth was that I was hooked on my scruffy Irish farmer. I should be with him, I thought.

'You're thinking about him.' Seb looked at me disapprovingly. 'Snap the fuck out of it, bitch. You should be as happy as a pig in shit right now.'

Seb was right. I downed the end of my Mojito, which I reluctantly observed wasn't nearly as good as Fred's. But I decided to put him firmly to the back of my head and enjoy the rest of my evening.

Terence arrived back and the three of us had another drink.

When we were finished, I suggested we ask for the bill, but Terence shook his head. 'Done,' he said firmly.

'Terence! You shouldn't have!' I said, but I was secretly flooded with relief. I would probably have had to sell Winnipeg just to afford the champagne we had drunk.

We thanked him effusively and then we all wandered outside into the warm night air. There was a little breeze though, so I wrapped my pashmina around my shoulders. Terence immediately took off his jacket and draped it around me.

I looked up at him. 'Thanks.' God, he was dreamy. Maybe he could make me forget about Fred, even for one night. No. It was a bad idea. A terrible idea! Firstly, this was a professional relationship. Secondly, I was not that sort of girl. Or was I?

'No problem,' he smiled.

'She'll talk you out of your shoes now if you're not careful,' Seb said as he fondly threw his arm across my shoulders. 'I nearly got frostbite in my toes from all the times I walked home barefoot carrying her ridiculous heels while she plodded along happily in my shoes.'

'Did you guys . . . ?' Terence looked confused, his eyes glancing from Seb to me.

'Yes, he's my ex. But now he's gay.'

'I'm bisexual,' Seb corrected. 'But don't worry – it's not weird at all!'

We laughed. Terence looked sceptical. Understandably.

As soon as the air hit me I became aware of how much we had drunk: at least five cocktails and a couple glasses of champagne each.

We laughed and joked all the way to Central Park and then continued strolling through the park. We watched a group of teenagers doing some incredible free running in a big playground area. They were so impressive. They were almost like Spiderman, but without the ropes coming out of their hands. For the first time all three of us were silent, except to cheer when someone did something extraordinary. Only in Manhattan, I thought, would you just happen upon a spectacle like this. There's always something to see. I was not ready for the night to end. Even though Seb and I were quarrelling like teenage siblings, I was glad he was there, because I wasn't sure I trusted myself to be left alone with Terence.

Seb hailed down a horse-drawn carriage and we climbed in, wrapping the soft blanket around us.

'We're going to play a potentially awkward game of "I Never".' Seb stated as he produced a bottle of Gran Centenario Tequila from somewhere inside his jacket. 'I'll go first.' He held the bottle high in the air. 'I never had sex with a man – a male man – with the dick part.' He smirked and slugged the tequila.

I rolled my eyes, swiped the bottle off him and drank from it. I shivered. Terence, as the only one of us who hadn't slept with a man, didn't take a drink. I glanced at Seb smugly.

'Well, there's a first time for everything,' Seb muttered.

As the game went on I shamefully knocked back the tequila way more than a lady should have. Seb wasn't wrong, the game had the potential to be highly uncomfortable. But, thankfully, we were a jolly group of drunks. But there was no lying with Seb there, and I had done some pretty disgraceful things while we were together, which Seb was only too happy to mention, knowing I'd be mortified. Well, there goes my chance with Terence anyway, I thought, a little bit relieved.

Chapter 32

I bolted awake in my old bed. The one I had shared with Seb for three years. Oh, *fuck*. I was in the middle of the bed, nestled between Seb and Terence. I was trapped. Oh, God help me! What had happened? I looked under the covers. I thanked God and all the angels and saints in heaven that I had all my clothes still on. I put my hand on my heart to calm it down. Now I just needed to sneak out, grab a taxi back to Sophie's and pretend it never happened, leaving a hilariously awkward situation for Seb and Terence to wake up to. I was actually sad to be missing that but not sad enough.

I slithered like a snake down through the centre of the bed. Stealth should be my middle name, I thought as I slid out from under the covers, almost grazing Terence's left foot with my nose. I was so close to freedom, but the only problem now was that I couldn't find my shoes anywhere. I would happily have cut my losses if they had been any pair of my cheapo shoes, but these were Sophie's gorgeous Mark Jacobs red sandals and she would be distraught. Where were they? Aha! Yes, I spotted a red heel peeping up in between the cushions of the couch. I plucked it out. But the other wasn't with it. I practically turned the couch upside down searching and I scampered around the apartment but it was nowhere. Then I heard movement coming from the bedroom so I grabbed a pair of Seb's socks off the clothes-horse in the hall and bolted out the front door. I did my best to close it silently behind me.

I took the stairs two at a time and jumped into the back of the first empty cab I saw outside. I sprawled out on the back seat of the cab taking big deep breaths as it whizzed up Thirteenth Street and turned right onto First Avenue, narrowly avoiding a collision with a big MTA bus. Even George Best would have been impressed.

'Girl, you better not throw up,' the driver announced. The man oozed sassy attitude, even more than Sasha.

'Well, you could slow down a bit,' I retorted. 'And maybe crack open a window back here! What is this? A fly-by sauna?' I sounded like a New Yorker. I surprised myself with how easily I slipped back into that persona.

We were only two blocks away from Sophie's building when my phone started buzzing. I dug it out of my purse. It was Seb.

'Hello?' I immediately regretted answering.

'Where are you?' He sounded pissed.

'What are you talking about? I'm at Sophie's. I've been here all night. We're just having breakfast.'

The driver pulled up outside the building, turned around and raised his eyebrows.

"Just a sec, Seb. Toast is burning."

I put my finger to my lips and tipped the driver an extra five bucks to buy his silence and cooperation. He smiled and mouthed 'Bye' with a wink as I climbed out of the car. He drove off slowly without roaring the engine.

Hmm, maybe Seb might forget what had happened and actually buy the story.

'Bullshit!' he spat. 'I woke up with the heel of your red shoe practically wedged in my asshole. Sadly I'm pretty sure it's the only action my asshole got last night – even if I did wake up

282

beside a very awkward hottie who, by the way, seemed a little too pissed off for my liking. And the other shoe is missing which means you took it with you and did a runner to avoid the shame of waking up in bed with us.'

Shit, Clouseau over there had me all figured out.

'Well, Cinderella? What do you have to say for yourself?'

'I have no idea what you're talking about,' I said, praying a car wouldn't drive by, proving him right. It was a good thing Sophie's building was on a street and not an avenue. 'I actually have both my shoes here. In fact I'm looking at them right now. However, I will take that one as a spare if you don't need it. I'll call over for it later.' I hung up.

Somehow, an hour later I was washed and dressed, in proper daytime attire, including a sandal on each foot, and I was jumping out of a cab outside the MMA. I felt like Superman, now transformed back into the clean-cut, sophisticated Clark Kent after a night of adventures. At the desk I asked for Joanna and was ushered over to a waiting area.

'Well, Katie, I have some great news.' Joanna's face remained expressionless.

I wondered if she'd had plastic surgery – her face never seemed to change with what she was saying. We were seated on plush emerald-green leather armchairs in her office, and her assistant was setting down a tray of tea and cookies on the glass coffee table between us.

'Mr Tobago has agreed to buy the whole collection. Have a look at this – this is the contract. We'll all be signing that tomorrow once we have seen the exhibition proposal.'

My eyes bulged out of my head as I looked at the figures. I wanted to jump around screaming but I kept my face frozen and composed, just like Joanna's.

'An exhibition room is being prepared as we speak – would you like to see it?'

We bustled through the corridors, me running to keep up with her, even though she was in her six-inch heels and I was in comfy flat sandals.

'Mr Tobago isn't here yet, as you can see. He called to say he was delayed.'

Yeah, because he woke up in Sebastian's bed about an hour ago, I thought, smirking to myself. But I was a bit relieved; I wasn't quite ready to look him in the eye after last night.

We arrived in a big white exhibition room with high ceilings and wooden floors. The canvases were already hanging on the walls covered in sheets and electricians were rigging up lights on the walls above them. Joanna went straight over to one of them that seemed to be completed.

'Is this ready?' she asked, looking around for an electrician.

'Yes, ma'am, that one's good to go!' a chunky bald man replied.

Joanna whipped off the sheet. It was *Billy Does Broadway*.

'Okay.' She put her hand to her face and tapped her fingers on her chin. 'Can we get the light on it?'

'Just give me a minute, ma'am.'

'Katie, we need to do a write-up about each piece that will go in this little mounting here.' She pointed to a little gold empty frame on the wall beside the painting. 'It will just say the name of the piece and a little about what inspired you or some little interesting bit of trivia. You don't have to describe the piece, we like to keep things open to interpretation, but something small about each one might be nice. Ah! Thank you.'

The light had switched on above the painting. It transformed it. It seemed to illuminate Billy's torso dramatically and the faces of the passersby seemed to catch the light, perfectly enhancing their various expressions. I almost felt guilty that it looked so good, better than it was in reality. But nevertheless I enjoyed the giddy feeling brimming in my belly. The lighting was perfect.

Joanna nodded and looked from me to the painting, and then looked back to me.

'I love how expressive these people are,' she said softly.

The irony struck me as her face was, as always, completely blank.

'This looks fantastic.' Terence seemed to glide into the room, his deep, commanding voice echoing around the space.

I smiled coyly at him, only barely making eye contact. But as soon as Johanna launched into all the cheek-kissing I did a mental eye-roll, knowing I was going to have to do it too. He leaned down to me once Joanna had released him and kissed my cheek. I jerked slightly as I felt his hand graze my ass. Did that happen? He couldn't have done it on purpose; it must have been an accident. He didn't look embarrassed though, but he had *definitely* grazed my ass with his hand.

As Joanna trotted off to ask the head electrician if there were any more paintings lit and ready to show to Terence and me, he leaned down towards me and whispered in my ear, 'How come I woke up in Sebastian's bed and not yours? That was an epic fail.'

I laughed awkwardly. 'Ha ha, yes, that must have been uncomfortable.'

Why was he behaving so oddly?

'Well, we'll have to rectify that little mistake tonight.'

His voice was quiet and husky and I could feel his breath on my ear, making the hairs on the back of my neck stand up. I tried not to react, but when his hand touched my ass again I instantly jumped away from him, forcing a little laugh. I looked around to see if anyone had seen it. What in God's name was he doing? He had been such a gentleman last night and now he was behaving like a complete and utter creep. It didn't even seem like the same guy. I did my best not to court this strange behaviour but he, on the other hand, seemed to be enjoying this little game of cat and mouse and was glued to my side as we went around the room. He made every effort to keep his hand attached to my lower back, no matter how many attempts I made to move away from him.

My heart was in my throat. How could this be happening? I asked myself. Had I led him on last night? I really didn't think I had and Seb would have told me. But it felt dangerous. Like it could mess everything up.

Joanna seemed completely oblivious. 'We have an exhibition opening tomorrow night in the room next to us. I would really appreciate it if you could come along, Katie, just to get an idea of what openings here are like. I think you'll really like the artist too. He's a Native American man, and he uses the most unusual materials. It's quite crude. He has an incredible talent though. You're more than welcome to pop in too, Mr Tobago. I'm sure you must have gotten an invite?'

'I did, thank you, Joanna. I have RSVP'd already saying I have other arrangements. But now that I think of it, perhaps I might be able to wiggle things around a bit.' He winked at me.

I thought I was going to throw up. I couldn't believe I had actually thought this man was attractive. He was so vile and repulsive with this behaviour, it completely changed his whole appearance.

Chapter 33

'No matter what I wear I look fat,' Sophie huffed.

I had talked her into coming with me to the exhibition to keep an eye on the situation and come to my rescue if Terence was being inappropriate. I really needed her help dealing with the situation, because professionally I had to keep him sweet, but I didn't want him thinking he could behave this way with me. I looked at Sophie and had to feel sorry for her. Normally she would love to be coming to something like this, but the pregnancy was really getting to her. She couldn't tell anyone and get all the compliments and congratulations. She just had to suffer in silence with the weight gain, and the morning sickness, and all anyone was thinking was that she was getting fat. Fat, and possibly eating too much. I understood how this would be upsetting.

'The chocolate-filled Krispy Kreme that you're stuffing into your face probably isn't going to help,' I said, and then quickly shut my mouth as she flashed me a killer glare.

'Chocolate is all the baby wants at the moment,' she whined, close to tears.

'Oh!' A smile spread across my face. 'I nearly forgot. I got this for you after I managed to escape Terence at the MMA earlier.' I dug a little package out of my rucksack. 'Sorry, I should have taken it out and hung it up – you might have to iron it.' It was the DVF wrap dress I had promised her. It was black with turquoise flowers, which I knew would set off her brown eyes beautifully.

'Katieeee,' she whimpered. 'Youshuddant'ave!' She was sobbing now. She took off the green dress she had on and stood there in her bra and knickers, holding the dress out. She sniffed. 'I can't believe you got me this. It's so fabulous. I look fabulous, don't I?' She was wrapping it around her now and prancing in front of the mirror.

'Jaysus, you really have become a proper emotional pregnant lady now, Soph! I hardly know what to expect from you. Sad tears then happy tears. You do look lovely though. But you should iron it really.'

She got naked again and pulled out the ironing board. I had been ready for ages. This was how it usually was with us. I was always ready in about ten minutes and then Sophie took well over an hour, and as every minute passed I got more and more worried I hadn't done enough with my look. Tonight I was happy enough though. I was wearing a Grecian navy-blue maxi dress with a sexy little slit up one leg, Angelina style. I wasn't planning on doing her ridiculous pose though. I hadn't done anything very extravagant with my hair and make-up because I felt the dress was dramatic enough without it. I stuck my iPhone into the dock above the fireplace and put on Queen's 'I Want To Break Free' and we danced around as she ironed her dress. It quickly put us both in a better mood, and by the time we were ready to go I had almost forgotten about the fact that I was facing an evening being hounded by the ultimate creep of the century. And Sophie had almost forgotten about her muffin top, which miraculously disappeared once she slipped into her DVF dress.

Sophie immediately spotted clients of hers as we walked into the entrance hall. An elderly gent with a fluffy white beard and an ageless woman with a bizarrely cat-like plastic face stretched around her skull and enormous lips protruding out the front.

'Mr and Mrs Lonsdale, so great to see you! How is the new apartment working out?' Sophie cooed, batting her eyelashes.

I knew I wouldn't be able to talk to them without staring at the woman's face so I did the pleasantries and then made my excuses. I wandered off on my own to see if I could spot Terence, keeping my back to the wall, so that he couldn't sneak up and get all handsy with my backside.

I found my way into the exhibition room and my breath caught in my chest. The most beautiful colours imaginable suddenly captivated me. I immediately forgot all about Terence as soon as I feasted my eyes on the astounding artwork. I had never seen yellow and amber colours looking so pure and vibrant in my life. They didn't seem in any way crude, as Joanna had described them. It did all seem raw, and his techniques were obviously quite unique. I was lost in his world. He depicted Native American men and women dancing and it instantly made me want to move. To join them. There was so much life jumping out of the paintings it was overwhelming.

'Katie! So glad you came!'

I turned around and it was Joanna.

My breath was still caught in my throat. I exhaled and slowly looked at her. 'Joanna, these are simply incredible.'

'Yes, Mr Mekwi is really wonderful. I'll introduce you to him later and you can tell him your thoughts.'

'I'd love that.' I found it difficult to peel my eyes off the captivating paintings to engage with Joanna's comparatively lifeless face.

'Great. Well, first let me introduce you to Mr Banks.'

A calm but powerful-looking man loomed behind her, and it was as if she just sensed his presence there. She turned to include him.

'Mr Banks, this is Katie McKenna, our latest discovery. It's a name you'll be hearing a lot more of. I showed you some of her work at the meeting on Thursday, the Irish Farmers series. And Katie, Mr Banks is the President of the Museum.'

'Ah Katie, I absolutely adore your collection.' He was a tall, bald African American man, in his sixties or seventies, sporting a canary-yellow bow tie. His face was warm and friendly, his eyes protruding intensely and his voice deep and gravelly like Morgan Freeman's.

'Wow! Thank you, Mr Banks. It's going to be a huge honour to exhibit it here. And it's wonderful to meet you of course.'

'Yes, well, this is something many young artists only dream of.'

I was nodding and smiling when suddenly I froze. I felt a hand on my lower back, just above my arse, dangerously close to the top of my butt crack. My whole body stiffened. I tried to slide away but the wall was to my right, Mr Banks in front of me and Joanna to my left. I wondered if they had noticed my face going red.

'Ah, Mr Tobago! How wonderful you could make it!' said Joanna.

Terence removed his hand to go in for all the kisses and handshakes, so I grabbed the opportunity and quickly made my excuses to go pee. Joanna shot me a surprised look and I realised that I probably should have said 'powder my nose' or something classy like that.

I looked everywhere for Sophie and couldn't spot her so I went and stood in the loo for a few minutes, as I couldn't think of anything else to do. I really didn't want to make a scene with Terence, or make the situation awkward, but at the same time he really made my skin crawl, and I didn't want to be that girl who lets an older influential guy do whatever he wants with her just in order to further her career. How could I find a middle ground? Was there one? I suspected he was well aware of the power he had over me, as we hadn't signed the contracts yet, and he was very cocky to presume I would go along with his so blatant advances. I figured he thought tonight would be the night to seal the deal before we sealed the real deal so to speak, because we had arranged to sign the papers tomorrow morning, before I flew back to Ireland in the evening. So if I got through this evening without shouting at him to piss off and stop sexually harassing me I'd be home and dry. But he obviously had other plans.

I concluded my only option was to escape. However, the speeches hadn't even started yet. It would be bad to leave so soon . . . unless I had an excuse.

As if she had read my mind Sophie busted into the toilets in a flood of tears.

'Some guy, some total dickhead told me I look old,' she panted.

'Huh?' I placed my hands on her shoulders to calm her down. 'What did he say?'

'Well, we were talking about cell phones and how did we ever get by without them blah blah blah, and he said, "Well, we grew up without them and we were fine, right?" and I just burst out crying. And I ran in here.'

'What? Why did that offend you? Did he say something else?'

'No, that was it.' She blew her nose.

'We did grow up without mobile phones.' I patted her back.

'I know. But it means he thinks I look like, you know, in my late twenties. It's just so sad. My life is all behind me now. You know up until a few months ago I used to get ID'd going into clubs? I don't any more. And I can never ever in my life wear miniskirts again. A mother should never wear a miniskirt, right? My miniskirt days are behind me . . .' There was a steady stream of tears running down her face and dripping off her chin. 'What if I want to dress up as a naughty schoolgirl for Halloween? I'll have to wear a knee-length skirt. It's so sad.'

I wasn't really sure what to say. Of course it was all completely ridiculous nonsense, obviously, but I couldn't exactly say that. So I did what suited me, and was probably best for the both of us anyway. I put my arm around her shoulder and asked her if she'd like to go home and get into bed and eat chocolate ice cream. She nodded.

'You're so smart, Katie. You always know just what I need,' she whimpered as we snuck out of the loo.

We managed to somehow avoid everyone and discreetly make our way out of the exhibition room and down the stairs. There was a queue of taxis waiting outside. Sophie jumped into the first one straight away but just as I was about to get in a hand grabbed my wrist. I looked around and it was Terence.

'Where are you heading off to so soon?' he asked, flashing his pearly whites in a broad, slightly threatening smile, his hand still wrapped rather tightly around my wrist.

'Oh, my friend's not really feeling well so I'm going to take her home,' I answered, forcing a big fake smile back at him.

'She hardly needs you to go with her, does she? Here!' He threw what seemed to be a fifty-dollar bill in the window to the driver, closed the door of the cab and tapped the back of it twice with the hand that was not attached to my wrist. It moved away.

'Hey! That was a little rude,' I said, frowning. I couldn't stop myself. I'd just had enough. Not only was he slimy and disgusting, but now he was behaving like a jerk.

'Well, I think you're a little rude leaving so soon. The only reason I came was to see you. I have a whole evening planned after this for the two of us, and a nice hotel to finish it all off.' He looked at me expectantly.

Ugh.

Thankfully I could see the taxi up ahead had stopped and

was reversing back towards us. I presumed Sophie was giving the driver an earful inside.

'Well, I don't know why you did that – I never agreed to go on a date with you.' I twisted my wrist out of his grasp and folded my arms across my chest so that he couldn't catch it again.

'Well, I don't know why I bothered either. Considering your ex was turned off women after being with you, you're obviously nothing special. You're just a typical slutty bitch who probably doesn't deliver. Go then. Fuck off with your fat friend.' And with that he walked back inside.

I watched him go with my jaw hanging open. He really had turned out to be a nasty piece of work. I numbly climbed into the taxi with Sophie to go home for some much-needed chocolate ice cream in bed.

At least he had paid for the taxi, although I had a sinking feeling that that was the last thing he would be paying for now.

I woke up to my phone buzzing. I focused my eyes on the screen and it read **Joanna Lenoir**.

I sat up, cleared my throat and answered.

'Hello, Joanna!' I chirped in the most awake voice I could manage.

'Katie! What happened last night? Goodness, what a nightmare. Mr Tobago has completely pulled out. I presume you know this – he said it wouldn't come as a surprise to you.'

I blinked a couple of times, and rubbed my eyes, holding the phone between my shoulder and cheek. I was dumbfounded. She was silent, waiting for some explanation.

'Well, yeah, because I didn't want to sleep –'

'Sorry, Katie, the connection's not great. Anyway, there's nothing that can be done now. But it's unfortunate really, Katie, because it turns out we're going to have to drop the exhibition altogether.'

'Why?'

'Well, you see we really value Terence's support – he's a good friend of Mr Banks and of the Museum. And . . . well, your collection . . . it just doesn't suit us at this time. That's it really. I'm very sorry it didn't work out, Katie. I'll have the pieces shipped back to Ireland tomorrow, or Wednesday at the latest. Our courier is quite busy at the moment but we'll do our best. My assistant will be in touch with you about that . . .' She trailed off and there was a brief silence where I thought maybe the line went dead. 'Well, from everyone at the MMA, good luck with your future, Katie. I have no doubt it's very bright.'

And then she was gone. Joanna Lenoir, with her frozen face and million-dollar opportunity, was out of my life just as quickly as she had come into it.

Five hours later I was at JFK, driving myself mad going through everything over and over in my head. How could I have handled it differently? I should have told him I was sick, or that I was having my period. Anything. A million different things I could have done that might have resulted in a different outcome. I was furious. The whole trip had been a big fat waste of time. Well, at least I got to spend some time with Sophie. That was the only good thing to have come from it. Now I was heading back to an isolated existence in a village in rural Ireland, where there was a crazy woman who wanted me gone, one way or another.

Chapter 34

I needed to see Fred. I felt totally jet-lagged and sleep-deprived and slightly demented from torturing myself with should have, would have, could have's the whole way home. Seb had also rung me while I was waiting to board the plane and again as soon as I turned on my phone at Shannon Airport. Both times he gave me an earful about why I should have just slept with Terence, that he was a very attractive man and he couldn't believe I'd been so stupid. He wanted to know what my problem was. I couldn't believe him. How had I attracted these disgraceful men?

It only further compounded my desire to see Fred. He was so totally and completely different from Seb and Terence. This time I needed to tell him exactly why I had been a crazy fool and beg him to give me another shot. I would get down on my knees and plead for a second chance if I had to.

I had developed a whole spiel in my head that would be very persuasive. He couldn't say no. My curls were back to normal and I had orchestrated them to fall around my face in such a way that he couldn't possibly turn me down. I was simply too adorable. I had also spent a few minutes perfecting my wide-eyed puppy-dog look in the mirror to assist the curls.

All that and some deep-pink lipstick Sophie had left behind, combined with my new Anthropologie dress, had to be a recipe for success. Unless I was completely deluded and in fact looked like one of those socially unaware adults who dressed like six-year-olds. That was also possible. I decided to tone down the puppy eyes, and maybe exchange my Converse for more sensible brogues.

I skipped up his drive nervously with a bottle of Oban, his favourite Scotch whisky in my hand. I couldn't believe it when I spotted it in the Duty Free at JFK for half price. It was like fate. I had also wrapped a big gold bow around it just for good measure.

But once again, my ding of his doorbell was met with silence. His car was also missing from the drive. My heart sank. It could be in the garage, I thought hopefully – not likely but I trotted around the fields looking for him, my heart gradually sinking lower and lower the more I searched. I took out my phone and contemplated calling him. Fuck it, what did I have to lose? Just as I expected, though, there was no answer. My eyes stung with tears, which I forced back. No worries, I convinced myself – maybe he's in Farrelly's and if not Jim would probably know where to find him. I set off for Farrelly's, fighting with all my might to hold onto the optimistic spring in my step.

I arrived at Farrelly's and Jim's eyes immediately lit up.

'Katie! Great to see you! Jesus, you look fantastic! Are you looking to get your job back?' He smiled widely.

I hadn't even considered that! It would be great – then Fred would be forced to spend more time with me, and I could win my way back into his affections!

'That sounds great, Jim – yeah, why not?' I beamed. Maybe the day was looking up after all.

I looked around for Fred but couldn't see him.

'That's perfect timing, Katie, what with Fred gone and everything. Perfect timing!' Jim clapped his hands together. 'Couldn't have worked out better now, could it?'

'What?' I could feel my heart thumping in my chest. 'Where has Fred gone?' I tried to keep the quivers out of my voice but a few sneaked in. I was really fighting to keep from breaking down.

'Did he not tell you? That's strange. He moved to Dublin,' Jim stated matter-of-factly.

I tried to look as unaffected as I could. I wondered was I effectively hiding the horror in my face. 'He's staying with his brother at the moment until he gets himself sorted with a job and such. Ah yes, it's a shame really. All the young people leaving Ballytiernan. But, sure then, what choice do they have? There's so little for them here. Kids these days are so ambitious. They want it all. And they want to live in a modern way. Free. You know? It's just not possible in Ballytiernan – what with – you know – there's the odd Hitler type still hanging around here, making it difficult to have any fun at all. So they take off . . . to greener, freer pastures and such. Although Dublin is hardly green, is it? It's more grey, really.'

I was crushed. I didn't think I could continue to stand there. My eyes darted around for an exit route.

Jim was rambling on as he restocked the cabinets. 'Fred had the sheep and the land to keep him here. But it's not enough, I suppose. Five years ago he had so much to stay for, with Jeanette, and the baby on the way . . . but then, well, everything went wrong, didn't it?'

What had he said?

'It did?' I asked softly.

'Oh absolutely. She really broke his heart, God love him. And he hasn't found anyone else since. Well then, I suppose he hasn't been looking. I actually thought you two might have got it together – that would have been nice. The pair of you always seemed to be having such a good laugh together. Quite a pair all right, you two, Always joking and laughing.' He winked at me.

I made an attempt at smiling back but it was strained at best.

Jim tilted an expensive bottle of Patron whiskey on its side and examined it.

'Would you say that's a third full?'

I nodded.

He pulled a pencil from behind his ear and jotted the info down on a scrap of paper beside the till.

'But it's good for him to be getting away from here, I suppose. Too many memories for him here, I'd say. I'm happy for the lad. I do hope it works out for him now . . . he's not a bad chap . . .'

He wandered into the back with an empty crate to gather more stock and I watched him stroll off with my mouth agape and my eyes stinging with tears. I couldn't believe what I had heard. I wanted to follow him and ask an endless amount of questions. What had happened with this Jeanette person? Were they expecting a baby? What went wrong?

I gathered myself together, shook the tears out of my eyes and sat up on the bar, more composed. When Jim came back I casually tried to coax it out of him.

'What happened with Jeanette, Jim? And the baby?'

'Oh, he didn't tell you? Well, they'd been together since school, the two of them, Fred and herself. And, well, it was only a few years ago, I suppose, that she became pregnant. It was a surprise, of course, but they were happy about it. There were some who weren't so happy though. There was a lot of talk, disapproval, nastiness, all that, because they weren't married. Jeanette – I think she got a bit depressed. She was very down. But Fred – I've never seen someone so excited about becoming a daddy. He did everything to cheer her up. He took her on a holiday, bought her flowers all the time. He painted and decorated a nursery in his house. He talked about the baby non-stop. And then, the child was stillborn, wasn't it?'

'Oh no!' I gasped.

Jim nodded. 'It destroyed them. It was an awful time really. We were all fierce cut up for them. But then there was a letter published in the *Ballytiernan Echo,* an anonymous letter, saying these things happen because of sin and sometimes things happen a certain way for a reason. It was a terrible thing. Mind you, it didn't directly mention them but everybody knew. Well, that just pushed Jeanette over the edge and she sank into a deep depression. Her family was distraught. Her dad used to come in here in bits, worried about her. Fred tried to keep it together. He even proposed to her, I think he wanted to give it a proper shot this time, get married and try again for a family. But she left. One day she was here, the next she was gone. Terrible sad. Anyway.' He nodded, his face sad and weary, remembering it all. 'She took off to Australia. She told him not to follow her, and we haven't seen her since. Her parents have been to visit, but she's never come back. Apparently she's married now to an Auzzie lad. There ya go. I don't know how Fred ever got over it all. Maybe he didn't.'

Chapter 35

I did nothing but check my phone obsessively to see if Fred had returned any of my hundreds of phone calls, voicemails and text messages. No luck. I stared at my phone, willing it to ring. Anything? Even some eejit ringing from a marketing call centre in Bristol, looking to do a survey would have been a welcome call. I sat at the table, staring at the stupid silent iPhone.

'Ring, you stupid little feck!' I told it. Nothing. It just lay there lifeless. Fuck it. I picked it up and rang him again. It was just plain rude at this stage for him not to answer. What if it was a life or death situation and my phone had been wiped of every number except his? Did he not even care if I might be dying?

I dialled for what felt like the millionth time.

'Katie.'

He answered. I couldn't believe it! He actually answered. Maybe he did care if I lived or died after all. Progress!

'Oh hi, Fred. What's up?'

'You rang me.'

'Oh yeah, sorry. Of course.' God, you'd think after all this time I'd have prepared what I would say if he actually answered the phone. 'Well, where are you?' I asked. Yes! That was a good place to start. Where the fuck are you, Fred? I didn't think I deserved this treatment. I told myself to cool down. I didn't want to shout at him and ruin the only chance I had to talk to him. That wouldn't help anything.

'I'm in Dublin.'

'Yeah, I knew that, sorry. Jim told me. I've been looking everywhere for you.'

'Twenty-three missed calls. You really don't go with the concept of playing it cool, do you?'

'Yeah. Sorry, I don't like playing it anything. And I don't think anyone is under the illusion that I'm a cool cucumber. I just really wanted to talk to you . . . obviously . . .'

'Okay.' He waited.

I didn't know where to start.

'Okay,' I repeated. Come on, Katie! It was now or never. I needed to focus on what I really needed to say. 'Well, I know you don't want to see me any more, you've made that clear. But, em, I just thought you should know that I really miss you.' I spoke softly and tried to build up the confidence in my voice to tell him everything. 'And maybe this isn't the best time to tell you this, over the phone . . . but I think I'm in love with you. I mean, I absolutely am. I've never felt this way about anyone.' I kept talking because if I left space for him to speak I was scared of what he might say. 'Really. I want to pull my heart out of my chest and, like, flush it down the loo just to stop it aching. You know? Sorry, that's gross. I don't know what I'm saying really. But it's the truth, whatever I'm jabbering about. Because it feels real.' I started to laugh and cry at the same time. 'If I can't have you – well, I don't know what I'll do. Yes, I know I'm not playing it cool or whatever. Yes, I rang you a load of times. I even rang you probably a dozen times from New York. I don't want to play games – I'm no good at them. Me – I'm just straightforward, Fred. Really. All of this bullshit with Seb. Really, all it was in the end – I was just helping a friend who needed me. That's all. There was nothing more to it, I swear. Cross my heart and hope to die.'

He was silent. I wished I could see him. Read his expression.

'I don't know what to say,' he said quietly then.

'Oh,' I closed my eyes and my heart sank. 'Do you not love me?' I pushed myself to say it because I needed clarity at this point. The minute I heard myself say it I cringed.

'I do. I just didn't want to say it for the first time over the phone. But, well, you went and forced it out of me, didn't you?'

I was still crying, but this time it was with relief and happiness.

'I'm a right old rascal,' I sniffed through tears and smiles.

'I didn't know you were that into me really,' he said softly. 'I thought it didn't mean as much to you as it did to me. Especially when Seb was there. And I just couldn't put myself through it. I thought it would be better to just get the hell out of that place.'

'Ballytiernan isn't the same without you,' I said. 'It's boring. Full of old people.'

'It was really boring before you came too,' he laughed. 'I don't know how I survived it. It was a real drag. But you livened things up like you wouldn't believe.'

'I did?' I asked with a giggle.

'Yep. Your big fuzzy ginger head caused quite a stir.'

'Hey! A girl doesn't like to be described as fuzzy.'

'It was a breath of fresh air! Sexy fuzzy fresh air.'

I was sure I could hear him smiling.

'Hmm,' I grumbled, then after a beat I gently said, 'I need to see you.'

'I'll come back,' he agreed. 'Are you in Winnipeg?'

'Yes.'

'Are you there on your own?'

'Of course.'

'Do they know you're back in the village?'

'Who?'

He paused. When he spoke his voice was low and serious. It sounded strained, possibly concerned. 'Don't worry . . . just . . . you need to take care of yourself, please? Maybe just . . . make sure the doors are locked and stuff.'

'Wow. That sounds a bit overly serious, don't ya think?' I laughed nervously.

'Trust me on this one.' He sounded sterner all of a sudden, which surprised me. 'I'm going to come to you as soon as I can.'

'Okay . . . I love you?' I said timidly.

'I love you too.'

I closed my eyes, relief flooding over me. I didn't care so much about my paintings any more. And really, I didn't care so much about Mo either. I did as I was told and locked up and then sank back into the couch to enjoy the happy moment of being in love, as unpolluted with negative thoughts as possible. I had Fred. That was all that really mattered. And I wouldn't let anything separate us again.

I crashed in front of the TV for the evening, mindlessly staring at the box, allowing myself to completely forget about the world outside it. I barely noticed my phone buzzing on the arm of the couch, I was in such a daze. It was a New York number. What now? I was so over New York I just wanted to hibernate in Ballytiernan for the rest of my life. I kept my eyes glued to the TV, ignoring the phone until it rang out. Then the only sound left in the room was the canned laughter on a really old episode of *Friends*. I laid my head down on a velvety soft cushion and my eyes slowly started to close.

I wasn't asleep for long when my phone buzzed near my ear, waking me. It was a text message from Fred.

'Hey, babe, I had a few things to sort out but I'm going to

hit the road now and come straight to Winnipeg. Can't wait to see you. I really don't like the thought of you being in that house on your own. I'll be there as soon as I can. Love u.'

Aw, he loves me, I thought, smiling. And he called me 'babe'.

Sasha was interrupting my thoughts with determined meows. I had paid Dennis Daly's ten-year-old grandson, who lived just around the corner, a tenner a day to drop by and feed her over the weekend. But I wasn't sure he'd done a very good job, because she had been doing a good impression of a famished abandoned cat ever since I got back. I was slightly worried the ISPCA were going to call around and arrest me due to her loud meowing. She's just missed me, I told myself . . . but it wasn't likely. Cats were rarely that loyal. Although Sasha wasn't the type of cat to behave as you'd expect her to. She hated being predictable. And we did have a special bond. I sleepily wandered into the kitchen, Sasha at my feet the whole way. I yawned as I opened a can of tuna and plopped its contents into her dish. I rubbed her little head as she tucked in, but she was no longer interested in me, now she had got what she wanted.

'So much for our special bond, Sash!' I stalked off up the stairs for a little lie-down, just so I'd be fully rested by the time Fred arrived. I lay on the bed, still fully dressed. I only just had the energy to take off my shoes. As soon as my head hit the pillow I was gone.

Chapter 36

It was night time in the MMA. Terence had me backed against a wall in a dark, abandoned corner of the gallery. His hands were groping my arse and he was trying to reach up my skirt. I squirmed to get away from him.

'Stop, Terence, leave me alone!' I was shouting but he didn't seem to hear anything I said. No noise was coming out of my mouth no matter how much I tried to scream.

'You're just a stupid slutty whore,' he whispered into my ear in his deep gravelly voice. 'And you're a cock-tease. Aren't you?'

'No.' I was whimpering and crying now.

'And your hair is on fire!'

'That's racist, Terence! Racist against people with red hair! You're a bully and a pervert, and I won't stand for it!' I was thrashing about now, swiping at him to get him away from me.

'*Your hair is on fire! The hair is on fire!*' He was grabbing my shoulders and shaking them violently.

I opened my eyes.

Fred was standing over the bed, shaking my shoulders.

'*The house is on fire! Get up, Katie! Please! Quick!*'

Why was my room full of smoke?

I started coughing. It felt like my throat was completely full of smoke. It was almost impossible to breathe. The smell of burning was overwhelming. Fred had his hoodie zipped right the way up, covering his mouth and his eyes were flashing with terror.

I jumped up.

'*Ooooooch!*' I yelped. The floorboards scalded the soles of my feet.

Fred grabbed a pair of Converse and shoved them on my feet.

I could hear the faint sound of sirens.

We ran out of the room and came to a halt at the top of the stairs. I gasped. Brutal flames were conquering the stairs with shocking speed. Downstairs was completely engulfed.

The heat was blistering and the smoke was overwhelming.

We were both coughing violently as we ran back into my room, slamming the door behind us. My lungs were almost consumed with smoke and my head was dizzy.

I stumbled towards the window and opened it as wide as it would go. Fred's hands were on my back, pushing me up and out. I hung on to him as I climbed out onto the windowsill and squatted next to the birdhouse.

I gasped, the cool air filling my lungs.

'Turn around!' Fred yelled.

I rotated on the windowsill, turning towards him, and, as he grasped my wrists, I understood what he intended to do. Our eyes locked as I pushed myself backwards and over the sill, until Fred was bearing all my weight. Then I was dangling above the ground which was still a terrifying distance below.

Fred eased me down as far as he could. Neither of us said anything but we knew he had to let go.

Then he did.

I fell to the ground, my knees buckling under me, and landed on my backside with a thud. My body aching, I dragged myself to my feet. The sound of sirens grew louder.

I looked up but barely made eye contact with Fred before my body was suddenly launched backwards like a rag-doll by a violent explosion blasting through the window of the kitchen.

I swiftly wiped the soot and smoke out of my eyes with my sleeve and looked back at the house. The flames were licking the outside of the cottage, reaching the window of the bedroom. Smoke billowed up in large black clouds.

'Fred!' I shrieked. But I couldn't see him any more.

I scrambled to my feet, ignoring the pain in my limbs.

I started screaming. My whole body convulsed in tears and rage. As I sprinted around the side of the house my eyes frantically darted here and there in search of Sasha. Looking up I could find no sight of Fred.

A crowd of people had gathered on the road.

A fire engine pulled up in front of Winnipeg and I bolted towards it.

'*Help!*' I shouted, grabbing one of the firemen. '*He's up there, Fred is up there!*' I gestured wildly at the upstairs of the house. '*Please get him out, please! Please!*'

'*Get him out!*' I begged another one.

I accosted another bystander. 'My cat, have you seen my cat?' I was wailing and sobbing. I couldn't control myself. '*Sasha! Fred!*'

The whole village was there to watch what was left of my life being destroyed. They stood there doing nothing. Just simply watching as my grandfather's home and all his memories and belongings were turned to ash. As my boyfriend was trapped inside – and maybe Sasha too.

Suddenly I could see everything for what it was. It was just like medieval times. The people of the village gathered in the village square to watch the witch be convicted, humiliated and then burnt at the stake. I was the Witch of Ballytiernan. Then it clicked. It all clicked right into place.

She did this.

'*I know who did this!*' I screamed at the crowd. I couldn't see her. It was dark and my vision was blurred from the tears. 'You are going to rot in hell! *You disgusting worthless vile creature!*' The words blasted out of me like fire out of a dragon's livid mouth. I was like a dragon scorned. On her period. I was uncontrollable. When I wasn't speaking I was screaming. My screams tasted of blood and salt and iron. I was standing in front of a mass of onlookers.

Mo appeared, suddenly right in my line of vision.

'*You'd better pray to Jesus or Satan or whoever you worship that Fred is alive – somehow – or so help me*!' I was shaking, my throat was raw but the words spat out of me with fury.

'Are your paintings in there?' a voice came from the crowd.

My eyeballs bulged. My fists clenched into balls of rage. Is this what it came down to? My stupid fucking paintings? Was this all just an attempt to destroy my paintings? My body was motionless as I composed myself.

'*Yes.*' I spoke calmly somehow, my voice deep but clear. I told her what she wanted to hear. 'Yes. My paintings have been destroyed. Go off and have a fucking party.'

They all looked back at me their mouths agape. Someone coughed.

'*Meooow*!'

I looked down and Sasha was at my feet.

'*Sasha!*' I bellowed. I picked her up in my arms and buried my head in her furry belly. She didn't complain or try to wiggle free. She knew I needed her more than ever.

I turned back to my beautiful burning cottage and fell to my knees on the grass in front of it. Sasha started walking around me in tight circles, guarding me. Men holding big hoses were blasting the cottage with torrents of water, gradually winning the fight with the flames. But it was much too late to save the building or any of my belongings. I gazed at what remained of my lovely home and I prayed for just one thing. Fred.

As if in answer to my prayers, two of the firemen emerged from the flames carrying a limp figure. I rushed over. I couldn't tell if he was alive or dead, or passed out. His face was black with soot.

'Stand back now, miss.'

They skilfully and carefully started strapping him to a stretcher.

'He needs intensive care immediately.'

They lifted the stretcher into the back of the ambulance.

'We'd like to get you looked at yourself. Can you get in the ambulance, please, miss?'

I looked down at Sasha, who was still circling my legs.

'Can my cat come?'

'Afraid not.'

At that moment Mac burst through the crowd and rushed towards me.

'Katie! My poor girl!' She enveloped me in a much-needed hug.

My knees buckled as I fell into her chest.

'I'm here, love. I'm here for you. Whatever you need.'

'We need to go.' A fireman standing near us had his gloved hand gently resting on my shoulder.

'Mac, could you look after Sasha? She's homeless. She has lost all of her belongings, and she doesn't have anywhere to live,' I sobbed.

The fireman urged me into the ambulance.

'Of course,' Mac called just before they closed the doors.

I looked out the back window as the engine started up.

The flames were gone from what was left of Winnipeg, which wasn't very much. The foundations were still there but otherwise it was completely unrecognisable. It wasn't much more than a steaming, scorched pile of rubble, with a black skeleton looming up out of it.

The paramedic sat down beside me and I finally got a proper look at Fred. From what I could see under all the ash and soot, his face was swollen and bruised. But it was still his face. His handsome, sweet, funny face.

'He dropped from an upstairs window, it seems,' said the paramedic. 'Didn't land as luckily as you. A broken arm and he hit his head against a rock so has a deep wound there.'

My face felt numb and stiff with hardened tears and my eyes were raw. I wanted to scratch my eyeballs to stop them itching.

Every time I thought about the cottage, what had happened and whether Fred would recover or what would become of him, my breath caught in my throat. I couldn't cope with it. So it was easier to remain numb and say nothing. Not allow myself to cry, speak or even think. So I blanked the paramedic. I sensed that he understood.

I kept my gaze focused on Fred. He didn't even stir. I wondered if he had fractured his skull or something dreadful like that. I thought about asking the paramedic this question, but couldn't bring myself to do it for fear the answer would send me into hysterics. So I remained silent for the whole journey. I told myself it would all be okay. I glanced briefly back out the window of the ambulance and caught sight of the stars in the sky, all bright and stoic. I started humming 'Starry Starry Night' – 'Vincent' by Don McLean. It was becoming the theme tune of my life.

It had to be okay, I assured myself. It was just a broken arm and a bump on the head – that was what the paramedic said. No more than that.

But why was he still unconsious?

Chapter 37

An avalanche of hard, irreversible realities flooded into my brain and I immediately wished I hadn't woken up. With a heavy heart I sat up and watched my mother fussing about the hotel room we were staying in. They had given me stitches at the hospital. There was a large wound on my left arm, and another on my left hip. I had been in quite a bit of pain, so they gave me painkillers and told me to go home and get some rest. I told them that I didn't have a home so they helped me to find a hotel nearby in Galway. I was happy to be staying in close proximity to Fred. My mother, God love her, came straight away to stay with me. For all her faults she was always there when I needed her. There was obviously a possibility she would make everything worse with her big often-insensitive mouth, but I was glad to have her there nonetheless.

She strutted over to me with an attitude like Gok Wan on a makeover show, with a firm belief that she was going to sort out my life and make it all better.

'Here you are, darling,' she said, calmly putting a cup of tea on the bedside table and some more painkillers, and then she bustled off around the room as though there were lots of urgent things to do. 'And please do eat something.' She returned with a fresh, warm croissant.

I didn't feel like eating, but I took a bite anyway and chewed it numbly in my mouth. Even after chewing for about two minutes it still felt like a rock going down my throat. Tears welled up in my eyes without any particular trigger. I blinked them back and zoned out again. It was much easier when I zoned out.

I watched my mother. Her white-blonde hair was perfectly blow-dried as always, and it bounced around on top of her head with the vitality of hair half its age. Eugene in Peter Mark did it for her twice a week and she never missed her appointment. I wondered whether this would be the one occasion, if she stayed with me a few days. Eugene will be worried, I mused. He'll probably phone my dad in a panic. She was wearing white waist-high jeans and a light-blue Ralph Lauren shirt. Her skin glowed more than mine ever did. She was pulling back the curtains and opening the windows now, whilst whistling a One Direction song. Ordinarily this sort of behaviour would drive me mad but it was now a pleasant distraction.

'Oh darling, I popped out and picked you up some clothes.' She picked up a Brown Thomas bag from the floor beside the door and dropped it beside me on the bed.

'This wasn't necessary, Mam – you could have just grabbed something from Penny's.'

'I would in my eye!' she gasped.

'Well, thank you anyway.' I smiled weakly and opened the bag.

'I know you probably don't care much about your bottom right now,' she whispered in a gentle soothing tone, 'but those Salsa jeans in there will give you a perky bum like you would not believe! It's just miraculous. Look at mine.'

She spun around and I admired my mother's posterior with a forced 'Oooh!'

As well as the jeans there were a dozen pairs of Calvin Klein knickers and a handful of bras thankfully because a bra would definitely be necessary with the sheer pink Diane Von Furstenberg blouse she had bought me. There were some ankle socks and a navy blazer in the bag too. I finally pulled a pair of Gucci pumps out of the bottom of the bag and slipped my feet into them. I stretched my legs out in front of me on the bed and admired my feet. It was like I was looking at Kate Middleton's feet instead of my own.

'Thanks, Mum, you really didn't need to spend so much,' I sighed.

'Don't be silly, darling! You could do with a bit of luxury. Sure you have no decent clothes.'

'I have no clothes full stop. My house just burned down.'

'Ah yes. Of course.' She tucked her hair behind her ear, revealing a large pearl earring that was hanging heavily off the lobe, which looked strained with the weight of it.

Fred was still in Intensive Care and I couldn't go in because I was not family, but Evie, his sister, came out to talk to me.

'Hi, Katie.' She gave me a hug. We hadn't met each other since we were children so it was a bit of an awkward hug, but she needed it as much as I did.

'Well?' I asked, trying to keep my voice from shaking.

She sighed. 'He's in a coma.'

I was speechless. My legs started to shake and I was suddenly seeing blue spots, so I found the nearest bench at the wall and sank down onto it. I really didn't want to cry. I wanted to focus and find out every detail.

My mother, who was hovering nearby, sat beside me and stroked my back.

'I'm Vivienne,' she said, gently extending a hand to Evie. 'I'm terribly sorry about Fred.'

'Thanks,' Evie nodded. 'There's a fracture in his skull as well as the wound. They don't know how it will go.' She spoke bluntly; she looked exhausted.

I wondered if she blamed me a little bit for what had happened. I found it hard to keep eye contact with her.

'He's staying in Intensive Care for a few more days, then being moved to another, more permanent room for a longer period . . .'

A fuzzy haze formed across my eyes and remained there for the rest of the day.

I sat on a wooden chair in the hospital café and dipped soggy bread in a bowl of tomato soup until it became so soaked it broke off and fell into the bowl. I didn't mind; I wasn't going to eat it anyway.

My mother said nothing. I knew she wouldn't force me to eat and she didn't.

My phone buzzed and for a lack of anything better to do I answered it.

'Hello, my lovely kitten, how are you?' Sophie's jolly booming voice felt like an assault on my senses. But I listened in silence as she rambled on. 'I've been trying to contact you. I have a little bit of news for you, petal, not sure how you'll feel about it. Do you remember the Lonsdales? Clients of mine. We met them at the MMA that awful night – do you remember? Anyway they were in the office today, raving about you! They were very curious as to why your exhibition hadn't gone ahead. That slut-faced bitch Joanna had given them a sneak preview that night while they were there and they absolutely *loved* what they saw! You're not going to believe this, Katie, but the Lonsdales are big art collectors, and they actually have a load of galleries. They even have one in Dublin. They have Irish family, you see. They also have a small but very highly regarded gallery here in Manhattan and another in London. Anyway, here's the thing! They want to exhibit *your work*. They want to tour the collection around all their galleries. They love the concept. They think that if they play their cards right it will generate huge media interest. It would be amazing! Sorry, I haven't given you a second to speak! What do you think?'

'Fred's in a coma,' I stated flatly.

'Oh.'

Chapter 38

The Lonsdales' gallery was in a beautiful Georgian building overlooking Stephen's Green. It was extraordinary. The crisp white walls stretched up high to meet ornate ceilings. The tall windows were draped in deep-blue velvet curtains. The wooden floors underfoot looked old but fabulously restored with a fresh glistening coat of varnish.

The gallery stretched up over three floors, so my collection would be on the top two floors, three paintings on each floor. The first painting to greet the viewer would be Billy, which would be followed by the two of Gerry. Then on the top floor Frank hung proudly at the top of the staircase, preceeded by the painting of Seán and Fred. The grand finale was Fred and the sheep. As quite large pieces they needed a lot of space. I liked the idea that the viewer could travel up the beautiful old building as they explored the story, having time to contemplate as they went.

Various people bustled around me, mounting the paintings on the walls, setting up lighting fixtures and arranging tables at the top of each floor for cupcakes and champagne. My parents had insisted on organising the champagne and various other nibbles and canapés. I left them to it, as they were definitely the right people for the job. The only request I had was cupcakes.

My mother was beyond excited and had invited all her socialite friends. She had dragged me in to Eugene for a blow-dry that morning, so that I wouldn't 'have to worry about bird's-nest hair.' I hadn't planned on worrying, and hadn't ever perceived my hair as a bird's nest although now I definitely would. But I didn't have the energy to debate it. He did a nice job anyway and Mum seemed pleased so I couldn't complain.

A box appeared on the floor at my feet and I crouched down to open it. It was the leaflets. Strikingly sleek glossy leaflets with images and paragraphs describing my art and the story behind the collection. I took out bundles and floated around the gallery, setting them on the tables.

I had grown accustomed to Mrs Lonsdale's cat face and was now able to look at it without staring with my mouth gaping open. She wore her usual bizarrely serene grin when she glided towards me as I slotted the leaflets into the display box at the reception desk.

'It's coming together marvellously now, Katie. We're nearly all ready for tonight. I expect a large amount of press. Your story has really attracted people's attention. This is a very exciting time. I do hope you'll enjoy it. Get yourself home now and spend some time pampering yourself. Those nails aren't going to paint themselves!' She nodded at my chipped nail varnish which was now on its second week of wear and was halfway down my nail at best.

'Thanks, Mrs Lonsdale, I'll do my best!' I took a deep breath and smiled at her. I had a feeling my mother and her were going to be like peas in a pod.

Outside the gallery Stephen's Green looked like something out of a fairytale. Little Christmas lights twinkled everywhere I looked, and people bustled around wrapped up in big woolly hats and scarves carrying shopping bags. I got into a taxi and whizzed home to slip into my navy-blue sparkly cocktail dress I had picked to match the curtains. My creativity was limited to painting, as my mother informed me. But she admitted it was a lovely dress.

I wrapped my mother's five-year-old, but pristine cream faux-fur jacket around my shoulders as I ascended the steps into the gallery that evening. My mother glided up behind me, a glimmering vision of blonde classic beauty. She breezed past and into the entrance hall, greeting her friends with delight. I wasn't quite so exuberant. I nervously made my way through the entrance hall, smiling politely at well-wishers. Even though I was wearing my lovely sparkly cocktail dress I felt naked, exposed. At least people had shown up though – that was a positive!

Mr and Mrs Lonsdale were right. There had been an extraordinary amount of press. The whole story of the collection had really captured interest. Especially the fire in the cottage – suspected arson – that was rumoured to have been intended to destroy every painting. The press were fascinated. I was just praying there wouldn't be any unwelcome visitors tonight. Maniac Mo was still on the loose as there was no hard evidence linking her to the fire. The whole affair had been disastrously disappointing. The whole village knew it had been her and yet there was no evidence and no one came forward with anything. My heart was well and truly broken from it all.

But, despite all these anxieties, those wonderful butterflies fluttered around in my belly with ardour.

When I reached the top of the stairs and saw bunches of people drinking champagne and admiring my paintings I relaxed a bit.

A heavily pregnant Sophie waddled towards me. 'Katie, it's just *so* exciting!' she gushed. 'The paintings look so wonderful displayed like this – I'm so proud of you, babe . . .' She trailed off. Her face changed, her brow furrowed. 'Listen, how's Fred?'

'Sure you might as well ask him yourself!' came a voice from behind me, as his fingers laced through mine.

I looked around, locked eyes with him and a smile spread across my face. Despite his arm still being in a cast he had certainly made a considerable effort to look swanky, bless his cotton socks. He wore a tailored grey suit and his navy skinny tie matched my dress – a lucky accident.

'Look, the star of the show has arrived!' Fred laughed as Frank sauntered into the gallery, modelling a gold-encrusted cane, and completing his dapper look with a gold dickie bow. He smiled broadly, displaying all three teeth.

I looked back at Fred as he slipped his arm around my waist. 'I can't believe you made it! You're only just out of hospital, you nutter! Are you sure you shouldn't be in bed?'

'As if I would miss this!' He shook his head and gave me his little half smile which made my toes wiggle. 'I've felt so out of the loop stuck in that place."

"Well, you're right back in the loop now!"

He looked at me. "So do Mo and the gang still think these paintings are amongst the rubble at Winnipeg Cottage?' he asked, his crooked smile still cheerfully playing on his face.

I shrugged. 'Well, if they do they'll get a lovely surprise when they read tomorrow's papers.'

I squeezed his hand.

The End